Rudyard Kipling

In Black and White

Rudyard Kipling

In Black and White

ISBN/EAN: 9783337891626

Printed in Europe, USA, Canada, Australia, Japan

Cover: Foto ©Andreas Hilbeck / pixelio.de

More available books at **www.hansebooks.com**

THE WRITINGS IN PROSE AND VERSE OF

RUDYARD KIPLING

IN BLACK AND WHITE

NEW YORK
CHARLES SCRIBNER'S SONS
1909

THE CITY WALL

THE WRITINGS IN PROSE AND VERSE OF

RUDYARD KIPLING

IN BLACK AND WHITE 🐦 🐦 🐦

NEW YORK
CHARLES SCRIBNER'S SONS
1909

PREFACE

IN Northern India stood a monastery called The Chubára of Dhunni Bhagat. No one remembered who or what Dhunni Bhagat had been. He had lived his life, made a little money and spent it all, as every good Hindu should do, on a work of piety—the Chubára. That was full of brick cells, gaily painted with the figures of Gods and kings and elephants, where worn-out priests could sit and meditate on the latter end of things: the paths were brick-paved, and the naked feet of thousands had worn them into gutters. Clumps of mangoes sprouted from between the bricks; great pipal trees overhung the well-windlass that whined all day; and hosts of parrots tore through the trees. Crows and squirrels were tame in that place, for they knew that never a priest would touch them.

The wandering mendicants, charm-sellers, and holy vagabonds for a hundred miles round used to make the Chubára their place of call and rest. Mahommedan, Sikh, and Hindu mixed equally under the trees. They were old men, and when man has come to the turnstiles of Night all the creeds in the world seem to him wonderfully alike and colourless.

Gobind the one-eyed told me this. He was a holy man who lived on an island in the middle of a river, and fed the fishes with little bread pellets twice a day. In flood-time, when swollen corpses stranded themselves at the foot of the island, Gobind would cause them to be piously burned, for the sake of the honour of mankind, and having regard to his own account with God hereafter. But when two-thirds of the island was torn away in a spate, Gobind came across the river to Dhunni Bhagat's Chubára, he and his brass drinking-vessel with the well-cord round the neck, his short arm-rest crutch studded with brass nails, his roll of bedding, his big pipe, his umbrella, and his tall sugar-loaf hat with the nodding peacock feathers in it. He wrapped himself up in his patched quilt made of every colour and material in the world, sat down in a sunny corner of the very quiet Chubára, and, resting his arm on his short-handled crutch, waited for death. The people brought him food and little clumps of marigold flowers, and he gave his blessing in return. He was nearly blind, and his face was seamed and lined and wrinkled beyond belief, for he had lived in his time, which was before the English came within five hundred miles of Dhunni Bhagat's Chubára.

PREFACE

When we grew to know each other well, Gobind would tell me tales in a voice most like the rumbling of heavy guns over a wooden bridge. His tales were true, but not one in twenty could be printed in an English book, because the English do not think as natives do. They brood over matters that a native would dismiss till a fitting occasion; and what they would not think twice about a native will brood over till a fitting occasion: then native and English stare at each other hopelessly across great gulfs of miscomprehension.

"And what," said Gobind one Sunday evening, "is your honoured craft, and by what manner of means earn you your daily bread?"

"I am," said I, "a *kerani* — one who writes with a pen upon paper, not being in the service of the Government."

"Then what do you write?" said Gobind. "Come nearer, for I cannot see your countenance, and the light fails."

"I write of all matters that lie within my understanding, and of many that do not. But chiefly I write of Life and Death, and men and women, and Love and Fate, according to the measure of my ability, telling the tale through the mouths of one, two, or more people. Then by the favour of God the tales are sold and money accrues to me that I may keep alive."

"Even so," said Gobind. "That is the work

of the bazar story-teller; but he speaks straight to men and women and does not write anything at all. Only when the tale has aroused expectation and calamities are about to befall the virtuous, he stops suddenly and demands payment ere he continues the narration. Is it so in your craft, my son ? "

" I have heard of such things when a tale is of great length, and is sold as a cucumber, in small pieces."

" Ay, I was once a famed teller of stories when I was begging on the road between Koshin and Etra, before the last pilgrimage that ever I took to Orissa. I told many tales and heard many more at the rest-houses in the evening when we were merry at the end of the march. It is in my heart that grown men are but as little children in the matter of tales, and the oldest tale is the most beloved."

" With your people that is truth," said I. " But in regard to our people they desire new tales, and when all is written they rise up and declare that the tale were better told in such and such a manner, and doubt either the truth or the invention thereof."

" But what folly is theirs ! " said Gobind, throwing out his knotted hand. " A tale that is told is a true tale as long as the telling lasts. And of their talk upon it — you know how Bilas Khan, that was the prince of tale-tellers, said to one who mocked him in the great rest-house on the Jhelum road: 'Go on, my brother, and finish that I have begun,' and he who mocked took up the tale, but having neither voice nor manner for the task, came to a standstill, and the pilgrims at supper made him eat abuse and stick half that night."

"Nay, but with our people, money having passed, it is their right; as we should turn against a shoeseller in regard to shoes if those wore out. If ever I make a book you shall see and judge."

"And the parrot said to the falling tree, Wait, brother, till I fetch a prop!" said Gobind with a grim chuckle. "God has given me eighty years, and it may be some over. I cannot look for more than day granted by day and as a favour at this tide. Be swift."

"In what manner is it best to set about the task," said I, "O chiefest of those who string pearls with their tongue?"

"How do I know? Yet"—he thought for a little—"how should I not know? God has made very many heads, but there is only one heart in all the world among your people or my people. They are children in the matter of tales."

"But none are so terrible as the little ones, if a man misplace a word, or in a second telling vary events by so much as one small devil."

"Ay, I also have told tales to the little ones,

ix

but do thou this —" His old eyes fell on the gaudy paintings of the wall, the blue and red dome, and the flames of the poinsettias beyond. "Tell them first of those things that thou hast seen and they have seen together. Thus their knowledge will piece out thy imperfections. Tell them of what thou alone hast seen, then what thou hast heard, and since they be children tell them of battles and kings, horses, devils, elephants, and angels, but omit not to tell them of love and such like. All the earth is full of tales to him who listens and does not drive away the poor from his door. The poor are the best of tale-tellers; for they must lay their ear to the ground every night."

After this conversation the idea grew in my head, and Gobind was pressing in his inquiries as to the health of the book.

Later, when we had been parted for months, it happened that I was to go away and far off, and I came to bid Gobind good-bye.

"It is farewell between us now, for I go a very long journey," I said.

"And I also. A longer one than thou. But what of the book?" said he.

"It will be born in due season if it is so ordained."

"I would I could see it," said the old man, huddling beneath his quilt. "But that will not be. I die three days hence, in the night, a little

x

before the dawn. The term of my years is accomplished."

In nine cases out of ten a native makes no miscalculation as to the day of his death. He has the foreknowledge of the beasts in this respect.

"Then thou wilt depart in peace, and it is good talk, for thou hast said that life is no delight to thee."

"But it is a pity that our book is not born. How shall I know that there is any record of my name?"

"Because I promise, in the forepart of the book, preceding everything else, that it shall be written, Gobind, sadhu, of the island in the river and awaiting God in Dhunni Bhagat's Chubára, first spoke of the book," said I.

"And gave counsel — an old man's counsel. Gobind, son of Gobind of the Chumi village in the Karaon tehsil, in the district of Mooltan. Will that be written also?"

"That will be written also."

"And the book will go across the Black Water to the houses of your people, and all the Sahibs will know of me who am eighty years old?"

"All who read the book shall know. I cannot promise for the rest."

"That is good talk. Call aloud to all who are in the monastery, and I will tell them this thing."

They trooped up, *faquirs, sadhus, sunnyasis, by-*

ragis, *nihangs*, and *mullahs*, priests of all faiths and every degree of raggedness, and Gobind, leaning upon his crutch, spoke so that they were visibly filled with envy, and a white-haired senior bade Gobind think of his latter end instead of transitory repute in the mouths of strangers. Then Gobind gave me his blessing, and I came away.

These tales have been collected from all places, and all sorts of people, from priests in the Chubára, from Ala Yar the carver, Jiwun Singh the carpenter, nameless men on steamers and trains round the world, women spinning outside their cottages in the twilight, officers and gentlemen now dead and buried, and a few, but these are the very best, my father gave me. The greater part of them have been published in magazines and newspapers, to whose editors I am indebted; but some are new on this side of the water, and some have not seen the light before.

The most remarkable stories are, of course, those which do not appear—for obvious reasons.

CONTENTS

xiii

CONTENTS

ILLUSTRATIONS

IN BLACK AND WHITE

DRAY WARA YOW DEE

*For jealousy is the rage of a man: therefore he will not
spare in the day of vengeance. — Prov. vi. 34.*

ALMONDS and raisins, Sahib? Grapes from
Kabul? Or a pony of the rarest if the
Sahib will only come with me. He is thirteen
three, Sahib, plays polo, goes in a cart, carries a
lady and—Holy Kurshed and the Blessed Imams,
it is the Sahib himself! My heart is made fat and
my eye glad. May you never be tired! As is
cold water in the Tirah, so is the sight of a friend
in a far place. And what do *you* in this accursed
land? South of Delhi, Sahib, you know the saying — "Rats are the men and trulls the women."
It was an order? Ahoo! An order is an order
till one is strong enough to disobey. O my
brother, O my friend, we have met in an auspicious
hour! Is all well in the heart and the body and
the house? In a lucky day have we two come
together again.

1

I am to go with you? Your favour is great. Will there be picket-room in the compound? I have three horses and the bundles and the horse-boy. Moreover, remember that the police here hold me a horse-thief. What do these Lowland bastards know of horse-thieves? Do you remember that time in Peshawur when Kamal hammered on the gates of Jumrud — mountebank that he was — and lifted the Colonel's horses all in one night? Kamal is dead now, but his nephew has taken up the matter, and there will be more horses amissing if the Khaiber Levies do not look to it.

The Peace of God and the favour of His Prophet be upon this house and all that is in it! Shafizullah, rope the mottled mare under the tree and draw water. The horses can stand in the sun, but double the felts over the loins. Nay, my friend, do not trouble to look them over. They are to sell to the Officer fools who know so many things of the horse. The mare is heavy in foal; the gray is a devil unlicked; and the dun — but you know the trick of the peg. When they are sold I go back to Pubbi, or, it may be, the Valley of Peshawur.

O friend of my heart, it is good to see you again. I have been bowing and lying all day to the Officer Sahibs in respect to those horses; and my mouth is dry for straight talk. *Auggrh!* Before a meal tobacco is good. Do not join me.

for we are not in our own country. Sit in the
verandah and I will spread my cloth here. But
first I will drink. *In the name of God returning
thanks, thrice!* This is sweet water, indeed —
sweet as the water of Sheoran when it comes from
the snows.

They are all well and pleased in the North —
Khoda Baksh and the others. Yar Khan has
come down with the horses from Kurdistan — six
and thirty head only, and a full half pack-ponies
— and has said openly in the Kashmir Serai that
you English should send guns and blow the Amir
into Hell. There are *fifteen* tolls now on the
Kabul road; and at Dakka, when he thought he
was clear, Yar Khan was stripped of all his Balkh
stallions by the Governor! This is a great injustice, and Yar Khan is hot with rage. And of
the others: Mahbub Ali is still at Pubbi, writing
God knows what. Tugluq Khan is in jail for the
business of the Kohat Police Post. Faiz Beg
came down from Ismail-ki-Dhera with a Bokhariot
belt for thee, my brother, at the closing of the year,
but none knew whither thou hadst gone: there
was no news left behind. The Cousins have taken
a new run near Pakpattan to breed mules for the
Government carts, and there is a story in Bazar of
a priest. Oho! Such a salt tale! Listen ——

Sahib, why do you ask that? My clothes are
fouled because of the dust on the road. My eyes

3

are sad because of the glare of the sun. My feet
are swollen because I have washed them in bitter
water, and my cheeks are hollow because the food
here is bad. Fire burn your money! What do
I want with it? I am rich and I thought you
were my friend; but you are like the others — a
Sahib. Is a man sad? Give him money, say the
Sahibs. Is he dishonoured? Give him money,
say the Sahibs. Hath he a wrong upon his head?
Give him money, say the Sahibs. Such are the
Sahibs, and such art thou — even thou.

Nay, do not look at the feet of the dun. Pity
it is that I ever taught you to know the legs of
a horse. Footsore? Be it so. What of that?
The roads are hard. And the mare footsore?
She bears a double burden, Sahib.

And now I pray you, give me permission to
depart. Great favour and honour has the Sahib
done me, and graciously has he shown his belief
that the horses are stolen. Will it please him to
send me to the Thana? To call a sweeper and
have me led away by one of these lizard-men?
I am the Sahib's friend. I have drunk water in
the shadow of his house, and he has blackened my
face. Remains there anything more to do? Will
the Sahib give me eight annas to make smooth the
injury and — complete the insult ——?

Forgive me, my brother. I knew not — I know
not now — what I say. Yes, I lied to you! I

will put dust on my head — and I am an Afridi!
The horses have been marched footsore from the
Valley to this place, and my eyes are dim, and my
body aches for the want of sleep, and my heart is
dried up with sorrow and shame. But as it was
my shame, so by God the Dispenser of Justice —
by Allah-al-Mumit — it shall be my own revenge!

We have spoken together with naked hearts
before this, and our hands have dipped into the
same dish and thou hast been to me as a brother.
Therefore I pay thee back with lies and ingrati-
tude — as a Pathan. Listen now! When the
grief of the soul is too heavy for endurance it
may be a little eased by speech, and, moreover,
the mind of a true man is as a well, and the pebble of confession dropped therein sinks and is no
more seen. From the Valley have I come on
foot, league by league, with a fire in my chest
like the fire of the Pit. And why? Hast thou,
then, so quickly forgotten our customs, among
this folk who sell their wives and their daughters
for silver? Come back with me to the North
and be among men once more. Come back,
when this matter is accomplished and I call for
thee! The bloom of the peach-orchards is upon
all the Valley, and *here* is only dust and a great
stink. There is a pleasant wind among the mul-
berry trees, and the streams are bright with snow-
water, and the caravans go up and the caravans go

down, and a hundred fires sparkle in the gut of
the Pass, and tent-peg answers hammer-nose, and
pack-horse squeals to pack-horse across the drift
smoke of the evening. It is good in the North
now. Come back with me. Let us return to our
own people! Come!

. . . . . .

Whence is my sorrow? Does a man tear out
his heart and make fritters thereof over a slow fire
for aught other than a woman? Do not laugh,
friend of mine, for your time will also be. A woman
of the Abazai was she, and I took her to wife to
staunch the feud between our village and the men
of Ghor. I am no longer young? The lime has
touched my beard? True. I had no need of the
wedding? Nay, but I loved her. What saith
Rahman: "Into whose heart Love enters, there is
Folly *and naught else*. By a glance of the eye she
hath blinded thee; and by the eyelids and the
fringe of the eyelids taken thee into the captivity
without ransom, *and naught else*." Dost thou remember that song at the sheep-roasting in the
Pindi camp among the Uzbegs of the Amir?

The Abazai are dogs and their women the servants of sin. There was a lover of her own people,
but of that her father told me naught. My friend,
curse for me in your prayers, as I curse at each
praying from the Fakr to the Isha, the name of
Daoud Shah, Abazai, whose head is still upon his

6

neck, whose hands are still upon his wrists, who has done me dishonour, who has made my name a laughing-stock among the women of Little Malikand.

I went into Hindustan at the end of two months — to Cherat. I was gone twelve days only; but I had said that I would be fifteen days absent. This I did to try her, for it is written: "Trust not the incapable." Coming up the gorge alone in the falling of the light, I heard the voice of a man singing at the door of my house; and it was the voice of Daoud Shah, and the song that he sang was "*Dray wara yow dee*" — "All three are one." It was as though a heel-rope had been slipped round my heart and all the Devils were drawing it tight past endurance. I crept silently up the hill-road, but the fuse of my matchlock was wetted with the rain, and I could not slay Daoud Shah from afar. Moreover, it was in my mind to kill the woman also. Thus he sang, sitting outside my house, and, anon, the woman opened the door, and I came nearer, crawling on my belly among the rocks. I had only my knife to my hand. But a stone slipped under my foot, and the two looked down the hillside, and he, leaving his matchlock, fled from my anger, because he was afraid for the life that was in him. But the woman moved not till I stood in front of her, crying: "O woman, what is this that thou hast done?" And she, void of fear, though

7

she knew my thought, laughed, saying: "It is a little thing. I loved him, and *thou* art a dog and cattle-thief coming by night. Strike!" And I, being still blinded by her beauty, for, O my friend, the women of the Abazai are very fair, said: "Hast thou no fear?" And she answered: "None — but only the fear that I do not die." Then said I: "Have no fear." And she bowed her head, and I smote it off at the neck-bone so that it leaped between my feet. Thereafter the rage of our people came upon me, and I hacked off the breasts, that the men of Little Malikand might know the crime, and cast the body into the water-course that flows to the Kabul river. *Dray wara yow dee! Dray wara yow dee!* The body without the head, the soul without light, and my own darkling heart — all three are one — all three are one!

That night, making no halt, I went to Ghor and demanded news of Daoud Shah. Men said: "He is gone to Pubbi for horses. What wouldst thou of him? There is peace between the villages." I made answer: "Aye! The peace of treachery and the love that the Devil Atala bore to Gurel." So I fired thrice into the gate and laughed and went my way.

In those hours, brother and friend of my heart's heart, the moon and the stars were as blood above me, and in my mouth was the taste of dry earth.

8

Also, I broke no bread, and my drink was the rain of the Valley of Ghor upon my face.

At Pubbi I found Mahbub Ali, the writer, sitting upon his charpoy, and gave up my arms according to your Law. But I was not grieved, for it was in my heart that I should kill Daoud Shah with my bare hands thus — as a man strips a bunch of raisins. Mahbub Ali said: "Daoud Shah has even now gone hot-foot to Peshawur, and he will pick up his horses upon the road to Delhi, for it is said that the Bombay Tramway Company are buying horses there by the truck-load; eight horses to the truck." And that was a true saying.

Then I saw that the hunting would be no little thing, for the man was gone into your borders to save himself against my wrath. And shall he save himself so? Am I not alive? Though he run northward to the Dora and the snow, or southerly to the Black Water, I will follow him, as a lover follows the footsteps of his mistress, and coming upon him I will take him tenderly — Aho! so tenderly!—in my arms, saying: "Well hast thou done and well shalt thou be repaid." And out of that embrace Daoud Shah shall not go forth with the breath in his nostrils. *Auggrh!* Where is the pitcher? I am as thirsty as a mother-mare in the first month.

Your Law! What is your Law to me? When the horses fight on the runs do they regard the

9

boundary pillars; or do the kites of Ali Musjid
forbear because the carrion lies under the shadow
of the Ghor Kuttri? The matter began across
the Border. It shall finish where God pleases.
Here, in my own country, or in Hell. All three
are one.

Listen now, sharer of the sorrow of my heart,
and I will tell of the hunting. I followed to Peshawur from Pubbi, and I went to and fro about
the streets of Peshawur like a houseless dog, seeking for my enemy. Once I thought that I saw
him washing his mouth in the conduit in the big
square, but when I came up he was gone. It may
be that it was he, and, seeing my face, he had fled.

A girl of the bazar said that he would go to
Nowshera. I said: "O heart's heart, does Daoud
Shah visit thee?" And she said: "Even so." I
said: "I would fain see him, for we be friends
parted for two years. Hide me, I pray, here in
the shadow of the window shutter, and I will wait
for his coming." And the girl said: "O Pathan,
look into my eyes!" And I turned, leaning upon
her breast, and looked into her eyes, swearing that
I spoke the very Truth of God. But she answered:
"Never friend waited friend with such eyes. Lie
to God and the Prophet, but to a woman ye cannot lie. Get hence! There shall no harm befall
Daoud Shah by cause of me."

I would have strangled that girl but for the fear

10

of your Police; and thus the hunting would have come to naught. Therefore I only laughed and departed, and she leaned over the window-bar in the night and mocked me down the street. Her name is Jamun. When I have made my account with the man I will return to Peshawur and—her lovers shall desire her no more for her beauty's sake. She shall not be *Jamun*, but *Ak*, the cripple among trees. Ho! Ho! *Ak* shall she be!

At Peshawur I bought the horses and grapes, and the almonds and dried fruits, that the reason of my wanderings might be open to the Government, and that there might be no hindrance upon the road. But when I came to Nowshera he was gone, and I knew not where to go. I stayed one day at Nowshera, and in the night a Voice spoke in my ears as I slept among the horses. All night it flew round my head and would not cease from whispering. I was upon my belly, sleeping as the Devils sleep, and it may have been that the Voice was the voice of a Devil. It said: "Go south, and thou shalt come upon Daoud Shah." Listen, my brother and chiefest among friends— listen! Is the tale a long one? Think how it was long to me. I have trodden every league of the road from Pubbi to this place; and from Nowshera my guide was only the Voice and the lust of vengeance.

To the Uttock I went, but that was no hin-

11

drance to me. Ho! Ho! A man may turn the word twice, even in his trouble. The Uttock was no *uttock* [obstacle] to me; and I heard the Voice above the noise of the waters beating on the big rock, saying: "Go to the right." So I went to Pindigheb, and in those days my sleep was taken from me utterly, and the head of the woman of the Abazai was before me night and day, even as it had fallen between my feet. *Dray wara yow dee! Dray wara yow dee!* Fire, ashes, and my couch, all three are one — all three are one!

Now I was far from the winter path of the dealers who had gone to Sialkot and so south by the rail and the Big Road to the line of cantonments; but there was a Sahib in camp at Pindigheb who bought from me a white mare at a good price, and told me that one Daoud Shah had passed to Shahpur with horses. Then I saw that the warning of the Voice was true, and made swift to come to the Salt Hills. The Jhelum was in flood, but I could not wait, and, in the crossing, a bay stallion was washed down and drowned. Herein was God hard to me — not in respect of the beast, of that I had no care — but in this snatching. While I was upon the right bank urging the horses into the water, Daoud Shah was upon the left; for — *Alghias! Alghias!* — the hoofs of my mare scattered the hot ashes of his fires when we

came up the hither bank in the light of morning.
But he had fled. His feet were made swift by
the terror of Death. And I went south from
Shahpur as the kite flies. I dared not turn aside,
lest I should miss my vengeance — which is my
right. From Shahpur I skirted by the Jhelum,
for I thought that he would avoid the Desert of
the Rechna. But, presently, at Sahiwal, I turned
away upon the road to Jhang, Samundri, and
Gugera, till, upon a night, the mottled mare
breasted the fence of the rail that runs to Montgomery. And that place was Okara, and the head
of the woman of the Abazai lay upon the sand
between my feet.

Thence I went to Fazilka, and they said that
I was mad to bring starved horses there. The
Voice was with me, and I was *not* mad, but only
wearied, because I could not find Daoud Shah.
It was written that I should not find him at Rania
nor Bahadurgarh, and I came into Delhi from the
west, and there also I found him not. My friend,
I have seen many strange things in my wanderings. I have seen Devils rioting across the Rechna
as the stallions riot in spring. I have heard the
Djinns calling to each other from holes in the
sand, and I have seen them pass before my face.
There are no Devils, say the Sahibs? They are
very wise, but they do not know all things about
devils or — horses. Ho! Ho! I say to you who

13

are laughing at my misery, that I have seen the Devils at high noon whooping and leaping on the shoals of the Chenab. And was I afraid? My brother, when the desire of a man is set upon one thing alone, he fears neither God nor Man nor Devil. If my vengeance failed, I would splinter the Gates of Paradise with the butt of my gun, or I would cut my way into Hell with my knife, and I would call upon Those who Govern there for the body of Daoud Shah. What love so deep as hate?

Do not speak. I know the thought in your heart. Is the white of this eye clouded? How does the blood beat at the wrist? There is no madness in my flesh, but only the vehemence of the desire that has eaten me up. Listen!

South of Delhi I knew not the country at all. Therefore I cannot say where I went, but I passed through many cities. I knew only that it was laid upon me to go south. When the horses could march no more, I threw myself upon the earth, and waited till the day. There was no sleep with me in that journeying; and that was a heavy burden. Dost thou know, brother of mine, the evil of wakefulness that cannot break — when the bones are sore for lack of sleep, and the skin of the temples twitches with weariness, and yet — there is no sleep — there is no sleep? *Dray wara yow dee! Dray wara yow dee!* The eye of the Sun, the eye

14

of the Moon, and my own unrestful eyes — all
three are one — all three are one!

There was a city the name whereof I have forgotten, and there the Voice called all night. That
was ten days ago. It has cheated me afresh.

I have come hither from a place called Hamir-
pur, and, behold, it is my Fate that I should meet
with thee to my comfort and the increase of friendship. This is a good omen. By the joy of looking upon thy face the weariness has gone from my
feet, and the sorrow of my so long travel is forgotten. Also my heart is peaceful; for I know
that the end is near.

It may be that I shall find Daoud Shah in this
city going northward, since a Hillman will ever
head back to his Hills when the spring warns.
And shall he see those hills of our country?
Surely I shall overtake him! Surely my vengeance is safe! Surely God hath him in the hollow of His hand against my claiming. There
shall no harm befall Daoud Shah till I come; for
I would fain kill him quick and whole with the
life sticking firm in his body. A pomegranate is
sweetest when the cloves break away unwilling
from the rind. Let it be in the daytime, that I
may see his face, and my delight may be crowned.

And when I have accomplished the matter and
my Honour is made clean, I shall return thanks
unto God, the Holder of the Scale of the Law,

and I shall sleep. From the night, through the day, and into the night again I shall sleep; and no dream shall trouble me.

And now, O my brother, the tale is all told. *Ahi! Ahi! Alghias! Ahi!*

There came to the beach a poor exile of Erin,
    The dew on his wet robe hung heavy and chill;
Ere the steamer that brought him had passed out of hearin',
    He was Alderman Mike inthrojuicin' a bill!

American Song.

ONCE upon a time there was a King who lived on the road to Thibet, very many miles in the Himalayas. His Kingdom was eleven thousand feet above the sea and exactly four miles square; but most of the miles stood on end owing to the nature of the country. His revenues were rather less than four hundred pounds yearly, and they were expended in the maintenance of one elephant and a standing army of five men. He was tributary to the Indian Government, who allowed him certain sums for keeping a section of the Himalaya-Thibet road in repair. He further increased his revenues by selling timber to the railway-companies; for he would cut the great deodar trees in his one forest, and they fell thundering into the Sutlej river and were swept down to the plains three hundred miles away and became railway-ties. Now and again this King, whose name does

17

not matter, would mount a ringstraked horse and ride scores of miles to Simla-town to confer with the Lieutenant-Governor on matters of state, or to assure the Viceroy that his sword was at the service of the Queen-Empress. Then the Viceroy would cause a ruffle of drums to be sounded, and the ringstraked horse and the cavalry of the State — two men in tatters — and the herald who bore the silver stick before the King would trot back to their own place, which lay between the tail of a heaven-climbing glacier and a dark birch-forest.

Now, from such a King, always remembering that he possessed one veritable elephant, and could count his descent for twelve hundred years, I expected, when it was my fate to wander through his dominions, no more than mere license to live.

The night had closed in rain, and rolling clouds blotted out the lights of the villages in the valley. Forty miles away, untouched by cloud or storm, the white shoulder of Donga Pa — the Mountain of the Council of the Gods — upheld the Evening Star. The monkeys sang sorrowfully to each other as they hunted for dry roosts in the fern-wreathed trees, and the last puff of the day-wind brought from the unseen villages the scent of damp wood-smoke, hot cakes, dripping undergrowth, and rotting pine-cones. That is the true smell of the Himalayas, and if once it creeps into the blood of a man, that man will at the last, forgetting all else, return to the hills to die. The clouds closed and the smell went away, and there remained nothing in all the world except chilling white mist and the boom of the Sutlej river racing through the valley below. A fat-tailed sheep, who did not want to die, bleated piteously at my tent door. He was scuffling with the Prime Minister and the Director-General of Public Education, and he was a royal gift to me and my camp servants. I expressed my thanks suitably, and asked if I might have audience of the King. The Prime Minister readjusted his turban, which had fallen off in the struggle, and assured me that the King would be very pleased to see me. Therefore I despatched two bottles as a foretaste, and when the sheep had entered upon another incarnation went to the King's Palace through the wet. He had sent his army to escort me, but the army stayed to talk with my cook. Soldiers are very much alike all the world over.

The Palace was a four-roomed and whitewashed mud and timber house, the finest in all the hills for a day's journey. The King was dressed in a purple velvet jacket, white muslin trousers, and a saffron-yellow turban of price. He gave me audience in a little carpeted room opening off the palace courtyard which was occupied by the Elephant of State. The great beast was sheeted and anchored from trunk to tail, and the curve of his back stood out grandly against the mist.

The Prime Minister and the Director-General of Public Education were present to introduce me, but all the court had been dismissed, lest the two bottles aforesaid should corrupt their morals. The King cast a wreath of heavy-scented flowers round my neck as I bowed, and inquired how my honoured presence had the felicity to be. I said that through seeing his auspicious countenance the mists of the night had turned into sunshine, and that by reason of his beneficent sheep his good deeds would be remembered by the Gods. He said that since I had set my magnificent foot in his Kingdom the crops would probably yield seventy per cent. more than the average. I said that the fame of the King had reached to the four corners of the earth, and that the nations gnashed their teeth when they heard daily of the glories of his realm and the wisdom of his moon-like Prime Minister and lotus-like Director-General of Public Education.

Then we sat down on clean white cushions, and I was at the King's right hand. Three minutes later he was telling me that the state of the maize crop was something disgraceful, and that the railway-companies would not pay him enough for his timber. The talk shifted to and fro with the bottles, and we discussed very many stately things, and the King became confidential on the subject of Government generally. Most of all he dwelt on the shortcomings of one of his subjects, who, from all I could gather, had been paralyzing the executive.

"In the old days," said the King, "I could have ordered the Elephant yonder to trample him to death. Now I must e'en send him seventy miles across the hills to be tried, and his keep would be upon the State. The Elephant eats everything."

"What be the man's crimes, Rajah Sahib?" said I.

"Firstly, he is an outlander and no man of mine own people. Secondly, since of my favour I gave him land upon his first coming, he refuses to pay revenue. Am I not the lord of the earth, above and below, entitled by right and custom to one-eighth of the crop? Yet this devil, establishing himself, refuses to pay a single tax; and he brings a poisonous spawn of babes."

"Cast him into jail," I said.

"Sahib," the King answered, shifting a little on the cushions, "once and only once in these forty years sickness came upon me so that I was not able to go abroad. In that hour I made a vow to my God that I would never again cut man or woman from the light of the sun and the air of God; for I perceived the nature of the punishment. How can I break my vow? Were it only the lopping of a hand or a foot I should not delay. But even that is impossible now that the English have rule. One or another of my people" — he looked obliquely at the Director-General of Public Education — " would at once write a letter to the Viceroy, and perhaps I should be deprived of my ruffle of drums."

He unscrewed the mouthpiece of his silver water-pipe, fitted a plain amber mouthpiece, and passed his pipe to me. " Not content with refusing revenue," he continued, " this outlander refuses also the *begar*" (this was the corvée or forced labour on the roads), "and stirs my people up to the like treason. Yet he is, when he wills, an expert log-snatcher. There is none better or bolder among my people to clear a block of the river when the logs stick fast."

" But he worships strange Gods," said the Prime Minister deferentially.

"For that I have no concern," said the King, who was as tolerant as Akbar in matters of belief. " To each man his own God and the fire or Mother Earth for us all at last. It is the rebellion that offends me."

" The King has an army," I suggested. "Has not the King burned the man's house and left him naked to the night dews ?"

"Nay, a hut is a hut, and it holds the life of a

22

man. But once I sent my army against him when his excuses became wearisome: of their heads he brake three across the top with a stick. The other two men ran away. Also the guns would not shoot."

I had seen the equipment of the infantry. One-third of it was an old muzzle-loading fowling-piece, with a ragged rust-hole where the nipples should have been, one-third a wire-bound match-lock with a worm-eaten stock, and one-third a four-bore flint duck-gun without a flint.

"But it is to be remembered," said the King, reaching out for the bottle, " that he is a very expert log-snatcher and a man of a merry face. What shall I do to him, Sahib?"

This was interesting. The timid hill-folk would as soon have refused taxes to their King as revenues to their Gods.

"If it be the King's permission," I said, "I will not strike my tents till the third day, and I will see this man. The mercy of the King is God-like, and rebellion is like unto the sin of witchcraft. Moreover, both the bottles and another be empty."

"You have my leave to go," said the King.

Next morning a crier went through the State proclaiming that there was a log-jam on the river, and that it behoved all loyal subjects to remove it. The people poured down from their villages to the moist warm valley of poppy-fields; and the

King and I went with them. Hundreds of dressed deodar-logs had caught on a snag of rock, and the river was bringing down more logs every minute to complete the blockade. The water snarled and wrenched and worried at the timber, and the population of the State began prodding the nearest logs with a pole in the hope of starting a general movement. Then there went up a shout of "Namgay Doola! Namgay Doola!" and a large red-haired villager hurried up, stripping off his clothes as he ran.

"That is he. That is the rebel," said the King. "Now will the dam be cleared."

"But why has he red hair?" I asked, since red hair among hill-folks is as common as blue or green.

"He is an outlander," said the King. "Well done! Oh, well done!"

Namgay Doola had scrambled out on the jam and was clawing out the butt of a log with a rude sort of boat-hook. It slid forward slowly as an alligator moves, three or four others followed it, and the green water spouted through the gaps they had made. Then the villagers howled and shouted and scrambled across the logs, pulling and pushing the obstinate timber, and the red head of Namgay Doola was chief among them all. The logs swayed and chafed and groaned as fresh consignments from up-stream battered the

24

new weakening dam. All gave way at last in a
smother of foam, racing logs, bobbing black heads
and confusion indescribable. The river tossed
everything before it. I saw the red head go down
with the last remnants of the jam and disappear between the great grinding tree-trunks. It rose close
to the bank and blowing like a grampus. Namgay
Doola wrung the water out of his eyes and made
obeisance to the King. I had time to observe him
closely. The virulent redness of his shock head
and beard was most startling; and in the thicket
of hair wrinkled above high cheek-bones shone
two very merry blue eyes. He was indeed an
outlander, but yet a Thibetan in language, habit,
and attire. He spoke the Lepcha dialect with an
indescribable softening of the gutturals. It was
not so much a lisp as an accent.

"Whence comest thou?" I asked.

"From Thibet." He pointed across the hills
and grinned. That grin went straight to my
heart. Mechanically I held out my hand and
Namgay Doola shook it. No pure Thibetan
would have understood the meaning of the ges-
ture. He went away to look for his clothes, and
as he climbed back to his village I heard a joyous
yell that seemed unaccountably familiar. It was
the whooping of Namgay Doola.

"You see now," said the King, "why I would
not kill him. He is a bold man among my logs,

but," and he shook his head like a schoolmaster, "I know that before long there will be complaints of him in the court. Let us return to the Palace and do justice." It was that King's custom to judge his subjects every day between eleven and three o'clock. I saw him decide equitably in weighty matters of trespass, slander, and a little wife-stealing. Then his brow clouded and he summoned me.

"Again it is Namgay Doola," he said despairingly. "Not content with refusing revenue on his own part, he has bound half his village by an oath to the like treason. Never before has such a thing befallen me! Nor are my taxes heavy."

A rabbit-faced villager, with a blush-rose stuck behind his ear, advanced trembling. He had been in the conspiracy, but had told everything and hoped for the King's favour.

"O King," said I. "If it be the King's will let this matter stand over till the morning. Only the Gods can do right swiftly, and it may be that yonder villager has lied."

"Nay, for I know the nature of Namgay Doola; but since a guest asks let the matter remain. Wilt thou speak harshly to this red-headed outlander? He may listen to thee."

I made an attempt that very evening, but for the life of me I could not keep my countenance. Namgay Doola grinned persuasively, and began to tell me about a big brown bear in a poppy-field by the river. Would I care to shoot it? I spoke austerely on the sin of conspiracy, and the certainty of punishment. Namgay Doola's face clouded for a moment. Shortly afterwards he withdrew from my tent, and I heard him singing to himself softly among the pines. The words were unintelligible to me, but the tune, like his liquid insinuating speech, seemed the ghost of something strangely familiar.

> " Dir hané mard-i-yemen dir
> To weeree ala gee,"

sang Namgay Doola again and again, and I racked my brain for that lost tune. It was not till after dinner that I discovered some one had cut a square foot of velvet from the centre of my best camera-cloth. This made me so angry that I wandered down the valley in the hope of meeting the big brown bear. I could hear him grunting like a discontented pig in the poppy-field, and I waited shoulder deep in the dew-dripping Indian corn to catch him after his meal. The moon was at full and drew out the rich scent of the tasselled crop. Then I heard the anguished bellow of a Himalayan cow, one of the little black crummies no bigger than Newfoundland dogs. Two shadows that looked like a bear and her cub hurried past me. I was in act to fire when I saw that

they had each a brilliant red head. The lesser
animal was trailing some rope behind it that left
a dark track on the path. They passed within
six feet of me, and the shadow of the moonlight
lay velvet-black on their faces. Velvet-black was
exactly the word, for by all the powers of moonlight they were masked in the velvet of my camera-cloth! I marvelled and went to bed.

Next morning the Kingdom was in uproar.
Namgay Doola, men said, had gone forth in the
night and with a sharp knife had cut off the tail
of a cow belonging to the rabbit-faced villager
who had betrayed him. It was sacrilege unspeakable against the Holy Cow. The State desired
his blood, but he had retreated into his hut, bar-
ricaded the doors and windows with big stones,
and defied the world.

The King and I and the populace approached
the hut cautiously. There was no hope of cap-
turing the man without loss of life, for from a hole
in the wall projected the muzzle of an extremely
well-cared-for gun — the only gun in the State that
could shoot. Namgay Doola had narrowly missed
a villager just before we came up. The Standing
Army stood. It could do no more, for when it
advanced pieces of sharp shale flew from the
windows. To these were added from time to
time showers of scalding water. We saw red
heads bobbing up and down in the hut. The

family of Namgay Doola were aiding their sire, and blood-curdling yells of defiance were the only answers to our prayers.

"Never," said the King, puffing, "has such a thing befallen my State. Next year I will certainly buy a little cannon." He looked at me imploringly.

"Is there any priest in the Kingdom to whom he will listen?" said I, for a light was beginning to break upon me.

"He worships his own God," said the Prime Minister. "We can starve him out."

"Let the white man approach," said Namgay Doola from within. "All others I will kill. Send me the white man."

The door was thrown open and I entered the smoky interior of a Thibetan hut crammed with children. And every child had flaming red hair. A raw cow's tail lay on the floor, and by its side two pieces of black velvet — my black velvet — rudely hacked into the semblance of masks.

"And what is this shame, Namgay Doola?" said I.

He grinned more winningly than ever. "There is no shame," said he. "I did but cut off the tail of that man's cow. He betrayed me. I was minded to shoot him, Sahib. But not to death. Indeed not to death. Only in the legs."

"And why at all, since it is the custom to pay revenue to the King? Why at all?"

"By the God of my father I cannot tell," said Namgay Doola.

"And who was thy father?"

"The same that had this gun." He showed me his weapon — a Tower musket bearing date 1832 and the stamp of the Honourable East India Company.

"And thy father's name?" said I.

"Timlay Doola," said he. "At the first, I being then a little child, it is in my mind that he wore a red coat."

"Of that I have no doubt. But repeat the name of thy father thrice or four times."

He obeyed, and I understood whence the puzzling accent in his speech came. "Thimla Dhula," said he excitedly. "To this hour I worship his God."

"May I see that God?"

"In a little while — at twilight time."

"Rememberest thou aught of thy father's speech?"

"It is long ago. But there is one word which he said often. Thus, '*Shun.*' Then I and my brethren stood upon our feet, our hands to our sides. Thus."

"Even so. And what was thy mother?"

"A woman of the hills. We be Lepchas of Darjeeling, but me they call an outlander because my hair is as thou seest."

30

The Thibetan woman, his wife, touched him on the arm gently. The long parley outside the fort had lasted far into the day. It was now close upon twilight—the hour of the Angelus. Very solemnly, the red-headed brats rose from the floor and formed a semicircle. Namgay Doola laid his gun against the wall, lighted a little oil lamp, and set it before a recess in the wall. Pulling aside a curtain of dirty cloth, he revealed a worn brass crucifix leaning against the helmet-badge of a long-forgotten East India regiment. "Thus did my father," he said, crossing himself clumsily. The wife and children followed suit. Then all together they struck up the wailing chant that I heard on the hillside —

> Dir hané mard-i-yemen dir
> To weeree ala gee.

I was puzzled no longer. Again and again they crooned, as if their hearts would break, their version of the chorus of the "Wearing of the Green"—

> They're hanging men and women too,
> For the wearing of the green.

A diabolical inspiration came to me. One of the brats, a boy about eight years old, was watching me as he sang. I pulled out a rupee, held the coin between finger and thumb, and looked—only looked — at the gun against the wall. A grin of brilliant and perfect comprehension overspread the face of the child. Never for an instant stopping the song, he held out his hand for the money, and then slid the gun to my hand. I might have shot Namgay Doola as he chanted. But I was satisfied. The blood-instinct of the race held true. Namgay Doola drew the curtain across the recess. Angelus was over.

"Thus my father sang. There is much more, but I have forgotten, and I do not know the purport of these words, but it may be that the God will understand. I am not of this people, and I will not pay revenue."

"And why?"

Again that soul-compelling grin. "What occupation would be to me between crop and crop? It is better than scaring bears. But these people do not understand." He picked the masks from the floor, and looked in my face as simply as a child.

"By what road didst thou attain knowledge to make these devilries?" I said, pointing.

"I cannot tell. I am but a Lepcha of Darjeeling, and yet the stuff —— "

"Which thou hast stolen."

"Nay, surely. Did I steal? I desired it so. The stuff — the stuff — what else should I have done with the stuff?" He twisted the velvet between his fingers.

"But the sin of maiming the cow — consider that."

"That is true; but oh, Sahib, that man betrayed me, and I had no thought — but the heifer's tail waved in the moonlight and I had my knife. What else should I have done? The tail came off ere I was aware. Sahib, thou knowest more than I."

"That is true," said I. "Stay within the door. I go to speak to the King."

The population of the State were ranged on the hillsides. I went forth and spoke to the King.

"O King," said I. "Touching this man there be two courses open to thy wisdom. Thou canst either hang him from a tree, he and his brood, till there remains no hair that is red within the land."

"Nay," said the King. "Why should I hurt the little children?"

They had poured out of the hut door and were making plump obeisance to everybody. Namgay Doola waited with his gun across his arm.

"Or thou canst, discarding the impiety of the cow-maiming, raise him to honour in thy Army. He comes of a race that will not pay revenue. A red flame is in his blood which comes out at the top of his head in that glowing hair. Make him chief of the Army. Give him honour as may befall, and full allowance of work, but look to it, O King, that neither he nor his hold a foot of earth

33

from thee henceforward. Feed him with words and favour, and also liquor from certain bottles that thou knowest of, and he will be a bulwark of defence. But deny him even a tuft of grass for his own. This is the nature that God has given him. Moreover, he has brethren —— "

The State groaned unanimously.

" But if his brethren come, they will surely fight with each other till they die; or else the one will always give information concerning the other. Shall he be of thy Army, O King? Choose."

The King bowed his head, and I said, " Come forth, Namgay Doola, and command the King's Army. Thy name shall no more be Namgay in the mouths of men, but Patsay Doola, for as thou hast said, I know."

Then Namgay Doola, new christened Patsay Doola, son of Timlay Doola, which is Tim Doolan gone very wrong indeed, clasped the King's feet, cuffed the Standing Army, and hurried in an agony of contrition from temple to temple, making offerings for the sin of cattle-maiming.

And the King was so pleased with my perspicacity that he offered to sell me a village for twenty pounds sterling. But I buy no villages in the Himalayas so long as one red head flares between the tail of the heaven-climbing glacier and the dark birch-forest.

I know that breed.

34

THE dense wet heat that hung over the face of land, like a blanket, prevented all hope of sleep in the first instance. The cicalas helped the heat; and the yelling jackals the cicalas. It was impossible to sit still in the dark, empty, echoing house and watch the punkah beat the dead air. So, at ten o'clock of the night, I set my walking-stick on end in the middle of the garden, and waited to see how it would fall. It pointed directly down the moonlit road that leads to the City of Dreadful Night. The sound of its fall disturbed a hare. She limped from her form and ran across to a disused Mahomedan burial-ground, where the jawless skulls and rough-butted shank-bones, heartlessly exposed by the July rains, glimmered like mother o' pearl on the rain-channelled soil. The heated air and the heavy earth had driven the very dead upward for coolness' sake. The hare limped on; snuffed curiously at a fragment of a smoke-stained lamp-shard, and died out in the shadow of a clump of tamarisk trees.

The mat-weaver's hut under the lee of the

Hindu temple was full of sleeping men who lay like sheeted corpses. Overhead blazed the unwinking eye of the Moon. Darkness gives at least a false impression of coolness. It was hard not to believe that the flood of light from above was warm. Not so hot as the Sun, but still sickly warm, and heating the heavy air beyond what was our due. Straight as a bar of polished steel ran the road to the City of Dreadful Night; and on either side of the road lay corpses disposed on beds in fantastic attitudes — one hundred and seventy bodies of men. Some shrouded all in white with bound-up mouths; some naked and black as ebony in the strong light; and one — that lay face upwards with dropped jaw, far away from the others — silvery white and ashen gray.

"A leper asleep; and the remainder wearied coolies, servants, small shopkeepers, and drivers from the hack-stand hard by. The scene — a main approach to Lahore city, and the night a warm one in August." This was all that there was to be seen; but by no means all that one could see. The witchery of the moonlight was everywhere; and the world was horribly changed. The long line of the naked dead, flanked by the rigid silver statue, was not pleasant to look upon. It was made up of men alone. Were the womenkind, then, forced to sleep in the shelter of the stifling mud-huts as best they might? The fretful wail of a child from a low mud-roof answered the question. Where the children are the mothers must be also to look after them. They need care on these sweltering nights. A black little bullet-head peeped over the coping, and a thin — a painfully thin — brown leg was slid over on to the gutter pipe. There was a sharp clink of glass bracelets; a woman's arm showed for an instant above the parapet, twined itself round the lean little neck, and the child was dragged back, protesting, to the shelter of the bedstead. His thin, high-pitched shriek died out in the thick air almost as soon as it was raised; for even the children of the soil found it too hot to weep.

More corpses; more stretches of moonlit, white road; a string of sleeping camels at rest by the wayside; a vision of scudding jackals; *ekka*-ponies asleep — the harness still on their backs, and the brass-studded country carts, winking in the moonlight — and again more corpses. Wherever a grain cart atilt, a tree trunk, a sawn log, a couple of bamboos and a few handfuls of thatch cast a shadow, the ground is covered with them. They lie — some face downwards, arms folded, in the dust; some with clasped hands flung up above their heads; some curled up dog-wise; some thrown like limp gunny-bags over the side of the grain-carts; and some bowed with their brows on their knees in the full glare of the Moon. It would be

37

a comfort if they were only given to snoring; but they are not, and the likeness to corpses is unbroken in all respects save one. The lean dogs snuff at them and turn away. Here and there a tiny child lies on his father's bedstead, and a protecting arm is thrown round it in every instance. But, for the most part, the children sleep with their mothers on the housetops. Yellow-skinned, white-toothed pariahs are not to be trusted within reach of brown bodies.

A stifling hot blast from the mouth of the Delhi Gate nearly ends my resolution of entering the City of Dreadful Night at this hour. It is a compound of all evil savours, animal and vegetable, that a walled city can brew in a day and a night. The temperature within the motionless groves of plantain and orange-trees outside the city walls seems chilly by comparison. Heaven help all sick persons and young children within the city to-night! The high house-walls are still radiating heat savagely, and from obscure side gullies fetid breezes eddy that ought to poison a buffalo. But the buffaloes do not heed. A drove of them are parading the vacant main street; stopping now and then to lay their ponderous muzzles against the closed shutters of a grain-dealer's shop, and to blow thereon like grampuses.

Then silence follows — the silence that is full of the night noises of a great city. A stringed instrument of some kind is just, and only just, audible. High overhead some one throws open a window, and the rattle of the wood-work echoes down the empty street. On one of the roofs a hookah is in full blast; and the men are talking softly as the pipe gutters. A little farther on, the noise of conversation is more distinct. A slit of light shows itself between the sliding shutters of a shop. Inside, a stubble-bearded, weary-eyed trader is balancing his account-books among the bales of cotton prints that surround him. Three sheeted figures bear him company, and throw in a remark from time to time. First he makes an entry, then a remark; then passes the back of his hand across his streaming forehead. The heat in the built-in street is fearful. Inside the shops it must be almost unendurable. But the work goes on steadily; entry, guttural growl, and uplifted hand-stroke succeeding each other with the precision of clockwork.

A policeman — turbanless and fast asleep — lies across the road on the way to the Mosque of Wazir Khan. A bar of moonlight falls across the forehead and eyes of the sleeper, but he never stirs. It is close upon midnight, and the heat seems to be increasing. The open square in front of the Mosque is crowded with corpses; and a man must pick his way carefully for fear of treading on them. The moonlight stripes the Mosque's

high front of coloured enamel work in broad diag-
onal bands; and each separate dreaming pigeon in
the niches and corners of the masonry throws a
squab little shadow.   Sheeted ghosts rise up
wearily from their pallets, and flit into the dark
depths of the building.   Is it possible to climb to
the top of the great Minars, and thence to look
down on the city?   At all events, the attempt is
worth making, and the chances are that the door of
the staircase will be unlocked.   Unlocked it is; but
a deeply-sleeping janitor lies across the threshold,
face turned to the Moon.   A rat dashes out of his
turban at the sound of approaching footsteps.
The man grunts, opens his eyes for a minute, turns
round and goes to sleep again.   All the heat of a
decade of fierce Indian summers is stored in the
pitch-black, polished walls of the corkscrew staircase.   Half-way up, there is something alive, warm,
and feathery; and it snores.   Driven from step to
step as it catches the sound of my advance, it flutters to the top and reveals itself as a yellow-eyed,
angry kite.   Dozens of kites are asleep on this and
the other Minars, and on the domes below.   There
is the shadow of a cool, or at least a less sultry
breeze at this height; and, refreshed thereby, turn
to look on the City of Dreadful Night.

Doré might have drawn it!   Zola could describe it—this spectacle of sleeping thousands in
the moonlight and in the shadow of the Moon.

The roof-tops are crammed with men, women, and children; and the air is full of undistinguishable noises. They are restless in the City of Dreadful Night; and small wonder. The marvel is that they can even breathe. If you gaze intently at the multitude, you can see that they are almost as uneasy as a daylight crowd; but the tumult is subdued. Everywhere, in the strong light, you can watch the sleepers turning to and fro; shifting their beds and again resettling them. In the pit-like courtyards of the houses there is the same movement.

The pitiless Moon shows it all. Shows, too, the plains outside the city, and here and there a hand's-breadth of the Ravee without the walls. Shows lastly a splash of glittering silver on a house-top almost directly below the mosque Minar. Some poor soul has risen to throw a jar of water over his fevered body; the tinkle of the falling water strikes faintly on the ear. Two or three other men, in far-off corners of the City of Dreadful Night, follow his example, and the water flashes like heliographic signals. A small cloud passes over the face of the Moon, and the city and its inhabitants — clear drawn in black and white before — fade into masses of black and deeper black. Still the unrestful noise continues, the sigh of a great city overwhelmed with the heat, and of a people seeking in vain for rest. It is only the lower-class women who sleep on the housetops. What must the torment be in the latticed zenanas, where a few lamps are still twinkling? There are footfalls in the court below. It is the *Muezzin* — faithful minister; but he ought to have been here an hour ago to tell the Faithful that prayer is better than sleep — the sleep that will not come to the city.

The *Muezzin* fumbles for a moment with the door of one of the Minars, disappears awhile, and a bull-like roar — a magnificent bass thunder — tells that he has reached the top of the Minar. They must hear the cry to the banks of the shrunken Ravee itself! Even across the court-yard it is almost overpowering. The cloud drifts by and shows him outlined in black against the sky, hands laid upon his ears, and broad chest heaving with the play of his lungs —"Allah ho Akbar"; then a pause while another *Muezzin* somewhere in the direction of the Golden Temple takes up the call —"Allah ho Akbar." Again and again; four times in all; and from the bedsteads a dozen men have risen up already.—"I bear witness that there is no God but God." What a splendid cry it is, the proclamation of the creed that brings men out of their beds by scores at midnight! Once again he thunders through the same phrase, shaking with the vehemence of his own voice; and then, far and near, the night

air rings with " Mahomed is the Prophet of God."
It is as though he were flinging his defiance to the
far-off horizon, where the summer lightning plays
and leaps like a bared sword. Every *Muezzin* in
the city is in full cry, and some men on the roof-
tops are beginning to kneel. A long pause pre-
cedes the last cry, " La ilaha Illallah," and the silence closes up on it, as the ram on the head of
a cotton-bale.

The *Muezzin* stumbles down the dark stairway
grumbling in his beard. He passes the arch of
the entrance and disappears. Then the stifling
silence settles down over the City of Dreadful
Night. The kites on the Minar sleep again, snoring more loudly, the hot breeze comes up in puffs
and lazy eddies, and the Moon slides down towards the horizon. Seated with both elbows on the
parapet of the tower, one can watch and wonder
over that heat-tortured hive till the dawn. " How
do they live down there? What do they think
of? When will they awake?" More tinkling
of sluiced water-pots; faint jarring of wooden bedsteads moved into or out of the shadows; uncouth
music of stringed instruments softened by distance
into a plaintive wail, and one low grumble of far-
off thunder. In the courtyard of the mosque the
janitor, who lay across the threshold of the Minar
when I came up, starts wildly in his sleep, throws
his hands above his head, mutters something, and

falls back again. Lulled by the snoring of the kites — they snore like over-gorged humans — I drop off into an uneasy doze, conscious that three o'clock has struck, and that there is a slight — a very slight — coolness in the atmosphere. The city is absolutely quiet now, but for some vagrant dog's love-song. Nothing save dead heavy sleep.

Several weeks of darkness pass after this. For the Moon has gone out. The very dogs are still, and I watch for the first light of the dawn before making my way homeward. Again the noise of shuffling feet. The morning call is about to begin, and my night watch is over. "Allah ho Akbar! Allah ho Akbar!" The east grows gray, and presently saffron; the dawn wind comes up as though the *Muezzin* had summoned it; and, as one man, the City of Dreadful Night rises from its bed and turns its face towards the dawning day. With return of life comes return of sound. First a low whisper, then a deep bass hum; for it must be remembered that the entire city is on the housetops. My eyelids weighed down with the arrears of long deferred sleep, I escape from the Minar through the courtyard and out into the square beyond, where the sleepers have risen, stowed away the bedsteads, and are discussing the morning hookah. The minute's freshness of the air has gone, and it is as hot as at first.

"Will the Sahib, out of his kindness, make

room?" What is it? Something borne on men's shoulders comes by in the half-light, and I stand back. A woman's corpse going down to the burning-ghat, and a bystander says, "She died at midnight from the heat." So the city was of Death as well as Night, after all.

THE JUDGMENT OF DUNGARA

See the pale martyr with his shirt on fire.—Printer's Error.

THEY tell the tale even now among the groves
of the Berbulda Hill, and for corroboration point
to the roofless and windowless Mission-house.
The great God Dungara, the God of Things as
They Are, Most Terrible, One-eyed, Bearing the
Red Elephant Tusk, did it all; and he who refuses to believe in Dungara will assuredly be smitten by the Madness of Yat — the madness that
fell upon the sons and the daughters of the Buria
Kol when they turned aside from Dungara and
put on clothes. So says Athon Dazé, who is
High Priest of the shrine and Warden of the
Red Elephant Tusk. But if you ask the Assistant Collector and Agent in Charge of the Buria
Kol, he will laugh — not because he bears any
malice against missions, but because he himself
saw the vengeance of Dungara executed upon the
spiritual children of the Reverend Justus Krenk,
Pastor of the Tubingen Mission, and upon Lotta,
his virtuous wife.

Yet if ever a man merited good treatment of

46

the Gods it was the Reverend Justus, one time
of Heidelberg, who, on the faith of a call, went
into the wilderness and took the blonde, blue-eyed
Lotta with him. "We will these Heathen now
by idolatrous practices so darkened better make,"
said Justus in the early days of his career. "Yes,"
he added with conviction, "they shall be good
and shall with their hands to work learn. For
all good Christians must work." And upon a
stipend more modest even than that of an English
lay-reader, Justus Krenk kept house beyond Ka-
mala and the gorge of Malair, beyond the Berbulda River close to the foot of the blue hill of
Panth on whose summit stands the Temple of
Dungara — in the heart of the country of the
Buria Kol — the naked, good-tempered, timid,
shameless, lazy Buria Kol.

Do you know what life at a Mission outpost
means ? Try to imagine a loneliness exceeding
that of the smallest station to which Government
has ever sent you — isolation that weighs upon
the waking eyelids and drives you by force head-
long into the labours of the day. There is no post,
there is no one of your own colour to speak to,
there are no roads : there is, indeed, food to keep
you alive, but it is not pleasant to eat ; and whatever of good or beauty or interest there is in your
life, must come from yourself and the grace that
may be planted in you.

47

In the morning, with a patter of soft feet, the converts, the doubtful, and the open scoffers, troop up to the verandah. You must be infinitely kind and patient, and, above all, clear-sighted, for you deal with the simplicity of childhood, the experience of man, and the subtlety of the savage. Your congregation have a hundred material wants to be considered; and it is for you, as you believe in your personal responsibility to your Maker, to pick out of the clamouring crowd any grain of spirituality that may lie therein. If to the cure of souls you add that of bodies, your task will be all the more difficult, for the sick and the maimed will profess any and every creed for the sake of healing, and will laugh at you because you are simple enough to believe them.

As the day wears and the impetus of the morning dies away, there will come upon you an overwhelming sense of the uselessness of your toil. This must be striven against, and the only spur in your side will be the belief that you are playing against the Devil for the living soul. It is a great, a joyous belief; but he who can hold it unwavering for four and twenty consecutive hours, must be blessed with an abundantly strong physique and equable nerve.

Ask the gray heads of the Bannockburn Medical Crusade what manner of life their preachers lead; speak to the Racine Gospel Agency, those lean Americans whose boast is that they go where no Englishman dare follow; get a Pastor of the Tubingen Mission to talk of his experiences — if you can. You will be referred to the printed reports, but these contain no mention of the men who have lost youth and health, all that a man may lose except faith, in the wilds; of English maidens who have gone forth and died in the fever-stricken jungle of the Panth Hills, knowing from the first that death was almost a certainty. Few Pastors will tell you of these things any more than they will speak of that young David of St. Bees, who, set apart for the Lord's work, broke down in the utter desolation, and returned half distraught to the Head Mission, crying: "There is no God, but I have walked with the Devil!"

The reports are silent here, because heroism, failure, doubt, despair, and self-abnegation on the part of a mere cultured white man are things of no weight as compared to the saving of one half-human soul from a fantastic faith in wood-spirits, goblins of the rock, and river-fiends.

And Gallio, the Assistant Collector of the country-side "cared for none of these things." He had been long in the district, and the Buria Kol loved him and brought him offerings of speared fish, orchids from the dim moist heart of the forests, and as much game as he could eat. In return, he gave them quinine, and with Athon

49

Dazé, the High Priest, controlled their simple policies.

"When you have been some years in the country," said Gallio at the Krenks' table, "you grow to find one creed as good as another. I'll give you all the assistance in my power, of course, but don't hurt my Buria Kol. They are a good people and they trust me."

"I will them the Word of the Lord teach," said Justus, his round face beaming with enthusiasm, "and I will assuredly to their prejudices no wrong hastily without thinking make. But, O my friend, this in the mind impartiality-of-creed-judgment-be-looking is very bad."

"Heigh-ho!" said Gallio, "I have their bodies and the district to see to, but you can try what you can do for their souls. Only don't behave as your predecessor did, or I'm afraid that I can't guarantee your life."

"And that?" said Lotta sturdily, handing him a cup of tea.

"He went up to the Temple of Dungara — to be sure, he was new to the country — and began hammering old Dungara over the head with an umbrella; so the Buria Kol turned out and hammered *him* rather savagely. I was in the district, and he sent a runner to me with a note saying: 'Persecuted for the Lord's sake. Send wing of regiment.' The nearest troops were about two hundred miles off, but I guessed what he had been doing. I rode to Panth and talked to old Athon Dazé like a father, telling him that a man of his wisdom ought to have known that the Sahib had sunstroke and was mad. You never saw a people more sorry in your life. Athon Dazé apologised, sent wood and milk and fowls and all sorts of things; and I gave five rupees to the shrine, and told Macnamara that he had been injudicious. He said that I had bowed down in the House of Rimmon; but if he had only just gone over the brow of the hill and insulted Palin Deo, the idol of the Suria Kol, he would have been impaled on a charred bamboo long before I could have done anything, and then I should have had to have hanged some of the poor brutes. Be gentle with them, Padri — but I don't think you'll do much."

"Not I," said Justus, "but my Master. We will with the little children begin. Many of them will be sick — that is so. After the children the mothers; and then the men. But I would greatly that you were in internal sympathies with us prefer."

Gallio departed to risk his life in mending the rotten bamboo bridges of his people, in killing a too persistent tiger here or there, in sleeping out in the reeking jungle, or in tracking the Suria Kol raiders who had taken a few heads from their brethren of the Buria clan. He was a knock-kneed, shambling young man, naturally devoid of creed or reverence, with a longing for absolute power which his undesirable district gratified.

" No one wants my post," he used to say grimly, "and my Collector only pokes his nose in when he's quite certain that there is no fever. I'm monarch of all I survey, and Athon Dazé is my viceroy."

Because Gallio prided himself on his supreme disregard of human life — though he never extended the theory beyond his own — he naturally rode forty miles to the Mission with a tiny brown girl-baby on his saddle-bow.

" Here is something for you, Padri," said he. " The Kols leave their surplus children to die. 'Don't see why they shouldn't, but you may rear this one. I picked it up beyond the Berbulda fork. I've a notion that the mother has been following me through the woods ever since."

" It is the first of the fold," said Justus, and Lotta caught up the screaming morsel to her bosom and hushed it craftily; while, as a wolf hangs in the field, Matui, who had borne it and in accordance with the law of her tribe had exposed it to die, panted weary and footsore in the bamboo-brake, watching the house with hungry mother-eyes. What would the omnipotent Assistant Collector do? Would the little man in the black coat eat her daughter alive, as Athon Dazé said was the custom of all men in black coats?

Matui waited among the bamboos through the
long night; and, in the morning, there came forth
a fair white woman, the like of whom Matui had
never seen, and in her arms was Matui's daughter
clad in spotless raiment.   Lotta knew little of the
tongue of the Buria Kol, but when mother calls
to mother, speech is easy to follow.   By the hands
stretched timidly to the hem of her gown, by the
passionate gutturals and the longing eyes, Lotta
understood with whom she had to deal.   So Matui
took her child again — would be a servant, even a
slave, to this wonderful white woman, for her own
tribe would recognise her no more.   And Lotta
wept with her exhaustively, after the German
fashion, which includes much blowing of the nose.

"First the child, then the mother, and last the
man, and to the Glory of God all," said Justus the
Hopeful.   And the man came, with a bow and
arrows, very angry indeed, for there was no one to
cook for him.

But the tale of the Mission is a long one, and I
have no space to show how Justus, forgetful of his
injudicious predecessor, grievously smote Moto,
the husband of Matui, for his brutality; how Moto
was startled, but being released from the fear of instant death, took heart and became the faithful ally
and first convert of Justus; how the little gathering
grew, to the huge disgust of Athon Dazé; how the
Priest of the God of Things as They Are argued

subtilely with the Priest of the God of Things as They Should Be, and was worsted; how the dues of the Temple of Dungara fell away in fowls and fish and honeycomb, how Lotta lightened the Curse of Eve among the women, and how Justus did his best to introduce the Curse of Adam; how the Buria Kol rebelled at this, saying that their God was an idle God, and how Justus partially overcame their scruples against work, and taught them that the black earth was rich in other produce than pig-nuts only.

All these things belong to the history of many months, and throughout those months the white-haired Athon Dazé meditated revenge for the tribal neglect of Dungara. With savage cunning he feigned friendship towards Justus, even hinting at his own conversion; but to the congregation of Dungara he said darkly: " They of the Padri's flock have put on clothes and worship a busy God. Therefore Dungara will afflict them grievously till they throw themselves, howling, into the waters of the Berbulda." At night the Red Elephant Tusk boomed and groaned among the hills, and the faithful waked and said: " The God of Things as They Are matures revenge against the back-sliders. Be merciful, Dungara, to us Thy children, and give us all their crops!"

Late in the cold weather, the Collector and his wife came into the Buria Kol country. "Go and look at Krenk's Mission," said Gallio. "He is doing good work in his own way, and I think he'd be pleased if you opened the bamboo chapel that he has managed to run up. At any rate, you'll see a civilised Buria Kol."

Great was the stir in the Mission. "Now he and the gracious lady will that we have done good work with their own eyes see, and — yes — we will him our converts in all their new clothes by their own hands constructed exhibit. It will a great day be — for the Lord always," said Justus; and Lotta said, "Amen." Justus had, in his quiet way, felt jealous of the Basel Weaving Mission, his own converts being unhandy; but Athon Dazé had latterly induced some of them to hackle the glossy silky fibres of a plant that grew plenteously on the Panth Hills. It yielded a cloth white and smooth almost as the *tappa* of the South Seas, and that day the converts were to wear for the first time clothes made therefrom. Justus was proud of his work. "They shall in white clothes clothed to meet the Collector and his well-born lady come down, sing-ing 'Now thank we all our God.' Then he will the Chapel open, and — yes — even Gallio to believe will begin. Stand so, my children, two by two, and — Lotta, why do they thus themselves be-scratch? It is not seemly to wriggle, Nala, my child. The Collector will be here and be pained."

The Collector, his wife, and Gallio climbed the

hill to the Mission-station. The converts were drawn up in two lines, a shining band nearly forty strong. "Hah!" said the Collector, whose acquisitive bent of mind led him to believe that he had fostered the institution from the first. "Advancing, I see, by leaps and bounds."

Never was truer word spoken! The Mission *was* advancing exactly as he had said — at first by little hops and shuffles of shamefaced uneasiness, but soon by the leaps of fly-stung horses and the bounds of maddened kangaroos. From the hill of Panth the Red Elephant Tusk delivered a dry and anguished blare. The ranks of the converts wavered, broke and scattered with yells and shrieks of pain, while Justus and Lotta stood horror-stricken.

"It is the Judgment of Dungara!" shouted a voice. "I burn! I burn! To the river or we die!"

The mob wheeled and headed for the rocks that overhung the Berbulda, writhing, stamping, twisting, and shedding its garments as it ran, pursued by the thunder of the trumpet of Dungara. Justus and Lotta fled to the Collector almost in tears.

"I cannot understand! Yesterday," panted Justus, "they had the Ten Commandments. What is this? Praise the Lord all good spirits by land and by sea. Nala! Oh, shame!"

With a bound and a scream there alighted on the

rocks above their heads, Nala, once the pride of the Mission, a maiden of fourteen summers, good, docile, and virtuous — now naked as the dawn and spitting like a wild-cat.

"Was it for this!" she raved, hurling her petticoat at Justus, "was it for this I left my people and Dungara—for the fires of your Bad Place? Blind ape, little earthworm, dried fish that you are, you said that I should never burn! O Dungara, I burn now! I burn now! Have mercy, God of Things as They Are!"

She turned and flung herself into the Berbulda, and the trumpet of Dungara bellowed jubilantly. The last of the converts of the Tubingen Mission had put a quarter of a mile of rapid river between herself and her teachers.

"Yesterday," gulped Justus, "she taught in the school A, B, C, D.—Oh! It is the work of Satan!"

But Gallio was curiously regarding the maiden's petticoat where it had fallen at his feet. He felt its texture, drew back his shirt-sleeve beyond the deep tan of his wrist and pressed a fold of the cloth against the flesh. A blotch of angry red rose on the white skin.

"Ah!" said Gallio calmly, "I thought so."

"What is it?" said Justus.

"I should call it the Shirt of Nessus, but — Where did you get the fibre of this cloth from?"

"Athon Dazé," said Justus. "He showed the boys how it should manufactured be."

"The old fox! Do you know that he has given you the Nilgiri Nettle — scorpion — *Girardenia heterophylla* — to work up? No wonder they squirmed! Why, it stings even when they make bridge-ropes of it, unless it's soaked for six weeks. The cunning brute! It would take about half an hour to burn through their thick hides, and then —— !"

Gallio burst into laughter, but Lotta was weeping in the arms of the Collector's wife, and Justus had covered his face with his hands.

"*Girardenia heterophylla!*" repeated Gallio. "Krenk, why *didn't* you tell me? I could have saved you this. Woven fire! Anybody but a naked Kol would have known it, and, if I'm a judge of their ways, you'll never get them back."

He looked across the river to where the converts were still wallowing and wailing in the shallows, and the laughter died out of his eyes, for he saw that the Tubingen Mission to the Buria Kol was dead.

Never again, though they hung mournfully round the deserted school for three months, could Lotta or Justus coax back even the most promising of their flock. No! The end of conversion was the fire of the Bad Place — fire that ran through the limbs and gnawed into the bones.

Who dare a second time tempt the anger of Dungara? Let the little man and his wife go elsewhere. The Buria Kol would have none of them. An unofficial message to Athon Dazé that if a hair of their heads were touched, Athon Dazé and the priests of Dungara would be hanged by Gallio at the temple shrine, protected Justus and Lotta from the stumpy poisoned arrows of the Buria Kol, but neither fish nor fowl, honeycomb, salt nor young pig were brought to their doors any more. And, alas! man cannot live by grace alone if meat be wanting.

"Let us go, mine wife," said Justus; "there is no good here, and the Lord has willed that some other man shall the work take—in good time—in His own good time. We will go away, and I will—yes—some botany bestudy."

If any one is anxious to convert the Buria Kol afresh, there lies at least the core of a mission-house under the hill of Panth. But the chapel and school have long since fallen back into jungle.

THE evening meal was ended in Dhunni Bhagat's Chubara, and the old priests were smoking or counting their beads. A little naked child pattered in, with its mouth wide open, a handful of marigold flowers in one hand, and a lump of conserved tobacco in the other. It tried to kneel and make obeisance to Gobind, but it was so fat that it fell forward on its shaven head, and rolled on its side, kicking and gasping, while the marigolds tumbled one way and the tobacco the other. Gobind laughed, set it up again, and blessed the marigold flowers as he received the tobacco.

"From my father," said the child. "He has the fever, and cannot come. Wilt thou pray for him, father?"

"Surely, littlest; but the smoke is on the ground, and the night-chill is in the air, and it is not good to go abroad naked in the autumn."

"I have no clothes," said the child, "and all to-day I have been carrying cow-dung cakes to the bazar. It was very hot, and I am very tired." It shivered a little, for the twilight was cool.

Gobind lifted an arm under his vast tattered quilt

of many colours, and made an inviting little nest by his side. The child crept in, and Gobind filled his brass-studded leather water-pipe with the new tobacco. When I came to the Chubara the shaven head with the tuft atop and the beady black eyes looked out of the folds of the quilt as a squirrel looks out from his nest, and Gobind was smiling while the child played with his beard.

I would have said something friendly, but remembered in time that if the child fell ill afterwards I should be credited with the Evil Eye, and that is a horrible possession.

"Sit thou still, Thumbling," I said as it made to get up and run away. "Where is thy slate, and why has the teacher let such an evil character loose on the streets when there are no police to protect us weaklings? In which ward dost thou try to break thy neck with flying kites from the house-tops?"

"Nay, Sahib, nay," said the child, burrowing its face into Gobind's beard, and twisting uneasily. "There was a holiday to-day among the schools, and I do not always fly kites. I play ker-li-kit like the rest."

Cricket is the national game among the school-boys of the Punjab, from the naked hedge-school children, who use an old kerosene-tin for wicket, to the B. A.'s of the University, who compete for the Championship belt.

61

" Thou play kerlikit! Thou art half the height of the bat!" I said.

The child nodded resolutely. "Yea, I *do* play. *Perlay-ball. Ow-at! Ran, ran, ran!* I know it all."

"But thou must not forget with all this to pray to the Gods according to custom," said Gobind, who did not altogether approve of cricket and western innovations.

"I do not forget," said the child in a hushed voice.

"Also to give reverence to thy teacher, and ' —Gobind's voice softened—"to abstain from pull ing holy men by the beard, little badling. Eh eh, eh?"

The child's face was altogether hidden in the great white beard, and it began to whimper till Gobind soothed it as children are soothed all the world over, with the promise of a story.

"I did not think to frighten thee, senseless little one. Look up! Am I angry? Aré, aré, aré! Shall I weep too, and of our tears make a great pond and drown us both, and then thy father will never get well, lacking thee to pull his beard? Peace, peace, and I will tell thee of the Gods. Thou hast heard many tales?"

"Very many, father."

"Now, this is a new one which thou hast not heard. Long and long ago when the Gods walked

with men as they do to-day, but that we have not
faith to see, Shiv, the greatest of Gods, and Parbati, his wife, were walking in the garden of a
temple."

"Which temple? That in the Nandgaon
ward?" said the child.

"Nay, very far away. Maybe at Trimbak or
Hurdwar, whither thou must make pilgrimage
when thou art a man. Now, there was sitting in
the garden under the jujube trees a mendicant that
had worshipped Shiv for forty years, and he lived
on the offerings of the pious, and meditated holi-
ness night and day."

"Oh, father, was it thou?" said the child, looking up with large eyes.

"Nay, I have said it was long ago, and, moreover, this mendicant was married."

"Did they put him on a horse with flowers on
his head, and forbid him to go to sleep all night
long? Thus they did to me when they made my
wedding," said the child, who had been married a
few months before.

"And what didst thou do?" said I.

"I wept, and they called me evil names, and
then I smote *her*, and we wept together."

"Thus did not the mendicant," said Gobind;
"for he was a holy man, and very poor. Parbati
perceived him sitting naked by the temple steps
where all went up and down, and she said to Shiv,

63

'What shall men think of the Gods when the Gods thus scorn their worshippers? For forty years yonder man has prayed to us, and yet there be only a few grains of rice and some broken cowries before him, after all. Men's hearts will be hardened by this thing.' And Shiv said, 'It shall be looked to,' and so he called to the temple which was the temple of his son, Ganesh of the elephant head, saying, 'Son, there is a mendicant without who is very poor. What wilt thou do for him?' Then that great elephant-headed One awoke in the dark and answered, 'In three days, if it be thy will, he shall have one lakh of rupees.' Then Shiv and Parbati went away.

"But there was a money-lender in the garden hidden among the marigolds" — the child looked at the ball of crumpled blossoms in its hands — "ay, among the yellow marigolds, and he heard the Gods talking. He was a covetous man, and of a black heart, and he desired that lakh of rupees for himself. So he went to the mendicant and said, 'O brother, how much do the pious give thee daily?' The mendicant said, 'I cannot tell. Sometimes a little rice, sometimes a little pulse, and a few cowries, and, it has been, pickled mangoes and dried fish.'"

"That is good," said the child, smacking its lips.

" Then said the money-lender, 'Because I have

long watched thee, and learned to love thee and
thy patience, I will give thee now five rupees
for all thy earnings of the three days to come.
There is only a bond to sign on the matter.' But
the mendicant said, 'Thou art mad. In two
months I do not receive the worth of five rupees,'
and he told the thing to his wife that evening.
She, being a woman, said, 'When did money-
lender ever make a bad bargain? The wolf runs
through the corn for the sake of the fat deer.
Our fate is in the hands of the Gods. Pledge it
not even for three days.'

"So the mendicant returned to the money-
lender, and would not sell. Then that wicked
man sat all day before him, offering more and
more for those three days' earnings. First, ten,
fifty, and a hundred rupees; and then, for he did
not know when the Gods would pour down their
gifts, rupees by the thousand, till he had offered
half a lakh of rupees. Upon this sum the mendicant's wife shifted her counsel, and the mendicant
signed the bond, and the money was paid in silver; great white bullocks bringing it by the cart-
load. But saving only all that money, the mendicant received nothing from the Gods at all, and
the heart of the money-lender was uneasy on account of expectation. Therefore at noon of the
third day the money-lender went into the temple
to spy upon the councils of the Gods, and to learn

in what manner that gift might arrive. Even as he was making his prayers, a crack between the stones of the floor gaped, and, closing, caught him by the heel. Then he heard the Gods walking in the temple in the darkness of the columns, and Shiv called to his son Ganesh, saying, 'Son, what hast thou done in regard to the lakh of rupees for the mendicant?' And Ganesh woke, for the money-lender heard the dry rustle of his trunk uncoiling, and he answered, 'Father, one half of the money has been paid, and the debtor for the other half I hold here fast by the heel.'"

The child bubbled with laughter. "And the money-lender paid the mendicant?" it said.

"Surely, for he whom the Gods hold by the heel must pay to the uttermost. The money was paid at evening, all silver, in great carts, and thus Ganesh did his work."

"Nathu! Ohē, Nathu!"

A woman was calling in the dusk by the door of the courtyard.

The child began to wriggle. "That is my mother," it said.

"Go then, littlest," answered Gobind; "but stay a moment."

He ripped a generous yard from his patchwork-quilt, put it over the child's shoulders, and the child ran away.

AT HOWLI THANA

His own shoe, his own head.—*Native Proverb.*

As a messenger, if the heart of the Presence be moved to so great favour. And on six rupees. Yes, Sahib, for I have three little little children whose stomachs are always empty, and corn is now but forty pounds to the rupee. I will make so clever a messenger that you shall all day long be pleased with me, and, at the end of the year, bestow a turban. I know all the roads of the Station and many other things. Aha, Sahib! I am clever. Give me service. I was aforetime in the Police. A bad character? Now without doubt an enemy has told this tale. Never was I a scamp. I am a man of clean heart, and all my words are true. They knew this when I was in the Police. They said: " Afzal Khan is a true speaker in whose words men may trust." I am a Delhi Pathan, Sahib — all Delhi Pathans are good men. You have seen Delhi? Yes, it is true that there be many scamps among the Delhi Pathans. How wise is the Sahib! Nothing is hid from his eyes, and he will make me his messenger, and I will take all his

67

notes secretly and without ostentation. Nay, Sahib, God is my witness that I meant no evil. I have long desired to serve under a true Sahib — a virtuous Sahib. Many young Sahibs are as devils unchained. With these Sahibs I would take no service — not though all the stomachs of my little children were crying for bread.

Why am I not still in the Police? I will speak true talk. An evil came to the Thana — to Ram Baksh, the Havildar, and Maula Baksh, and Juggut Ram and Bhim Singh and Suruj Bul. Ram Baksh is in the jail for a space, and so also is Maula Baksh.

It was at the Thana of Howli, on the road that leads to Gokral-Seetarun, wherein are many dacoits. We were all brave men — Rustums. Wherefore we were sent to that Thana, which was eight miles from the next Thana. All day and all night we watched for dacoits. Why does the Sahib laugh? Nay, I will make a confession. The dacoits were too clever, and, seeing this, we made no further trouble. It was in the hot weather. What can a man do in the hot days? Is the Sahib who is so strong — is he, even, vigorous in that hour? We made an arrangement with the dacoits for the sake of peace. That was the work of the Havildar, who was fat. Ho! Ho! Sahib, he is now getting thin in the jail among the carpets. The Havildar said: "Give us no trouble, and we will give you no trouble. At the end of the reaping send us a man to lead before the judge, a man of infirm mind against whom the trumped-up case will break down. Thus we shall save our honour." To this talk the dacoits agreed, and we had no trouble at the Thana, and could eat melons in peace, sitting upon our charpoys all day long. Sweet as sugar-cane are the melons of Howli.

Now there was an assistant commissioner — a Stunt Sahib, in that district, called Yunkum Sahib. Aha! He was hard — hard even as is the Sahib who, without doubt, will give me the shadow of his protection. Many eyes had Yunkum Sahib, and moved quickly through his district. Men called him The Tiger of Gokral-Seetarun, because he would arrive unannounced and make his kill, and, before sunset, would be giving trouble to the Tehsildars thirty miles away. No one knew the comings or the goings of Yunkum Sahib. He had no camp, and when his horse was weary he rode upon a devil-carriage. I do not know its name, but the Sahib sat in the midst of three silver wheels that made no creaking, and drave them with his legs, prancing like a bean-fed horse — thus. A shadow of a hawk upon the fields was not more without noise than the devil-carriage of Yunkum Sahib. It was here: it was there: it was gone: and the rapport was made, and there was trouble. Ask the Tehsildar of Rohestri how the hen-stealing came to be known, Sahib.

It fell upon a night that we of the Thana slept according to custom upon our charpoys, having eaten the evening meal and drunk tobacco. When we awoke in the morning, behold, of our six rifles not one remained! Also, the big Police-book that was in the Havildar's charge was gone. Seeing these things, we were very much afraid, thinking on our parts that the dacoits, regardless of honour, had come by night and put us to shame. Then said Ram Baksh, the Havildar: "Be silent! The business is an evil business, but it may yet go well. Let us make the case complete. Bring a kid and my tulwar. See you not *now*, O fools? A kick for a horse, but a word is enough for a man."

We of the Thana, perceiving quickly what was in the mind of the Havildar, and greatly fearing that the service would be lost, made haste to take the kid into the inner room, and attended to the words of the Havildar. " Twenty dacoits came," said the Havildar, and we, taking his words, re-peated after him according to custom. " There was a great fight," said the Havildar, "and of us no man escaped unhurt. The bars of the window were broken. Suruj Bul, see thou to that; and, O men, put speed into your work, for a runner must go with the news to The Tiger of Gokral-

Seetarun." Thereon, Suruj Bul, leaning with his shoulder, brake in the bars of the window, and I, beating her with a whip, made the Havildar's mare skip among the melon-beds till they were much trodden with hoof-prints.

These things being made, I returned to the Thana, and the goat was slain, and certain portions of the walls were blackened with fire, and each man dipped his clothes a little into the blood of the goat. Know, O Sahib, that a wound made by man upon his own body can, by those skilled, be easily discerned from a wound wrought by another man. Therefore, the Havildar, taking his tulwar, smote one of us lightly on the forearm in the fat, and another on the leg, and a third on the back of the hand. Thus dealt he with all of us till the blood came; and Suruj Bul, more eager than the others, took out much hair. O Sahib, never was so perfect an arrangement. Yea, even I would have sworn that the Thana had been treated as we said. There was smoke and breaking and blood and trampled earth.

"Ride now, Maula Baksh," said the Havildar, "to the house of the Stunt Sahib, and carry the news of the dacoity. Do you also, O Afzal Khan, run there, and take heed that you are mired with sweat and dust on your in-coming. The blood will be dry on the clothes. I will stay and send a straight report to the Dipty Sahib, and we will

catch certain that ye know of, villagers, so that all
may be ready against the Dipty Sahib's arrival."

Thus Maula Baksh rode and I ran hanging on
the stirrup, and together we came in an evil plight
before The Tiger of Gokral-Seetarun in the Rohestri tehsil.   Our tale was long and correct, Sahib, for we gave even the names of the dacoits
and the issue of the fight, and besought him to
come.   But The Tiger made no sign, and only
smiled after the manner of Sahibs when they have
a wickedness in their hearts.   "Swear ye to the
rapport?" said he, and we said: "Thy servants
swear.   The blood of the fight is but newly dry
upon us.   Judge thou if it be the blood of the
servants of the Presence, or not."   And he said:
"I see.   Ye have done well."   But he did not
call for his horse or his devil-carriage, and scour
the land as was his custom.   He said: "Rest now
and eat bread, for ye be wearied men.   I will wait
the coming of the Dipty Sahib."

Now it is the order that the Havildar of the
Thana should send a straight report of all dacoi-
ties to the Dipty Sahib.   At noon came he, a fat
man and an old, and overbearing withal, but we
of the Thana had no fear of his anger; dreading
more the silences of The Tiger of Gokral-Seetarun.   With him came Ram Baksh, the Havildar, and the others, guarding ten men of the village of Howli — all men evil affected towards the

Police of the Sirkar. As prisoners they came, the irons upon their hands, crying for mercy — Imam Baksh, the farmer, who had denied his wife to the Havildar, and others, ill-conditioned rascals against whom we of the Thana bore spite. It was well done, and the Havildar was proud. But the Dipty Sahib was angry with the Stunt for lack of zeal, and said " Dam-Dam" after the custom of the English people, and extolled the Havildar. Yunkum Sahib lay still in his long chair. " Have the men sworn?" said Yunkum Sahib. " Aye, and captured ten evildoers," said the Dipty Sahib. " There be more abroad in *your* charge. Take horse — ride, and go in the name of the Sirkar!" " Truly there be more evildoers abroad," said Yunkum Sahib, " but there is no need of a horse. Come all men with me."

I saw the mark of a string on the temples of Imam Baksh. Does the Presence know the torture of the Cold Draw? I saw also the face of The Tiger of Gokral-Seetarun, the evil smile was upon it, and I stood back ready for what might befall. Well it was, Sahib, that I did this thing. Yunkum Sahib unlocked the door of his bathroom, and smiled anew. Within lay the six rifles and the big Police-book of the Thana of Howli! He had come by night in the devil-carriage that is noiseless as a ghoul, and moving among us asleep, had taken away both the guns and the book!

73

Twice had he come to the Thana, taking each time three rifles. The liver of the Havildar was turned to water, and he fell scrabbling in the dirt about the boots of Yunkum Sahib, crying — "Have mercy!"

And I? Sahib, I am a Delhi Pathan, and a young man with little children. The Havildar's mare was in the compound. I ran to her and rode: the black wrath of the Sirkar was behind me, and I knew not whither to go. Till she dropped and died I rode the red mare; and by the blessing of God, who is without doubt on the side of all just men, I escaped. But the Havildar and the rest are now in jail.

I am a scamp? It is as the Presence pleases. God will make the Presence a Lord, and give him a rich *Memsahib* as fair as a Peri to wife, and many strong sons, if he makes me his orderly. The Mercy of Heaven be upon the Sahib! Yes, I will only go to the bazar and bring my children to these so-palace-like quarters, and then — the Presence is my Father and my Mother, and I, Afzal Khan, am his slave.

Ohe, *Sirdar-ji!* I also am of the household of the Sahib.

IN FLOOD TIME

Tweed said tae Till:
" What gars ye rin sae still ? "
Till said tae Tweed :
" Though ye rin wi' speed
An' I rin slaw—
Yet where ye droon ae man
I droon twa."

THERE is no getting over the river to-night, Sahib.
They say that a bullock-cart has been washed down
already, and the *ekka* that went over a half hour
before you came has not yet reached the far side.
Is the Sahib in haste ?   I will drive the ford-ele-
phant in to show him.   Ohe, mahout there in the
shed !   Bring out Ram Pershad, and if he will face
the current, good.   An elephant never lies, Sahib,
and Ram Pershad is separated from his friend Kala
Nag.   He, too, wishes to cross to the far side.
Well done !   Well done ! my King !   Go half
way across, *mahoutji*, and see what the river says.
Well done, Ram Pershad !   Pearl among elephants, go into the river !   Hit him on the head,
fool !   Was the goad made only to scratch thy
own fat back with, bastard ?   Strike !   Strike !

75

What are the boulders to thee, Ram Pershad,
my Rustum, my mountain of strength? Go in!
Go in!

No, Sahib! It is useless. You can hear him
trumpet. He is telling Kala Nag that he cannot
come over. See! He has swung round and is
shaking his head. He is no fool. He knows
what the Barhwi means when it is angry. Aha!
Indeed, thou art no fool, my child! *Salaam*, Ram
Pershad, Bahadur! Take him under the trees,
mahout, and see that he gets his spices. Well
done, thou chiefest among tuskers! *Salaam* to
the Sirkar and go to sleep.

What is to be done? The Sahib must wait till
the river goes down. It will shrink to-morrow morning, if God pleases, or the day after at the latest.
Now why does the Sahib get so angry? I am his
servant. Before God, *I* did not create this stream!
What can I do! My hut and all that is therein
is at the service of the Sahib, and it is beginning
to rain. Come away, my Lord. How will the
river go down for your throwing abuse at it? In
the old days the English people were not thus.
The fire-carriage has made them soft. In the old
days, when they drave behind horses by day or by
night, they said naught if a river barred the way,
or a carriage sat down in the mud. It was the
will of God — not like a fire-carriage which goes
and goes and goes, and would go though all the

devils in the land hung on to its tail. The fire-carriage hath spoiled the English people. After all, what is a day lost, or, for that matter, what are two days? Is the Sahib going to his own wedding, that he is so mad with haste? Ho! Ho! Ho! I am an old man and see few Sahibs. Forgive me if I have forgotten the respect that is due to them. The Sahib is not angry?

His own wedding! Ho! Ho! Ho! The mind of an old man is like the *numah*-tree. Fruit, bud, blossom, and the dead leaves of all the years of the past flourish together. Old and new and that which is gone out of remembrance, all three are there! Sit on the bedstead, Sahib, and drink milk. Or — would the Sahib in truth care to drink my tobacco? It is good. It is the tobacco of Nuklao. My son, who is in service there, sent it to me. Drink, then, Sahib, if you know how to handle the tube. The Sahib takes it like a Musalman. Wah! Wah! Where did he learn that? His own wedding! Ho! Ho! Ho! The Sahib says that there is no wedding in the matter at all? Now *is* it likely that the Sahib would speak true talk to me who am only a black man? Small wonder, then, that he is in haste. Thirty years have I beaten the gong at this ford, but never have I seen a Sahib in such haste. Thirty years, Sahib! That is a very long time. Thirty years ago this ford was on the track of the *bunjaras*, and I have

77

seen two thousand pack-bullocks cross in one night,
Now the rail has come, and the fire-carriage says
buz-buz-buz, and a hundred lakhs of maunds slide
across that big bridge. It is very wonderful; but
the ford is lonely now that there are no *bunjaras* to
camp under the trees.

Nay, do not trouble to look at the sky without.
It will rain till the dawn. Listen! The boulders
are talking to-night in the bed of the river. Hear
them! They would be husking your bones,
Sahib, had you tried to cross. See, I will shut the
door and no rain can enter. *Wahi! Ahi! Ugh!*
Thirty years on the banks of the ford! An old
man am I, and — where is the oil for the lamp?

.   .   .   .   .   .

Your pardon, but, because of my years, I sleep
no sounder than a dog; and you moved to the
door. Look then, Sahib. Look and listen. A
full half *kos* from bank to bank is the stream now
— you can see it under the stars — and there are
ten feet of water therein. It will not shrink because of the anger in your eyes, and it will not be
quiet on account of your curses. Which is louder,
Sahib — your voice or the voice of the river?
Call to it — perhaps it will be ashamed. Lie
down and sleep afresh, Sahib. I know the anger
of the Barhwi when there has fallen rain in the
foot-hills. I swam the flood, once, on a night ten-
fold worse than this, and by the Favour of God I

was released from death when I had come to the very gates thereof.

May I tell the tale? Very good talk. I will fill the pipe anew.

Thirty years ago it was, when I was a young man and had but newly come to the ford. I was strong then, and the *bunjaras* had no doubt when I said, " This ford is clear." I have toiled all night up to my shoulder-blades in running water amid a hundred bullocks mad with fear, and have brought them across, losing not a hoof. When all was done I fetched the shivering men, and they gave me for reward the pick of their cattle — the bell-bullock of the drove. So great was the honour in which I was held! But to-day, when the rain falls and the river rises, I creep into my hut and whimper like a dog. My strength is gone from me. I am an old man, and the fire-carriage has made the ford desolate. They were wont to call me the Strong One of the Barhwi.

Behold my face, Sahib — it is the face of a monkey. And my arm — it is the arm of an old woman. I swear to you, Sahib, that a woman has loved this face and has rested in the hollow of this arm. Twenty years ago, Sahib. Believe me, this was true talk — twenty years ago.

Come to the door and look across. Can you see a thin fire very far away down the stream? That is the temple-fire in the shrine of Hanuman,

of the village of Pateera. North, under the big
star, is the village itself, but 't is hidden by a bend
of the river. Is that far to swim, Sahib? Would
you take off your clothes and adventure? Yet I
swam to Pateera — not once, but many times; and
there are *muggers* in the river too.

Love knows no caste; else why should I, a
Musalman and the son of a Musalman, have sought
a Hindu woman — a widow of the Hindus — the
sister of the headman of Pateera? But it was even
so. They of the headman's household came on a
pilgrimage to Muttra when She was but newly a
bride. Silver tires were upon the wheels of the
bullock-cart, and silken curtains hid the woman.
Sahib, I made no haste in their conveyance, for the
wind parted the curtains and I saw Her. When
they returned from pilgrimage the boy that was
Her husband had died, and I saw Her again in
the bullock-cart. By God, these Hindus are fools!
What was it to me whether She was Hindu or
Jain — scavenger, leper, or whole? I would have
married Her and made Her a home by the ford.
The Seventh of the Nine Bars says that a man
may not marry one of the idolaters? Is that
truth? Both Shiahs and Sunnis say that a Musalman may not marry one of the idolaters? Is the
Sahib a priest, then, that he knows so much? I
will tell him something that he does not know.
There is neither Shiah nor Sunni, forbidden nor

idolater, in Love; and the Nine Bars are but nine
little fagots that the flame of Love utterly burns
away. In truth, I would have taken Her; but
what could I do? The headman would have
sent his men to break my head with staves. I
am not — I was not — afraid of any five men;
but against half a village who can prevail?

Therefore it was my custom, these things having been arranged between us twain, to go by
night to the village of Pateera, and there we met
among the crops; no man knowing aught of the
matter. Behold, now! I was wont to cross here,
skirting the jungle to the river bend where the
railway bridge is, and thence across the elbow of
land to Pateera. The light of the shrine was my
guide when the nights were dark. That jungle
near the river is very full of snakes — little *ka-
raits* that sleep on the sand — and moreover, Her
brothers would have slain me had they found me
in the crops. But none knew — none knew save
She and I; and the blown sand of the river-bed
covered the track of my feet. In the hot months
it was an easy thing to pass from the ford to Pateera, and in the first Rains, when the river rose
slowly, it was an easy thing also. I set the
strength of my body against the strength of the
stream, and nightly I ate in my hut here and
drank at Pateera yonder. She had said that one
Hirnam Singh, a thief, had sought Her, and he

was of a village up the river but on the same bank. All Sikhs are dogs, and they have refused in their folly that good gift of God — tobacco. I was ready to destroy Hirnam Singh that ever he had come nigh Her; and the more because he had sworn to Her that She had a lover, and that he would lie in wait and give the name to the headman unless She went away with him. What curs are these Sikhs!

After that news, I swam always with a little sharp knife in my belt, and evil would it have been for a man had he stayed me. I knew not the face of Hirnam Singh, but I would have killed any who came between me and Her.

Upon a night in the beginning of the Rains, I was minded to go across to Pateera, albeit the river was angry. Now the nature of the Barhwi is this, Sahib. In twenty breaths it comes down from the Hills, a wall three feet high, and I have seen it, between the lighting of a fire and the cooking of a *chupatty*, grow from a runnel to a sister of the Jumna.

When I left this bank there was a shoal a half mile down, and I made shift to fetch it and draw breath there ere going forward; for I felt the hands of the river heavy upon my heels. Yet what will a young man not do for Love's sake? There was but little light from the stars, and midway to the shoal a branch of the stinking deodar tree brushed my mouth as I swam. That was a sign of heavy rain in the foot-hills and beyond, for the deodar is a strong tree, not easily shaken from the hillsides. I made haste, the river aiding me, but ere I had touched the shoal, the pulse of the stream beat, as it were, within me and around, and, behold, the shoal was gone and I rode high on the crest of a wave that ran from bank to bank. Has the Sahib ever been cast into much water that fights and will not let a man use his limbs? To me, my head upon the water, it seemed as though there were naught but water to the world's end, and the river drave me with its driftwood. A man is a very little thing in the belly of a flood. And *this* flood, though I knew it not, was the Great Flood about which men talk still. My liver was dissolved and I lay like a log upon my back in the fear of Death. There were living things in the water, crying and howling griev- ously — beasts of the forest and cattle, and once the voice of a man asking for help. But the rain came and lashed the water white, and I heard no more save the roar of the boulders below and the roar of the rain above. Thus I was whirled down- stream, wrestling for the breath in me. It is very hard to die when one is young. Can the Sahib, standing here, see the railway bridge? Look, there are the lights of the mail-train going to Pe- shawur! The bridge is now twenty feet above the river, but upon that night the water was roaring against the lattice-work and against the lattice came I feet first. But much driftwood was piled there and upon the piers, and I took no great hurt. Only the river pressed me as a strong man presses a weaker. Scarcely could I take hold of the lattice-work and crawl to the upper boom. Sahib, the water was foaming across the rails a foot deep! Judge therefore what manner of flood it must have been. I could not hear. I could not see. I could but lie on the boom and pant for breath.

After a while the rain ceased and there came out in the sky certain new washed stars, and by their light I saw that there was no end to the black water as far as the eye could travel, and the water had risen upon the rails. There were dead beasts in the driftwood on the piers, and others caught by the neck in the lattice-work, and others not yet drowned who strove to find a foothold on the lattice-work — buffaloes and kine, and wild pig, and deer one or two, and snakes and jackals past all counting. Their bodies were black upon the left side of the bridge, but the smaller of them were forced through the lattice-work and whirled down-stream.

Thereafter the stars died and the rain came down afresh and the river rose yet more, and I felt the bridge begin to stir under me as a man stirs in his sleep ere he wakes. But I was not

afraid, Sahib. I swear to you that I was not
afraid, though I had no power in my limbs. I
knew that I should not die till I had seen Her
once more. But I was very cold, and I felt that
the bridge must go.

There was a trembling in the water, such a
trembling as goes before the coming of a great
wave, and the bridge lifted its flank to the rush of
that coming so that the right lattice dipped under
water and the left rose clear. On my beard,
Sahib, I am speaking God's truth! As a Mirz-
apore stone-boat careens to the wind, so the Barhwi
Bridge turned. Thus and in no other manner.

I slid from the boom into deep water, and behind me came the wave of the wrath of the river. I
heard its voice and the scream of the middle part
of the bridge as it moved from the piers and sank,
and I knew no more till I rose in the middle of
the great flood. I put forth my hand to swim,
and lo! it fell upon the knotted hair of the head
of a man. He was dead, for no one but I, the
Strong One of Barhwi, could have lived in that
race. He had been dead full two days, for he rode
high, wallowing, and was an aid to me. I laughed
then, knowing for a surety that I should yet see
Her and take no harm; and I twisted my fingers
in the hair of the man, for I was far spent, and
together we went down the stream — he the dead
and I the living. Lacking that help I should

85

have sunk: the cold was in my marrow, and my flesh was ribbed and sodden on my bones. But *he* had no fear who had known the uttermost of the power of the river; and I let him go where he chose. At last we came into the power of a side-current that set to the right bank, and I strove with my feet to draw with it. But the dead man swung heavily in the whirl, and I feared that some branch had struck him and that he would sink. The tops of the tamarisk brushed my knees, so I knew we were come into flood-water above the crops, and, after, I let down my legs and felt bottom — the ridge of a field — and, after, the dead man stayed upon a knoll under a fig-tree, and I drew my body from the water rejoicing.

Does the Sahib know whither the backwash of the flood had borne me? To the knoll which is the eastern boundary-mark of the village of Pateera! No other place. I drew the dead man up on the grass for the service that he had done me, and also because I knew not whether I should need him again. Then I went, crying thrice like a jackal, to the appointed place which was near the byre of the headman's house. But my Love was already there, weeping. She feared that the flood had swept my hut at the Barhwi Ford. When I came softly through the ankle-deep water, She thought it was a ghost and would have fled, but I put my arms round Her, and — I was no ghost in

86

those days, though I am an old man now. Ho!
Ho! Dried corn, in truth. Maize without juice.
Ho! Ho![1]

I told Her the story of the breaking of the Barhwi
Bridge, and She said that I was greater than mortal
man, for none may cross the Barhwi in full flood,
and I had seen what never man had seen before.
Hand in hand we went to the knoll where the
dead lay, and I showed Her by what help I had
made the ford. She looked also upon the body
under the stars, for the latter end of the night was
clear, and hid Her face in Her hands, crying: "It
is the body of Hirnam Singh!" I said: "The
swine is of more use dead than living, my Beloved," and She said: "Surely, for he has saved the
dearest life in the world to my love. None the
less, he cannot stay here, for that would bring
shame upon me." The body was not a gunshot
from Her door.

Then said I, rolling the body with my hands:
"God hath judged between us, Hirnam Singh,
that thy blood might not be upon my head.
Now, whether I have done thee a wrong in keeping thee from the burning-ghat, do thou and the
crows settle together." So I cast him adrift into
the flood-water, and he was drawn out to the open,
ever wagging his thick black beard like a priest

---

[1] I grieve to say that the Warden of Barhwi Ford is responsible here
for two very bad puns in the vernacular.—R. K.

under the pulpit-board. And I saw no more of Hirnam Singh.

Before the breaking of the day we two parted, and I moved towards such of the jungle as was not flooded. With the full light I saw what I had done in the darkness, and the bones of my body were loosened in my flesh, for there ran two *kos* of raging water between the village of Pateera and the trees of the far bank, and, in the middle, the piers of the Barhwi Bridge showed like broken teeth in the jaw of an old man. Nor was there any life upon the waters—neither birds nor boats, but only an army of drowned things — bullocks and horses and men — and the river was redder than blood from the clay of the foot-hills. Never had I seen such a flood — never since that year have I seen the like — and, O Sahib, no man living had done what I had done. There was no return for me that day. Not for all the lands of the headman would I venture a second time without the shield of darkness that cloaks danger. I went a *kos* up the river to the house of a blacksmith, saying that the flood had swept me from my hut, and they gave me food. Seven days I stayed with the blacksmith, till a boat came and I returned to my house. There was no trace of wall, or roof, or floor—naught but a patch of slimy mud. Judge, therefore, Sahib, how far the river must have risen.

It was written that I should not die either in my house, or in the heart of the Barhwi, or under the wreck of the Barhwi Bridge, for God sent down Hirnam Singh two days dead, though I know not how the man died, to be my buoy and support. Hirnam Singh has been in Hell these twenty years, and the thought of that night must be the flower of his torment.

Listen, Sahib! The river has changed its voice. It is going to sleep before the dawn, to which there is yet one hour. With the light it will come down afresh. How do I know? Have I been here thirty years without knowing the voice of the river as a father knows the voice of his son? Every moment it is talking less angrily. I swear that there will be no danger for one hour or, perhaps, two. I cannot answer for the morning. Be quick, Sahib! I will call Ram Pershad, and he will not turn back this time. Is the paulin tightly corded upon all the baggage? Ohe, mahout with a mud head, the elephant for the Sahib, and tell them on the far side that there will be no crossing after daylight.

Money? Nay, Sahib. I am not of that kind. No, not even to give sweetmeats to the baby-folk. My house, look you, is empty, and I am an old man.

Dutt, Ram Pershad! *Dutt! Dutt! Dutt!* Good luck go with you, Sahib.

89

ONCE upon a time there was a coffee-planter in
India who wished to clear some forest land for
coffee-planting. When he had cut down all the
trees and burned the under-wood the stumps still
remained. Dynamite is expensive and slow-fire
slow. The happy medium for stump-clearing is
the lord of all beasts, who is the elephant. He
will either push the stump out of the ground with
his tusks, if he has any, or drag it out with ropes.
The planter, therefore, hired elephants by ones and
twos and threes, and fell to work. The very best
of all the elephants belonged to the very worst of
all the drivers or mahouts; and the superior beast's
name was Moti Guj. He was the absolute property
of his mahout, which would never have been the
case under native rule, for Moti Guj was a creature
to be desired by kings; and his name, being translated, meant the Pearl Elephant. Because the
British Government was in the land, Deesa, the
mahout, enjoyed his property undisturbed. He
was dissipated. When he had made much money
through the strength of his elephant, he would get
extremely drunk and give Moti Guj a beating

with a tent-peg over the tender nails of the forefeet.
Moti Guj never trampled the life out of Deesa on
these occasions, for he knew that after the beating
was over Deesa would embrace his trunk and
weep and call him his love and his life and the
liver of his soul, and give him some liquor. Moti
Guj was very fond of liquor — arrack for choice,
though he would drink palm-tree toddy if nothing
better offered. Then Deesa would go to sleep between Moti Guj's forefeet, and as Deesa generally
chose the middle of the public road, and as Moti
Guj mounted guard over him and would not per-
mit horse, foot, or cart to pass by, traffic was con-
gested till Deesa saw fit to wake up.

There was no sleeping in the daytime on the
planter's clearing: the wages were too high to risk.
Deesa sat on Moti Guj's neck and gave him orders, while Moti Guj rooted up the stumps — for
he owned a magnificent pair of tusks; or pulled at
the end of a rope — for he had a magnificent pair
of shoulders, while Deesa kicked him behind the
ears and said he was the king of elephants. At
evening time Moti Guj would wash down his three
hundred pounds' weight of green food with a quart
of arrack, and Deesa would take a share and sing
songs between Moti Guj's legs till it was time to
go to bed. Once a week Deesa led Moti Guj
down to the river, and Moti Guj lay on his side
luxuriously in the shallows, while Deesa went over

him with a coir-swab and a brick. Moti Guj
never mistook the pounding blow of the latter for
the smack of the former that warned him to get
up and turn over on the other side. Then Deesa
would look at his feet, and examine his eyes, and
turn up the fringes of his mighty ears in case of
sores or budding ophthalmia. After inspection,
the two would "come up with a song from the
sea," Moti Guj all black and shining, waving a
torn tree branch twelve feet long in his trunk, and
Deesa knotting up his own long wet hair.

It was a peaceful, well-paid life till Deesa felt
the return of the desire to drink deep. He wished
for an orgie. The little draughts that led nowhere
were taking the manhood out of him.

He went to the planter, and "My mother's
dead," said he, weeping.

"She died on the last plantation two months
ago; and she died once before that when you were
working for me last year," said the planter, who
knew something of the ways of nativedom.

"Then it's my aunt, and she was just the same
as a mother to me," said Deesa, weeping more than
ever. "She has left eighteen small children entirely without bread, and it is I who must fill their
little stomachs," said Deesa, beating his head on
the floor.

"Who brought you the news?" said the planter.

"The post," said Deesa.

" There hasn't been a post here for the past week. Get back to your lines!"

" A devastating sickness has fallen on my village, and all my wives are dying," yelled Deesa, really in tears this time.

" Call Chihun, who comes from Deesa's village," said the planter. " Chihun, has this man a wife?"

" He!" said Chihun. " No. Not a woman of our village would look at him. They'd sooner marry the elephant." Chihun snorted. Deesa wept and bellowed.

" You will get into a difficulty in a minute," said the planter. " Go back to your work!"

"Now I will speak Heaven's truth," gulped Deesa, with an inspiration. " I haven't been drunk for two months. I desire to depart in order to get properly drunk afar off and distant from this heavenly plantation. Thus I shall cause no trouble."

A flickering smile crossed the planter's face. "Deesa," said he, " you've spoken the truth, and I'd give you leave on the spot if anything could be done with Moti Guj while you're away. You know that he will only obey your orders."

" May the Light of the Heavens live forty thousand years. I shall be absent but ten little days. After that, upon my faith and honour and soul, I return. As to the inconsiderable interval, have I the gracious permission of the Heaven-born to call up Moti Guj?"

Permission was granted, and, in answer to Deesa's shrill yell, the lordly tusker swung out of the shade of a clump of trees where he had been squirting dust over himself till his master should return.

"Light of my heart, Protector of the Drunken, Mountain of Might, give ear," said Deesa, standing in front of him.

Moti Guj gave ear, and saluted with his trunk. "I am going away," said Deesa.

Moti Guj's eyes twinkled. He liked jaunts as well as his master. One could snatch all manner of nice things from the roadside then.

"But you, you fubsy old pig, must stay behind and work."

The twinkle died out as Moti Guj tried to look delighted. He hated stump-hauling on the plantation. It hurt his teeth.

"I shall be gone for ten days, O Delectable One. Hold up your near forefoot and I'll impress the fact upon it, warty toad of a dried mud-puddle." Deesa took a tent-peg and banged Moti Guj ten times on the nails. Moti Guj grunted and shuffled from foot to foot.

"Ten days," said Deesa, "you must work and haul and root trees as Chihun here shall order you. Take up Chihun and set him on your neck!" Moti Guj curled the tip of his trunk, Chihun put his foot there and was swung on to the neck.

Deesa handed Chihun the heavy *ankus*, the iron elephant-goad.

Chihun thumped Moti Guj's bald head as a paviour thumps a kerbstone.

Moti Guj trumpeted.

"Be still, hog of the backwoods. Chihun's your mahout for ten days. And now bid me good-bye, beast after mine own heart. Oh, my lord, my king! Jewel of all created elephants, lily of the herd, preserve your honoured health; be virtuous. Adieu!"

Moti Guj lapped his trunk round Deesa and swung him into the air twice. That was his way of bidding the man good-bye.

"He'll work now," said Deesa to the planter. "Have I leave to go?"

The planter nodded, and Deesa dived into the woods. Moti Guj went back to haul stumps.

Chihun was very kind to him, but he felt unhappy and forlorn notwithstanding. Chihun gave him balls of spices, and tickled him under the chin, and Chihun's little baby cooed to him after work was over, and Chihun's wife called him a darling; but Moti Guj was a bachelor by instinct, as Deesa was. He did not understand the domestic emotions. He wanted the light of his universe back again — the drink and the drunken slumber, the savage beatings and the savage caresses.

None the less he worked well, and the planter

wondered. Deesa had vagabonded along the roads till he met a marriage procession of his own caste and, drinking, dancing, and tippling, had drifted past all knowledge of the lapse of time.

The morning of the eleventh day dawned, and there returned no Deesa. Moti Guj was loosed from his ropes for the daily stint. He swung clear, looked round, shrugged his shoulders, and began to walk away, as one having business elsewhere.

"Hi! ho! Come back, you," shouted Chihun. "Come back, and put me on your neck, Misborn Mountain. Return, Splendour of the Hillsides. Adornment of all India, heave to, or I'll bang every toe off your fat forefoot!"

Moti Guj gurgled gently, but did not obey. Chihun ran after him with a rope and caught him up. Moti Guj put his ears forward, and Chihun knew what that meant, though he tried to carry it off with high words.

"None of your nonsense with me," said he. "To your pickets, Devil-son."

"Hrrump!" said Moti Guj, and that was all — that and the forebent ears.

Moti Guj put his hands in his pockets, chewed a branch for a toothpick, and strolled about the clearing, making jest of the other elephants, who had just set to work.

Chihun reported the state of affairs to the planter,

who came out with a dog-whip and cracked it furiously. Moti Guj paid the white man the compliment of charging him nearly a quarter of a mile across the clearing and "Hrrumping" him into the verandah. Then he stood outside the house chuckling to himself, and shaking all over with the fun of it, as an elephant will.

"We'll thrash him," said the planter. "He shall have the finest thrashing that ever elephant received. Give Kala Nag and Nazim twelve foot of chain apiece, and tell them to lay on twenty blows."

Kala Nag — which means Black Snake — and Nazim were two of the biggest elephants in the lines, and one of their duties was to administer the graver punishments, since no man can beat an elephant properly.

They took the whipping-chains and rattled them in their trunks as they sidled up to Moti Guj, meaning to hustle him between them. Moti Guj had never, in all his life of thirty-nine years, been whipped, and he did not intend to open new experiences. So he waited, weaving his head from right to left, and measuring the precise spot in Kala Nag's fat side where a blunt tusk would sink deepest. Kala Nag had no tusks; the chain was his badge of authority; but he judged it good to swing wide of Moti Guj at the last minute, and seem to appear as if he had brought out the chain for amusement.

97

Nazim turned round and went home early. He did not feel fighting-fit that morning, and so Moti Guj was left standing alone with his ears cocked.

That decided the planter to argue no more, and Moti Guj rolled back to his inspection of the clearing. An elephant who will not work, and is not tied up, is not quite so manageable as an eighty-one ton gun loose in a heavy sea-way. He slapped old friends on the back and asked them if the stumps were coming away easily; he talked nonsense concerning labour and the inalienable rights of elephants to a long "nooning"; and, wandering to and fro, thoroughly demoralized the garden till sundown, when he returned to his pickets for food.

"If you won't work you sha'n't eat," said Chihun angrily. "You're a wild elephant, and no educated animal at all. Go back to your jungle."

Chihun's little brown baby, rolling on the floor of the hut, stretched its fat arms to the huge shadow in the doorway. Moti Guj knew well that it was the dearest thing on earth to Chihun. He swung out his trunk with a fascinating crook at the end, and the brown baby threw itself shouting upon it. Moti Guj made fast and pulled up till the brown baby was crowing in the air twelve feet above his father's head.

"Great Chief!" said Chihun. "Flour cakes of

the best, twelve in number, two feet across, and soaked in rum shall be yours on the instant, and two hundred pounds' weight of fresh-cut young sugar-cane therewith. Deign only to put down safely that insignificant brat who is my heart and my life to me."

Moti Guj tucked the brown baby comfortably between his forefeet, that could have knocked into toothpicks all Chihun's hut, and waited for his food. He ate it, and the brown baby crawled away. Moti Guj dozed, and thought of Deesa. One of many mysteries connected with the elephant is that his huge body needs less sleep than anything else that lives. Four or five hours in the night suffice — two just before midnight, lying down on one side; two just after one o'clock, lying down on the other. The rest of the silent hours are filled with eating and fidgeting and long grumbling soliloquies.

At midnight, therefore, Moti Guj strode out of his pickets, for a thought had come to him that Deesa might be lying drunk somewhere in the dark forest with none to look after him. So all that night he chased through the undergrowth, blowing and trumpeting and shaking his ears. He went down to the river and blared across the shallows where Deesa used to wash him, but there was no answer. He could not find Deesa, but he disturbed all the elephants in the lines, and nearly frightened to death some gypsies in the woods.

At dawn Deesa returned to the plantation. He had been very drunk indeed, and he expected to fall into trouble for outstaying his leave. He drew a long breath when he saw that the bungalow and the plantation were still uninjured; for he knew something of Moti Guj's temper; and reported himself with many lies and salaams. Moti Guj had gone to his pickets for breakfast. His night exercise had made him hungry.

" Call up your beast," said the planter, and Deesa shouted in the mysterious elephant-language, that some mahouts believe came from China at the birth of the world, when elephants and not men were masters. Moti Guj heard and came. Elephants do not gallop. They move from spots at varying rates of speed. If an elephant wished to catch an express train he could not gallop, but he could catch the train. Thus Moti Guj was at the planter's door almost before Chihun noticed that he had left his pickets. He fell into Deesa's arms trumpeting with joy, and the man and beast wept and slobbered over each other, and handled each other from head to heel to see that no harm had befallen.

" Now we will get to work," said Deesa. "Lift me up, my son and my joy."

Moti Guj swung him up, and the two went to the coffee-clearing to look for irksome stumps.

The planter was too astonished to be very angry.

WITHOUT BENEFIT OF CLERGY

Before my Spring I garnered Autumn's gain,
Out of her time my field was white with grain,
  The year gave up her secrets to my woe.
Forced and deflowered each sick season lay,
In mystery of increase and decay ;
I saw the sunset ere men saw the day,
  Who am too wise in that I should not know.

                 Bitter Waters.

I

"But if it be a girl?"

"Lord of my life, it cannot be. I have prayed for so many nights, and sent gifts to Sheikh Badl's shrine so often, that I know God will give us a son — a man-child that shall grow into a man. Think of this and be glad. My mother shall be his mother till I can take him again, and the mullah of the Pattan mosque shall cast his nativity — God send he be born in an auspicious hour! — and then, and then thou wilt never weary of me, thy slave."

"Since when hast thou been a slave, my queen?"

"Since the beginning — till this mercy came to

101

me. How could I be sure of thy love when I knew that I had been bought with silver?"

"Nay, that was the dowry. I paid it to thy mother."

"And she has buried it, and sits upon it all day long like a hen. What talk is yours of dower! I was bought as though I had been a Lucknow dancing-girl instead of a child."

"Art thou sorry for the sale?"

"I have sorrowed; but to-day I am glad. Thou wilt never cease to love me now?—answer, my king."

"Never—never. No."

"Not even though the *mem-log*—the white women of thy own blood—love thee? And remember, I have watched them driving in the evening; they are very fair."

"I have seen fire-balloons by the hundred. I have seen the moon, and—then I saw no more fire-balloons."

Ameera clapped her hands and laughed. "Very good talk," she said. Then with an assumption of great stateliness, "It is enough. Thou hast my permission to depart,—if thou wilt."

The man did not move. He was sitting on a low red-lacquered couch in a room furnished only with a blue and white floor-cloth, some rugs, and a very complete collection of native cushions. At his feet sat a woman of sixteen, and she was all but all the world in his eyes. By every rule and law she should have been otherwise, for he was an Englishman, and she a Mussulman's daughter bought two years before from her mother, who, being left without money, would have sold Ameera shrieking to the Prince of Darkness if the price had been sufficient.

It was a contract entered into with a light heart; but even before the girl had reached her bloom she came to fill the greater portion of John Holden's life. For her, and the withered hag her mother, he had taken a little house overlooking the great red-walled city, and found,— when the marigolds had sprung up by the well in the courtyard and Ameera had established herself according to her own ideas of comfort, and her mother had ceased grumbling at the inadequacy of the cooking-places, the distance from the daily market, and at matters of housekeeping in general, —that the house was to him his home. Any one could enter his bachelor's bungalow by day or night, and the life that he led there was an unlovely one. In the house in the city his feet only could pass beyond the outer courtyard to the women's rooms; and when the big wooden gate was bolted behind him he was king in his own territory, with Ameera for queen. And there was going to be added to this kingdom a third person whose arrival Holden felt inclined to resent. It interfered with his perfect happiness. It disarranged the orderly peace of the house that was his own. But Ameera was wild with delight at the thought of it, and her mother not less so. The love of a man, and particularly a white man, was at the best an inconstant affair, but it might, both women argued, be held fast by a baby's hands. "And then," Ameera would always say, "then he will never care for the white *mem-log*. I hate them all — I hate them all."

"He will go back to his own people in time," said the mother; "but by the blessing of God that time is yet afar off."

Holden sat silent on the couch thinking of the future, and his thoughts were not pleasant. The drawbacks of a double life are manifold. The Government, with singular care, had ordered him out of the station for a fortnight on special duty in the place of a man who was watching by the bedside of a sick wife. The verbal notification of the transfer had been edged by a cheerful remark that Holden ought to think himself lucky in being a bachelor and a free man. He came to break the news to Ameera.

"It is not good," she said slowly, "but it is not all bad. There is my mother here, and no harm will come to me — unless indeed I die of pure joy. Go thou to thy work and think no troublesome thoughts. When the days are done I believe . . . nay, I am sure. And — and then I shall lay *him* in thy arms, and thou wilt love me for ever. The train goes to-night, at midnight is it not? Go now, and do not let thy heart be heavy by cause of me. But thou wilt not delay in returning? Thou wilt not stay on the road to talk to the bold white *mem-log*. Come back to me swiftly, my life."

As he left the courtyard to reach his horse that was tethered to the gate-post, Holden spoke to the white-haired old watchman who guarded the house, and bade him under certain contingencies despatch the filled-up telegraph-form that Holden gave him. It was all that could be done, and with the sensations of a man who has attended his own funeral Holden went away by the night mail to his exile. Every hour of the day he dreaded the arrival of the telegram, and every hour of the night he pictured to himself the death of Ameera. In consequence his work for the State was not of first-rate quality, nor was his temper towards his colleagues of the most amiable. The fortnight ended without a sign from his home, and, torn to pieces by his anxieties, Holden returned to be swallowed up for two precious hours by a dinner at the club, wherein he heard, as a man hears in a swoon, voices telling him how execrably he had performed the other man's duties, and how he had endeared himself to all his associates. Then he fled on horseback through the night with his heart in his mouth. There was no answer at first to his blows on the gate, and he had just wheeled his horse round to kick it in when Pir Khan appeared with a lantern and held his stirrup.

"Has aught occurred?" said Holden.

"The news does not come from my mouth, Protector of the Poor, but ——" He held out his shaking hand as befitted the bearer of good news who is entitled to a reward.

Holden hurried through the courtyard. A light burned in the upper room. His horse neighed in the gateway, and he heard a shrill little wail that sent all the blood into the apple of his throat. It was a new voice, but it did not prove that Ameera was alive.

"Who is there?" he called up the narrow brick staircase.

There was a cry of delight from Ameera, and then the voice of the mother, tremulous with old age and pride —"We be two women and — the — man — thy — son."

On the threshold of the room Holden stepped on a naked dagger, that was laid there to avert ill-luck, and it broke at the hilt under his impatient heel.

"God is great!" cooed Ameera in the half-light. "Thou hast taken his misfortunes on thy head."

"Ay, but how is it with thee, life of my life? Old woman, how is it with her?"

" She has forgotten her sufferings for joy that the child is born. There is no harm; but speak softly," said the mother.

" It only needed thy presence to make me all well," said Ameera. " My king, thou hast been very long away. What gifts hast thou for me ? Ah, ah ! It is I that bring gifts this time. Look, my life, look. Was there ever such a babe ? Nay, I am too weak even to clear my arm from him."

" Rest then, and do not talk. I am here, *bachari* [little woman]."

" Well said, for there is a bond and a heel-rope [*peecharee*] between us now that nothing can break. Look — canst thou see in this light ? He is without spot or blemish. Never was such a man-child. *Ya illah !* he shall be a pundit — no, a trooper of the Queen. And, my life, dost thou love me as well as ever, though I am faint and sick and worn ? Answer truly."

" Yea. I love as I have loved, with all my soul. Lie still, pearl, and rest."

" Then do not go. Sit by my side here — so. Mother, the lord of this house needs a cushion. Bring it." There was an almost imperceptible movement on the part of the new life that lay in the hollow of Ameera's arm. " Aho ! " she said, her voice breaking with love. " The babe is a champion from his birth. He is kicking me in the side with mighty kicks. Was there ever such a babe? And he is ours to us—thine and mine. Put thy hand on his head, but carefully, for he is very young, and men are unskilled in such matters."

Very cautiously Holden touched with the tips of his fingers the downy head.

"He is of the faith," said Ameera; "for lying here in the night-watches I whispered the call to prayer and the profession of faith into his ears. And it is most marvellous that he was born upon a Friday, as I was born. Be careful of him, my life; but he can almost grip with his hands."

Holden found one helpless little hand that closed feebly on his finger. And the clutch ran through his body till it settled about his heart. Till then his sole thought had been for Ameera. He began to realise that there was some one else in the world, but he could not feel that it was a veritable son with a soul. He sat down to think, and Ameera dozed lightly.

"Get hence, Sahib," said her mother under her breath. "It is not good that she should find you here on waking. She must be still."

"I go," said Holden submissively. "Here be rupees. See that my *baba* gets fat and finds all that he needs."

The chink of the silver roused Ameera. "I am his mother, and no hireling," she said weakly. "Shall I look to him more or less for the sake of money? Mother, give it back. I have born my lord a son."

The deep sleep of weakness came upon her almost before the sentence was completed. Holden went down to the courtyard very softly with his heart at ease. Pir Khan, the old watchman, was chuckling with delight. "This house is now complete," he said, and without further comment thrust into Holden's hands the hilt of a sabre worn many years ago when he, Pir Khan, served the Queen in the police. The bleat of a tethered goat came from the well-kerb.

"There be two," said Pir Khan, "two goats of the best. I bought them, and they cost much money; and since there is no birth-party assembled their flesh will be all mine. Strike craftily, Sahib! 'Tis an ill-balanced sabre at the best. Wait till they raise their heads from cropping the marigolds."

"And why?" said Holden, bewildered.

"For the birth-sacrifice. What else? Otherwise the child being unguarded from fate may die. The Protector of the Poor knows the fitting words to be said."

Holden had learned them once with little thought that he would ever speak them in earnest. The touch of the cold sabre-hilt in his palm turned suddenly to the clinging grip of the child up-stairs— the child that was his own son—and a dread of loss filled him.

"Strike!" said Pir Khan. "Never life came into the world but life was paid for it. See, the goats have raised their heads. Now! With a drawing cut!"

Hardly knowing what he did Holden cut twice as he muttered the Mahomedan prayer that runs: "Almighty! In place of this my son I offer life for life, blood for blood, head for head, bone for bone, hair for hair, skin for skin." The waiting horse snorted and bounded in his pickets at the smell of the raw blood that spurted over Holden's riding-boots.

"Well smitten!" said Pir Khan, wiping the sabre. "A swordsman was lost in thee. Go with a light heart, Heaven-born. I am thy servant, and the servant of thy son. May the Presence live a thousand years and . . . the flesh of the goats is all mine?" Pir Khan drew back richer by a month's pay. Holden swung himself into the saddle and rode off through the low-hanging wood-smoke of the evening. He was full of riotous exultation, alternating with a vast vague tenderness directed towards no particular object, that made him choke as he bent over the neck of his uneasy horse. "I never felt like this in my life," he thought. "I'll go to the club and pull myself together."

A game of pool was beginning, and the room was full of men. Holden entered, eager to get to

the light and the company of his fellows, singing
at the top of his voice —

    In Baltimore a-walking, a lady I did meet!

"Did you?" said the club-secretary from his
corner. "Did she happen to tell you that your
boots were wringing wet? Great goodness, man,
it's blood!"

"Bosh!" said Holden, picking his cue from the
rack. "May I cut in? It's dew. I've been riding through high crops. My faith! my boots are
in a mess though!

   "And if it be a girl she shall wear a wedding-ring,
     And if it be a boy he shall fight for his king,
     With his dirk, and his cap, and his little jacket blue,
     He shall walk the quarter-deck —"

"Yellow on blue — green next player," said the
marker monotonously.

"'He shall walk the quarter-deck,'— Am I
green, marker? 'He shall walk the quarter-
deck,'— eh! that's a bad shot,—'As his daddy
used to do!'"

"I don't see that you have anything to crow
about," said a zealous junior civilian acidly. "The
Government is not exactly pleased with your work
when you relieved Sanders."

"Does that mean a wigging from headquarters?"

said Holden with an abstracted smile. " I think
I can stand it."

The talk beat up round the ever-fresh subject
of each man's work, and steadied Holden till it
was time to go to his dark empty bungalow, where
his butler received him as one who knew all his
affairs. Holden remained awake for the greater
part of the night, and his dreams were pleasant
ones.

II

" How old is he now ? "

" *Ya illah!* What a man's question ! He is
all but six weeks old; and on this night I go up
to the housetop with thee, my life, to count the
stars. For that is auspicious. And he was born
on a Friday under the sign of the Sun, and it has
been told to me that he will outlive us both and
get wealth. Can we wish for aught better, beloved ? "

" There is nothing better. Let us go up to the
roof, and thou shalt count the stars — but a few
only, for the sky is heavy with cloud."

" The winter rains are late, and maybe they
come out of season. Come, before all the stars
are hid. I have put on my richest jewels."

" Thou hast forgotten the best of all."

"*Ai!* Ours. He comes also. He has never
yet seen the skies."

112

Ameera climbed the narrow staircase that led to the flat roof. The child, placid and unwinking, lay in the hollow of her right arm, gorgeous in silver-fringed muslin with a small skull-cap on his head. Ameera wore all that she valued most. The diamond nose-stud that takes the place of the Western patch in drawing attention to the curve of the nostril, the gold ornament in the centre of the forehead studded with tallow-drop emeralds and flawed rubies, the heavy circlet of beaten gold that was fastened round her neck by the softness of the pure metal, and the chinking curb-patterned silver anklets hanging low over the rosy ankle-bone. She was dressed in jade-green muslin as befitted a daughter of the Faith, and from shoulder to elbow and elbow to wrist ran bracelets of silver tied with floss silk, frail glass bangles slipped over the wrist in proof of the slenderness of the hand, and certain heavy gold bracelets that had no part in her country's ornaments but, since they were Holden's gift and fastened with a cunning European snap, delighted her immensely.

They sat down by the low white parapet of the roof, overlooking the city and its lights.

"They are happy down there," said Ameera. "But I do not think that they are as happy as we. Nor do I think the white *mem-log* are as happy. And thou?"

" I know they are not."

" How dost thou know? "

" They give their children over to the nurses."

" I have never seen that," said Ameera with a sigh, "nor do I wish to see. *Ahi!* "—she dropped her head on Holden's shoulder—" I have counted forty stars, and I am tired. Look at the child, love of my life, he is counting too."

The baby was staring with round eyes at the dark of the heavens. Ameera placed him in Holden's arms, and he lay there without a cry.

" What shall we call him among ourselves? " she said. "Look! Art thou ever tired of looking? He carries thy very eyes. But the mouth —— "

" Is thine, most dear. Who should know better than I? "

" 'Tis such a feeble mouth. Oh, so small! And yet it holds my heart between its lips. Give him to me now. He has been too long away."

" Nay, let him lie; he has not yet begun to cry."

" When he cries thou wilt give him back—eh? What a man of mankind thou art! If he cried he were only the dearer to me. But, my life, what little name shall we give him? "

The small body lay close to Holden's heart. It was utterly helpless and very soft. He scarcely dared to breathe for fear of crushing it. The caged green parrot that is regarded as a sort of guardian-spirit in most native households moved on its perch and fluttered a drowsy wing.

"There is the answer," said Holden. "Mian Mittu has spoken. He shall be the parrot. When he is ready he will talk mightily and run about. Mian Mittu is the parrot in thy — in the Mussulman tongue, is it not?"

"Why put me so far off?" said Ameera fretfully. "Let it be like unto some English name — but not wholly. For he is mine."

"Then call him Tota, for that is likest English."

"Ay, Tota, and that is still the parrot. Forgive me, my lord, for a minute ago, but in truth he is too little to wear all the weight of Mian Mittu for name. He shall be Tota — our Tota to us. Hearest thou, O small one? Littlest, thou art Tota." She touched the child's cheek, and he waking wailed, and it was necessary to return him to his mother, who soothed him with the wonderful rhyme of *Aré koko, Jaré koko!* which says:

Oh crow! Go crow! Baby's sleeping sound,
And the wild plums grow in the jungle, only a penny a pound.
Only a penny a pound, *baba*, only a penny a pound.

Reassured many times as to the price of those plums, Tota cuddled himself down to sleep. The two sleek, white well-bullocks in the courtyard were steadily chewing the cud of their evening meal; old Pir Khan squatted at the head of Hol-

den's horse, his police sabre across his knees, pulling drowsily at a big water-pipe that croaked like
a bull-frog in a pond. Ameera's mother sat spinning in the lower verandah, and the wooden gate
was shut and barred. The music of a marriage-
procession came to the roof above the gentle hum
of the city, and a string of flying-foxes crossed the
face of the low moon.

"I have prayed," said Ameera after a long pause,
"I have prayed for two things. First, that I may
die in thy stead if thy death is demanded, and in
the second that I may die in the place of the child.
I have prayed to the Prophet and to Beebee Miriam [the Virgin Mary]. Thinkest thou either will
hear?"

"From thy lips who would not hear the lightest
word?"

"I asked for straight talk, and thou hast given
me sweet talk. Will my prayers be heard?"

"How can I say? God is very good."

"Of that I am not sure. Listen now. When
I die, or the child dies, what is thy fate? Living,
thou wilt return to the bold white *mem-log*, for kind
calls to kind."

"Not always."

"With a woman, no; with a man it is otherwise. Thou wilt in this life, later on, go back to
thine own folk. That I could almost endure, for
I should be dead. But in thy very death thou

wilt be taken away to a strange place and a paradise that I do not know."

"Will it be paradise?"

"Surely, for who would harm thee? But we
two—I and the child—shall be elsewhere, and
we cannot come to thee, nor canst thou come to
us. In the old days, before the child was born, I
did not think of these things; but now I think of
them always. It is very hard talk."

"It will fall as it will fall. To-morrow we do
not know, but to-day and love we know well.
Surely we are happy now."

"So happy that it were well to make our happiness assured. And thy Beebee Miriam should
listen to me; for she is also a woman. But then
she would envy me! It is not seemly for men to
worship a woman."

Holden laughed aloud at Ameera's little spasm
of jealousy.

"Is it not seemly? Why didst thou not turn
me from worship of thee, then?"

"Thou a worshipper! And of me? My king,
for all thy sweet words, well I know that I am thy
servant and thy slave, and the dust under thy feet.
And I would not have it otherwise. See!"

Before Holden could prevent her she stooped
forward and touched his feet; recovering herself
with a little laugh she hugged Tota closer to her
bosom. Then, almost savagely——

"Is it true that the bold white *mem-log* live for three times the length of my life? Is it true that they make their marriages not before they are old women?"

"They marry as do others — when they are women."

"That I know, but they wed when they are twenty-five. Is that true?"

"That is true."

"*Ya illah!* At twenty-five! Who would of his own will take a wife even of eighteen? She is a woman — aging every hour. Twenty-five! I shall be an old woman at that age, and —— Those *mem-log* remain young for ever. How I hate them!"

"What have they to do with us?"

"I cannot tell. I know only that there may now be alive on this earth a woman ten years older than I who may come to thee and take thy love ten years after I am an old woman, gray-headed, and the nurse of Tota's son. That is un-just and evil. They should die too."

"Now, for all thy years thou art a child, and shalt be picked up and carried down the staircase."

"Tota! Have a care for Tota, my lord! Thou at least art as foolish as any babe!" Ameera tucked Tota out of harm's way in the hollow of her neck, and was carried downstairs laughing in

Holden's arms, while Tota opened his eyes and smiled after the manner of the lesser angels.

He was a silent infant, and, almost before Holden could realise that he was in the world, developed into a small gold-coloured little god and unquestioned despot of the house overlooking the city. Those were months of absolute happiness to Holden and Ameera — happiness withdrawn from the world, shut in behind the wooden gate that Pir Khan guarded. By day Holden did his work with an immense pity for such as were not so fortunate as himself, and a sympathy for small children that amazed and amused many mothers at the little station-gatherings. At nightfall he returned to Ameera,— Ameera, full of the wondrous doings of Tota; how he had been seen to clap his hands together and move his fingers with intention and purpose — which was manifestly a miracle — how later, he had of his own initiative crawled out of his low bedstead on to the floor and swayed on both feet for the space of three breaths.

" And they were long breaths, for my heart stood still with delight," said Ameera.

Then Tota took the beasts into his councils — the well-bullocks, the little gray squirrels, the mongoose that lived in a hole near the well, and especially Mian Mittu, the parrot, whose tail he grievously pulled, and Mian Mittu screamed till Ameera and Holden arrived.

"O villain! Child of strength! This to thy brother on the house-top! *Tobah, tobah!* Fie! Fie! But I know a charm to make him wise as Suleiman and Aflatoun [Solomon and Plato]. Now look," said Ameera. She drew from an embroidered bag a handful of almonds. "See! we count seven. In the name of God!"

She placed Mian Mittu, very angry and rumpled, on the top of his cage, and seating herself between the babe and the bird she cracked and peeled an almond less white than her teeth. "This is a true charm, my life, and do not laugh. See! I give the parrot one half and Tota the other." Mian Mittu with careful beak took his share from between Ameera's lips, and she kissed the other half into the mouth of the child, who ate it slowly with wondering eyes. "This I will do each day of seven, and without doubt he who is ours will be a bold speaker and wise. Eh, Tota, what wilt thou be when thou art a man and I am gray-headed?" Tota tucked his fat legs into adorable creases. He could crawl, but he was not going to waste the spring of his youth in idle speech. He wanted Mian Mittu's tail to tweak.

When he was advanced to the dignity of a silver belt — which, with a magic square engraved on silver and hung round his neck, made up the greater part of his clothing — he staggered on a perilous journey down the garden to Pir Khan and proffered him all his jewels in exchange for one little ride on Holden's horse, having seen his mother's mother chaffering with pedlars in the verandah. Pir Khan wept and set the untried feet on his own gray head in sign of fealty, and brought the bold adventurer to his mother's arms, vowing that Tota would be a leader of men ere his beard was grown.

One hot evening, while he sat on the roof between his father and mother watching the never-ending warfare of the kites that the city boys flew, he demanded a kite of his own with Pir Khan to fly it, because he had a fear of dealing with anything larger than himself, and when Holden called him a "spark," he rose to his feet and answered slowly in defence of his new-found individuality, "*Hum 'park nahin hai. Hum admi hai* [I am no spark, but a man]."

The protest made Holden choke and devote himself very seriously to a consideration of Tota's future. He need hardly have taken the trouble. The delight of that life was too perfect to endure. Therefore it was taken away as many things are taken away in India — suddenly and without warning. The little lord of the house, as Pir Khan called him, grew sorrowful and complained of pains who had never known the meaning of pain. Ameera, wild with terror, watched him through the night, and in the dawning of the second day the life was shaken out of him by fever — the seasonal autumn fever. It seemed altogether impossible that he could die, and neither Ameera nor Holden at first believed the evidence of the little body on the bedstead. Then Ameera beat her head against the wall and would have flung herself down the well in the garden had Holden not restrained her by main force.

One mercy only was granted to Holden. He rode to his office in broad daylight and found waiting him an unusually heavy mail that demanded concentrated attention and hard work. He was not, however, alive to this kindness of the gods.

III

The first shock of a bullet is no more than a brisk pinch. The wrecked body does not send in its protest to the soul till ten or fifteen seconds later. Holden realised his pain slowly, exactly as he had realised his happiness, and with the same imperious necessity for hiding all trace of it. In the beginning he only felt that there had been a loss, and that Ameera needed comforting, where she sat with her head on her knees shivering as Mian Mittu from the house-top called *Tota ! Tota! Tota !* Later all his world and the daily life of it rose up to hurt him. It was an outrage that any one of

the children at the band-stand in the evening should
be alive and clamorous, when his own child lay
dead.   It was more than mere pain when one of
them touched him, and stories told by over-fond
fathers of their children's latest performances cut
him to the quick.   He could not declare his pain.
He had neither help, comfort, nor sympathy; and
Ameera at the end of each weary day would lead
him through the hell of self-questioning reproach
which is reserved for those who have lost a child,
and believe that with a little —just a little—more
care it might have been saved.

" Perhaps," Ameera would say, " I did not take
sufficient heed.   Did I, or did I not ?   The sun
on the roof that day when he played so long alone
and I was — *ahi!* braiding my hair — it may be
that the sun then bred the fever.   If I had warned
him from the sun he might have lived.   But, oh
my life, say that I am guiltless!   Thou knowest
that I loved him as I love thee.   Say that there is
no blame on me, or I shall die — I shall die! "

" There is no blame,— before God, none.   It
was written and how could we do aught to save ?
What has been, has been.   Let it go, beloved."

" He was all my heart to me.   How can I let
the thought go when my arm tells me every night
that he is not here ?   *Ahi!   Ahi!*   O Tota, come
back to me — come back again, and let us be all
together as it was before ! "

"Peace, peace! For thine own sake, and for mine also, if thou lovest me — rest."

"By this I know thou dost not care; and how shouldst thou? The white men have hearts of stone and souls of iron. Oh, that I had married a man of mine own people — though he beat me — and had never eaten the bread of an alien!"

"Am I an alien — mother of my son?"

"What else — Sahib? . . . Oh, forgive me — forgive! The death has driven me mad. Thou art the life of my heart, and the light of my eyes, and the breath of my life, and — and I have put thee from me, though it was but for a moment. If thou goest away to whom shall I look for help? Do not be angry. Indeed, it was the pain that spoke and not thy slave."

"I know, I know. We be two who were three. The greater need therefore that we should be one."

They were sitting on the roof as of custom. The night was a warm one in early spring, and sheet-lightning was dancing on the horizon to a broken tune played by far-off thunder. Ameera settled herself in Holden's arms.

"The dry earth is lowing like a cow for the rain, and I — I am afraid. It was not like this when we counted the stars. But thou lovest me as much as before, though a bond is taken away? Answer!"

"I love more because a new bond has come

out of the sorrow that we have eaten together, and that thou knowest."

"Yea, I knew," said Ameera in a very small whisper. "But it is good to hear thee say so, my life, who art so strong to help. I will be a child no more, but a woman and an aid to thee. Listen! Give me my *sitar* and I will sing bravely."

She took the light silver-studded *sitar* and began a song of the great hero Rajah Rasalu. The hand failed on the strings, the tune halted, checked, and at a low note turned off to the poor little nursery-rhyme about the wicked crow —

And the wild plums grow in the jungle, only a penny a
    pound.
Only a penny a pound, *baba* — only . . .

Then came the tears, and the piteous rebellion against fate till she slept, moaning a little in her sleep, with the right arm thrown clear of the body as though it protected something that was not there. It was after this night that life became a little easier for Holden. The ever-present pain of loss drove him into his work, and the work repaid him by filling up his mind for nine or ten hours a day. Ameera sat alone in the house and brooded, but grew happier when she understood that Holden was more at ease, according to the custom of women. They touched happiness again, but this time with caution.

"It was because we loved Tota that he died. The jealousy of God was upon us," said Ameera. "I have hung up a large black jar before our window to turn the evil eye from us, and we must make no protestations of delight, but go softly underneath the stars, lest God find us out. Is that not good talk, worthless one?"

She had shifted the accent on the word that means "beloved," in proof of the sincerity of her purpose. But the kiss that followed the new christening was a thing that any deity might have envied. They went about henceforward saying, "It is naught, it is naught;" and hoping that all the Powers heard.

The Powers were busy on other things. They had allowed thirty million people four years of plenty wherein men fed well and the crops were certain, and the birth-rate rose year by year; the districts reported a purely agricultural population varying from nine hundred to two thousand to the square mile of the overburdened earth; and the Member for Lower Tooting, wandering about India in pot-hat and frock-coat, talked largely of the benefits of British rule and suggested as the one thing needful the establishment of a duly qualified electoral system and a general bestowal of the franchise. His long-suffering hosts smiled and made him welcome, and when he paused to admire, with pretty picked words, the blossom of

the blood-red *dhak*-tree that had flowered untimely
for a sign of what was coming, they smiled more
than ever.

It was the Deputy Commissioner of Kot-Kumharsen, staying at the club for a day, who lightly
told a tale that made Holden's blood run cold as
he overheard the end.

"He won't bother any one any more. Never
saw a man so astonished in my life. By Jove, I
thought he meant to ask a question in the House
about it. Fellow-passenger in his ship — dined
next him — bowled over by cholera and died in
eighteen hours. You needn't laugh, you fellows.
The Member for Lower Tooting is awfully
angry about it; but he's more scared. I think
he's going to take his enlightened self out of
India."

"I'd give a good deal if he were knocked over.
It might keep a few vestrymen of his kidney to
their own parish. But what's this about cholera?
It's full early for anything of that kind," said
the warden of an unprofitable salt-lick.

"Don't know," said the Deputy Commissioner
reflectively. "We've got locusts with us. There's
sporadic cholera all along the north — at least
we're calling it sporadic for decency's sake. The
spring crops are short in five districts, and nobody
seems to know where the rains are. It's nearly
March now. I don't want to scare anybody,

but it seems to me that Nature's going to audit her accounts with a big red pencil this summer."

"Just when I wanted to take leave, too!" said a voice across the room.

"There won't be much leave this year, but there ought to be a great deal of promotion. I've come in to persuade the Government to put my pet canal on the list of famine-relief works. It's an ill wind that blows no good. I shall get that canal finished at last."

"Is it the old programme then," said Holden; "famine, fever, and cholera?"

"Oh, no. Only local scarcity and an unusual prevalence of seasonal sickness. You'll find it all in the reports if you live till next year. You're a lucky chap. *You* haven't got a wife to send out of harm's way. The hill-stations ought to be full of women this year."

"I think you're inclined to exaggerate the talk in the *bazars*," said a young civilian in the Secretariat. "Now I have observed —— "

"I daresay you have," said the Deputy Commissioner, "but you've a great deal more to observe, my son. In the meantime, I wish to observe to you —— " and he drew him aside to discuss the construction of the canal that was so dear to his heart. Holden went to his bungalow and began to understand that he was not alone in the world, and also that he was afraid for the sake of another — which is the most soul-satisfying fear known to man.

Two months later, as the Deputy had foretold, Nature began to audit her accounts with a red pencil. On the heels of the spring-reapings came a cry for bread, and the Government, which had decreed that no man should die of want, sent wheat. Then came the cholera from all four quarters of the compass. It struck a pilgrim-gathering of half a million at a sacred shrine. Many died at the feet of their god; the others broke and ran over the face of the land, carrying the pestilence with them. It smote a walled city and killed two hundred a day. The people crowded the trains, hanging on to the footboards and squatting on the roofs of the carriages, and the cholera followed them, for at each station they dragged out the dead and the dying. They died by the roadside, and the horses of the Englishmen shied at the corpses in the grass. The rains did not come, and the earth turned to iron lest man should escape death by hiding in her. The English sent their wives away to the hills and went about their work, coming forward as they were bidden to fill the gaps in the fighting-line. Holden, sick with fear of losing his chiefest treasure on earth, had done his best to persuade Ameera to go away with her mother to the Himalayas.

"Why should I go?" said she one evening on the roof.

"There is sickness, and people are dying, and all the white *mem-log* have gone."

"All of them?"

"All — unless perhaps there remain some old scald-head who vexes her husband's heart by running risk of death."

"Nay; who stays is my sister, and thou must not abuse her, for I will be a scald-head too. I am glad all the bold *mem-log* are gone."

"Do I speak to a woman or a babe? Go to the hills and I will see to it that thou goest like a queen's daughter. Think, child. In a red-lacquered bullock-cart, veiled and curtained, with brass peacocks upon the pole and red cloth hangings. I will send two orderlies for guard, and —— "

"Peace! Thou art the babe in speaking thus. What use are those toys to me? *He* would have patted the bullocks and played with the housings. For his sake, perhaps, — thou hast made me very English — I might have gone. Now, I will not. Let the *mem-log* run."

"Their husbands are sending them, beloved."

"Very good talk. Since when hast thou been my husband to tell me what to do? I have but borne thee a son. Thou art only all the desire of my soul to me. How shall I depart when I know

that if evil befall thee by the breadth of so much
as my littlest finger-nail — is that not small? — I
should be aware of it though I were in paradise.
And here, this summer thou mayest die—*ai, janee,*
die!—and in dying they might call to tend thee a
white woman, and she would rob me in the last
of thy love!"

"But love is not born in a moment or on a
death-bed!"

"What dost thou know of love, stoneheart?
She would take thy thanks at least, and, by God
and the Prophet and Beebee Miriam the mother
of thy Prophet, that I will never endure. My
lord and my love, let there be no more foolish
talk of going away. Where thou art, I am. It
is enough." She put an arm round his neck and
a hand on his mouth.

There are not many happinesses so complete as
those that are snatched under the shadow of the
sword. They sat together and laughed, calling
each other openly by every pet name that could
move the wrath of the gods. The city below
them was locked up in its own torments. Sulphur fires blazed in the streets; the conches in the
Hindu temples screamed and bellowed, for the
gods were inattentive in those days. There was
a service in the great Mahomedan shrine, and the
call to prayer from the minarets was almost un-
ceasing. They heard the wailing in the houses

of the dead, and once the shriek of a mother who had lost a child and was calling for its return. In the gray dawn they saw the dead borne out through the city gates, each litter with its own little knot of mourners. Wherefore they kissed each other and shivered.

It was a red and heavy audit, for the land was very sick and needed a little breathing-space ere the torrent of cheap life should flood it anew. The children of immature fathers and undeveloped mothers made no resistance. They were cowed and sat still, waiting till the sword should be sheathed in November if it were so willed. There were gaps among the English, but the gaps were filled. The work of superintending famine-relief, cholera-sheds, medicine-distribution, and what little sanitation was possible, went forward because it was so ordered.

Holden had been told to keep himself in readiness to move to replace the next man who should fall. There were twelve hours in each day when he could not see Ameera, and she might die in three. He was considering what his pain would be if he could not see her for three months, or if she died out of his sight. He was absolutely certain that her death would be demanded — so certain that when he looked up from the telegram and saw Pir Khan breathless in the doorway, he laughed aloud. "And?" said he,——

"When there is a cry in the night and the spirit flutters into the throat, who has a charm that will restore? Come swiftly, Heaven-born! It is the black cholera."

Holden galloped to his home. The sky was heavy with clouds, for the long-deferred rains were near and the heat was stifling. Ameera's mother met him in the courtyard, whimpering, "She is dying. She is nursing herself into death. She is all but dead. What shall I do, Sahib?"

Ameera was lying in the room in which Tota had been born. She made no sign when Holden entered, because the human soul is a very lonely thing, and, when it is getting ready to go away, hides itself in a misty borderland where the living may not follow. The black cholera does its work quietly and without explanation. Ameera was being thrust out of life as though the Angel of Death had himself put his hand upon her. The quick breathing seemed to show that she was either afraid or in pain, but neither eyes nor mouth gave any answer to Holden's kisses. There was nothing to be said or done. Holden could only wait and suffer. The first drops of the rain began to fall on the roof, and he could hear shouts of joy in the parched city.

The soul came back a little and the lips moved. Holden bent down to listen. "Keep nothing of mine," said Ameera. "Take no hair from my

133

head. *She* would make thee burn it later on.
That flame I should feel. Lower! Stoop lower!
Remember only that I was thine and bore thee a
son. Though thou wed a white woman to-morrow, the pleasure of receiving in thy arms thy first
son is taken from thee for ever. Remember me
when thy son is born—the one that shall carry thy
name before all men. His misfortunes be on my
head. I bear witness—I bear witness "—the lips
were forming the words on his ear—"that there
is no God but—thee, beloved!"

Then she died. Holden sat still, and all thought
was taken from him,—till he heard Ameera's
mother lift the curtain.

"Is she dead, Sahib?"

"She is dead."

"Then I will mourn, and afterwards take an in-
ventory of the furniture in this house. For that
will be mine. The Sahib does not mean to resume
it? It is so little, so very little, Sahib, and I am
an old woman. I would like to lie softly."

"For the mercy of God be silent a while. Go
out and mourn where I cannot hear."

"Sahib, she will be buried in four hours."

"I know the custom. I shall go ere she is taken
away. That matter is in thy hands. Look to it,
that the bed on which—on which she lies——"

"Aha! That beautiful red-lacquered bed. I
have long desired——"

"That the bed is left here untouched for my disposal. All else in the house is thine. Hire a cart, take everything, go hence, and before sunrise let there be nothing in this house but that which I have ordered thee to respect."

"I am an old woman. I would stay at least for the days of mourning, and the rains have just broken. Whither shall I go?"

"What is that to me? My order is that there is a going. The house gear is worth a thousand rupees, and my orderly shall bring thee a hundred rupees to-night."

"That is very little. Think of the cart-hire."

"It shall be nothing unless thou goest, and with speed. O woman, get hence and leave me with my dead!"

The mother shuffled down the staircase, and in her anxiety to take stock of the house-fittings forgot to mourn. Holden stayed by Ameera's side and the rain roared on the roof. He could not think connectedly by reason of the noise, though he made many attempts to do so. Then four sheeted ghosts glided dripping into the room and stared at him through their veils. They were the washers of the dead. Holden left the room and went out to his horse. He had come in a dead, stifling calm through ankle-deep dust. He found the courtyard a rain-lashed pond alive with frogs; a torrent of yellow water ran under the gate, and a roaring wind drove the bolts of the rain like buck-shot against the mud walls. Pir Khan was shivering in his little hut by the gate, and the horse was stamping uneasily in the water.

"I have been told the Sahib's order," said Pir Khan. "It is well. This house is now desolate. I go also, for my monkey-face would be a reminder of that which has been. Concerning the bed, I will bring that to thy house yonder in the morning; but remember, Sahib, it will be to thee a knife turning in a green wound. I go upon a pilgrimage, and I will take no money. I have grown fat in the protection of the Presence whose sorrow is my sorrow. For the last time I hold his stirrup."

He touched Holden's foot with both hands and the horse sprang out into the road, where the creaking bamboos were whipping the sky, and all the frogs were chuckling. Holden could not see for the rain in his face. He put his hands before his eyes and muttered —

"Oh, you brute! You utter brute!"

The news of his trouble was already in his bungalow. He read the knowledge in his butler's eyes when Ahmed Khan brought in food, and for the first and last time in his life laid a hand upon his master's shoulder, saying, "Eat, Sahib, eat. Meat is good against sorrow. I also have known. Moreover, the shadows come and go, Sahib; the shadows come and go. These be curried eggs."

Holden could neither eat nor sleep. The heavens sent down eight inches of rain in that night and washed the earth clean. The waters tore down walls, broke roads, and scoured open the shallow graves on the Mahomedan burying-ground. All next day it rained, and Holden sat still in his house considering his sorrow. On the morning of the third day he received a telegram which said only, "Ricketts, Myndonie. Dying. Holden relieve. Immediate." Then he thought that before he departed he would look at the house wherein he had been master and lord. There was a break in the weather, and the rank earth steamed with vapour.

He found that the rains had torn down the mud pillars of the gateway, and the heavy wooden gate that had guarded his life hung lazily from one hinge. There was grass three inches high in the courtyard; Pir Khan's lodge was empty, and the sodden thatch sagged between the beams. A gray squirrel was in possession of the verandah, as if the house had been untenanted for thirty years instead of three days. Ameera's mother had removed everything except some mildewed matting. The *tick-tick* of the little scorpions as they hurried across the floor was the only sound in the house. Ameera's room and the other one where Tota had lived were heavy with mildew; and the narrow staircase leading to the roof was streaked and stained with rain-borne mud. Holden saw all these things, and came out again to meet in the road Durga Dass, his landlord,— portly, affable, clothed in white muslin, and driving a Cee-spring buggy. He was overlooking his property to see how the roofs stood the stress of the first rains.

"I have heard," said he, "you will not take this place any more, Sahib?"

"What are you going to do with it?"

"Perhaps I shall let it again."

"Then I will keep it on while I am away."

Durga Dass was silent for some time. "You shall not take it on, Sahib," he said. "When I was a young man I also ——, but to-day I am a member of the Municipality. Ho! Ho! No. When the birds have gone what need to keep the nest? I will have it pulled down — the timber will sell for something always. It shall be pulled down, and the Municipality shall make a road across, as they desire, from the burning-ghaut to the city wall, so that no man may say where this house stood."

NABOTH

THIS was how it happened; and the truth is also an allegory of Empire.

I met him at the corner of my garden, an empty basket on his head, and an unclean cloth round his loins. That was all the property to which Naboth had the shadow of a claim when I first saw him. He opened our acquaintance by begging. He was very thin and showed nearly as many ribs as his basket; and he told me a long story about fever and a lawsuit, and an iron cauldron that had been seized by the court in execution of a decree. I put my hand into my pocket to help Naboth, as kings of the East have helped alien adventurers to the loss of their kingdoms. A rupee had hidden in my waistcoat lining. I never knew it was there, and gave the trove to Naboth as a direct gift from Heaven. He replied that I was the only legitimate Protector of the Poor he had ever known.

Next morning he reappeared, a little fatter in the round, and curled himself into knots in the front verandah. He said I was his father and his mother, and the direct descendant of all the gods in his Pantheon, besides controlling the destinies of the universe. He himself was but a sweetmeat-seller, and much less important than the dirt under my feet. I had heard this sort of thing before, so I asked him what he wanted. My rupee, quoth Naboth, had raised him to the everlasting heavens, and he wished to prefer a request. He wished to establish a sweetmeat-pitch near the house of his benefactor, to gaze on my revered countenance as I went to and fro illumining the world. I was graciously pleased to give permission, and he went away with his head between his knees.

Now at the far end of my garden the ground slopes toward the public road, and the slope is crowned with a thick shrubbery. There is a short carriage-road from the house to the Mall, which passes close to the shrubbery. Next afternoon I saw that Naboth had seated himself at the bottom of the slope, down in the dust of the public road, and in the full glare of the sun, with a starved basket of greasy sweets in front of him. He had gone into trade once more on the strength of my munificent donation, and the ground was as Paradise by my honoured favour. Remember, there was only Naboth, his basket, the sunshine, and the gray dust when the sap of my Empire first began.

Next day he had moved himself up the slope

nearer to my shrubbery, and waved a palm-leaf
fan to keep the flies off the sweets. So I judged
that he must have done a fair trade.

Four days later I noticed that he had backed
himself and his basket under the shadow of the
shrubbery, and had tied an Isabella-coloured rag
between two branches in order to make more
shade. There were plenty of sweets in his basket.
I thought that trade must certainly be looking up.

Seven weeks later the Government took up a
plot of ground for a Chief Court close to the end
of my compound, and employed nearly four hundred coolies on the foundations. Naboth bought
a blue and white striped blanket, a brass lamp-
stand, and a small boy to cope with the rush of
trade, which was tremendous.

Five days later he bought a huge, fat, red-backed
account-book and a glass inkstand. Thus I saw
that the coolies had been getting into his debt, and
that commerce was increasing on legitimate lines
of credit. Also I saw that the one basket had
grown into three, and that Naboth had backed
and hacked into the shrubbery, and made himself
a nice little clearing for the proper display of the
basket, the blanket, the books, and the boy.

One week and five days later he had built a
mud fireplace in the clearing, and the fat account-
book was overflowing. He said that God created
few Englishmen of my kind, and that I was the

incarnation of all human virtues. He offered me
some of his sweets as tribute, and by accepting
these I acknowledged him as my feudatory under
the skirt of my protection.

Three weeks later I noticed that the boy was in
the habit of cooking Naboth's mid-day meal for
him, and Naboth was beginning to grow a stomach. He had hacked away more of my shrubbery,
and owned another and a fatter account-book.

Eleven weeks later Naboth had eaten his way
nearly through that shrubbery, and there was a reed
hut with a bedstead outside it, standing in the
little glade that he had eroded. Two dogs and a
baby slept on the bedstead. So I fancied Naboth
had taken a wife. He said that he had, by my
favour, done this thing, and that I was several
times finer than Krishna.

Six weeks and two days later a mud wall had
grown up at the back of the hut. There were
fowls in front and it smelt a little. The Municipal
Secretary said that a cess-pool was forming in the
public road from the drainage of my compound,
and that I must take steps to clear it away. I
spoke to Naboth. He said I was Lord Paramount
of his earthly concerns, and the garden was all my
own property, and sent me some more sweets in a
second-hand duster.

Two months later a coolie bricklayer was killed
in a scuffle that took place opposite Naboth's Vine-

yard. The Inspector of Police said it was a serious case; went into my servants' quarters; insulted my butler's wife, and wanted to arrest my butler. The curious thing about the murder was that most of the coolies were drunk at the time. Naboth pointed out that my name was a strong shield between him and his enemies, and he expected that another baby would be born to him shortly.

Four months later the hut was *all* mud walls, very solidly built, and Naboth had used most of my shrubbery for his five goats. A silver watch and an aluminium chain shone upon his very round stomach. My servants were alarmingly drunk several times, and used to waste the day with Naboth when they got the chance. I spoke to Naboth. He said, by my favour and the glory of my countenance, he would make all his women-folk ladies, and that if any one hinted that he was running an illicit still under the shadow of the tamarisks, why, I, his Suzerain, was to prosecute.

A week later he hired a man to make several dozen square yards of trellis-work to put round the back of his hut, that his women-folk might be screened from the public gaze. The man went away in the evening, and left his day's work to pave the short cut from the public road to my house. I was driving home in the dusk, and turned the corner by Naboth's Vineyard quickly. The next thing I knew was that the horses of the phaeton were stamping and plunging in the strongest sort of bamboo net-work. Both beasts came down. One rose with nothing more than chipped knees. The other was so badly kicked that I was forced to shoot him.

Naboth is gone now, and his hut is ploughed into its native mud with sweetmeats instead of salt for a sign that the place is accursed. I have built a summer-house to overlook the end of the garden, and it is as a fort on my frontier whence I guard my Empire.

I know exactly how Ahab felt. He has been shamefully misrepresented in the Scriptures.

THE SENDING OF DANA DA

When the Devil rides on your chest remember the *chamar*.
— *Native Proverb*.

ONCE upon a time, some people in India made a new Heaven and a new Earth out of broken tea-cups, a missing brooch or two, and a hair-brush. These were hidden under bushes, or stuffed into holes in the hillside, and an entire Civil Service of subordinate Gods used to find or mend them again; and every one said: "There are more things in Heaven and Earth than are dreamt of in our philosophy." Several other things happened also, but the Religion never seemed to get much beyond its first manifestations; though it added an air-line postal service, and orchestral effects in order to keep abreast of the times and choke off competition.

This Religion was too elastic for ordinary use. It stretched itself and embraced pieces of everything that the medicine-men of all ages have manufactured. It approved of and stole from Freemasonry; looted the Latter-day Rosicrucians of half their pet words; took any fragments of Egyp-

tian philosophy that it found in the " Encyclo-
pædia Britannica "; annexed as many of the Vedas
as had been translated into French or English, and
talked of all the rest; built in the German versions
of what is left of the Zend Avesta; encouraged
White, Gray and Black Magic, including spiri-
tualism, palmistry, fortune-telling by cards, hot
chestnuts, double-kernelled nuts and tallow-drop-
pings; would have adopted Voodoo and Oboe had
it known anything about them, and showed itself,
in every way, one of the most accommodating arrangements that had ever been invented since the
birth of the Sea.

When it was in thorough working order, with
all the machinery, down to the subscriptions, complete, Dana Da came from nowhere, with nothing
in his hands, and wrote a chapter in its history
which has hitherto been unpublished. He said
that his first name was Dana, and his second was
Da. Now, setting aside Dana of the New York
" Sun," Dana is a Bhil name, and Da fits no native
of India unless you accept the Bengali Dé as the
original spelling. Da is Lap or Finnish; and
Dana Da was neither Finn, Chin, Bhil, Bengali,
Lap, Nair, Gond, Romaney, Magh, Bokhariot,
Kurd, Armenian, Levantine, Jew, Persian, Punjabi,
Madrasi, Parsee, nor anything else known to eth-
nologists. He was simply Dana Da, and declined
to give further information. For the sake of

brevity and as roughly indicating his origin, he was called " The Native." He might have been the original Old Man of the Mountains, who is said to be the only authorized head of the Tea-cup Creed. Some people said that he was; but Dana Da used to smile and deny any connection with the cult; explaining that he was an " Independent Experimenter."

As I have said, he came from nowhere, with his hands behind his back, and studied the Creed for three weeks; sitting at the feet of those best competent to explain its mysteries. Then he laughed aloud and went away, but the laugh might have been either of devotion or derision.

When he returned he was without money, but his pride was unabated. He declared that he knew more about the Things in Heaven and Earth than those who taught him, and for this contumacy was abandoned altogether.

His next appearance in public life was at a big cantonment in Upper India, and he was then telling fortunes with the help of three leaden dice, a very dirty old cloth, and a little tin box of opium pills. He told better fortunes when he was allowed half a bottle of whiskey; but the things which he invented on the opium were quite worth the money. He was in reduced circumstances. Among other people's he told the fortune of an Englishman who had once been interested in the

Simla Creed, but who, later on, had married and forgotten all his old knowledge in the study of babies and things. The Englishman allowed Dana Da to tell a fortune for charity's sake, and gave him five rupees, a dinner, and some old clothes. When he had eaten, Dana Da professed gratitude, and asked if there were anything he could do for his host — in the esoteric line.

"Is there any one that you love?" said Dana Da. The Englishman loved his wife, but had no desire to drag her name into the conversation. He therefore shook his head.

"Is there any one that you hate?" said Dana Da. The Englishman said that there were several men whom he hated deeply.

"Very good," said Dana Da, upon whom the whiskey and the opium were beginning to tell. "Only give me their names, and I will despatch a Sending to them and kill them."

Now a Sending is a horrible arrangement, first invented, they say, in Iceland. It is a Thing sent by a wizard, and may take any form, but, most generally, wanders about the land in the shape of a little purple cloud till it finds the Sendee, and him it kills by changing into the form of a horse, or a cat, or a man without a face. It is not strictly a native patent, though *chamars* of the skin and hide castes can, if irritated, despatch a Sending which sits on the breast of their enemy by night and nearly kills him. Very few natives care to irritate *chamars* for this reason.

"Let me despatch a Sending," said Dana Da; "I am nearly dead now with want, and drink, and opium; but I should like to kill a man before I die. I can send a Sending anywhere you choose, and in any form except in the shape of a man."

The Englishman had no friends that he wished to kill, but partly to soothe Dana Da, whose eyes were rolling, and partly to see what would be done, he asked whether a modified Sending could not be arranged for — such a Sending as should make a man's life a burden to him, and yet do him no harm. If this were possible, he notified his willingness to give Dana Da ten rupees for the job.

"I am not what I was once," said Dana Da, "and I must take the money because I am poor. To what Englishman shall I send it?"

"Send a Sending to Lone Sahib," said the Englishman, naming a man who had been most bitter in rebuking him for his apostasy from the Teacup Creed. Dana Da laughed and nodded.

"I could have chosen no better man myself," said he. "I will see that he finds the Sending about his path and about his bed."

He lay down on the hearth-rug, turned up the whites of his eyes, shivered all over and began to snort. This was Magic, or Opium, or the Sending, or all three. When he opened his eyes he vowed that the Sending had started upon the war-path, and was at that moment flying up to the town where Lone Sahib lives.

" Give me my ten rupees," said Dana Da wearily, "and write a letter to Lone Sahib, telling him, and all who believe with him, that you and a friend are using a power greater than theirs. They will see that you are speaking the truth."

He departed unsteadily, with the promise of some more rupees if anything came of the Sending.

The Englishman sent a letter to Lone Sahib, couched in what he remembered of the terminology of the Creed. He wrote: " I also, in the days of what you held to be my backsliding, have obtained Enlightenment, and with Enlightenment has come Power." Then he grew so deeply mysterious that the recipient of the letter could make neither head nor tail of it, and was proportionately impressed; for he fancied that his friend had become a " fifth-rounder." When a man is a " fifth-rounder " he can do more than Slade and Houdin combined.

Lone Sahib read the letter in five different fashions, and was beginning a sixth interpretation when his bearer dashed in with the news that there was a cat on the bed. Now if there was one thing that Lone Sahib hated more than another, it was a cat. He scolded the bearer for not turning it out of the house. The bearer said that he was afraid. All the doors of the bedroom had been shut throughout the morning, and no *real* cat could possibly have entered the room. He would prefer not to meddle with the creature.

Lone Sahib entered the room gingerly, and there, on the pillow of his bed, sprawled and whimpered a wee white kitten; not a jumpsome, frisky little beast, but a slug-like crawler with its eyes barely opened and its paws lacking strength or direction. — a kitten that ought to have been in a basket with its mamma. Lone Sahib caught it by the scruff of its neck, handed it over to the sweeper to be drowned, and fined the bearer four annas.

That evening, as he was reading in his room, he fancied that he saw something moving about on the hearth-rug, outside the circle of light from his reading-lamp. When the thing began to myowl, he realised that it was a kitten — a wee white kitten, nearly blind and very miserable. He was seriously angry, and spoke bitterly to his bearer, who said that there was no kitten in the room when he brought in the lamp, and *real* kittens of tender age generally had mother-cats in attendance.

" If the Presence will go out into the verandah and listen," said the bearer, " he will hear no cats. How, therefore, can the kitten on the bed and the kitten on the hearth-rug be real kittens ? "

Lone Sahib went out to listen, and the bearer

followed him, but there was no sound of any one
mewing for her children. He returned to his room,
having hurled the kitten down the hillside, and
wrote out the incidents of the day for the benefit
of his co-religionists. Those people were so absolutely free from superstition that they ascribed
anything a little out of the common to Agencies.
As it was their business to know all about the
Agencies, they were on terms of almost indecent
familiarity with Manifestations of every kind.
Their letters dropped from the ceiling — un-
stamped — and Spirits used to squatter up and
down their staircases all night; but they had never
come into contact with kittens. Lone Sahib wrote
out the facts, noting the hour and the minute, as
every Psychical Observer is bound to do, and ap-
pending the Englishman's letter because it was the
most mysterious document and might have had a
bearing upon anything in this world or the next.
An outsider would have translated all the tangle
thus: " Look out! You laughed at me once, and
now I am going to make you sit up."

Lone Sahib's co-religionists found that meaning
in it; but their translation was refined and full of
four-syllable words. They held a sederunt, and
were filled with tremulous joy, for, in spite of their
familiarity with all the other worlds and cycles,
they had a very human awe of things sent from
Ghost-land. They met in Lone Sahib's room in

shrouded and sepulchral gloom, and their conclave was broken up by a clinking among the photo-frames on the mantelpiece. A wee white kitten, nearly blind, was looping and writhing itself between the clock and the candlesticks. That stopped all investigations or doubtings. Here was the Manifestation in the flesh. It was, so far as could be seen, devoid of purpose, but it was a Manifestation of undoubted authenticity.

They drafted a Round Robin to the English-man, the backslider of old days, adjuring him in the interests of the Creed to explain whether there was any connection between the embodiment of some Egyptian God or other (I have forgotten the name) and his communication. They called the kitten Ra, or Toth, or Tum, or something; and when Lone Sahib confessed that the first one had, at his most misguided instance, been drowned by the sweeper, they said consolingly that in his next life he would be a "bounder," and not even a "rounder" of the lowest grade. These words may not be quite correct, but they accurately express the sense of the house.

When the Englishman received the Round Robin — it came by post — he was startled and bewildered. He sent into the bazar for Dana Da, who read the letter and laughed. "That is my Sending," said he. "I told you I would work well. Now give me another ten rupees."

"But what in the world is this gibberish about Egyptian Gods?" asked the Englishman.

"Cats," said Dana Da with a hiccough, for he had discovered the Englishman's whiskey-bottle. "Cats, and cats, and cats! Never was such a Sending. A hundred of cats. Now give me ten more rupees and write as I dictate."

Dana Da's letter was a curiosity. It bore the Englishman's signature, and hinted at cats — at a Sending of Cats. The mere words on paper were creepy and uncanny to behold.

"What have you done, though?" said the Englishman. "I am as much in the dark as ever. Do you mean to say that you can actually send this absurd Sending you talk about?"

"Judge for yourself," said Dana Da. "What does that letter mean? In a little time they will all be at my feet and yours, and I — O Glory! — will be drugged or drunk all day long."

Dana Da knew his people.

When a man who hates cats wakes up in the morning and finds a little squirming kitten on his breast, or puts his hand into his ulster-pocket and finds a little half-dead kitten where his gloves should be, or opens his trunk and finds a vile kitten among his dress-shirts, or goes for a long ride with his mackintosh strapped on his saddle-bow and shakes a little squawling kitten from its folds when he opens it, or goes out to dinner and finds a little blind kitten under his chair, or stays at home and finds a writhing kitten under the quilt, or wriggling among his boots, or hanging, head downwards, in his tobacco-jar, or being mangled by his terrier in the verandah,— when such a man finds one kitten, neither more nor less, once a day in a place where no kitten rightly could or should be, he is naturally upset. When he dare not mur-der his daily trove because he believes it to be a Manifestation, an Emissary, an Embodiment, and half a dozen other things all out of the regular course of nature, he is more than upset. He is actually distressed. Some of Lone Sahib's co-re-ligionists thought that he was a highly favoured individual; but many said that if he had treated the first kitten with proper respect — as suited a Toth-Ra-Tum-Sennacherib Embodiment — all this trouble would have been averted. They compared him to the Ancient Mariner, but none the less they were proud of him and proud of the English-man who had sent the Manifestation. They did not call it a Sending because Icelandic magic was not in their programme.

After sixteen kittens, that is to say after one fortnight, for there were three kittens on the first day to impress the fact of the Sending, the whole camp was uplifted by a letter — it came flying through a· window — from the Old Man of the Mountains — the Head of all the Creed — explain-

155

ing the Manifestation in the most beautiful language and soaking up all the credit for it himself. The Englishman, said the letter, was not there at all. He was a backslider without Power or Asceticism, who couldn't even raise a table by force of volition, much less project an army of kittens through space. The entire arrangement, said the letter, was strictly orthodox, worked and sanctioned by the highest authorities within the pale of the Creed. There was great joy at this, for some of the weaker brethren seeing, that an outsider who had been working on independent lines could create kittens, whereas their own rulers had never gone beyond crockery—and broken at best—were showing a desire to break line on their own trail. In fact, there was the promise of a schism. A second Round Robin was drafted to the Englishman, beginning: "O Scoffer," and ending with a selection of curses from the Rites of Mizraim and Memphis and the Commination of Jugana, who was a "fifth rounder" upon whose name an upstart "third-rounder" once traded. A papal excommunication is a *billet-doux* compared to the Commination of Jugana. The Englishman had been proved, under the hand and seal of the Old Man of the Mountains, to have appropriated Virtue and pretended to have Power which, in reality, belonged only to the Supreme Head. Naturally the Round Robin did not spare him.

He handed the letter to Dana Da to translate into decent English. The effect on Dana Da was curious. At first he was furiously angry, and then he laughed for five minutes.

"I had thought," he said, "that they would have come to me. In another week I would have shown that I sent the Sending, and they would have discrowned the Old Man of the Mountains who has sent this Sending of mine. Do you do nothing. The time has come for me to act. Write as I dictate, and I will put them to shame. But give me ten more rupees."

At Dana Da's dictation the Englishman wrote nothing less than a formal challenge to the Old Man of the Mountains. It wound up: "And if this Manifestation be from your hand, then let it go forward; but if it be from my hand, I will that the Sending shall cease in two days' time. On that day there shall be twelve kittens and thenceforward none at all. The people shall judge between us." This was signed by Dana Da, who added pentacles and pentagrams, and a *crux ansata*, and half a dozen *swastikas*, and a Triple Tau to his name, just to show that he was all he laid claim to be.

The challenge was read out to the gentlemen and ladies, and they remembered then that Dana Da had laughed at them some years ago. It was officially announced that the Old Man of the Moun-

tains would treat the matter with contempt; Dana
Da being an Independent Investigator without a
single " round " at the back of him. But this did
not soothe his people. They wanted to see a fight.
They were very human for all their spirituality.
Lone Sahib, who was really being worn out with
kittens, submitted meekly to his fate. He felt
that he was being " kittened to prove the power
of Dana Da," as the poet says.

When the stated day dawned, the shower of
kittens began. Some were white and some were
tabby, and all were about the same loathsome age.
Three were on his hearth-rug, three in his bathroom, and the other six turned up at intervals
among the visitors who came to see the prophecy
break down. Never was a more satisfactory Sending. On the next day there were no kittens, and
the next day and all the other days were kittenless
and quiet. The people murmured and looked to
the Old Man of the Mountains for an explanation.
A letter, written on a palm-leaf, dropped from the
ceiling, but every one except Lone Sahib felt that
letters were not what the occasion demanded.
There should have been cats, there should have been
cats,— full-grown ones. The letter proved conclu-
sively that there had been a hitch in the Psychic
Current which, colliding with a Dual Identity, had
interfered with the Percipient Activity all along
the main line. The kittens were still going on,

but owing to some failure in the Developing Fluid, they were not materialised. The air was thick with letters for a few days afterwards. Unseen hands played Glück and Beethoven on finger-bowls and clock-shades; but all men felt that Psychic Life was a mockery without materialised Kittens. Even Lone Sahib shouted with the majority on this head. Dana Da's letters were very insulting, and if he had then offered to lead a new departure, there is no knowing what might not have happened.

But Dana Da was dying of whiskey and opium in the Englishman's godown, and had small heart for honours.

"They have been put to shame," said he. "Never was such a Sending. It has killed me."

"Nonsense," said the Englishman, "you are going to die, Dana Da, and that sort of stuff must be left behind. I'll admit that you have made some queer things come about. Tell me honestly, now, how was it done?"

"Give me ten more rupees," said Dana Da faintly, "and if I die before I spend them, bury them with me." The silver was counted out while Dana Da was fighting with Death. His hand closed upon the money and he smiled a grim smile.

"Bend low," he whispered. The Englishman bent.

"*Bunnia* — Mission-school — expelled — *box-wallah* (peddler) — Ceylon pearl-merchant — all mine English education — out-casted, and made up name Dana Da — England with American thought-reading man and — and — you gave me ten rupees several times — I gave the Sahib's bearer two-eight a month for cats — little, little cats. I wrote, and he put them about — very clever man. Very few kittens now in the bazar. Ask Lone Sahib's sweeper's wife."

So saying, Dana Da gasped and passed away into a land where, if all be true, there are no materialisations and the making of new creeds is discouraged.

But consider the gorgeous simplicity of it all!

THE Policeman rode through the Himalayan forest, under the moss-draped oaks, and his orderly trotted after him.

"It's an ugly business, Bhere Singh," said the Policeman. "Where are they?"

"It is a very ugly business," said Bhere Singh; "and as for *them*, they are, doubtless, now frying in a hotter fire than was ever made of spruce-branches."

"Let us hope not," said the Policeman, "for, allowing for the difference between race and race, it's the story of Francesca da Rimini, Bhere Singh."

Bhere Singh knew nothing about Francesca da Rimini, so he held his peace until they came to the charcoal-burners' clearing where the dying flames said "*whit, whit, whit*" as they fluttered and whispered over the white ashes. It must have been a great fire when at full height. Men had seen it at Donga Pa across the valley winking and blazing through the night, and said that the charcoal-burners of Kodru were getting drunk. But it was only Suket Singh, Sepoy of the 102d Pun-

jab Native Infantry, and Athira, a woman, burning — burning —burning.

This was how things befell; and the Policeman's Diary will bear me out.

Athira was the wife of Madu, who was a char-
coal-burner, one-eyed and of a malignant disposi-
tion.   A week after their marriage, he beat Athira
with a heavy stick.   A month later, Suket Singh,
Sepoy, came that way to the cool hills on leave
from his regiment, and electrified the villagers of
Kodru with tales of service and glory under the
Government, and the honour in which he, Suket
Singh, was held by the Colonel Sahib Bahadur.
And Desdemona listened to Othello as Desde-
monas have done all the world over, and, as she
listened, she loved.

"I've a wife of my own," said Suket Singh,
"though that is no matter when you come to think
of it.   I am also due to return to my regiment
after a time, and I cannot be a deserter — I who
intend to be Havildar."   There is no Himalayan
version of "I could not love thee, dear, as much,
Loved I not Honour more "; but Suket Singh
came near to making one.

"Never mind," said Athira, "stay with me, and,
if Madu tries to beat me, you beat him."

"Very good," said Suket Singh; and he beat
Madu severely, to the delight of all the charcoal-
burners of Kodru.

"That is enough," said Suket Singh, as he rolled Madu down the hillside. "Now we shall have peace." But Madu crawled up the grass slope again, and hovered round his hut with angry eyes.

"He'll kill me dead," said Athira to Suket Singh. "You must take me away."

"There'll be a trouble in the Lines. My wife will pull out my beard; but never mind," said Suket Singh, "I will take you."

There was loud trouble in the Lines, and Suket Singh's beard was pulled, and Suket Singh's wife went to live with her mother and took away the children. "That's all right," said Athira; and Suket Singh said, "Yes, that's all right."

So there was only Madu left in the hut that looks across the valley to Donga Pa; and, since the beginning of time, no one has had any sympathy for husbands so unfortunate as Madu.

He went to Juseen Dazé, the wizard-man who keeps the Talking Monkey's Head.

"Get me back my wife," said Madu.

"I can't," said Juseen Dazé, "until you have made the Sutlej in the valley run up the Donga Pa."

"No riddles," said Madu, and he shook his hatchet above Juseen Dazé's white head.

"Give all your money to the headmen of the village," said Juseen Dazé; "and they will hold a communal Council, and the Council will send a message that your wife must come back."

So Madu gave up all his worldly wealth, amounting to twenty-seven rupees, eight annas, three pice, and a silver chain, to the Council of Kodru. And it fell as Juseen Dazé foretold.

They sent Athira's brother down into Suket Singh's regiment to call Athira home. Suket Singh kicked him once round the Lines, and then handed him over to the Havildar, who beat him with a belt.

"Come back," yelled Athira's brother.

"Where to?" said Athira.

"To Madu," said he.

"Never," said she.

"Then Juseen Dazé will send a curse, and you will wither away like a barked tree in the springtime," said Athira's brother. Athira slept over these things.

Next morning she had rheumatism. "I am beginning to wither away like a barked tree in the springtime," she said. "That is the curse of Juseen Dazé."

And she really began to wither away because her heart was dried up with fear, and those who believe in curses die from curses. Suket Singh, too, was afraid because he loved Athira better than his very life. Two months passed, and Athira's brother stood outside the regimental Lines again and yelped, "Aha! You are withering away. Come back."

" I will come back," said Athira.

" Say rather that *we* will come back," said Suket Singh.

" Ai; but when?" said Athira's brother.

" Upon a day very early in the morning," said Suket Singh; and he tramped off to apply to the Colonel Sahib Bahadur for one week's leave.

" I am withering away like a barked tree in the spring," moaned Athira.

" You will be better soon," said Suket Singh; and he told her what was in his heart, and the two laughed together softly, for they loved each other. But Athira grew better from that hour.

They went away together, travelling third-class by train as the regulations provided, and then in a cart to the low hills, and on foot to the high ones. Athira sniffed the scent of the pines of her own hills, the wet Himalayan hills. " It is good to be alive," said Athira.

" Hah!" said Suket Singh. " Where is the Kodru road and where is the Forest Ranger's house?" . . .

" It cost forty rupees twelve years ago," said the Forest Ranger, handing the gun.

" Here are twenty," said Suket Singh, " and you must give me the best bullets."

" It is *very* good to be alive," said Athira wistfully, sniffing the scent of the pine-mould; and they waited till the night had fallen upon Kodru and the Donga Pa. Madu had stacked the dry wood for the next day's charcoal-burning on the spur above his house. "It is courteous in Madu to save us this trouble," said Suket Singh as he stumbled on the pile, which was twelve foot square and four high. "We must wait till the moon rises."

When the moon rose, Athira knelt upon the pile. "If it were only a Government Snider," said Suket Singh ruefully, squinting down the wire-bound barrel of the Forest Ranger's gun.

"Be quick," said Athira; and Suket Singh was quick; but Athira was quick no longer. Then he lit the pile at the four corners and climbed on to it, reloading the gun.

The little flames began to peer up between the big logs atop of the brushwood. "The Government should teach us to pull the triggers with our toes," said Suket Singh grimly to the moon. That was the last public observation of Sepoy Suket Singh.

.   .   .   .   .   .

Upon a day, early in the morning, Madu came to the pyre and shrieked very grievously, and ran away to catch the Policeman who was on tour in the district.

"The base-born has ruined four rupees' worth of charcoal wood," Madu gasped. "He has also killed my wife, and he has left a letter which I cannot read, tied to a pine bough."

In the stiff, formal hand taught in the regimental school, Sepoy Suket Singh had written —

"Let us be burned together, if anything remain over, for we have made the necessary prayers. We have also cursed Madu, and Malak the brother of Athira — both evil men. Send my service to the Colonel Sahib Bahadur."

The Policeman looked long and curiously at the marriage-bed of red and white ashes on which lay, dull black, the barrel of the Ranger's gun. He drove his spurred heel absently into a half-charred log, and the chattering sparks flew upwards. "Most extraordinary people," said the Policeman.

"*Whe-w, whew, ouiou,*" said the little flames.

The Policeman entered the dry bones of the case, for the Punjab Government does not approve of romancing, in his Diary.

"But who will pay me those four rupees?" said Madu.

THE HEAD OF THE DISTRICT

There's a convict more in the Central Jail,
  Behind the old mud wall;
There's a lifter less on the Border trail,
  And the Queen's Peace over all,
      Dear boys,
  The Queen's Peace over all.

For we must bear our leader's blame,
  On us the shame will fall,
If we lift our hand from a fettered land,
  And the Queen's Peace over all,
      Dear boys,
  The Queen's Peace over all!
        The Running of Shindand.

I

THE Indus had risen in flood without warning.
Last night it was a fordable shallow; to-night five
miles of raving muddy water parted bank and
caving bank, and the river was still rising under
the moon. A litter borne by six bearded men, all
unused to the work, stopped in the white sand that
bordered the whiter plain.

"It's God's will," they said. "We dare not

cross to-night, even in a boat. Let us light a fire and cook food. We be tired men."

They looked at the litter inquiringly. Within, the Deputy Commissioner of the Kot-Kumharsen district lay dying of fever. They had brought him across country, six fighting-men of a frontier clan that he had won over to the paths of a moderate righteousness, when he had broken down at the foot of their inhospitable hills. And Tallantire, his assistant, rode with them, heavy-hearted as heavy-eyed with sorrow and lack of sleep. He had served under the sick man for three years, and had learned to love him as men associated in toil of the hardest learn to love — or hate. Dropping from his horse, he parted the curtains of the litter and peered inside.

"Orde — Orde, old man, can you hear? We have to wait till the river goes down, worse luck."

"I hear," returned a dry whisper. "Wait till the river goes down. I thought we should reach camp before the dawn. Polly knows. She'll meet me."

One of the litter-men stared across the river and caught a faint twinkle of light on the far side. He whispered to Tallantire, "There are his camp-fires, and his wife. They will cross in the morning, for they have better boats. Can he live so long?"

Tallantire shook his head. Yardley-Orde was very near to death. What need to vex his soul with hopes of a meeting that could not be? The river gulped at the banks, brought down a cliff of sand, and snarled the more hungrily. The littermen sought for fuel in the waste — dried camel-thorn and refuse of the camps that had waited at the ford. Their sword-belts clinked as they moved softly in the haze of the moonlight, and Tallantire's horse coughed to explain that he would like a blanket.

"I'm cold too," said the voice from the litter. "I fancy this is the end. Poor Polly!"

Tallantire rearranged the blankets; Khoda Dad Khan, seeing this, stripped off his own heavy-wadded sheepskin coat and added it to the pile. "I shall be warm by the fire presently," said he. Tallantire took the wasted body of his chief into his arms and held it against his breast. Perhaps if they kept him very warm Orde might live to see his wife once more. If only blind Providence would send a three-foot fall in the river!

"That's better," said Orde faintly. "Sorry to be a nuisance, but is — is there anything to drink?"

They gave him milk and whiskey, and Tallantire felt a little warmth against his own breast. Orde began to mutter.

"It isn't that I mind dying," he said. "It's leaving Polly and the district. Thank God! we have no children. Dick, you know, I'm dipped — awfully dipped — debts in my first five years' ser-

vice. It isn't much of a pension, but enough for
her. She has her mother at home. Getting there
is the difficulty. And — and — you see, not being
a soldier's wife —— "

" We'll arrange the passage home, of course,"
said Tallantire quietly.

" It's not nice to think of sending round the
hat; but, good Lord! how many men I lie here
and remember that had to do it! Morten's dead
— he was of my year. Shaughnessy is dead, and
he had children; I remember he used to read us
their school-letters; what a bore we thought him!
Evans is dead — Kot-Kumharsen killed him!
Ricketts of Myndonie is dead — and I'm going
too. 'Man that is born of a woman is small po-
tatoes and few in the hill.' That reminds me,
Dick; the four Khusru Kheyl villages in our border want a one-third remittance this spring. That's
fair; their crops are bad. See that they get it, and
speak to Ferris about the canal. I should like to
have lived till that was finished; it means so much
for the North-Indus villages — but Ferris is an
idle beggar — wake him up. You'll have charge
of the district till my successor comes. I wish
they would appoint you permanently; you know
the folk. I suppose it will be Bullows, though.
'Good man, but too weak for frontier work; and
he doesn't understand the priests. The blind priest
at Jagai will bear watching. You'll find it in

171

my papers,— in the uniform-case, I think. Call the Khusru Kheyl men up; I'll hold my last public audience. Khoda Dad Khan!"

The leader of the men sprang to the side of the litter, his companions following.

"Men, I'm dying," said Orde quickly, in the vernacular; "and soon there will be no more Orde Sahib to twist your tails and prevent you from raiding cattle."

"God forbid this thing!" broke out the deep bass chorus: "The Sahib is not going to die."

"Yes, he is; and then he will know whether Mahomed speaks truth, or Moses. But you must be good men when I am not here. Such of you as live in our borders must pay your taxes quietly as before. I have spoken of the villages to be gently treated this year. Such of you as live in the hills must refrain from cattle-lifting, and burn no more thatch, and turn a deaf ear to the voice of the priests, who, not knowing the strength of the Government, would lead you into foolish wars, wherein you will surely die and your crops be eaten by strangers. And you must not sack any caravans, and must leave your arms at the police-post when you come in; as has been your custom, and my order. And Tallantire Sahib will be with you, but I do not know who takes my place. I speak now true talk, for I am as it were already dead, my children,—for though ye be strong men, ye are children."

"And thou art our father and our mother," broke in Khoda Dad Khan with an oath. "What shall we do, now there is no one to speak for us, or to teach us to go wisely!"

"There remains Tallantire Sahib. Go to him; he knows your talk and your heart. Keep the young men quiet, listen to the old men, and obey. Khoda Dad Khan, take my ring. The watch and chain go to thy brother. Keep those things for my sake, and I will speak to whatever God I may encounter and tell him that the Khusru Kheyl are good men. Ye have my leave to go."

Khoda Dad Khan, the ring upon his finger, choked audibly as he caught the well-known formula that closed an interview. His brother turned to look across the river. The dawn was breaking, and a speck of white showed on the dull silver of the stream. "She comes," said the man under his breath. "Can he live for another two hours?" And he pulled the newly-acquired watch out of his belt and looked uncomprehendingly at the dial, as he had seen Englishmen do.

For two hours the bellying sail tacked and blundered up and down the river, Tallantire still clasping Orde in his arms, and Khoda Dad Khan chafing his feet. He spoke now and again of the district and his wife, but, as the end neared, more frequently of the latter. They hoped he did not know that she was even then risking her life in a crazy native boat to regain him. But the awful foreknowledge of the dying deceived them. Wrenching himself forward, Orde looked through the curtains and saw how near was the sail. "That's Polly," he said simply, though his mouth was wried with agony. "Polly and — the grimmest practical joke ever played on a man. Dick — you'll — have — to — explain."

And an hour later Tallantire met on the bank a woman in a gingham riding-habit and a sun-hat who cried out to him for her husband — her boy and her darling — while Khoda Dad Khan threw himself face-down on the sand and covered his eyes.

II

The very simplicity of the notion was its charm. What more easy to win a reputation for far-seeing statesmanship, originality, and, above all, deference to the desires of the people, than by appointing a child of the country to the rule of that country? Two hundred millions of the most loving and grateful folk under Her Majesty's dominion would laud the fact, and their praise would endure for ever. Yet he was indifferent to praise or blame, as befitted the Very Greatest of All the Viceroys. His administration was based upon

174

principle, and the principle must be enforced in season and out of season. His pen and tongue had created the New India, teeming with possibilities — loud-voiced, insistent, a nation among nations — all his very own. Wherefore the Very Greatest of All the Viceroys took another step in advance, and with it counsel of those who should have advised him on the appointment of a successor to Yardley-Orde. There was a gentleman and a member of the Bengal Civil Service who had won his place and a university degree to boot in fair and open competition with the sons of the English. He was cultured, of the world, and, if report spoke truly, had wisely and, above all, sympathetically ruled a crowded district in South-Eastern Bengal. He had been to England and charmed many drawing-rooms there. His name, if the Viceroy recollected aright, was Mr. Grish Chunder Dé, M. A. In short, did anybody see any objection to the appointment, always on principle, of a man of the people to rule the people? The district in South-Eastern Bengal might with advantage, he apprehended, pass over to a younger civilian of Mr. G. C. Dé's nationality (who had written a remarkably clever pamphlet on the political value of sympathy in administration); and Mr. G. C. Dé could be transferred northward to Kot-Kumharsen. The Viceroy was averse, on principle, to interfering with appointments under

control of the Provincial Governments. He wished
it to be understood that he merely recommended
and advised in this instance. As regarded the
mere question of race, Mr. Grish Chunder Dé
was more English than the English, and yet possessed of that peculiar sympathy and insight which
the best among the best Service in the world could
only win to at the end of their service.

The stern, black-bearded kings who sit about
the Council-board of India divided on the step,
with the inevitable result of driving the Very
Greatest of All the Viceroys into the borders of
hysteria, and a bewildered obstinacy pathetic as
that of a child.

"The principle is sound enough," said the
weary-eyed Head of the Red Provinces in which
Kot-Kumharsen lay, for he too held theories.
"The only difficulty is —— "

" Put the screw on the District officials ; brigade
Dé with a very strong Deputy Commissioner on
each side of him ; give him the best assistant in
the Province; rub the fear of God into the people
beforehand ; and if anything goes wrong, say that
his colleagues didn't back him up. All these
lovely little experiments recoil on the District-
Officer in the end," said the Knight of the Drawn
Sword with a truthful brutality that made the
Head of the Red Provinces shudder. And on a
tacit understanding of this kind the transfer was

accomplished, as quietly as might be for many reasons.

It is sad to think that what goes for public opinion in India did not generally see the wisdom of the Viceroy's appointment. There were not lacking indeed hireling organs, notoriously in the pay of a tyrannous bureaucracy, who more than hinted that His Excellency was a fool, a dreamer of dreams, a doctrinaire, and, worst of all, a trifler with the lives of men. "The Viceroy's Excellence Gazette," published in Calcutta, was at pains to thank "Our beloved Viceroy for once more and again thus gloriously vindicating the potentialities of the Bengali nations for extended executive and administrative duties in foreign parts beyond our ken. We do not at all doubt that our excellent fellow-townsman, Mr. Grish Chunder Dé, Esq., M. A., will uphold the prestige of the Bengali, notwithstanding what underhand intrigue and *peshbundi* may be set on foot to insidiously nip his fame and blast his prospects among the proud civilians, some of which will now have to serve under a despised native and take orders too. How will you like that, Misters? We entreat our beloved Viceroy still to substantiate himself superiorly to race-prejudice and colour-blindness, and to allow the flower of this now *our* Civil Service all the full pays and allowances granted to his more fortunate brethren."

177

III

" When does this man take over charge ? I'm
alone just now, and I gather that I'm to stand fast
under him."

" Would you have cared for a transfer ? " said
Bullows keenly. Then, laying his hand on Tallantire's shoulder : " We're all in the same boat;
don't desert us. And yet, why the devil should
you stay, if you can get another charge ? "

" It was Orde's," said Tallantire simply.

" Well, it's Dé's now. He's a Bengali of the
Bengalis, crammed with code and case law; a
beautiful man so far as routine and deskwork go,
and pleasant to talk to. They naturally have always kept him in his own home district, where all
his sisters and his cousins and his aunts lived,
somewhere south of Dacca. He did no more than
turn the place into a pleasant little family preserve,
allowed his subordinates to do what they liked, and
let everybody have a chance at the shekels. Consequently he's immensely popular down there."

" I've nothing to do with that. How on earth
am I to explain to the district that they are going
to be governed by a Bengali ? Do you — does
the Government, I mean — suppose that the
Khusru Kheyl will sit quiet when they once know?
What will the Mahomedan heads of villages say ?
How will the police — Muzbi Sikhs and Pathans

— how will *they* work under him? We couldn't say anything if the Government appointed a sweeper; but my people will say a good deal, you know that. It's a piece of cruel folly!'"

"My dear boy, I know all that, and more. I've represented it, and have been told that I am exhibiting 'culpable and puerile prejudice.' By Jove, if the Khusru Kheyl don't exhibit something worse than that I don't know the Border! The chances are that you will have the district alight on your hands, and I shall have to leave my work and help you pull through. I needn't ask you to stand by the Bengali man in every possible way. You'll do that for your own sake."

"For Orde's. I can't say that I care twopence personally."

"Don't be an ass. It's grievous enough, God knows, and the Government will know later on; but that's no reason for your sulking. *You* must try to run the district; *you* must stand between him and as much insult as possible; *you* must show him the ropes; *you* must pacify the Khusru Kheyl, and just warn Curbar of the Police to look out for trouble by the way. I'm always at the end of a telegraph-wire, and willing to peril my reputation to hold the district together. You'll lose yours, of course. If you keep things straight, and he isn't actually beaten with a stick when he's on tour, he'll get all the credit. If anything goes wrong, you'll be told that you didn't support him loyally."

"I know what I've got to do," said Tallantire wearily, "and I'm going to do it. But it's hard."

"The work is with us, the event is with Allah, —as Orde used to say when he was more than usually in hot water." And Bullows rode away.

That two gentlemen in Her Majesty's Bengal Civil Service should thus discuss a third, also in that service, and a cultured and affable man withal, seems strange and saddening. Yet listen to the artless babble of the Blind Mullah of Jagai, the priest of the Khusru Kheyl, sitting upon a rock overlooking the Border. Five years before, a chance-hurled shell from a screw-gun battery had dashed earth in the face of the Mullah, then urging a rush of Ghazis against half a dozen British bayonets. So he became blind, and hated the English none the less for the little accident. Yardely-Orde knew his failing, and had many times laughed at him therefor.

"Dogs you are," said the Blind Mullah to the listening tribesmen round the fire. "Whipped dogs! Because you listened to Orde Sahib and called him father and behaved as his children, the British Government have proven how they regard you. Orde Sahib ye know is dead."

"Ai! ai! ai!" said half a dozen voices.

"He was a man. Comes now in his stead, whom

think ye? A Bengali of Bengal — an eater of fish from the South."

"A lie!" said Khoda Dad Khan. "And but for the small matter of thy priesthood, I'd drive my gun, butt first, down thy throat."

"Oho, art thou there, lickspittle of the English? Go in to-morrow across the Border to pay service to Orde Sahib's successor, and thou shalt slip thy shoes at the tent-door of a Bengali, as thou shalt hand thy offering to a Bengali's black fist. This I know; and in my youth, when a young man spoke evil to a Mullah holding the doors of Heaven and Hell, the gun-butt was not rammed down the Mullah's gullet. No!"

The Blind Mullah hated Khoda Dad Khan with Afghan hatred, both being rivals for the headship of the tribe; but the latter was feared for bodily as the other for spiritual gifts. Khoda Dad Khan looked at Orde's ring and grunted, "I go in to-morrow because I am not an old fool, preaching war against the English. If the Government, smitten with madness, have done this, then . . ."

"Then," croaked the Mullah, "thou wilt take out the young men and strike at the four villages within the Border?"

"Or wring thy neck, black raven of Jehannum, for a bearer of ill-tidings."

Khoda Dad Khan oiled his long locks with great care, put on his best Bokhara belt, a new turban-cap and fine green shoes, and accompanied by a few friends came down from the hills to pay a visit to the new Deputy Commissioner of Kot-Kumharsen. Also he bore tribute — four or five priceless gold mohurs of Akbar's time in a white handkerchief. These the Deputy Commissioner would touch and remit. The little ceremony used to be a sign that, so far as Khoda Dad Khan's personal influence went, the Khusru Kheyl would be good boys, — till the next time ; especially if Khoda Dad Khan happened to like the new Deputy Commissioner. In Yardely-Orde's consul-ship his visit concluded with a sumptuous dinner and perhaps forbidden liquors ; certainly with some wonderful tales and great good-fellowship. Then Khoda Dad Khan would swagger back to his hold, vowing that Orde Sahib was one prince and Tallan-tire Sahib another, and that whosoever went a-raid-ing into British territory would be flayed alive. On this occasion he found the Deputy Commissioner's tents looking much as usual. Regarding himself as privileged, he strode through the open door to confront a suave, portly Bengali in English cos-tume, writing at a table. Unversed in the elevat-ing influence of education, and not in the least caring for university degrees, Khoda Dad Khan promptly set the man down for a Babu — the native clerk of the Deputy Commissioner — a hated and despised animal.

"Ugh!" said he cheerfully. "Where's your master, Babujee?"

"I am the Deputy Commissioner," said the gentleman in English.

Now he overvalued the effects of university degrees, and stared Khoda Dad Khan in the face. But if from your earliest infancy you have been accustomed to look on battle, murder, and sudden death, if spilt blood affects your nerves as much as red paint, and, above all, if you have faithfully believed that the Bengali was the servant of all Hindustan, and that all Hindustan was vastly inferior to your own large, lustful self, you can endure, even though uneducated, a very large amount of looking over. You can even stare down a graduate of an Oxford college if the latter has been born in a hothouse, of stock bred in a hothouse, and fearing physical pain as some men fear sin; especially if your opponent's mother has frightened him to sleep in his youth with horrible stories of devils inhabiting Afghanistan, and dismal legends of the black North. The eyes behind the gold spectacles sought the floor. Khoda Dad Khan chuckled, and swung out to find Tallantire hard by. "Here," said he roughly, thrusting the coins before him, "touch and remit. That answers for *my* good behaviour. But, O Sahib, has the Government gone mad to send a black Bengali dog to us? And am I to pay service to

such an one? And are you to work under him?
What does it mean?"

"It is an order," said Tallantire. He had expected something of this kind. "He is a very
clever S-sahib."

"He a Sahib! He's a *kala admi*—a black man
—unfit to run at the tail of a potter's donkey.
All the peoples of the earth have harried Bengal.
It is written. Thou knowest when we of the
North wanted women or plunder whither went we?
To Bengal—where else? What child's talk is
this of Sahibdom—after Orde Sahib too! Of a
truth the Blind Mullah was right."

"What of him?" asked Tallantire uneasily.
He mistrusted that old man with his dead eyes
and his deadly tongue.

"Nay, now, because of the oath that I sware to
Orde Sahib when we watched him die by the river
yonder, I will tell. In the first place, is it true
that the English have set the heel of the Bengali
on their own neck, and that there is no more
English rule in the land?"

"I am here," said Tallantire, "and I serve the
Maharanee of England."

"The Mullah said otherwise, and further that
because we loved Orde Sahib the Government sent
us a pig to show that we were dogs who till now
have been held by the strong hand. Also that
they were taking away the white soldiers, that

more Hindustanis might come, and that all was changing."

This is the worst of ill-considered handling of a very large country. What looks so feasible in Calcutta, so right in Bombay, so unassailable in Madras, is misunderstood by the North and entirely changes its complexion on the banks of the Indus. Khoda Dad Khan explained as clearly as he could that, though he himself intended to be good, he really could not answer for the more reckless members of his tribe under the leadership of the Blind Mullah. They might or they might not give trouble, but they certainly had no intention whatever of obeying the new Deputy Commissioner. Was Tallantire perfectly sure that in the event of any systematic border-raiding the force in the district could put it down promptly?

" Tell the Mullah if he talks any more fool's talk," said Tallantire curtly, "that he takes his men on to certain death, and his tribe to blockade, trespass-fine, and blood-money. But why do I talk to one who no longer carries weight in the counsels of the tribe ? "

Khoda Dad Khan pocketed that insult. He had learned something that he much wanted to know, and returned to his hills to be sarcastically complimented by the Mullah, whose tongue raging round the camp-fires was deadlier flame than ever dung-cake fed.

Be pleased to consider here for a moment the
unknown district of Kot-Kumharsen. It lay cut
lengthways by the Indus under the line of the
Khusru hills — ramparts of useless earth and tumbled stone. It was seventy miles long by fifty
broad, maintained a population of something less
than two hundred thousand, and paid taxes to the
extent of forty thousand pounds a year on an area
that was by rather more than half sheer, hopeless
waste. The cultivators were not gentle people,
the miners for salt were less gentle still, and the
cattle-breeders least gentle of all. A police-post in
the top right-hand corner and a tiny mud fort in
the top left-hand corner prevented as much salt-
smuggling and cattle-lifting as the influence of the
civilians could not put down; and in the bottom
right-hand corner lay Jumala, the district headquarters — a pitiful knot of lime-washed barns
facetiously rented as houses, reeking with frontier fever, leaking in the rain, and ovens in the
summer.

It was to this place that Grish Chunder Dé was
travelling, there formally to take over charge of
the district. But the news of his coming had gone
before. Bengalis were as scarce as poodles among
the simple Borderers, who cut each other's heads
open with their long spades and worshipped im-

partially at Hindu and Mahomedan shrines. They crowded to see him, pointing at him, and diversely comparing him to a gravid milch-buffalo, or a broken-down horse, as their limited range of metaphor prompted. They laughed at his police-guard, and wished to know how long the burly Sikhs were going to lead Bengali apes. They inquired whether he had brought his women with him, and advised him explicitly not to tamper with theirs. It remained for a wrinkled hag by the roadside to slap her lean breasts as he passed, crying, "I have suckled six that could have eaten six thousand of *him*. The Government shot them, and made this That a king!" Whereat a blue-turbaned huge-boned plough-mender shouted, "Have hope, mother o' mine! He may yet go the way of thy wastrels." And the children, the little brown puff-balls, regarded curiously. It was generally a good thing for infancy to stray into Orde Sahib's tent, where copper coins were to be won for the mere wishing, and tales of the most authentic, such as even their mothers knew but the first half of. No! This fat black man could never tell them how Pir Prith hauled the eye-teeth out of ten devils; how the big stones came to lie all in a row on top of the Khusru hills, and what happened if you shouted through the village-gate to the gray wolf at even, "Badl Khas is dead." Meantime Grish Chunder Dé talked hastily and much to Tallantire, after the

187

manner of those who are " more English than the
English,"—of Oxford and " home," with much curious book-knowledge of bump-suppers, cricket-
matches, hunting-runs, and other unholy sports of
the alien. " We must get these fellows in hand,"
he said once or twice uneasily; " get them well in
hand, and drive them on a tight rein. No use,
you know, being slack with your district."

And a moment later Tallantire heard Debendra
Nath Dé, who brotherliwise had followed his kins-
man's fortune and hoped for the shadow of his
protection as a pleader, whisper in Bengali,
" Better are dried fish at Dacca than drawn swords
at Delhi. Brother of mine, these men are devils,
as our mother said. And you will always have to
ride upon a horse ! "

That night there was a public audience in a
broken-down little town thirty miles from Jumala,
when the new Deputy Commissioner, in reply to
the greetings of the subordinate native officials,
delivered a speech. It was a carefully thought out
speech, which would have been very valuable had
not his third sentence begun with three innocent
words, " *Hamara hookum hai* — It is my order."
Then there was a laugh, clear and bell-like, from
the back of the big tent, where a few border landholders sat, and the laugh grew and scorn mingled
with it, and the lean, keen face of Debendra Nath
Dé paled, and Grish Chunder, turning to Tallantire,

spake : " *You* — you put up this arrangement."
Upon that instant the noise of hoofs rang without,
and there entered Curbar, the District Superintendent of Police, sweating and dusty. The
State had tossed him into a corner of the province
for seventeen weary years, there to check smuggling
of salt, and to hope for promotion that never came.
He had forgotten how to keep his white uniform
clean, had screwed rusty spurs into patent-leather
shoes, and clothed his head indifferently with a
helmet or a turban. Soured, old, worn with
heat and cold, he waited till he should be
entitled to sufficient pension to keep him from
starving.

"Tallantire," said he, disregarding Grish
Chunder Dé, " come outside. I want to speak to
you." They withdrew. "It's this," continued
Curbar. " The Khusru Kheyl have rushed and
cut up half a dozen of the coolies on Ferris's new
canal-embankment; killed a couple of men and
carried off a woman. I wouldn't trouble you
about that — Ferris is after them and Hugonin,
my assistant, with ten mounted police. But that's
only the beginning, I fancy. Their fires are out
on the Hassan Ardeb heights, and unless we're
pretty quick there'll be a flare-up all along our
Border. They are sure to raid the four Khusru
villages on our side of the line; there's been bad
blood between them for years; and you know the

Blind Mullah has been preaching a holy war since
Orde went out.   What's your notion?"

"Damn!"   said   Tallantire   thoughtfully.
"They've begun quick.   Well, it seems to me
I'd better ride off to Fort Ziar and get what men
I can there to picket among the lowland villages,
if it's not too late.   Tommy Dodd commands at
Fort Ziar, I think.   Ferris and Hugonin ought to
teach the canal-thieves a lesson, and —— No, we
can't have the Head of the Police ostentatiously
guarding the Treasury.   You go back to the canal.
I'll wire Bullows to come into Jumala with a
strong police-guard, and sit on the Treasury.   They
won't touch the place, but it looks well."

"I — I — I insist upon knowing what this
means," said the voice of the Deputy Commissioner, who had followed the speakers.

"Oh!" said Curbar, who, being in the Police,
could not understand that fifteen years of education must, on principle, change the Bengali into
a Briton.   "There has been a fight on the Border,
and heaps of men are killed.   There's going
to be another fight, and heaps more will be
killed."

"What for?"

"Because the teeming millions of this district
don't exactly approve of you, and think that under your benign rule they are going to have a
good time.   It strikes me that you had better

make arrangements. I act, as you know, by your orders. What do you advise?"

"I—I take you all to witness that I have not yet assumed charge of the district," stammered the Deputy Commissioner, not in the tones of the " more English."

"Ah, I thought so. Well, as I was saying, Tallantire, your plan is sound. Carry it out. Do you want an escort?"

"No; only a decent horse. But how about wiring to headquarters?"

"I fancy, from the colour of his cheeks, that your superior officer will send some wonderful telegrams before the night's over. Let him do that, and we shall have half the troops of the province coming up to see what's the trouble. Well, run along, and take care of yourself—the Khusru Kheyl jab upwards from below, remember. Ho! Mir Khan, give Tallantire Sahib the best of the horses, and tell five men to ride to Jumala with the Deputy Commissioner Sahib Bahadur. There is a hurry toward."

There was; and it was not in the least bettered by Debendra Nath Dé clinging to a policeman's bridle and demanding the shortest, the very shortest way to Jumala. Now originality is fatal to the Bengali. Debendra Nath should have stayed with his brother, who rode steadfastly for Jumala on the railway-line, thanking gods entirely un-

known to the most catholic of universities that
he had not taken charge of the district, and could
still — happy resource of a fertile race! — fall sick.

And I grieve to say that when he reached his
goal two policemen, not devoid of rude wit, who
had been conferring together as they bumped in
their saddles, arranged an entertainment for his
behoof. It consisted of first one and then the
other entering his room with prodigious details
of war, the massing of bloodthirsty and devilish
tribes, and the burning of towns. It was almost
as good, said these scamps, as riding with Curbar
after evasive Afghans. Each invention kept the
hearer at work for half an hour on telegrams which
the sack of Delhi would hardly have justified. To
every power that could move a bayonet or transfer
a terrified man, Grish Chunder Dé appealed tele-
graphically. He was alone, his assistants had
fled, and in truth he had not taken over charge
of the district. Had the telegrams been despatched many things would have occurred; but
since the only signaller in Jumala had gone to
bed, and the station-master, after one look at the
tremendous pile of paper, discovered that railway
regulations forbade the forwarding of imperial
messages, policemen Ram Singh and Nihal Singh
were fain to turn the stuff into a pillow and slept
on it very comfortably.

Tallantire drove his spurs into a rampant skew-

bald stallion with china-blue eyes, and settled
himself for the forty-mile ride to Fort Ziar.
Knowing his district blindfold, he wasted no time
hunting for short cuts, but headed across the richer
grazing-ground to the ford where Orde had died
and been buried. The dusty ground deadened
the noise of his horse's hoofs, the moon threw his
shadow, a restless goblin, before him, and the
heavy dew drenched him to the skin. Hillock,
scrub that brushed against the horse's belly, un-
metalled road where the whip-like foliage of the
tamarisks lashed his forehead, illimitable levels of
lowland furred with bent and speckled with drows-
ing cattle, waste, and hillock anew, dragged themselves past, and the skewbald was labouring in
the deep sand of the Indus-ford. Tallantire was
conscious of no distinct thought till the nose of
the dawdling ferry-boat grounded on the farther
side, and his horse shied snorting at the white
headstone of Orde's grave. Then he uncovered,
and shouted that the dead might hear, "They're
out, old man! Wish me luck." In the chill of
the dawn he was hammering with a stirrup-iron
at the gate of Fort Ziar, where fifty sabres of that
tattered regiment, the Belooch Beshaklis, were
supposed to guard Her Majesty's interests along
a few hundred miles of Border. This particular
fort was commanded by a subaltern, who, born
of the ancient family of the Derouletts, naturally

answered to the name of Tommy Dodd. Him Tallantire found robed in a sheepskin coat, shaking with fever like an aspen, and trying to read the native apothecary's list of invalids.

"So you've come, too," said he. "Well, we're all sick here, and I don't think I can horse thirty men; but we're bub-bub-bub-blessed willing. Stop, does this impress you as a trap or a lie?" He tossed a scrap of paper to Tallantire, on which was written painfully in crabbed Gurmukhi, "We cannot hold young horses. They will feed after the moon goes down in the four border villages issuing from the Jagai pass on the next night." Then in English round hand — "Your sincere friend."

"Good man!" said Tallantire. "That's Khoda Dad Khan's work, I know. It's the only piece of English he could ever keep in his head, and he is immensely proud of it. He is playing against the Blind Mullah for his own hand — the treacherous young ruffian!"

"Don't know the politics of the Khusru Kheyl, but if you're satisfied, I am. That was pitched in over the gate-head last night, and I thought we might pull ourselves together and see what was on. Oh, but we're sick with fever here, and no mistake! Is this going to be a big business, think you?" said Tommy Dodd.

Tallantire gave him briefly the outlines of the

case, and Tommy Dodd whistled and shook with
fever alternately.   That day he devoted to strategy,
the art of war, and the enlivenment of the invalids,
till at dusk there stood ready forty-two troopers,
lean, worn, and dishevelled, whom Tommy Dodd
surveyed with pride, and addressed thus: "O
men! If you die you will go to Hell. Therefore
endeavour to keep alive. But if you go to Hell
that place cannot be hotter than this place, and we
are not told that we shall there suffer from fever.
Consequently be not afraid of dying. File out
there!" They grinned, and went.

v

It will be long ere the Khusru Kheyl forget
their night attack on the lowland villages. The
Mullah had promised an easy victory and un-
limited plunder; but behold, armed troopers of
the Queen had risen out of the very earth, cutting,
slashing, and riding down under the stars, so that
no man knew where to turn, and all feared that
they had brought an army about their ears, and
ran back to the hills. In the panic of that flight
more men were seen to drop from wounds inflicted
by an Afghan knife jabbed upwards, and yet more
from long-range carbine-fire. Then there rose a
cry of treachery, and when they reached their own
guarded heights, they had left, with some forty

195

dead and sixty wounded, all their confidence in
the Blind Mullah on the plains below. They
clamoured, swore, and argued round the fires;
the women wailing for the lost, and the Mullah
shrieking curses on the returned.

Then Khoda Dad Khan, eloquent and un-
breathed, for he had taken no part in the fight,
rose to improve the occasion. He pointed out
that the tribe owed every item of its present mis-
fortune to the Blind Mullah, who had lied in every
possible particular and talked them into a trap. It
was undoubtedly an insult that a Bengali, the son
of a Bengali, should presume to administer the
Border, but that fact did not, as the Mullah pretended, herald a general time of license and lifting;
and the inexplicable madness of the English had
not in the least impaired their power of guarding
their marches. On the contrary, the baffled and
out-generalled tribe would now, just when their
food-stock was lowest, be blockaded from any
trade with Hindustan until they had sent hostages
for good behaviour, paid compensation for disturbance, and blood-money at the rate of thirty-six
English pounds per head for every villager that
they might have slain. "And ye know that those
lowland dogs will make oath that we have slain
scores. Will the Mullah pay the fines or must we
sell our guns?" A low growl ran round the fires.
"Now, seeing that all this is the Mullah's work,

and that we have gained nothing but promises of Paradise thereby, it is in my heart that we of the Khusru Kheyl lack a shrine whereat to pray. We are weakened, and henceforth how shall we dare to cross into the Madar Kheyl border, as has been our custom, to kneel to Pir Sajji's tomb? The Madar men will fall upon us, and rightly. But our Mullah is a holy man. He has helped two score of us into Paradise this night. Let him therefore accompany his flock, and we will build over his body a dome of the blue tiles of Mooltan, and burn lamps at his feet every Friday night. He shall be a saint; we shall have a shrine; and there our women shall pray for fresh seed to fill the gaps in our fighting-tale. How think you?"

A grim chuckle followed the suggestion, and the soft *wheep*, *wheep* of unscabbarded knives followed the chuckle. It was an excellent notion, and met a long-felt want of the tribe. The Mullah sprang to his feet, glaring with withered eyeballs at the drawn death he could not see, and calling down the curses of God and Mahomed on the tribe. Then began a game of blind man's buff round and between the fires, whereof Khuruk Shah, the tribal poet, has sung in verse that will not die.

They tickled him gently under the armpit with the knife-point. He leaped aside screaming, only to feel a cold blade drawn lightly over the back of his neck, or a rifle-muzzle rubbing his beard.

197

He called on his adherents to aid him, but most of these lay dead on the plains, for Khoda Dad Khan had been at some pains to arrange their decease. Men described to him the glories of the shrine they would build, and the little children, clapping their hands, cried, " Run, Mullah, run! There's a man behind you!" In the end, when the sport wearied, Khoda Dad Khan's brother sent a knife home between his ribs. "Wherefore," said Khoda Dad Khan with charming simplicity, "I am now Chief of the Khusru Kheyl!" No man gainsaid him; and they all went to sleep very stiff and sore.

On the plain below Tommy Dodd was lecturing on the beauties of a cavalry charge by night, and Tallantire, bowed on his saddle, was gasping hysterically because there was a sword dangling from his wrist flecked with the blood of the Khusru Kheyl, the tribe that Orde had kept in leash so well. When a Rajpoot trooper pointed out that the skewbald's right ear had been taken off at the root by some blind slash of its unskilled rider, Tallantire broke down altogether, and laughed and sobbed till Tommy Dodd made him lie down and rest.

" We must wait about till the morning," said he. " I wired to the Colonel, just before we left, to send a wing of the Beshaklis after us. He'll be furious with me for monopolizing the fun, though. Those

198

beggars in the hills won't give us any more trouble."

"Then tell the Beshaklis to go on and see what has happened to Curbar on the canal. We must patrol the whole line of the Border. You're quite sure, Tommy, that — that stuff was — was only the skewbald's ear?"

"Oh, quite," said Tommy. "You just missed cutting off his head. *I* saw you when we went into the mess. Sleep, old man."

Noon brought two squadrons of Beshaklis and a knot of furious brother officers demanding the court-martial of Tommy Dodd for "spoiling the picnic," and a gallop across country to the canal-works where Ferris, Curbar, and Hugonin were haranguing the terror-stricken coolies on the enormity of abandoning good work and high pay, merely because half a dozen of their fellows had been cut down. The sight of a troop of the Beshaklis restored wavering confidence, and the police-hunted section of the Khusru Kheyl had the joy of watching the canal-bank humming with life as usual, while such of their men as had taken refuge in the water-courses and ravines were being driven out by the troopers. By sundown began the remorseless patrol of the Border by police and trooper, most like the cow-boys' eternal ride round restless cattle.

"Now," said Khoda Dad Khan to his fellows,

pointing out a line of twinkling fires below, " ye may see how far the old order changes. After their horse will come the little devil-guns that they can drag up to the tops of the hills, and, for aught I know, to the clouds when we crown the hills. If the tribe-council thinks good, I will go to Tallantire Sahib — who loves me — and see if I can stave off at least the blockade. Do I speak for the tribe ? "

" Ay, speak for the tribe in God's name. How those accursed fires wink ! Do the English send their troops on the wire — or is this the work of the Bengali ? "

As Khoda Dad Khan went down the hill he was delayed by an interview with a hard-pressed tribesman, which caused him to return hastily for something he had forgotten. Then, handing himself over to the two troopers who had been chasing his friend, he claimed escort to Tallantire Sahib, then with Bullows at Jumala. The Border was safe, and the time for reasons in writing had begun.

" Thank Heaven," said Bullows, " that the trouble came at once. Of course we can never put down the reason in black and white, but all India will understand. And it is better to have a sharp, short outbreak than five years of impotent administration inside the Border. It costs less. Grish Chunder Dé has reported himself sick, and has been transferred to his own province without any sort of reprimand. He was strong on not having taken over the district."

"Of course," said Tallantire bitterly. "Well, what am I supposed to have done that was wrong?"

"Oh, you will be told that you exceeded all your powers, and should have reported, and written, and advised for three weeks until the Khusru Kheyl could really come down in force. But I don't think the authorities will dare to make a fuss about it. They've had their lesson. Have you seen Curbar's version of the affair? He can't write a report, but he can speak the truth."

"What's the use of the truth? He'd much better tear up the report. I'm sick and heart-broken over it all. It was so utterly unnecessary — except in that it rid us of the Babu."

Entered unabashed Khoda Dad Khan, a stuffed forage-net in his hand, and the troopers behind him.

"May you never be tired!" said he cheerily. "Well, Sahibs, that was a good fight, and Naim Shah's mother is in debt to you, Tallantire Sahib. A clean cut, they tell me, through jaw, wadded coat, and deep into the collar-bone. Well done! But I speak for the tribe. There has been a fault — a great fault. Thou knowest that I and mine, Tallantire Sahib, kept the oath we sware to Orde Sahib on the banks of the Indus."

"As an Afghan keeps his knife — sharp on one side, blunt on the other," said Tallantire.

" The better swing in the blow, then. But I speak God's truth. Only the Blind Mullah carried the young men on the tip of his tongue, and said that there was no more Border-law because a Bengali had been sent, and we need not fear the English at all. So they came down to avenge that insult and get plunder. Ye know what befell, and how far I helped. Now five score of us are dead or wounded, and we are all shamed and sorry, and desire no further war. Moreover, that ye may better listen to us, we have taken off the head of the Blind Mullah, whose evil counsels have led us to folly. I bring it for proof," — and he heaved on the floor the head. " He will give no more trouble, for *I* am chief now, and so I sit in a higher place at all audiences. Yet there is an offset to this head. That was another fault. One of the men found that black Bengali beast, through whom this trouble arose, wandering on horseback and weeping. Reflecting that he had caused loss of much good life, Alla Dad Khan, whom, if you choose, I will to-morrow shoot, whipped off this head, and I bring it to you to cover your shame, that ye may bury it. See, no man kept the spectacles, though they were of gold."

Slowly rolled to Tallantire's feet the crop-haired head of a spectacled Bengali gentleman, open-eyed, open-mouthed — the head of Terror incarnate. Bullows bent down. "Yet another blood-fine and a heavy one, Khoda Dad Khan, for this is the head of Debendra Nath, the man's brother. The Babu is safe long since. All but the fools of the Khusru Kheyl know that."

"Well, I care not for carrion. Quick meat for me. The thing was under our hills asking the road to Jumala, and Alla Dad Khan showed him the road to Jehannum, being, as thou sayest, but a fool. Remains now what the Government will do to us. As to the blockade —— "

"Who art thou, seller of dog's flesh," thundered Tallantire, "to speak of terms and treaties? Get hence to the hills — go and wait there, starving, till it shall please the Government to call thy people out for punishment — children and fools that ye be! Count your dead, and be still. Rest assured that the Government will send you a *man!*"

"Ay," returned Khoda Dad Khan, "for we also be men."

As he looked Tallantire between the eyes, he added, "And by God, Sahib, may thou be that man!"

THE AMIR'S HOMILY

His Royal Highness Abdur Rahman, Amir of Afghanistan, **G. C. S. I.**, and trusted ally of Her Imperial Majesty the Queen of England and Empress of India, is a gentleman for whom all right-thinking people should have a profound regard. Like most other rulers, he governs not as he would, but as he can, and the mantle of his authority covers the most turbulent race under the stars. To the Afghan neither life, property, law, nor kingship are sacred when his own lusts prompt him to rebel. He is a thief by instinct, a murderer by heredity and training, and frankly and bestially immoral by all three. None the less he has his own crooked notions of honour, and his character is fascinating to study. On occasion he will fight without reason given till he is hacked in pieces; on other occasions he will refuse to show fight till he is driven into a corner. Herein he is as unaccountable as the gray wolf, who is his blood-brother.

And these men His Highness rules by the only weapon that they understand — the fear of death, which among some Orientals is the beginning of

204

wisdom. Some say that the Amir's authority reaches no farther than a rifle-bullet can range; but as none are quite certain when their king may be in their midst, and as he alone holds every one of the threads of Government, his respect is increased among men. Gholam Hyder, the Commander-in-chief of the Afghan army, is feared reasonably, for he can impale; all Kabul city fears the Governor of Kabul, who has power of life and death through all the wards; but the Amir of Afghanistan, though outlying tribes pretend otherwise when his back is turned, is dreaded beyond chief and governor together. His word is red law; by the gust of his passion falls the leaf of man's life, and his favour is terrible. He has suffered many things, and been a hunted fugitive before he came to the throne, and he understands all the classes of his people. By the custom of the East any man or woman having a complaint to make, or an enemy against whom to be avenged, has the right of speaking face to face with the king at the daily public audience. This is personal government, as it was in the days of Harun al Raschid of blessed memory, whose times exist still and will exist long after the English have passed away.

The privilege of open speech is of course exercised at certain personal risk. The king may be pleased, and raise the speaker to honour for that very bluntness of speech which three minutes later brings a too imitative petitioner to the edge of the ever-ready blade. And the people love to have it so, for it is their right.

It happened upon a day in Kabul that the Amir chose to do his day's work in the Baber Gardens, which lie a short distance from the city of Kabul. A light table stood before him, and round the table in the open air were grouped generals and finance ministers according to their degree. The Court and the long tail of feudal chiefs — men of blood, fed and cowed by blood — stood in an irregular semicircle round the table, and the wind from the Kabul orchards blew among them. All day long sweating couriers dashed in with letters from the outlying districts with rumours of rebellion, intrigue, famine, failure of payments, or announcements of treasure on the road; and all day long the Amir would read the dockets, and pass such of these as were less private to the officials whom they directly concerned, or call up a waiting chief for a word of explanation. It is well to speak clearly to the ruler of Afghanistan. Then the grim head, under the black astrachan cap with the diamond star in front, would nod gravely, and that chief would return to his fellows. Once that afternoon a woman clamoured for divorce against her husband, who was bald, and the Amir, hearing both sides of the case, bade her pour curds over the bare scalp, and lick them off, that the hair might grow again, and she be contented. Here the Court laughed, and the woman withdrew, cursing her king under her breath.

But when twilight was falling, and the order of the Court was a little relaxed, there came before the king, in custody, a trembling, haggard wretch, sore with much buffeting, but of stout enough build, who had stolen three rupees — of such small matters does His Highness take cognisance.

" Why did you steal ? " said he ; and when the king asks questions they do themselves service who answer directly.

" I was poor, and no one gave. Hungry, and there was no food."

" Why did you not work ? "

" I could find no work, Protector of the Poor, and I was starving."

" You lie. You stole for drink, for lust, for idleness, for anything but hunger, since any man who will may find work and daily bread."

The prisoner dropped his eyes. He had attended the Court before, and he knew the ring of the death-tone.

"Any man may get work. Who knows this so well as I do? for I too have been hungered — not like you, bastard scum, but as any honest man may be, by the turn of Fate and the will of God."

Growing warm, the Amir turned to his nobles all arow, and thrust the hilt of his sabre aside with his elbow.

"You have heard this Son of Lies? Hear me tell a true tale. I also was once starved, and tightened my belt on the sharp belly-pinch. Nor was I alone, for with me was another, who did not fail me in my evil days, when I was hunted, before ever I came to this throne. And wandering like a houseless dog by Kandahar, my money melted, melted, melted till —— " He flung out a bare palm before the audience. " And day upon day, faint and sick, I went back to that one who waited, and God knows how we lived, till on a day I took our best *libaf*—silk it was, fine work of Iran, such as no needle now works, warm, and a coverlet for two, and all that we had. I brought it to a money-lender in a by-lane, and I asked for three rupees upon it. He said to me, who am now the King, 'You are a thief. This is worth three hundred.' 'I am no thief,' I answered, 'but a prince of good blood, and I am hungry.'—'Prince of wandering beggars,' said that money-lender, 'I have no money with me, but go to my house with my clerk and he will give you two rupees eight annas, for that is all I will lend.' So I went with the clerk to the house, and we talked on the way, and he gave me the money. We lived on it till it was spent, and we fared hard. And then that

clerk said, being a young man of a good heart,
'Surely the money-lender will lend yet more on
that *lihaf*,' and he offered me two rupees. These
I refused, saying, 'Nay; but get me some work.'
And he got me work, and I, even I, Abdur Rahman, Amir of Afghanistan, wrought day by day
as a coolie, bearing burdens, and labouring of my
hands, receiving four annas wage a day for my
sweat and backache. But he, this bastard son of
naught, must steal! For a year and four months
I worked, and none dare say that I lie, for I have
a witness, even that clerk who is now my friend."

Then there rose in his place among the Sirdars
and the nobles one clad in silk, who folded his
hands and said, "This is the truth of God, for I,
who, by the favour of God and the Amir, am such
as you know, was once clerk to that money-
lender."

There was a pause, and the Amir cried hoarsely
to the prisoner, throwing scorn upon him, till he
ended with the dread, "*Dar arid*," which clinches
justice.

So they led the thief away, and the whole of
him was seen no more together; and the Court
rustled out of its silence, whispering, "Before God
and the Prophet, but this is a man!"

Narrow as the womb, deep as the Pit, and dark as the heart
of a man.—*Sonthal Miner's Proverb*.

"A WEAVER went out to reap, but stayed to un-
ravel the corn-stalks. Ha! Ha! Ha! Is there
any sense in a weaver?"

Janki Meah glared at Kundoo, but, as Janki
Meah was blind, Kundoo was not impressed. He
had come to argue with Janki Meah, and, if
chance favoured, to make love to the old man's
pretty young wife.

This was Kundoo's grievance, and he spoke in
the name of all the five men who, with Janki
Meah, composed the gang in Number Seven gallery of Twenty-Two. Janki Meah had been blind
for the thirty years during which he had served
the Jimahari Collieries with pick and crowbar.
All through those thirty years he had regularly,
every morning before going down, drawn from
the overseer his allowance of lamp-oil — just as
if he had been an eyed miner. What Kundoo's
gang resented, as hundreds of gangs had resented
before, was Janki Meah's selfishness. He would

not add the oil to the common stock of his gang, but would save and sell it.

"I knew these workings before you were born," Janki Meah used to reply: "I don't want the light to get my coal out by, and I am not going to help you. The oil is mine, and I intend to keep it."

A strange man in many ways was Janki Meah, the white-haired, hot-tempered, sightless weaver who had turned pitman. All day long — except Sundays and Mondays, when he was usually drunk — he worked in the Twenty-Two shaft of the Jimahari Colliery as cleverly as a man with all the senses. At evening he went up in the great steam-hauled cage to the pit-bank, and there called for his pony — a rusty, coal-dusty beast, nearly as old as Janki Meah. The pony would come to his side, and Janki Meah would clamber on to its back and be taken at once to the plot of land which he, like the other miners, received from the Jimahari Company. The pony knew that place, and when, after six years, the Company changed all the allotments to prevent the miners from acquiring proprietary rights, Janki Meah represented, with tears in his eyes, that were his holding shifted, he would never be able to find his way to the new one. "My horse only knows that place," pleaded Janki Meah, and so he was allowed to keep his land.

On the strength of this concession and his ac-
cumulated oil-savings, Janki Meah took a second
wife — a girl of the Jolaha main stock of the
Meahs, and singularly beautiful. Janki Meah
could not see her beauty; wherefore he took her
on trust, and forbade her to go down the pit. He
had not worked for thirty years in the dark without knowing that the pit was no place for pretty
women. He loaded her with ornaments — not
brass or pewter, but real silver ones — and she re-
warded him by flirting outrageously with Kundoo
of Number Seven gallery gang. Kundoo was
really the gang-head, but Janki Meah insisted
upon all the work being entered in his own name,
and chose the men that he worked with. Custom
— stronger even than the Jimahari Company —
dictated that Janki, by right of his years, should
manage these things, and should, also, work de-
spite his blindness. In Indian mines, where they
cut into the solid coal with the pick and clear it out
from floor to ceiling, he could come to no great
harm. At Home, where they undercut the coal
and bring it down in crashing avalanches from the
roof, he would never have been allowed to set foot
in a pit. He was not a popular man, because of
his oil-savings; but all the gangs admitted that
Janki knew all the *khads*, or workings, that had ever
been sunk or worked since the Jimahari Company
first started operations on the Tarachunda fields.

Pretty little Unda only knew that her old husband was a fool who could be managed. She took no interest in the collieries except in so far as they swallowed up Kundoo five days out of the seven, and covered him with coal-dust. Kundoo was a great workman, and did his best not to get drunk, because, when he had saved forty rupees, Unda was to steal everything that she could find in Janki's house and run with Kundoo to a land where there were no mines, and every one kept three fat bullocks and a milch-buffalo. While this scheme ripened it was his custom to drop in upon Janki and worry him about the oil-savings. Unda sat in a corner and nodded approval. On the night when Kundoo had quoted that objectionable proverb about weavers, Janki grew angry.

"Listen, you pig," said he, "blind I am, and old I am, but, before ever you were born, I was gray among the coal. Even in the days when the Twenty-Two *khad* was unsunk and there were not two thousand men here, I was known to have all knowledge of the pits. What *khad* is there that I do not know, from the bottom of the shaft to the end of the last drive? Is it the Baromba *khad*, the oldest, or the Twenty-Two where Tibu's gallery runs up to Number Five?"

"Hear the old fool talk!" said Kundoo, nodding to Unda. "No gallery of Twenty-Two will cut into Five before the end of the Rains. We have a month's solid coal before us. The Babuji says so."

"Babuji! Pigji! Dogji! What do these fat slugs from Calcutta know? He draws and draws and draws, and talks and talks and talks, and his maps are all wrong. I, Janki, know that this is so. When a man has been shut up in the dark for thirty years, God gives him knowledge. The old gallery that Tibu's gang made is not six feet from Number Five."

"Without doubt God gives the blind knowledge," said Kundoo, with a look at Unda. "Let it be as you say. I, for my part, do not know where lies the gallery of Tibu's gang, but *I* am not a withered monkey who needs oil to grease his joints with."

Kundoo swung out of the hut laughing, and Unda giggled. Janki turned his sightless eyes toward his wife and swore. "I have land, and I have sold a great deal of lamp-oil," mused Janki; "but I was a fool to marry this child."

A week later the Rains set in with a vengeance, and the gangs paddled about in coal-slush at the pit-banks. Then the big mine-pumps were made ready, and the Manager of the Colliery ploughed through the wet towards the Tarachunda River swelling between its soppy banks. "Lord send that this beastly beck doesn't misbehave," said the

Manager piously, and he went to take counsel with his Assistant about the pumps.

But the Tarachunda misbehaved very much indeed. After a fall .of three inches of rain in an hour it was obliged to do something. It topped its bank and joined the flood-water that was hemmed between two low hills just where the embankment of the Colliery main line crossed. When a large part of a rain-fed river, and a few acres of flood-water, make a dead set for a nine-foot culvert, the culvert may spout its finest, but the water cannot *all* get out. The Manager pranced upon one leg with excitement, and his language was improper.

He had reason to swear, because he knew that one inch of water on land meant a pressure of one hundred tons to the acre; and here were about five feet of water forming, behind the railway embankment, over the shallower workings of Twenty-Two. You must understand that, in a coal-mine, the coal nearest the surface is worked first from the central shaft. That is to say, the miners may clear out the stuff to within ten, twenty, or thirty feet of the surface, and, when all is worked out, leave only a skin of earth upheld by some few pillars of coal. In a deep mine where they know that they have any amount of material at hand, men prefer to get all their mineral out at one shaft, rather than make a number of little holes to tap the comparatively unimportant surface-coal.

And the Manager watched the flood.

The culvert spouted a nine-foot gush; but the water still formed, and word was sent to clear the men out of Twenty-two. The cages came up crammed and crammed again with the men nearest the pit-eye, as they call the place where you can see daylight from the bottom of the main shaft. All away and away up the long black galleries the flare-lamps were winking and dancing like so many fireflies, and the men and the women waited for the clanking, rattling, thundering cages to come down and fly up again. But the out-workings were very far off, and word could not be passed quickly, though the heads of the gangs and the Assistant shouted and swore and tramped and stumbled. The Manager kept one eye on the great troubled pool behind the embankment, and prayed that the culvert would give way and let the water through in time. With the other eye he watched the cages come up and saw the headmen counting the roll of the gangs. With all his heart and soul he swore at the winder who controlled the iron drum that wound up the wire rope on which hung the cages.

In a little time there was a down-draw in the water behind the embankment — a sucking whirlpool, all yellow and yeasty. The water had smashed through the skin of the earth and was pouring into the old shallow workings of Twenty-Two.

Deep down below, a rush of black water caught
the last gang waiting for the cage, and as they
clambered in the whirl was about their waists. The
cage reached the pit-bank, and the Manager called
the roll. The gangs were all safe except Gang
Janki, Gang Mogul, and Gang Rahim, eighteen
men, with perhaps ten basket-women who loaded
the coal into the little iron carriages that ran on
the tramways of the main galleries. These gangs
were in the out-workings, three-quarters of a mile
away, on the extreme fringe of the mine. Once
more the cage went down, but with only two Englishmen in it, and dropped into a swirling, roaring
current that had almost touched the roof of some
of the lower side-galleries. One of the wooden
balks with which they had propped the old workings shot past on the current, just missing the cage.

"If we don't want our ribs knocked out, we'd
better go," said the Manager. "We can't even
save the Company's props."

The cage drew out of the water with a splash,
and a few minutes later it was officially reported
that there were at least ten feet of water in the
pit's eye. Now ten feet of water there meant that
all other places in the mine were flooded except
such galleries as were more than ten feet above
the level of the bottom of the shaft. The deep
workings would be full, the main galleries would
be full, but in the high workings reached by in-

clines from the main roads there would be a certain amount of air cut off, so to speak, by the water and squeezed up by it. The little science-primers explain how water behaves when you pour it down test-tubes. The flooding of Twenty-Two was an illustration on a large scale.

.   .   .   .   .   .

" By the Holy Grove, what has happened to the air ! " It was a Sonthal gangman of Gang Mogul in Number Nine gallery, and he was driving a six-foot way through the coal. Then there was a rush from the other galleries, and Gang Janki and Gang Rahim stumbled up with their basket-women.

" Water has come in the mine," they said, " and there is no way of getting out."

" I went down," said Janki — " down the slope of my gallery, and I felt the water."

" There has been no water in the cutting in our time," clamoured the women. " Why cannot we go away ? "

" Be silent ! " said Janki. " Long ago, when my father was here, water came to Ten — no, Eleven — cutting, and there was great trouble. Let us get away to where the air is better."

The three gangs and the basket-women left Number Nine gallery and went further up Number Sixteen. At one turn of the road they could see the pitchy black water lapping on the coal. It had touched the roof of a gallery that they knew well — a gallery where they used to smoke their *huqas* and manage their flirtations. Seeing this, they called aloud upon their Gods, and the Mehas, who are thrice bastard Muhammadans, strove to recollect the name of the Prophet. They came to a great open square whence nearly all the coal had been extracted. It was the end of the out-workings, and the end of the mine.

Far away down the gallery a small pumping-engine, used for keeping dry a deep working and fed with steam from above, was throbbing faithfully. They heard it cease.

" They have cut off the steam," said Kundoo hopefully. " They have given the order to use all the steam for the pit-bank pumps. They will clear out the water."

" If the water has reached the smoking-gallery," said Janki, " all the Company's pumps can do nothing for three days."

" It is very hot," moaned Jasoda, the Meah basket-woman. " There is a very bad air here because of the lamps."

" Put them out," said Janki; " why do you want lamps? " The lamps were put out and the company sat still in the utter dark. Somebody rose quietly and began walking over the coals. It was Janki, who was touching the walls with his hands. " Where is the ledge? " he murmured to himself.

"Sit, sit!" said Kundoo. "If we die, we die. The air is very bad."

But Janki still stumbled and crept and tapped with his pick upon the walls. The women rose to their feet.

"Stay all where you are. Without the lamps you cannot see, and I — I am always seeing," said Janki. Then he paused, and called out: "Oh, you who have been in the cutting more than ten years, what is the name of this open place? I am an old man and I have forgotten."

"Bullia's Room," answered the Sonthal who had complained of the vileness of the air.

"Again," said Janki.

"Bullia's Room."

"Then I have found it," said Janki. "The name only had slipped my memory. Tibu's gang's gallery is here."

"A lie," said Kundoo. "There have been no galleries in this place since my day."

"Three paces was the depth of the ledge," muttered Janki without heeding — "and — oh, my poor bones! — I have found it! It is here, up this ledge. Come all you, one by one, to the place of my voice, and I will count you."

There was a rush in the dark, and Janki felt the first man's face hit his knees as the Sonthal scrambled up the ledge.

"Who?" cried Janki.

"I, Sunua Manji."

"Sit you down," said Janki. "Who next?"

One by one the women and the men crawled up the ledge which ran along one side of "Bullia's Room." Degraded Muhammadan, pig-eating Musahr and wild Sonthal, Janki ran his hand over them all.

"Now follow after," said he, "catching hold of my heel, and the women catching the men's clothes." He did not ask whether the men had brought their picks with them. A miner, black or white, does not drop his pick. One by one, Janki leading, they crept into the old gallery — a six-foot way with a scant four feet from thill to roof.

"The air is better here," said Jasoda. They could hear her heart beating in thick, sick bumps.

"Slowly, slowly," said Janki. "I am an old man, and I forget many things. This is Tibu's gallery, but where are the four bricks where they used to put their *huqa* fire on when the Sahibs never saw? Slowly, slowly, O you people behind."

They heard his hands disturbing the small coal on the floor of the gallery and then a dull sound. "This is one unbaked brick, and this is another and another. Kundoo is a young man — let him come forward. Put a knee upon this brick and strike here. When Tibu's gang were at dinner on the last day before the good coal ended, they heard the men of Five on the other side, and Five worked *their* gallery two Sundays later — or it may have been one. Strike there, Kundoo, but give me room to go back."

Kundoo, doubting, drove the pick, but the first soft crush of the coal was a call to him. He was fighting for his life and for Unda — pretty little Unda with rings on all her toes — for Unda and the forty rupees. The women sang the Song of the Pick — the terrible, slow, swinging melody with the muttered chorus that repeats the sliding of the loosened coal, and, to each cadence, Kundoo smote in the black dark. When he could do no more, Sunua Manji took the pick, and struck for his life and his wife, and his village beyond the blue hills over the Tarachunda River. An hour the men worked, and then the women cleared away the coal.

"It is farther than I thought," said Janki. "The air is very bad; but strike, Kundoo, strike hard."

For the fifth time Kundoo took up the pick as the Sonthal crawled back. The song had scarcely recommenced when it was broken by a yell from Kundoo that echoed down the gallery: "*Par hua! Par hua!* We are through, we are through!" The imprisoned air in the mine shot through the opening, and the women at the far end of the gallery heard the water rush through the pillars of

" Bullia's Room " and roar against the ledge. Having fulfilled the law under which it worked, it rose no farther. The women screamed and pressed forward. " The water has come — we shall be killed! Let us go."

Kundoo crawled through the gap and found himself in a propped gallery by the simple process of hitting his head against a beam.

" Do I know the pits or do I not ? " chuckled Janki. " This is the Number Five ; go you out slowly, giving me your names. Ho ! Rahim, count your gang ! Now let us go forward, each catching hold of the other as before."

They formed a line in the darkness and Janki led them — for a pit-man in a strange pit is only one degree less liable to err than an ordinary mortal underground for the first time. At last they saw a flare-lamp, and Gangs Janki, Mogul, and Rahim of Twenty-Two stumbled dazed into the glare of the draught-furnace at the bottom of Five : Janki feeling his way and the rest behind.

" Water has come into Twenty-Two. God knows where are the others. I have brought these men from Tibu's gallery in our cutting ; making connection through the north side of the gallery. Take us to the cage," said Janki Meah.

.   .   .   .

At the pit-bank of Twenty-Two some thousand people clamoured and wept and shouted. One hundred men — one thousand men — had been drowned in the cutting. They would all go to their homes to-morrow. Where were their men? Little Unda, her cloth drenched with the rain, stood at the pit-mouth, calling down the shaft for Kundoo. They had swung the cages clear of the mouth, and her only answer was the murmur of the flood in the pit's eye two hundred and sixty feet below.

"Look after that woman! She'll chuck herself down the shaft in a minute," shouted the Manager.

But he need not have troubled; Unda was afraid of Death. She wanted Kundoo. The Assistant was watching the flood and seeing how far he could wade into it. There was a lull in the water, and the whirlpool had slackened. The mine was full, and the people at the pit-bank howled.

"My faith, we shall be lucky if we have five hundred hands on the place to-morrow!" said the Manager. "There's some chance yet of running a temporary dam across that water. Shove in anything — tubs and bullock-carts if you haven't enough bricks. Make them work *now* if they never worked before. Hi! you gangers, make them work."

Little by little the crowd was broken into detachments, and pushed towards the water with promises of overtime. The dam-making began, and when it was fairly under way, the Manager thought that the hour had come for the pumps. There was no fresh inrush into the mine. The tall, red, iron-clamped pump-beam rose and fell, and the pumps snored and guttered and shrieked as the first water poured out of the pipe.

"We must run her all to-night," said the Manager wearily, "but there's no hope for the poor devils down below. Look here, Gur Sahai, if you are proud of your engines, show me what they can do now."

Gur Sahai grinned and nodded, with his right hand upon the lever and an oil-can in his left. He could do no more than he was doing, but he could keep that up till the dawn. Were the Company's pumps to be beaten by the vagaries of that troublesome Tarachunda River? Never, never! And the pumps sobbed and panted: "Never, never!" The Manager sat in the shelter of the pit-bank roofing, trying to dry himself by the pump-boiler fire, and, in the dreary dusk, he saw the crowds on the dam scatter and fly.

"That's the end," he groaned. "'Twill take us six weeks to persuade 'em that we haven't tried to drown their mates on purpose. Oh, for a decent, rational Geordie!"

But the flight had no panic in it. Men had run over from Five with astounding news, and the foremen could not hold their gangs together. Presently, surrounded by a clamorous crew, Gangs

Rahim, Mogul, and Janki, and ten basket-women walked up to report themselves, and pretty little Unda stole away to Janki's hut to prepare his evening meal.

"Alone I found the way," explained Janki Meah, "and now will the Company give me pension?"

The simple pit-folk shouted and leaped and went back to the dam, reassured in their old belief that, whatever happened, so great was the power of the Company whose salt they ate, none of them could be killed. But Gur Sahai only bared his white teeth and kept his hand upon the lever and proved his pumps to the uttermost.

.   .   .   .   .   .

"I say," said the Assistant to the Manager, a week later, "do you recollect 'Germinal'?"

"Yes. 'Queer thing. I thought of it in the cage when that balk went by. Why?"

"Oh, this business seems to be 'Germinal' upside down. Janki was in my verandah all this morning, telling me that Kundoo had eloped with his wife — Unda or Anda, I think her name was."

"Hillo! And those were the cattle that you risked your life to clear out of Twenty-Two!"

"No — I was thinking of the Company's props, not the Company's men."

"Sounds better to say so *now;* but I don't believe you, old fellow."

My newly purchased house furniture was, at the least, insecure; the legs parted from the chairs, and the tops from the tables, on the slightest provocation. But such as it was, it was to be paid for, and Ephraim, agent and collector for the local auctioneer, waited in the verandah with the receipt. He was announced by the Mahomedan servant as " Ephraim, Yahudi " — Ephraim the Jew. He who believes in the Brotherhood of Man should hear my Elahi Bukhsh grinding the second word through his white teeth with all the scorn he dare show before his master. Ephraim was, personally, meek in manner — so meek indeed that one could not understand how he had fallen into the profession of bill-collecting. He resembled an over-fed sheep, and his voice suited his figure. There was a fixed, unvarying mask of childish wonder upon his face. If you paid him, he was as one marvelling at your wealth; if you sent him away, he seemed puzzled at your hard-heartedness. Never was Jew more unlike his dread breed.

Ephraim wore list slippers and coats of duster-

227

cloth, so preposterously patterned that the most brazen of British subalterns would have shied from them in fear. Very slow and deliberate was his speech, and carefully guarded to give offense to no one. After many weeks, Ephraim was induced to speak to me of his friends.

"There be eight of us in Shushan, and we are waiting till there are ten. Then we shall apply for a synagogue, and get leave from Calcutta. To-day we have no synagogue; and I, only I, am Priest and Butcher to our people. I am of the tribe of Judah — I think, but I am not sure. My father was of the tribe of Judah, and we wish much to get our synagogue. I shall be a priest of that synagogue."

Shushan is a big city in the North of India, counting its dwellers by the ten thousand; and these eight of the Chosen People were shut up in its midst, waiting till time or chance sent them their full congregation.

Miriam, the wife of Ephraim, two little children, an orphan boy of their people, Ephraim's uncle Jackrael Israel, a white-haired old man, his wife Hester, a Jew from Cutch, one Hyem Benjamin, and Ephraim, Priest and Butcher, made up the list of the Jews in Shushan. They lived in one house, on the outskirts of the great city, amid heaps of saltpetre, rotten bricks, herds of kine, and a fixed pillar of dust caused by the incessant passing of the beasts to the river to drink. In the evening, the children of the City came to the waste place to fly their kites, and Ephraim's sons held aloof, watching the sport from the roof, but never descending to take part in it. At the back of the house stood a small brick enclosure, in which Ephraim prepared the daily meat for his people after the custom of the Jews. Once the rude door of the square was suddenly smashed open by a struggle from inside, and showed the meek bill-collector at his work, nostrils dilated, lips drawn back over his teeth, and his hands upon a half-maddened sheep. He was attired in strange raiment, having no relation whatever to duster coats or list slippers, and a knife was in his mouth. As he struggled with the animal between the walls, the breath came from him in thick sobs, and the nature of the man seemed changed. When the ordained slaughter was ended, he saw that the door was open and shut it hastily, his hand leaving a red mark on the timber, while his children from the neighbouring house-top looked down awe-stricken and open-eyed. A glimpse of Ephraim busied in one of his religious capacities was no thing to be desired twice.

Summer came upon Shushan, turning the trodden waste-ground to iron, and bringing sickness to the city.

" It will not touch us," said Ephraim confi-

dently. "Before the winter we shall have our
synagogue. My brother and his wife and children
are coming up from Calcutta, and *then* I shall be
the priest of the synagogue."

Jackrael Israel, the old man, would crawl out in
the stifling evenings to sit on the rubbish-heap and
watch the corpses being borne down to the river.

"It will not come near us," said Jackrael Israel
feebly, "for we are the people of God, and my
nephew will be priest of our synagogue. Let
them die." He crept back to his house again
and barred the door to shut himself off from the
world of the Gentile.

But Miriam, the wife of Ephraim, looked out
of the window at the dead as the biers passed, and
said that she was afraid. Ephraim comforted her
with hopes of the synagogue to be, and collected
bills as was his custom.

In one night the two children died and were
buried early in the morning by Ephraim. The
deaths never appeared in the City returns. "The
sorrow is my sorrow," said Ephraim; and this to
him seemed a sufficient reason for setting at naught
the sanitary regulations of a large, flourishing, and
remarkably well-governed Empire.

The orphan boy, dependent on the charity of
Ephraim and his wife, could have felt no gratitude, and must have been a ruffian. He begged
for whatever money his protectors would give him,

and with that fled down country for his life. **A**
week after the death of her children Miriam left
her bed at night and wandered over the country
to find them. She heard them crying behind
every bush, or drowning in every pool of water
in the fields, and she begged the cartmen on the
Grand Trunk Road not to steal her little ones
from her. In the morning the sun rose and beat
upon her bare head, and she turned into the cool,
wet crops to lie down, and never came back,
though Hyem Benjamin and Ephraim sought her
for two nights.

The look of patient wonder on Ephraim's face
deepened, but he presently found an explanation.
" There are so few of us here, and these people are
so many," said he, " that, it may be, our God has
forgotten us."

In the house on the outskirts of the city old
Jackrael Israel and Hester grumbled that there
was no one to wait on them, and that Miriam had
been untrue to her race. Ephraim went out and
collected bills, and in the evenings smoked with
Hyem Benjamin till, one dawning, Hyem Benjamin died, having first paid all his debts to Ephraim.
Jackrael Israel and Hester sat alone in the empty
house all day, and, when Ephraim returned, wept
the easy tears of age till they cried themselves
asleep.

A week later Ephraim, staggering under a huge

bundle of clothes and cooking-pots, led the old man and woman to the railway station, where the bustle and confusion made them whimper.

" We are going back to Calcutta," said Ephraim, to whose sleeve Hester was clinging. " There are more of us there, and here my house is empty."

He helped Hester into the carriage and, turning back, said to me, " I should have been priest of the synagogue if there had been ten of us. Surely we must have been forgotten by our God."

The remnant of the broken colony passed out of the station on their journey south ; while a sub-altern, turning over the books on the bookstall, was whistling to himself " The Ten Little Nigger Boys."

But the tune sounded as solemn as the Dead March.

It was the dirge of the Jews in Shushan.

GEORGIE PORGIE

Georgie Porgie, pudding and pie,
Kissed the girls and made them cry.
When the girls came out to play
Georgie Porgie ran away.

If you will admit that a man has no right to enter his drawing-room early in the morning, when
the housemaid is setting things right and clearing
away the dust, you will concede that civilised
people who eat out of china and own card-cases
have no right to apply their standard of right and
wrong to an unsettled land.   When the place is
made fit for their reception, by those men who are
told off to the work, they can come up, bringing
in their trunks their own society and the Deca-
logue, and all the other apparatus.   Where the
Queen's Law does not carry, it is irrational to expect an observance of other and weaker rules.
The men who run ahead of the cars of Decency
and Propriety, and make the jungle ways straight,
cannot be judged in the same manner as the stay-
at-home folk of the ranks of the regular *Tchin.*

Not many months ago the Queen's Law stopped

a few miles north of Thayetmyo on the Irrawaddy. There was no very strong Public Opinion up to that limit, but it existed to keep men in order. When the Government said that the Queen's Law must carry up to Bhamo and the Chinese border, the order was given, and some men whose desire was to be ever a little in advance of the rush of Respectability flocked forward with the troops. These were the men who could never pass examinations, and would have been too pronounced in their ideas for the administration of bureau-worked Provinces. The Supreme Government stepped in as soon as might be, with codes and regulations, and all but reduced New Burma to the dead Indian level; but there was a short time during which strong men were necessary and ploughed a field for themselves.

Among the fore-runners of Civilisation was Georgie Porgie, reckoned by all who knew him a strong man. He held an appointment in Lower Burma when the order came to break the Frontier, and his friends called him Georgie Porgie because of the singularly Burmese-like manner in which he sang a song whose first line is something like the words "Georgie Porgie." Most men who have been in Burma will know the song. It means: "Puff, puff, puff, puff, great steamboat!" Georgie sang it to his banjo, and his friends shouted with delight, so that you could hear them far away in the teak-forest.

When he went to Upper Burma he had no special regard for God or Man, but he knew how to
make himself respected, and to carry out the mixed
Military-Civil duties that fell to most men's share
in those months. He did his office work and en-
tertained, now and again, the detachments of fever-
shaken soldiers who blundered through his part of
the world in search of a flying party of dacoits.
Sometimes he turned out and dressed down dacoits on his own account; for the country was still
smouldering and would blaze when least expected.
He enjoyed these charivaris, but the dacoits were
not so amused. All the officials who came in contact with him departed with the idea that Georgie
Porgie was a valuable person, well able to take
care of himself, and, on that belief, he was left to
his own devices.

At the end of a few months he wearied of his
solitude, and cast about for company and refine-
ment. The Queen's Law had hardly begun to be
felt in the country, and Public Opinion, which is
more powerful than the Queen's Law, had yet to
come. Also, there was a custom in the country
which allowed a white man to take to himself a
wife of the Daughters of Heth upon due payment.
The marriage was not quite so binding as is the
nikkah ceremony among Mahomedans, but the wife
was very pleasant.

When all our troops are back from Burma there

will be a proverb in their mouths, "As thrifty as
a Burmese wife," and pretty English ladies will
wonder what in the world it means.

The headman of the village next to Georgie
Porgie's post had a fair daughter who had seen
Georgie Porgie and loved him from afar. When
news went abroad that the Englishman with the
heavy hand who lived in the stockade was looking
for a housekeeper, the headman came in and explained that, for five hundred rupees down, he
would entrust his daughter to Georgie Porgie's
keeping, to be maintained in all honour, respect,
and comfort, with pretty dresses, according to the
custom of the country. This thing was done, and
Georgie Porgie never repented it.

He found his rough-and-tumble house put
straight and made comfortable, his hitherto un-
checked expenses cut down by one half, and himself petted and made much of by his new acquisi-
tion, who sat at the head of his table and sang
songs to him and ordered his Madrassee servants
about, and was in every way as sweet and merry
and honest and winning a little woman as the most
exacting of bachelors could have desired. No
race, men say who know, produces such good
wives and heads of households as the Burmese.
When the next detachment tramped by on the
war-path the Subaltern in Command found at
Georgie Porgie's table a hostess to be deferential

to, a woman to be treated in every way as one occupying an assured position. When he gathered his men together next dawn and replunged into the jungle, he thought regretfully of the nice little dinner and the pretty face, and envied Georgie Porgie from the bottom of his heart. Yet *he* was engaged to a girl at Home, and that is how some men are constructed.

The Burmese girl's name was not a pretty one; but as she was promptly christened Georgina by Georgie Porgie, the blemish did not matter. Georgie Porgie thought well of the petting and the general comfort, and vowed that he had never spent five hundred rupees to a better end.

After three months of domestic life, a great idea struck him. Matrimony — English matrimony — could not be such a bad thing after all. If he were so thoroughly comfortable at the Back of Beyond with this Burmese girl who smoked cheroots, how much more comfortable would he be with a sweet English maiden who would not smoke cheroots, and would play upon a piano instead of a banjo? Also he had a desire to return to his kind, to hear a Band once more, and to feel how it felt to wear a dress-suit again. Decidedly, Matrimony would be a very good thing. He thought the matter out at length of evenings, while Georgina sang to him, or asked him why he was so silent, and whether she had done anything to offend him. As he thought he smoked, and as he smoked he looked at Georgina, and in his fancy turned her into a fair, thrifty, amusing, merry little English girl, with hair coming low down on her forehead, and perhaps a cigarette between her lips. Certainly not a big, thick, Burma cheroot, of the brand that Georgina smoked. He would wed a girl with Georgina's eyes and most of her ways. But not all. She could be improved upon. Then he blew thick smoke-wreaths through his nostrils and stretched himself. He would taste marriage. Georgina had helped him to save money, and there were six months' leave due to him.

"See here, little woman," he said, "we must put by more money for these next three months. I want it." That was a direct slur on Georgina's housekeeping; for she prided herself on her thrift; but since her God wanted money she would do her best.

"You want money?" she said with a little laugh. "I *have* money. Look!" She ran to her own room and fetched out a small bag of rupees. "Of all that you give me, I keep back some. See! One hundred and seven rupees. Can you want more money than that? Take it. It is my pleasure if you use it." She spread out the money on the table and pushed it towards him with her quick, little, pale yellow fingers.

Georgie Porgie never referred to economy in the household again.

Three months later, after the despatch and receipt of several mysterious letters which Georgina could not understand, and hated for that reason, Georgie Porgie said that he was going away and she must return to her father's house and stay there.

Georgina wept. She would go with her God from the world's end to the world's end. Why should she leave him? She loved him.

"I am only going to Rangoon," said Georgie Porgie. "I shall be back in a month, but it is safer to stay with your father. I will leave you two hundred rupees."

"If you go for a month, what need of two hundred? Fifty are more than enough. There is some evil here. Do not go, or at least let me go with you."

Georgie Porgie does not like to remember that scene even at this date. In the end he got rid of Georgina by a compromise of seventy-five rupees. She would not take more. Then he went by steamer and rail to Rangoon.

The mysterious letters had granted him six months' leave. The actual flight and an idea that he might have been treacherous hurt severely at the time, but as soon as the big steamer was well out into the blue, things were easier, and Georgina's

239

face, and the queer little stockaded house, and the
memory of the rushes of shouting dacoits by night,
the cry and struggle of the first man that he had
ever killed with his own hand, and a hundred other
more intimate things, faded and faded out of
Georgie Porgie's heart, and the vision of approaching England took its place.   The steamer was full
of men on leave, all rampantly jovial souls who
had shaken off the dust and sweat of Upper Burma
and were as merry as schoolboys.   They helped
Georgie Porgie to forget.

Then came England with its luxuries and de-
cencies and comforts, and Georgie Porgie walked
in a pleasant dream upon pavements of which he
had nearly forgotten the ring, wondering why men
in their senses ever left Town.   He accepted his
keen delight in his furlough as the reward of his
services.   Providence further arranged for him
another and greater delight — all the pleasures of
a quiet English wooing, quite different from the
brazen businesses of the East, when half the community stand back and bet on the result, and the
other half wonder what Mrs. So-and-So will say
to it.

It was a pleasant girl and a perfect summer, and
a big country-house near Petworth where there are
acres and acres of purple heather and high-grassed
water-meadows to wander through.   Georgie Porgie felt that he had at last found something worth

the living for, and naturally assumed that the next thing to do was to ask the girl to share his life in India. She, in her ignorance, was willing to go. On this occasion there was no bartering with a village headman. There was a fine middle-class wedding in the country, with a stout Papa and a weeping Mamma, and a best man in purple and fine linen, and six snub-nosed girls from the Sunday-School to throw roses on the path between the tombstones up to the Church door. The local paper described the affair at great length, even down to giving the hymns in full. But that was because the Direction were starving for want of material.

Then came a honeymoon at Arundel, and the Mamma wept copiously before she allowed her one daughter to sail away to India under the care of Georgie Porgie the Bridegroom. Beyond any question, Georgie Porgie was immensely fond of his wife, and she was devoted to him as the best and greatest man in the world. When he reported himself at Bombay he felt justified in demanding a good station for his wife's sake; and, because he had made a little mark in Burma and was beginning to be appreciated, they allowed him nearly all that he asked for, and posted him to a station which we will call Sutrain. It stood upon several hills, and was styled officially a " Sanitarium," for the good reason that the drainage was utterly

neglected. Here Georgie Porgie settled down,
and found married life come very naturally to him.
He did not rave, as do many bridegrooms, over
the strangeness and delight of seeing his own true
love sitting down to breakfast with him every
morning " as though it were the most natural thing
in the world." " He had been there before," as the
Americans say, and, checking the merits of his
own present grace by those of Georgina, he was
more and more inclined to think that he had done
well.

But there was no peace or comfort across the
Bay of Bengal, under the teak-trees where Georgina lived with her father, waiting for Georgie
Porgie to return. The headman was old, and remembered the war of '51. He had been to Rangoon, and knew something of the ways of the
Kullahs. Sitting in front of his door in the evenings, he taught Georgina a dry philosophy which
did not console her in the least.

The trouble was that she loved Georgie Porgie
just as much as the French girl in the English
History books loved the priest whose head was
broken by the King's bullies. One day she dis-
appeared from the village, with all the rupees that
Georgie Porgie had given her, and a very small
smattering of English—also gained from Georgie
Porgie.

The headman was angry at first, but lit a fresh

cheroot and said something uncomplimentary about the sex in general. Georgina had started on a search for Georgie Porgie, who might be in Rangoon, or across the Black Water, or dead, for aught that she knew. Chance favoured her. An old Sikh policeman told her that Georgie Porgie had crossed the Black Water. She took a steer-age-passage from Rangoon and went to Calcutta, keeping the secret of her search to herself.

In India every trace of her was lost for six weeks, and no one knows what trouble of heart she must have undergone.

She reappeared, four hundred miles north of Calcutta, steadily heading northwards, very worn and haggard, but very fixed in her determination to find Georgie Porgie. She could not understand the language of the people; but India is infinitely charitable, and the women-folk along the Grand Trunk gave her food. Something made her believe that Georgie Porgie was to be found at the end of that pitiless road. She may have seen a sepoy who knew him in Burma, but of this no one can be certain. At last she found a regiment on the line of march, and met there one of the many subalterns whom Georgie Porgie had invited to dinner in the far-off, old days of the dacoit-hunting. There was a certain amount of amusement among the tents when Georgina threw herself at the man's feet and began to cry.

There was no amusement when her story was told; but a collection was made, and that was more to the point. One of the subalterns knew of Georgie Porgie's whereabouts, but not of his marriage. So he told Georgina and she went her way joyfully to the north, in a railway carriage where there was rest for tired feet and shade for a dusty little head. The marches from the train through the hills into Sutrain were trying, but Georgina had money, and families journeying in bullock-carts gave her help. It was an almost miraculous journey, and Georgina felt sure that the good spirits of Burma were looking after her. The hill-road to Sutrain is a chilly stretch, and Georgina caught a bad cold. Still there was Georgie Porgie at the end of all the trouble to take her up in his arms and pet her, as he used to do in the old days when the stockade was shut for the night and he had approved of the evening meal. Georgina went forward as fast as she could; and her good spirits did her one last favour.

An Englishman stopped her, in the twilight, just at the turn of the road into Sutrain, saying, "Good Heavens! What are you doing here?"

He was Gillis, the man who had been Georgie Porgie's assistant in Upper Burma, and who oc-cupied the next post to Georgie Porgie's in the jungle. Georgie Porgie had applied to have him to work with at Sutrain because he liked him.

"I have come," said Georgina simply. "It was such a long way, and I have been months in coming. Where is his house?"

Gillis gasped. He had seen enough of Georgina in the old times to know that explanations would be useless. You cannot explain things to the Oriental. You must show.

"I'll take you there," said Gillis, and he led Georgina off the road, up the cliff, by a little pathway, to the back of a house set on a platform cut into the hillside.

The lamps were just lit, but the curtains were not drawn. "Now look," said Gillis, stopping in front of the drawing-room window. Georgina looked and saw Georgie Porgie and the Bride.

She put her hand up to her hair, which had come out of its top-knot and was straggling about her face. She tried to set her ragged dress in order, but the dress was past pulling straight, and she coughed a queer little cough, for she really had taken a very bad cold. Gillis looked, too, but while Georgina only looked at the Bride once, turning her eyes always on Georgie Porgie, Gillis looked at the Bride all the time.

"What are you going to do?" said Gillis, who held Georgina by the wrist, in case of any unexpected rush into the lamplight. "Will you go in and tell that English woman that you lived with her husband?"

"No," said Georgina faintly. "Let me go. I am going away. I swear that I am going away." She twisted herself free and ran off into the dark.

"Poor little beast!" said Gillis, dropping on to the main road. "I'd ha' given her something to get back to Burma with. What a narrow shave, though! And that angel would never have forgiven it."

This seems to prove that the devotion of Gillis was not entirely due to his affection for Georgie Porgie.

The Bride and the Bridegroom came out into the verandah after dinner, in order that the smoke of Georgie Porgie's cheroots might not hang in the new drawing-room curtains.

"What is that noise down there?" said the Bride. Both listened.

"Oh," said Georgie Porgie, "I suppose some brute of a hillman has been beating his wife."

"Beating—his—wife! How ghastly!" said the Bride. "Fancy *your* beating *me!*" She slipped an arm round her husband's waist, and, leaning her head against his shoulder, looked out across the cloud-filled valley in deep content and security.

But it was Georgina crying, all by herself, down the hillside, among the stones of the water-course where the washermen wash the clothes.

LITTLE TOBRAH

"Prisoner's head did not reach to the top of the dock," as the English newspapers say. This case, however, was not reported because nobody cared by so much as a hempen rope for the life or death of Little Tobrah. The assessors in the red court-house sat upon him all through the long hot afternoon, and whenever they asked him a question he salaamed and whined. Their verdict was that the evidence was inconclusive, and the Judge concurred. It was true that the dead body of Little Tobrah's sister had been found at the bottom of the well, and Little Tobrah was the only human being within a half-mile radius at the time; but the child might have fallen in by accident. Therefore Little Tobrah was acquitted, and told to go where he pleased. This permission was not so generous as it sounds, for he had nowhere to go to, nothing in particular to eat, and nothing whatever to wear.

He trotted into the court-compound, and sat upon the well-curb, wondering whether an unsuccessful dive into the black water below would

end in a forced voyage across the other Black
Water. A groom put down an emptied nose-bag
on the bricks, and Little Tobrah, being hungry,
set himself to scrape out what wet grain the horse
had overlooked.

"O Thief — and but newly set free from the
terror of the Law! Come along!" said the groom,
and Little Tobrah was led by the ear to a large
and fat Englishman, who heard the tale of the
theft.

"Hah!" said the Englishman three times (only
he said a stronger word). "Put him into the net
and take him home." So Little Tobrah was thrown
into the net of the cart, and, nothing doubting that
he should be stuck like a pig, was driven to the
Englishman's house. "Hah!" said the Englishman as before. "Wet grain, by Jove! Feed
the little beggar, some of you, and we'll make a
riding-boy of him? See? Wet grain, good Lord!"

"Give an account of yourself," said the head
of the Grooms to Little Tobrah after the meal had
been eaten and the servants lay at ease in their
quarters behind the house. "You are not of the
groom caste, unless it be for the stomach's sake.
How came you into the court, and why? Answer,
little devil's spawn!"

"There was not enough to eat," said Little
Tobrah calmly. "This is a good place."

"Talk straight talk," said the Head Groom,

"or I will make you clean out the stable of that large red stallion who bites like a camel."

"We be *Telis*, oil-pressers," said Little Tobrah, scratching his toes in the dust. "We were *Telis* — my father, my mother, my brother, the elder by four years, myself, and the sister."

"She who was found dead in the well?" said one who had heard something of the trial.

"Even so," said Little Tobrah gravely. "She who was found dead in the well. It befell upon a time, which is not in my memory, that the sickness came to the village where our oil-press stood, and first my sister was smitten as to her eyes, and went without sight, for it was *mata* — the smallpox. Thereafter, my father and my mother died of that same sickness, so we were alone — my brother who had twelve years, I who had eight, and the sister who could not see. Yet were there the bullock and the oil-press remaining, and we made shift to press the oil as before. But Surjun Dass, the grain-seller, cheated us in his dealings; and it was always a stubborn bullock to drive. We put marigold flowers for the Gods upon the neck of the bullock, and upon the great grinding-beam that rose through the roof; but we gained nothing thereby, and Surjun Dass was a hard man."

"*Bapri-bap*," muttered the grooms' wives, "to cheat a child so! But *we* know what the *bunnia*-folk are, sisters."

249

"The press was an old press, and we were not strong men — my brother and I; nor could we fix the neck of the beam firmly in the shackle."

"Nay, indeed," said the gorgeously-clad wife of the Head Groom, joining the circle. "That is a strong man's work. When I was a maid in my father's house —— "

"Peace, woman," said the Head Groom. "Go on, boy."

"It is nothing," said Little Tobrah. "The big beam tore down the roof upon a day which is not in my memory, and with the roof fell much of the hinder wall, and both together upon our bullock, whose back was broken. Thus we had neither home, nor press, nor bullock — my brother, myself, and the sister who was blind. We went crying away from that place, hand-in-hand, across the fields; and our money was seven annas and six pie. There was a famine in the land. I do not know the name of the land. So, on a night when we were sleeping, my brother took the five annas that remained to us and ran away. I do not know whither he went. The curse of my father be upon him. But I and the sister begged food in the villages, and there was none to give. Only all men said — 'Go to the Englishmen and they will give.' I did not know what the Englishmen were; but they said that they were white, living in tents. I went forward; but I cannot say whither I went, and there was no more food for myself or the sister. And upon a hot night, she weeping and calling for food, we came to a well, and I bade her sit upon the curb, and thrust her in, for, in truth, she could not see; and it is better to die than to starve."

"Ai! Ahi!" wailed the grooms' wives in chorus; "he thrust her in, for it is better to die than to starve!"

"I would have thrown myself in also, but that she was not dead and called to me from the bottom of the well, and I was afraid and ran. And one came out of the crops saying that I had killed her and defiled the well, and they took me before an Englishman, white and terrible, living in a tent, and me he sent here. But there were no witnesses, and it is better to die than to starve. She, furthermore, could not see with her eyes, and was but a little child."

"Was but a little child," echoed the Head Groom's wife. "But who art thou, weak as a fowl and small as a day-old colt, what art *thou*?"

"I who was empty am now full," said Little Tobrah, stretching himself upon the dust. "And I would sleep."

The groom's wife spread a cloth over him while Little Tobrah slept the sleep of the just.

GEMINI

Great is the justice of the White Man — greater the power of a lie. — *Native Proverb*.

THIS is your English Justice, Protector of the Poor. Look at my back and loins which are beaten with sticks — heavy sticks! I am a poor man, and there is no justice in Courts.

There were two of us, and we were born of one birth, but I swear to you that I was born the first, and Ram Dass is the younger by three full breaths. The astrologer said so, and it is written in my horoscope — the horoscope of Durga Dass.

But we were alike — I and my brother who is a beast without honour — so alike that none knew, together or apart, which was Durga Dass. I am a Mahajun of Pali in Marwar, and an honest man. This is true talk. When we were men, we left our father's house in Pali, and went to the Punjab, where all the people are mud-heads and sons of asses. We took shop together in Isser Jang — I and my brother — near the big well where the Governor's camp draws water. But Ram Dass, who is without truth, made quarrel with me, and

252

we were divided. He took his books, and his
pots, and his Mark, and became a *bunnia* — a
money-lender — in the long street of Isser Jang,
near the gateway of the road that goes to Montgomery. It was not my fault that we pulled each
other's turbans. I am a Mahajun of Pali, and I
always speak true talk. Ram Dass was the thief
and the liar.

Now no man, not even the little children, could
at one glance see which was Ram Dass and which
was Durga Dass. But all the people of Isser Jang
— may they die without sons ! — said that we were
thieves. They used much bad talk, but I took
money on their bedsteads and their cooking-pots
and the standing crop and the calf unborn, from
the well in the big square to the gate of the Montgomery road. They were fools, these people —
unfit to cut the toe-nails of a Marwari from Pali.
I lent money to them all. A little, very little
only — here a pice and there a pice. God is my
witness that I am a poor man ! The money is
all with Ram Dass — may his sons turn Christian,
and his daughter be a burning fire and a shame in
the house from generation to generation ! May
she die unwed, and be the mother of a multitude
of bastards ! Let the light go out in the house of
Ram Dass, my brother. This I pray daily twice
— with offerings and charms.

Thus the trouble began. We divided the town

of Isser Jang between us — I and my brother.
There was a landholder beyond the gates, living
but one short mile out, on the road that leads to
Montgomery, and his name was Muhammad Shah,
son of a Nawab. He was a great devil and drank
wine. So long as there were women in his house,
and wine and money for the marriage-feasts, he
was merry and wiped his mouth. Ram Dass lent
him the money, a lakh or half a lakh — how do I
know? — and so long as the money was lent, the
landholder cared not what he signed.

The people of Isser Jang were my portion, and
the landholder and the out-town were the portion
of Ram Dass; for so we had arranged. I was the
poor man, for the people of Isser Jang were without wealth. I did what I could, but Ram Dass
had only to wait without the door of the landholder's garden-court, and to lend him the money;
taking the bonds from the hand of the steward.

In the autumn of the year after the lending,
Ram Dass said to the landholder: "Pay me my
money," but the landholder gave him abuse. But
Ram Dass went into the Courts with the papers
and the bonds — all correct — and took out decrees against the landholder; and the name of the
Government was across the stamps of the decrees.
Ram Dass took field by field, and mango-tree by
mango-tree, and well by well; putting in his own
men — debtors of the out-town of Isser Jang —

—to cultivate the crops. So he crept up across the land, for he had the papers, and the name of the Government was across the stamps, till his men held the crops for him on all sides of the big white house of the landholder. It was well done; but when the landholder saw these things he was very angry and cursed Ram Dass after the manner of the Muhammadans.

And thus the landholder was angry, but Ram Dass laughed and claimed more fields, as was written upon the bonds. This was in the month of Phagun. I took my horse and went out to speak to the man who makes lac-bangles upon the road that leads to Montgomery, because he owed me a debt. There was in front of me, upon his horse, my brother Ram Dass. And when he saw me, he turned aside into the high crops, because there was hatred between us. And I went forward till I came to the orange-bushes by the landholder's house. The bats were flying, and the evening smoke was low down upon the land. Here met me four men — swashbucklers and Muhammadans — with their faces bound up, laying hold of my horse's bridle and crying out: "This is Ram Dass! Beat!" Me they beat with their staves — heavy staves bound about with wire at the end, such weapons as those swine of Punjabis use — till, having cried for mercy, I fell down senseless. But these shameless ones still beat me, saying: "O Ram

Dass, this is your interest — well weighed and counted into your hand, Ram Dass." I cried aloud that I was not Ram Dass, but Durga Dass, his brother, yet they only beat me the more, and when I could make no more outcry they left me. But I saw their faces. There was Elahi Baksh who runs by the side of the landholder's white horse, and Nur Ali the keeper of the door, and Wajib Ali the very strong cook, and Abdul Latif the messenger — all of the household of the landholder. These things I can swear on the Cow's Tail if need be, but — *Ahi! Ahi!* — it has been already sworn, and I am a poor man whose honour is lost.

When these four had gone away laughing, my brother Ram Dass came out of the crops and mourned over me as one dead. But I opened my eyes, and prayed him to get me water. When I had drunk, he carried me on his back, and by byways brought me into the town of Isser Jang. My heart was turned to Ram Dass, my brother, in that hour, because of his kindness, and I lost my enmity.

But a snake is a snake till it is dead; and a liar is a liar till the Judgment of the Gods takes hold of his heel. I was wrong in that I trusted my brother — the son of my mother.

When we had come to his house and I was a little restored, I told him my tale, and he said : " Without doubt it is me whom they would have beaten. But the Law Courts are open, and there is the Justice of the Sirkar above all; and to the Law Courts do thou go when this sickness is over-past."

Now when we two had left Pali in the old years, there fell a famine that ran from Jeysulmir to Gurgaon and touched Gogunda in the south. At that time the sister of my father came away and lived with us in Isser Jang; for a man must above all see that his folk do not die of want. When the quarrel between us twain came about, the sister of my father—a lean she-dog without teeth—said that Ram Dass had the right, and went with him. Into her hands—because she knew medicines and many cures—Ram Dass, my brother, put me faint with the beating, and much bruised even to the pouring of blood from the mouth. When I had two days' sickness the fever came upon me; and I set aside the fever to the account written in my mind against the landholder.

The Punjabis of Isser Jang are all the sons of Belial and a she-ass, but they are very good witnesses, bearing testimony unshakingly whatever the pleaders may say. I would purchase witnesses by the score, and each man should give evidence, not only against Nur Ali, Wajib Ali, Abdul Latif, and Elahi Baksh, but against the landholder, saying that he upon his white horse had called his men to beat me; and, further that they had robbed me of two hundred rupees. For the latter testimony I would remit a little of the debt of the man who sold the lac-bangles, and he should say that he had put the money into my hands, and had seen the robbery from afar, but, being afraid, had run away. This plan I told to my brother Ram Dass; and he said that the arrangement was good, and bade me take comfort and make swift work to be abroad again. My heart was opened to my brother in my sickness, and I told him the names of those whom I would call as witnesses—all men in my debt, but of that the Magistrate Sahib could have no knowledge, nor the landholder. The fever stayed with me, and after the fever I was taken with colic, and gripings very terrible. In that day I thought that my end was at hand, but I know now that she who gave me the medicines, the sister of my father—a widow with a widow's heart—had brought about my second sickness. Ram Dass, my brother, said that my house was shut and locked, and brought me the big door-key and my books, together with all the moneys that were in my house—even the money that was buried under the floor; for I was in great fear lest thieves should break in and dig. I speak true talk; there was but very little money in my house. Perhaps ten rupees—perhaps twenty. How can I tell? God is my witness that I am a poor man.

One night when I had told Ram Dass all that

was in my heart of the lawsuit that I would bring against the landholder, and Ram Dass had said that he had made the arrangements with the witnesses, giving me their names written, I was taken with a new great sickness, and they put me on the bed. When I was a little recovered—I cannot tell how many days afterwards—I made enquiry for Ram Dass, and the sister of my father said that he had gone to Montgomery upon a lawsuit. I took medicine and slept very heavily without waking. When my eyes were opened, there was a great stillness in the house of Ram Dass, and none answered when I called — not even the sister of my father. This filled me with fear, for I knew not what had happened.

Taking a stick in my hand, I went out slowly, till I came to the great square by the well, and my heart was hot in me against the landholder because of the pain of every step I took.

I called for Jowar Singh, the carpenter, whose name was first upon the list of those who should bear evidence against the landholder, saying: "Are all things ready, and do you know what should be said?"

Jowar Singh answered: "What is this, and whence do you come, Durga Dass?"

I said: "From my bed, where I have so long lain sick because of the landholder. Where is Ram Dass, my brother, who was to have made the arrangement for the witnesses? Surely you and yours know these things!"

Then Jowar Singh said: "What has this to do with us, O Liar? I have borne witness and I have been paid, and the landholder has, by the order of the Court, paid both the five hundred rupees that he robbed from Ram Dass and yet other five hundred because of the great injury he did to your brother."

The well and the jujube-tree above it and the square of Isser Jang became dark in my eyes, but I leaned on my stick and said: "Nay! This is child's talk and senseless. It was I who suffered at the hands of the landholder, and I am come to make ready the case. Where is my brother Ram Dass?"

But Jowar Singh shook his head, and a woman cried: "What lie is here? What quarrel had the landholder with you, *bunnia?* It is only a shameless one and one without faith who profits by his brother's smarts. Have these *bunnias* no bowels?"

I cried again, saying: "By the Cow — by the Oath of the Cow, by the Temple of the Blue-throated Mahadeo, I and I only was beaten — beaten to the death! Let your talk be straight, O people of Isser Jang, and I will pay for the witnesses." And I tottered where I stood, for the sickness and the pain of the beating were heavy upon me.

Then Ram Narain, who has his carpet spread under the jujube-tree by the well, and writes all letters for the men of the town, came up and said: "To-day is the one and fortieth day since the beating, and since these six days the case has been judged in the Court, and the Assistant Commissioner Sahib has given it for your brother Ram Dass, allowing the robbery, to which, too, I bore witness, and all things else as the witnesses said. There were many witnesses, and twice Ram Dass became senseless in the Court because of his wounds, and the Stunt Sahib — the *baba* Stunt Sahib — gave him a chair before all the pleaders. Why do you howl, Durga Dass? These things fell as I have said. Was it not so?"

And Jowar Singh said: "That is truth. I was there, and there was a red cushion in the chair."

And Ram Narain said: "Great shame has come upon the landholder because of this judgment, and fearing his anger, Ram Dass and all his house have gone back to Pali. Ram Dass told us that you also had gone first, the enmity being healed between you, to open a shop in Pali. Indeed, it were well for you that you go even now, for the landholder has sworn that if he catch any one of your house, he will hang him by the heels from the well-beam, and, swinging him to and fro, will beat him with staves till the blood runs from his ears. What I have said in respect to the case is

261

true, as these men here can testify — even to the five hundred rupees."

I said: "Was it five hundred?" And Kirpa Ram, the Jat, said: "Five hundred; for I bore witness also."

And I groaned, for it had been in my heart to have said two hundred only.

Then a new fear came upon me and my bowels turned to water, and, running swiftly to the house of Ram Dass, I sought for my books and my money in the great wooden chest under my bedstead. There remained nothing : not even a cowrie's value. All had been taken by the devil who said he was my brother. I went to my own house also and opened the boards of the shutters; but there also was nothing save the rats among the grain-baskets. In that hour my senses left me, and, tearing my clothes, I ran to the well-place, crying out for the Justice of the English on my brother Ram Dass, and, in my madness, telling all that the books were lost. When men saw that I would have jumped down the well, they believed the truth of my talk; more especially because upon my back and bosom were still the marks of the staves of the landholder.

Jowar Singh the carpenter withstood me, and turning me in his hands — for he is a very strong man — showed the scars upon my body, and bowed down with laughter upon the well-curb. He cried aloud so that all heard him, from the well-square to the Caravanserai of the Pilgrims: "Oho! The jackals have quarrelled, and the gray one has been caught in the trap. In truth, this man has been grievously beaten, and his brother has taken the money which the Court decreed! Oh, *bunnia*, this shall be told for years against you! The jackals have quarrelled, and, moreover, the books are burned. O people indebted to Durga Dass — and I know that ye be many — the books are burned!"

Then all Isser Jang took up the cry that the books were burned — *Ahi! Ahi!* that in my folly I had let that escape my mouth — and they laughed throughout the city. They gave me the abuse of the Punjabi, which is a terrible abuse and very hot; pelting me also with sticks and cow-dung till I fell down and cried for mercy.

Ram Narain, the letter-writer, bade the people cease, for fear that the news should get into Montgomery, and the Policemen might come down to enquire. He said, using many bad words: "This much mercy will I do to you, Durga Dass, though there was no mercy in your dealings with my sister's son over the matter of the dun heifer. Has any man a pony on which he sets no store, that this fellow may escape? If the landholder hears that one of the twain (and God knows whether he beat one or both, but this man is certainly beaten) be in the city, there will be a murder done, and then will come the Police, making inquisition into each man's house and eating the sweet-seller's stuff all day long."

Kirpa Ram, the Jat, said: "I have a pony very sick. But with beating he can be made to walk for two miles. If he dies, the hide-sellers will have the body."

Then Chumbo, the hide-seller, said: "I will pay three annas for the body, and will walk by this man's side till such time as the pony dies. If it be more than two miles, I will pay two annas only."

Kirpa Ram said: "Be it so." Men brought out the pony, and I asked leave to draw a little water from the well, because I was dried up with fear.

Then Ram Narain said: "Here be four annas. God has brought you very low, Durga Dass, and I would not send you away empty, even though the matter of my sister's son's dun heifer be an open sore between us. It is a long way to your own country. Go, and if it be so willed, live; but, above all, do not take the pony's bridle, for that is mine."

And I went out of Isser Jang, amid the laughing of the huge-thighed Jats, and the hide-seller walked by my side waiting for the pony to fall dead. In one mile it died, and being full of fear of the landholder, I ran till I could run no more, and came to this place.

But I swear by the Cow, I swear by all things whereon Hindus and Musalmans, and even the Sahibs swear, that I, and not my brother, was beaten by the landholder. But the case is shut and the doors of the Law Courts are shut, and God knows where the *baba* Stunt Sahib — the mother's milk is not yet dry upon his hairless lip — is gone. *Ahi! Ahi!* I have no witnesses, and the scars will heal, and I am a poor man. But, on my Father's Soul, on the oath of a Mahajun from Pali, I, and not my brother, I was beaten by the landholder!

What can I do? The Justice of the English is as a great river. Having gone forward, it does not return. Howbeit, do you, Sahib, take a pen and write clearly what I have said, that the Dipty Sahib may see, and remove the Stunt Sahib, who is a colt yet unlicked by the mare, so young is he. I, and not my brother, was beaten, and he is gone to the west — I do not know where.

But, above all things, write—so that Sahibs may read, and his disgrace be accomplished — that Ram Dass, my brother, son of Purun Dass, Mahajun of Pali, is a swine and a night-thief, a taker of life, an eater of flesh, a jackal-spawn without beauty, or faith, or cleanliness, or honour!

IF you consider the circumstances of the case, it was the only thing that he could do. But Pambé Serang has been hanged by the neck till he is dead, and Nurkeed is dead also.

Three years ago, when the Elsass-Lothringen steamer *Saarbruck* was coaling at Aden and the weather was very hot indeed, Nurkeed, the big fat Zanzibar stoker who fed the second right furnace thirty feet down in the hold, got leave to go ashore. He departed "a Seedee boy," as they call the stokers; he returned the full-blooded Sultan of Zanzibar — His Highness Sayyid Burgash, with a bottle in each hand. Then he sat on the fore-hatch grating, eating salt fish and onions, and singing the songs of a far country. The food belonged to Pambé, the serang or head man of the lascar sailors. He had just cooked it for himself, turned to borrow some salt, and when he came back Nurkeed's dirty black fingers were spading into the rice.

A serang is a person of importance, far above a stoker, though the stoker draws better pay. He

sets the chorus of "Hya! Hulla! Hee-ah! Heh!"
when the captain's gig is pulled up to the davits; he
heaves the lead too; and sometimes, when all the
ship is lazy, he puts on his whitest muslin and a big
red sash, and plays with the passengers' children
on the quarter-deck. Then the passengers give
him money, and he saves it all up for an orgy at
Bombay or Calcutta, or Pulu Penang.

"Ho! you fat black barrel, you're eating my
food!" said Pambé, in the Other Lingua Franca
that begins where the Levant tongue stops, and
runs from Port Said eastward till east is west, and
the sealing-brigs of the Kurile Islands gossip with
the strayed Hakodate junks.

"Son of Eblis, monkey-face, dried shark's liver,
pig-man, I am the Sultan Sayyid Burgash, and
the commander of all this ship. Take away your
garbage"; and Nurkeed thrust the empty pewter
rice-plate into Pambé's hand.

Pambé beat it into a basin over Nurkeed's
woolly head. Nurkeed drew his sheath-knife and
stabbed Pambé in the leg. Pambé drew *his* sheath-
knife; but Nurkeed dropped down into the darkness of the hold and spat through the grating at
Pambé, who was staining the clean fore-deck with
his blood.

Only the white moon saw these things; for the
officers were looking after the coaling, and the
passengers were tossing in their close cabins. "All

right," said Pambé — and went forward to tie up his leg — "we will settle the account later on."

He was a Malay born in India: married once in Burma, where his wife had a cigar-shop on the Shwe-Dagon road; once in Singapore, to a Chinese girl; and once in Madras, to a Mahomedan woman who sold fowls. The English sailor cannot, owing to postal and telegraph facilities, marry as profusely as he used to do; but native sailors can, being uninfluenced by the barbarous inventions of the Western savage. Pambé was a good husband when he happened to remember the existence of a wife; but he was also a very good Malay; and it is not wise to offend a Malay, because he does not forget anything. Moreover, in Pambé's case blood had been drawn and food spoiled.

Next morning Nurkeed rose with a blank mind. He was no longer Sultan of Zanzibar, but a very hot stoker. So he went on deck and opened his jacket to the morning breeze, till a sheath-knife came like a flying-fish and stuck into the woodwork of the cook's galley half an inch from his right armpit. He ran down below before his time, trying to remember what he could have said to the owner of the weapon. At noon, when all the ship's lascars were feeding, Nurkeed advanced into their midst, and, being a placid man with a large regard for his own skin, he opened negotiations, saying, "Men of the ship, last night I was

268

drunk, and this morning I know that I behaved unseemly to some one or another of you. Who was that man, that I may meet him face to face and say that I was drunk?"

Pambé measured the distance to Nurkeed's naked breast. If he sprang at him he might be tripped up, and a blind blow at the chest sometimes only means a gash on the breast-bone. Ribs are difficult to thrust between unless the subject be asleep. So he said nothing; nor did the other lascars. Their faces immediately dropped all expression, as is the custom of the Oriental when there is killing on the carpet or any chance of trouble. Nurkeed looked long at the white eyeballs. He was only an African, and could not read characters. A big sigh — almost a groan — broke from him, and he went back to the furnaces. The lascars took up the conversation where he had interrupted it. They talked of the best methods of cooking rice.

Nurkeed suffered considerably from lack of fresh air during the run to Bombay. He only came on deck to breathe when all the world was about; and even then a heavy block once dropped from a derrick within a foot of his head, and an apparently firm-lashed grating on which he set his foot began to turn over with the intention of dropping him on the cased cargo fifteen feet below; and one insupportable night the sheath-knife dropped

from the fo'c's'le, and this time it drew blood. So
Nurkeed made complaint; and, when the *Saarbruck* reached Bombay, fled and buried himself
among eight hundred thousand people, and did
not sign articles till the ship had been a month
gone from the port.   Pambé waited too; but his
Bombay wife grew clamorous, and he was forced
to sign in the *Spicheren* to Hongkong, because he
realised that all play and no work gives Jack a
ragged shirt.   In the foggy China seas he thought
a great deal of Nurkeed, and, when Elsass-Lothringen steamers lay in port with the *Spicheren*, inquired after him and found he had gone to England *via* the Cape, on the *Gravelotte*.   Pambé came
to England on the *Worth*.   The *Spicheren* met her
by the Nore Light.   Nurkeed was going out with
the *Spicheren* to the Calicut coast.

" Want to find a friend, my trap-mouthed coal-
scuttle ? " said a gentleman in the mercantile service.   "Nothing easier.   Wait at the Nyanza
Docks till he comes.   Every one comes to the
Nyanza Docks.   Wait, you poor heathen."   The
gentleman spoke truth.   There are three great
doors in the world where, if you stand long enough,
you shall meet any one you wish.   The head of
the Suez Canal is one, but there Death comes also;
Charing Cross Station is the second — for inland
work ; and the Nyanza Docks is the third.   At
each of these places are men and women looking

eternally for those who will surely come. So
Pambé waited at the docks. Time was no object
to him; and the wives could wait, as he did from
day to day, week to week, and month to month,
by the Blue Diamond funnels, the Red Dot smoke-
stacks, the Yellow Streaks, and the nameless dingy '
gypsies of the sea that loaded and unloaded, jostled,
whistled, and roared in the everlasting fog. When
money failed, a kind gentleman told Pambé to become a Christian; and Pambé became one with
great speed, getting his religious teachings between
ship and ship's arrival, and six or seven shillings a
week for distributing tracts to mariners. What
the faith was Pambé did not in the least care; but
he knew if he said "Native Ki-lis-ti-an, Sar," to
men with long black coats he might get a few
coppers; and the tracts were vendible at a little
public-house that sold shag by the "dottel," which
is even smaller weight than the half-screw, which
is less than the half-ounce, and a most profitable
retail trade.

But after eight months Pambé fell sick with
pneumonia, contracted from long standing still in
slush; and much against his will he was forced to
lie down in his two-and-sixpenny room raging
against Fate.

The kind gentleman sat by his bedside, and
grieved to find that Pambé talked in strange
tongues, instead of listening to good books, and

271

almost seemed to become a benighted heathen
again — till one day he was roused from semi-
stupor by a voice in the street by the dock-
head. "My friend — he," whispered Pambé.
"Call now — call Nurkeed. Quick! God has
sent him!"

"He wanted one of his own race," said the kind
gentleman; and, going out, he called "Nurkeed!"
at the top of his voice. An excessively coloured
man in a rasping white shirt and brand-new slops,
a shining hat, and a breast-pin, turned round.
Many voyages had taught Nurkeed how to spend
his money and made him a citizen of the world.

"Hi! Yes!" said he, when the situation was
explained. "Command him — black nigger —
when I was in the *Saarbruck*. Ole Pambé, good
ole Pambé. Dam lascar. Show him up, Sar";
and he followed into the room. One glance told
the stoker what the kind gentleman had overlooked. Pambé was desperately poor. Nurkeed
drove his hands deep into his pockets, then advanced with clenched fists on the sick, shouting,
"Hya, Pambé. Hya! Hee-ah! Hulla! Heh!
Takilo! Takilo! Make fast aft, Pambé. You
know, Pambé. You know me. Dekho, jee!
Look! Dam big fat lazy lascar!"

Pambé beckoned with his left hand. His right
was under his pillow. Nurkeed removed his gorgeous hat and stooped over Pambé till he could

272

catch a faint whisper. "How beautiful!" said the kind gentleman. "How these Orientals love like children!"

"Spit him out," said Nurkeed, leaning over Pambé yet more closely.

"Touching the matter of that fish and onions," said Pambé — and sent the knife home under the edge of the rib-bone upwards and forwards.

There was a thick, sick cough, and the body of the African slid slowly from the bed, his clutching hands letting fall a shower of silver pieces that ran across the room.

"Now I can die!" said Pambé.

But he did not die. He was nursed back to life with all the skill that money could buy, for the Law wanted him; and in the end he grew sufficiently healthy to be hanged in due and proper form.

Pambé did not care particularly; but it was a sad blow to the kind gentleman.

ONE VIEW OF THE QUESTION

From Shafiz Ullah Khan, son of Hyat Ullah Khan. in the honoured service of His Highness the Rao Sahib of Jagesur, which is in the northern borders of Hindustan, and Orderly to His Highness, this to Kazi Jamal-ud-Din, son of Kazi Ferisht ud Din Khan, in the service of the Rao Sahib, a minister much honoured. From that place which they call the Northbrook Club, in the town of London, under the shadow of the Empress, it is written:

BETWEEN brother and chosen brother be no long protestations of Love and Sincerity. Heart speaks naked to Heart, and the Head answers for all. Glory and Honour on thy house till the ending of the years, and a tent in the borders of Paradise.

MY BROTHER,— In regard to that for which I was despatched follows the account. I have purchased for the Rao Sahib, and paid sixty pounds in every hundred, the things he most desired. Thus, two of the great fawn-coloured tiger-dogs, male and female, their pedigree being written upon paper, and silver collars adorning their necks. For the Rao Sahib's greater pleasure I send them at once by the steamer, in charge of a man who will render account of them at Bombay to the bankers there. They are the best of all dogs in this place. Of guns I have bought five — two silver-sprigged in the stock, with gold scroll-work about the hammer, both double-barrelled, hard-striking, cased in velvet and red leather; three of unequalled workmanship, but lacking adornment; a pump-gun that fires fourteen times — this when the Rao Sahib drives pig; a double-barrelled shell-gun for tiger, and that is a miracle of workmanship; and a fowling-piece no lighter than a feather, with green and blue cartridges by the thousand. Also a very small rifle for blackbuck, that yet would slay a man at four hundred paces. The harness with the golden crests for the Rao Sahib's coach is not yet complete, by reason of the difficulty of lining the red velvet into leather; but the two-horse harness and the great saddle with the golden holsters that is for state use have been put with camphor into a tin box, and I have signed it with my ring. Of the grained-leather case of women's tools and tweezers for the hair and beard, of the perfumes and the silks, and all that was wanted by the women behind the curtains, I have no knowledge. They are matters of long coming, and the hawk-bells, hoods, and jesses with the golden lettering are as much delayed as they. Read this in the Rao Sahib's ear, and speak of my diligence and zeal, that favour may not be abated by absence, and keep the eye of constraint upon that jesting dog without teeth — Bahadur Shah — for by thy aid and voice, and what I have done in regard to the guns, I look, as thou knowest, for the headship of the army of Jagesur. That conscienceless one desires it also, and I have heard that the Rao Sahib leans thatward. Have ye done, then, with the drinking of wine in your house, my brother, or has Bahadur Shah become a forswearer of brandy? I would not that drink should end him, but the well-mixed draught leads to madness. Consider.

And now in regard to this land of the Sahibs, follows that thou hast demanded. God is my witness that I have striven to understand all that I saw and a little of what I heard. My words and intention are those of truth, yet it may be that I write of nothing but lies.

Since the first wonder and bewilderment of my beholding is gone — we note the jewels in the ceiling-dome, but later the filth on the floor — I see clearly that this town, London, which is as large as all Jagesur, is accursed, being dark and unclean, devoid of sun, and full of low-born, who are perpetually drunk, and howl in the streets like

jackals, men and women together. At nightfall
it is the custom of countless thousands of women
to descend into the streets and sweep them, roaring, making jests, and demanding liquor. At the
hour of this attack it is the custom of the house-
holders to take their wives and children to the
playhouses and the places of entertainment; evil
and good thus returning home together as do kine
from the pools at sundown. I have never seen
any sight like this sight in all the world, and I
doubt that a double is to be found on the hither
side of the gates of Hell. Touching the mystery
of their craft, it is an ancient one, but the house-
holders assemble in herds, being men and women,
and cry aloud to their God that it is not there;
the said women pounding at the doors without. Moreover, upon the day when they go to
prayer the drink-places are only opened when the
mosques are shut; as who should dam the Jumna
river for Friday only. Therefore the men and
women, being forced to accomplish their desires
in the shorter space, become the more furiously
drunk, and roll in the gutter together. They are
there regarded by those going to pray. Further,
and for visible sign that the place is forgotten of
God, there falls upon certain days, without warning, a cold darkness, whereby the sun's light is altogether cut off from all the city and the people,
male and female, and the drivers of the vehicles

grope and howl in this Pit at high noon, none seeing the other. The air being filled with the smoke of Hell—sulphur and pitch as it is written —they die speedily with gaspings, and so are buried in the dark. This is a terror beyond the pen, but by my hand I write of what I have seen!

It is not true that the Sahibs worship one God, as do we of the Faith, or that the differences in their creed be like those now running between Shiah and Sunni. I am but a fighting man, and no darvesh, caring, as thou knowest, as much for Shiah as Sunni. But I have spoken to many people of the nature of their Gods. One there is who is the head of the Mukht-i-Fauj,[1] and he is worshipped by men in blood-red clothes, who shout and become without sense. Another is an image, before whom they burn candles and incense in just such a place as I have seen when I went to Rangoon to buy Burma ponies for the Rao. Yet a third has naked altars facing a great assembly of dead. To him they sing chiefly; and for others there is a woman who was the mother of the great prophet that was before Mahomed. The common folk have no God, but worship those who may speak to them hanging from the lamps in the street. The most wise people worship themselves and such things as they have made with their mouths and their hands, and this is to be

[1] Salvation Army.

found notably among the barren women, of whom there are many. Thou wilt not believe this, my brother. Nor did I when I was first told, but now it is nothing to me; so greatly has the foot of travel let out the stirrup-holes of belief.

But thou wilt say, "What matter to us whether Ahmed's beard or Mahmud's be the longer! Speak what thou canst of the Accomplishment of Desire." Would that thou wert here to talk face to face; to walk abroad with me and learn.

With this people it is a matter of Heaven and Hell whether Ahmed's beard and Mahmud's tally or differ but by a hair. Thou knowest the system of their statecraft? It is this. Certain men, appointing themselves, go about and speak to the low-born, the peasants, the leather-workers, and the cloth-dealers, and the women, saying: "Give us leave by your favour to speak for you in the council." Securing that permission by large promises, they return to the council-place, and, sitting unarmed, some six hundred together, speak at random each for himself and his own ball of low-born. The viziers and dewans of the Empress must ever beg money at their hands, for unless more than a half of the six hundred be of one heart towards the spending of the revenues, neither horse can be shod, rifle loaded, or man clothed throughout the land. Remember this very continually. The six hundred are above the Empress, above the Viceroy of India, above the Head of the Army and every other power that thou hast ever known. Because they hold the revenues.

They are divided into two hordes — the one perpetually hurling abuse at the other, and bidding the low-born hamper and rebel against all that the other may devise for government. Except that they sit unarmed, and so call each other liar, dog, and bastard without fear, even under the shadow of the Empress's throne, they are at bitter war which is without any end. They pit lie against lie, till the low-born and common folk grow drunk with lies, and in their turn begin to lie and refuse to pay the revenues. Further, they divide their women into bands, and send them into this fight with yellow flowers in their hands, and since the belief of a woman is but her lover's belief stripped of judgment, very many wild words are added. Well said the slave girl to Mámún in the delectable pages of the Son of Abdullah:—

> "Oppression and the sword slay fast —
> Thy breath kills slowly but at last."

If they desire a thing they declare that it is true. If they desire it not, though that were Death itself, they cry aloud, "It has never been." Thus their talk is the talk of children, and like children they snatch at what they covet, not considering whether it be their own or another's. And in their councils, when the army of unreason has come to the defile of dispute, and there is no more talk left on either side, they, dividing, count heads, and the will of that side which has the larger number of heads makes that law. But the outnumbered side run speedily among the common people and bid them trample on that law, and slay the officers thereof. Follow slaughter by night of men un-armed, and the slaughter of cattle and insults to women. They do not cut off the noses of women, but they crop their hair and scrape the flesh with pins. Then those shameless ones of the council stand up before the judges wiping their mouths and making oath. They say: " Before God we are free from blame. Did we say ' Heave that stone out of that road and kill that one and no other' ? " So they are not made shorter by the head because they said only : "Here are stones and yonder is such a fellow obeying the Law which is no law because we do not desire it."

Read this in the Rao Sahib's ear, and ask him if he remembers that season when the Manglôt headmen refused revenue, not because they could not pay, but because they judged the cess extreme. I and thou went out with the troopers all one day and the black lances raised the thatch, so that there was hardly any need of firing; and no man was slain. But this land is at secret war and veiled killing. In five years of peace they have slain within their own borders and of their own kin more men than would have fallen had the ball of dissension been left to the mallet of the army. And yet there is no hope of peace, for soon the sides again divide, and then they will cause to be slain more men unarmed and in the fields. And so much for that matter, which is to our advantage. There is a better thing to be told, and one tending to the Accomplishment of Desire. Read here with a fresh mind after sleep. I write as I understand.

Above all this war without honour lies that which I find hard to put into writing, and thou knowest I am unhandy of the pen. I will ride the steed of Inability sideways at the wall of Expression. The earth underfoot is sick and sour with the much handling of man, as a grazing-ground sours under cattle; and the air is sick too. Upon the ground they have laid in this town, as it were, the stinking boards of a stable, and through these boards, between a thousand thousand houses, the rank humours of the earth sweat through to the over-burdened air that returns them to their breeding-place; for the smoke of their cooking-fires keeps all in as the cover the juices of the sheep. And in like manner there is a green-sickness among the people, and especially among the six hundred men who talk. Neither winter nor autumn abates that malady of the soul. I have seen it among women in our own country, and in boys not yet blooded to the sword; but I have never seen so much thereof before. Through the peculiar operation of this air the people, abandoning honour and steadfastness, question all authority, not as men question, but as girls, whimperingly, with pinchings in the back when the back is turned, and mowing. If one cries in the streets, " There has been an injustice," they take him not to make complaint to those appointed, but all who pass, drinking his words, fly clamorously to the house of the accused and write evil things of him, his wives and his daughters; for they take no thought to the weighing of evidence, but are as women. And with one hand they beat their constables who guard the streets, and with the other beat the constables for resenting that beating, and fine them. When they have in all things made light of the State they cry to the State for help, and it is given; so that the next time they will cry more. Such as are oppressed riot through the streets, bearing banners that hold four days' labour and a week's bread in cost and toil; and when neither horse nor foot can pass by they are satisfied. Others, receiving wages, refuse to work till they get more, and the priests help them, and also men of the six hundred—for where rebellion is

one of those men will come as a kite to a dead
bullock —and priests, talker, and men together declare that it is right because these will not work
that no others may attempt.   In this manner they
have so confused the loading and the unloading of
the ships that come to this town that, in sending
the Rao Sahib's guns and harness, I saw fit to send
the cases by the train to another ship that sailed
from another place.   There is now no certainty in
any sending.   But who injures the merchants shuts
the door of well-being on the city and the army.
And ye know what Sa'adi saith :—

> " How may the merchant westward fare
>   When he hears the tale of the tumults there?"

No man can keep faith, because he cannot tell
how his underlings will go.   They have made the
servant greater than the master, for that he is the
servant; not reckoning that each is equal under
God to the appointed task.   That is a thing to be
put aside in the cupboard of the mind.

Further, the misery and outcry of the common
folk, of whom the earth's bosom is weary, has so
wrought upon the minds of certain people who
have never slept under fear nor seen the flat edge
of the sword on the heads of a mob, that they cry
out: " Let us abate everything that is, and altogether labour with our bare hands."   Their hands

in that employ would fester at the second stroke; and I have seen, for all their unrest at the agonies of others, that they abandon no whit of soft living. Unknowing the common folk, or indeed the minds of men, they offer strong drink of words, such as they themselves use, to empty bellies; and that wine breeds drunkenness of soul. The distressful persons stand all day long at the door of the drink-places to the number of very many thousands. The well-wishing people of small discernment give them words or pitifully attempt in schools to turn them into craftsmen, weavers, or builders, of whom there be more than enough. Yet they have not the wisdom to look at the hands of the taught, whereon a man's craft and that of his father is written by God and Necessity. They believe that the son of a drunkard shall drive a straight chisel and the charioteer do plaster-work. They take no thought in the dispensation of generosity, which is as the closed fingers of a water-scooping palm. Therefore the rough timber of a very great army drifts unhewn through the slime of their streets. If the Government, which is to-day and to-morrow changes, spent on these hopeless ones some money to clothe and equip, I should not write what I write. But these people despise the trade of arms, and rest content with the memory of old battles; the women and the talking-men aiding them.

Thou wilt say: "Why speak continually of
women and fools?" I answer by God, the Fash-
ioner of the Heart, the fools sit among the six
hundred, and the women sway their councils. Hast
thou forgotten when the order came across the
seas that rotted out the armies of the English with
us, so that soldiers fell sick by the hundred where
but ten had sickened before? That was the work
of not more than twenty of the men and some
fifty of the barren women. I have seen three or
four of them, male and female, and they triumph
openly, in the name of their God, because three
regiments of the white troops are not. This is to
our advantage, because the sword with the rust-
spot breaks over the turban of the enemy. But if
they thus tear their own flesh and blood ere their
madness be risen to its height, what will they do
when the moon is full?

Seeing that power lay in the hands of the six
hundred, and not in the Viceroy or elsewhere, I
have throughout my stay sought the shadow of
those among them who talk most and most ex-
travagantly. They lead the common folk, and
receive permission of their good-will. It is the
desire of some of these men — indeed, of almost
as many as caused the rotting of the English army
— that our lands and peoples should accurately
resemble those of the English upon this very day.
May God, the Contemner of Folly, forbid! I

myself am accounted a show among them, and of us and ours they know naught, some calling me Hindu and others Rajput, and using towards me, in ignorance, slave-talk and expressions of great disrespect. Some of them are well-born, but the greater part are low-born, coarse-skinned, waving their arms, high-voiced, without dignity, slack in the mouth, shifty-eyed, and, as I have said, swayed by the wind of a woman's cloak.

Now this is a tale but two days old. There was a company at meat, and a high-voiced woman spoke to me, in the face of the men, of the affairs of our womankind. It was her ignorance that made each word an edged insult. Remembering this, I held my peace till she had spoken a new law as to the control of our zenanas, and of all who are behind the curtains.

Then I — " Hast thou ever felt the life stir under thy heart or laid a little son between thy breasts, O most unhappy ? " Thereto she, hotly, with a haggard eye — " No, for I am a free woman, and no servant of babes." Then I, softly —" God deal lightly with thee, my sister, for thou art in heavier bondage than any slave, and the fuller half of the earth is hidden from thee. The first ten years of the life of a man are his mother's, and from the dusk to the dawn surely the wife may command the husband. Is it a great thing to stand back in the waking hours while the men go abroad unhampered by thy hands on the bridle-rein ? " Then she wondered that a heathen should speak thus : yet she is a woman honoured among these men, and openly professes that she hath no profession of faith in her mouth. Read this in the ear of the Rao Sahib, and demand how it would fare with me if I brought such a woman for his use. It were worse than that yellow desert-bred girl from Cutch, who set the girls to fighting for her own pleasure, and slippered the young prince across the mouth. Rememberest thou ?

In truth the fountain-head of power is putrid with long standing still. These men and women would make of all India a dung-cake, and would fain leave the mark of the fingers upon it. And they have power and the control of the revenues, and that is why I am so particular in description. *They have power over all India.* Of what they speak they understand nothing, for the low-born's soul is bounded by his field, and he grasps not the connection of affairs from pole to pole. They boast openly that the Viceroy and the others are their servants. When the masters are mad, what shall the servants do ?

Some hold that all war is sin, and Death the greatest fear under God. Others declare with the Prophet that it is evil to drink, to which teaching their streets bear evident witness; and others there are, specially the low-born, who aver that all dominion is wicked and sovereignty of the sword accursed. These protested to me, making, as it were, an apology that their kin should hold Hindustan, and hoping that some day they would withdraw. Knowing well the breed of white man in our borders, I would have laughed, but forbore, remembering that these speakers had power in the counting of heads. Yet others cry aloud against the taxation of Hindustan under the Sahibs' rule. To this I assent, remembering the yearly mercy of the Rao Sahib when the turbans of the troopers come through the blighted corn, and the women's anklets go into the melting-pot. But I am no good speaker. *That* is the duty of the boys from Bengal — hill-asses with an eastern bray — Mahrattas from Poona, and the like. These, moving among fools, represent themselves as the sons of some one, being beggar-taught, offspring of grain-dealers, curriers, sellers of bottles, and money-lenders, as thou knowest. Now, we of Jagesur owe naught save friendship to the English who took us by the sword, and having taken us let us go, assuring the Rao Sahib's succession for all time. But *these* base-born, having won their learning through the mercy of the Government, attired in English clothes, forswearing the faith of their fathers for gain, spread rumour and debate against the Government, and are therefore very dear to certain of the six hundred. I have heard these cattle speak as princes and rulers of men, and I have laughed, but not altogether.

Once it happened that a son of some grain-bag sat with me at meat, who was arrayed and speaking after the manner of the English. At each mouthful he committed perjury against the salt that he had eaten, the men and women applauding. When, craftily falsifying, he had magnified oppression and invented untold wrong, together with the desecration of his tun-bellied gods, he demanded in the name of his people the government of all our land, and turning, laid palm to my shoulder, saying —"Here is one who is with us, albeit he professes another faith; he will bear out my words." This he delivered in English, and, as it were, exhibited me to that company. Preserving a smiling countenance, I answered in our own tongue—" Take away that hand, man without a father, or the folly of these folk shall not save thee, nor my silence guard thy reputation. Sit off, herd!" And in their speech I said— " He speaks truth. When the favour and wisdom of the English allows us yet a little larger share in the burden and the reward, the Musalman will deal with the Hindu." He alone saw what was in my heart. I was merciful towards him because he was accomplishing our desires; but remember that his father is one Durga Charan Laha, in Calcutta. Lay thy hand upon *his* shoulder if ever chance sends. It is not good that bottle-dealers and auctioneers should paw the sons of princes. I walk abroad sometimes with the man, that all the world may know the Hindu and Musalman are one, but when we come to the unfrequented streets I bid him walk behind me, and that is sufficient honour.

And why did I eat dirt?

Thus, my brother, it seems to my heart, which has almost burst in the consideration of these matters. The Bengalis and the beggar-taught boys know well that the Sahibs' power to govern comes neither from the Viceroy nor the head of the army, but from the hands of the six hundred in this town, and peculiarly those who talk most. They will therefore yearly address themselves more and more to that protection, and working on the green-sickness of the land, as has ever been their custom, will in time cause, through the perpetually instigated interference of the six hundred, the hand of the Indian Government to become inoperative, so that no measure nor order may be carried through without clamour and argument on their part; for that is the delight of the English at this hour. Have I overset the bounds of possibility? No. Even thou must have heard that one of the six hundred, having neither knowledge, fear, nor reverence before his eyes, has made in sport a new and a written scheme for the government of Ben-

gal, and openly shows it abroad as a king might
read his crowning proclamation. And this man,
meddling in affairs of State, speaks in the council
for an assemblage of leather-dressers, makers of
boots and harness, and openly glories in that he
has no God. Has either minister of the Empress,
Empress, Viceroy, or any other raised a voice
against this leather-man? Is not his power therefore to be sought, and that of his like-thinkers with
it? Thou seest.

The telegraph is the servant of the six hundred,
and all the Sahibs in India, omitting not one, are
the servants of the telegraph. Yearly, too, thou
knowest, the beggar-taught will hold that which
they call their Congress, first at one place and then
at another, leavening Hindustan with rumour,
echoing the talk among the low-born people here,
and demanding that they, like the six hundred,
control the revenues. And they will bring every
point and letter over the heads of the Governors
and the Lieutenant-Governors, and whoever hold
authority, and cast it clamorously at the feet of the
six hundred here; and certain of those word-con-
founders and the barren women will assent to their
demands, and others will weary of disagreement.
Thus fresh confusion will be thrown into the councils of the Empress, even as an island near by is
helped and comforted into the smothered war of
which I have written. Then yearly, as they have

begun and we have seen, the low-born men of the six hundred anxious for honour will embark for our land, and, staying a little while, will gather round them and fawn before the beggar-taught, and these departing from their side will assuredly inform the peasants, and the fighting men for whom there is no employ, that there is a change toward and a coming of help from over the seas. That rumour will not grow smaller in the spreading. And, most of all, the Congress, when it is not under the eye of the six hundred — who, though they foment dissension and death, pretend great reverence for the law which is no law — will, stepping aside, deliver uneasy words to the peasants, speaking, as it has done already, of the remission of taxation, and promising a new rule. That is to our advantage, but the flower of danger is in the seed of it. Thou knowest what evil a rumour may do; though in the Black Year, when thou and I were young, our standing to the English brought gain to Jagesur and enlarged our borders, for the Government gave us land on both sides. Of the Congress itself nothing is to be feared that ten troopers could not remove, but if its words too soon perturb the minds of those waiting or *of princes in idleness*, a flame may come *before the time*, and since there are now many white hands to quench it, all will return to the former condition. If the flame be kept under we need have no fear, because, sweating and panting, the one trampling on the other, the white people here are digging their own graves. The hand of the Viceroy will be tied, the hearts of the Sahibs will be downcast, and all eyes will turn to England disregarding any orders. Meantime, keeping tally on the sword-hilt against the hour when the score must be made smooth by the blade, it is well for us to assist and greatly befriend the Bengali that he may get control of the revenues and the posts. We must even write to England that we be of one blood with the schoolmen. It is not long to wait; by my head it is not long! This people are like the great king Ferisht, who, eaten with the scab of long idleness, plucked off his crown and danced naked among the dung-hills. But I have not forgotten the profitable end of that tale. The vizier set him upon a horse and led him into battle. Presently his health returned, and he caused to be engraven on the crown :—

" Though I was cast away by the king
   Yet, through God, I returned and he added to my brilliance
   Two great rubies (Balkh and Iran)."

If this people be purged and bled out by battle, their sickness may go and their eyes be cleared to the necessities of things. But they are now far gone in rottenness. Even the stallion, too long heel-roped, forgets how to fight: and these men

are mules. I do not lie when I say that unless
they are bled and taught with the whip, they will
hear and obey all that is said by the Congress and
the black men here, hoping to turn our land into
their own orderless Jehannum. For the men of
the six hundred, being chiefly low-born and unused to authority, desire much to exercise rule,
extending their arms to the sun and moon, and
shouting very greatly in order to hear the echo
of their voices, each one saying some new strange
thing and parting the goods and honour of others
among the rapacious, that he may obtain the favour of the common folk. And all this is to our
advantage.

Therefore write, that they may read, of gratitude
and of love and the law. I myself, when I return,
will show how the dish should be dressed to take
the taste here; for it is here that we must come.
Cause to be established in Jagesur a newspaper,
and fill it with translations of their papers. A
beggar-taught may be brought from Calcutta for
thirty rupees a month, and if he writes in Gurmukhi our people cannot read. Create, further,
councils other than the panchayats of headmen,
village by village and district by district, instruct-
ing them beforehand what to say according to the
order of the Rao. Print all these things in a book
in English, and send it to this place, and to every
man of the six hundred. Bid the beggar-taught

write in front of all that Jagesur follows fast on the English plan. If thou squeezest the Hindu shrine at Theegkot, and it is ripe, remit the head-tax, and perhaps the marriage-tax, with great publicity. But above all things keep the troops ready, and in good pay, even though we glean the stubble with the wheat and stint the Rao Sahib's women. All must go softly. Protest thou thy love for the voice of the common people in all things, and affect to despise the troops. That shall be taken for a witness in this land. The headship of the troops must be mine. See that Bahadur Shah's wits go wandering over the wine, but do not send him to God. I am an old man, but I may yet live to lead.

If this people be not bled out and regain strength, we, watching how the tide runs, when we see that the shadow of their hand is all but lifted from Hindustan, must bid the Bengali demand the removal of the residue or set going an uneasiness to that end. We must have a care neither to hurt the life of the Englishmen nor the honour of their women, for in that case six times the six hundred here could not hold those who remain from making the land swim. We must care that they are not mobbed by the Bengalis, but honourably escorted, while the land is held down with the threat of the sword if a hair of their heads fall. Thus we shall gain a good name,

and when rebellion is unaccompanied by bloodshed, as has lately befallen in a far country, the
English, disregarding honour, call it by a new
name: even one who has been a minister of the
Empress, but is now at war against the law, praises
it openly before the common folk. So greatly
are they changed since the days of Nikhal Seyn![1]
And then, if all go well and the Sahibs, who
through continual checking and browbeating will
have grown sick at heart, see themselves abandoned by their kin—for this people have allowed
their greatest to die on dry sand through delay
and fear of expense—we may go forward. This
people are swayed by names. A new name therefore must be given to the rule of Hindustan (and
that the Bengalis may settle among themselves),
and there will be many writings and oaths of love,
such as the little island over seas makes when it
would fight more bitterly; and after that the residue are diminished the hour comes, and we must
strike so that the Sword is never any more ques-
tioned.

.   By the favour of God and the conservation of
the Sahibs these many years, Hindustan contains
very much plunder, which we can in no way eat
hurriedly.   There will be to our hand the scaffolding of the house of state, for the Bengali shall con-
tinue to do our work, and must account to us for

[1] Nicholson, a gentleman once of some notoriety in India.

the revenue, and learn his seat in the order of
things. Whether the Hindu kings of the West
will break in to share that spoil before we have
swept it altogether, thou knowest better than I;
but be certain that, *then*, strong hands will seek
their own thrones, and it may be that the days of
the king of Delhi will return if we only, curbing
our desires, pay due obedience to the outward
appearances and the names. Thou rememberest
the old song : —

"Hadst thou not called it Love, I had said it were a drawn
    sword,
But since thou hast spoken, I believe and — I die."

It is in my heart that there will remain in our
land a few Sahibs undesirous of returning to England. These we must cherish and protect, that by
their skill and cunning we may hold together and
preserve unity in time of war. The Hindu kings
will never trust a Sahib in the core of their counsels. I say again that if we of the Faith confide
in them, we shall trample upon our enemies.

Is all this a dream to thee, gray fox of my
mother's bearing? I have written of what I have
seen and heard, but from the same clay two men
will never fashion platters alike, nor from the same
facts draw equal conclusions. Once more, there
is a green-sickness upon all the people of this
country. They eat dirt even now to stay their

cravings. Honour and stability have departed from their councils, and the knife of dissension has brought down upon their heads the flapping tent-flies of confusion. The Empress is old. They speak disrespectfully of her and hers in the street. They despise the sword, and believe that the tongue and the pen sway all. The measure of their ignorance and their soft belief is greater than the measure of the wisdom of Solomon, the son of David. All these things I have seen whom they regard as a wild beast and a spectacle. By God the Enlightener of Intelligence, if the Sahibs in India could breed sons who lived so that their houses might be established, I would almost fling my sword at the Viceroy's feet, saying: " Let us here fight for a kingdom together, thine and mine, disregarding the babble across the water. Write a letter to England, saying that we love them, but would depart from their camps and make all clean under a new crown." But the Sahibs die out at the third generation in our land, and it may be that I dream dreams. Yet not altogether. Until a white calamity of steel and bloodshed, the bearing of burdens, the trembling for life, and the hot rage of insult — *for pestilence would unman them if eyes not unused to men see clear* — befall this people, our path is safe. They are sick. The Fountain of Power is a gutter which all may defile ; and the voices of the men are overborne by the squealings of mules and the whinnying of barren mares. If through adversity they become wise, then, my brother, strike with and for them, and later, when thou and I are dead, and the disease grows up again (the young men bred in the school of fear and trembling and word-confounding have yet to live out their appointed span), those who have fought on the side of the English may ask and receive what they choose. At present seek quietly to confuse, and delay, and evade, and make of no effect. In this business four score of the six hundred are our true helpers.

Now the pen, and the ink, and the hand weary together, as thy eyes will weary in this reading. Be it known to my house that I return soon, but do not speak of the hour. Letters without name have come to me touching my honour. The honour of my house is thine. If they be, as I believe, the work of a dismissed groom, Futteh Lal, that ran at the tail of my wine-coloured Katthiawar stallion, his village is beyond Manglôt; look to it that his tongue no longer lengthens itself on the names of those who are mine. If it be otherwise, put a guard upon my house till I come, and especially see that no sellers of jewelry, astrologers, or midwives have entrance to the women's rooms. We rise by our slaves, and by our slaves we fall, as it was said. To all who are of my remembrance I bring gifts according to their worth.

I have written twice of the gift that I would cause to be given to Bahadur Shah.

The blessing of God and his Prophet on thee and thine till the end which is appointed. Give me felicity by informing me of the state of thy health. My head is at the Rao Sahib's feet; my sword is at his left side, a little above my heart. Follows my seal.

LALUN is a member of the most ancient profession in the world. Lilith was her very-great-grandmamma, and that was before the days of Eve, as every one knows. In the West, people say rude things about Lalun's profession, and write lectures about it, and distribute the lectures to young persons in order that Morality may be preserved. In the East, where the profession is hereditary, descending from mother to daughter, nobody writes lectures or takes any notice; and that is a distinct proof of the inability of the East to manage its own affairs.

Lalun's real husband, for even ladies of Lalun's profession in the East must have husbands, was a big jujube-tree. Her Mamma, who had married a fig-tree, spent ten thousand rupees on Lalun's wedding, which was blessed by forty-seven clergymen of Mamma's church, and distributed five thousand rupees in charity to the poor. And that was the custom of the land. The advantages of having a jujube-tree for a husband are obvious. You cannot hurt his feelings, and he looks imposing.

Lalun's husband stood on the plain outside the City walls, and Lalun's house was upon the east wall, facing the river. If you fell from the broad window-seat you dropped thirty feet sheer into the City Ditch. But if you stayed where you should and looked forth, you saw all the cattle of the City being driven down to water, the students of the Government College playing cricket, the high grass and trees that fringed the river-bank, the great sand-bars that ribbed the river, the red tombs of dead Emperors beyond the river, and very far away through the blue heat-haze, a glint of the snows of the Himalayas.

Wali Dad used to lie in the window-seat for hours at a time, watching this view. He was a young Muhammadan who was suffering acutely from education of the English variety, and knew it. His father had sent him to a Mission-school to get wisdom, and Wali Dad had absorbed more than ever his father or the Missionaries intended he should. When his father died, Wali Dad was independent and spent two years experimenting with the creeds of the Earth and reading books that are of no use to anybody.

After he had made an unsuccessful attempt to enter the Roman Catholic Church and the Presbyterian fold at the same time (the Missionaries found him out and called him names, but they did not understand his trouble), he discovered Lalun on the City wall and became the most constant of her few admirers. He possessed a head that English artists at home would rave over and paint amid impossible surroundings — a face that female novelists would use with delight through nine hundred pages. In reality he was only a clean-bred young Muhammadan, with penciled eyebrows, small-cut nostrils, little feet and hands, and a very tired look in his eyes. By virtue of his twenty-two years he had grown a neat black beard which he stroked with pride and kept delicately scented. His life seemed to be divided between borrowing books from me and making love to Lalun in the window-seat. He composed songs about her, and some of the songs are sung to this day in the City from the Street of the Mutton-Butchers to the Copper-Smiths' ward.

One song, the prettiest of all, says that the beauty of Lalun was so great that it troubled the hearts of the British Government and caused them to lose their peace of mind. That is the way the song is sung in the streets; but, if you examine it carefully and know the key to the explanation, you will find that there are three puns in it — on " beauty," " heart," and " peace of mind,"—so that it runs: " By the subtlety of Lalun the administration of the Government was troubled and it lost such and such a man." When Wali Dad sings that song his eyes glow like hot coals, and Lalun leans back among the cushions and throws bunches of jasmine-buds at Wali Dad.

But first it is necessary to explain something about the Supreme Government which is above all and below all and behind all. Gentlemen come from England, spend a few weeks in India, walk round this great Sphinx of the Plains, and write books upon its ways and its works, denouncing or praising it as their own ignorance prompts. Consequently all the world knows how the Supreme Government conducts itself. But no one, not even the Supreme Government, knows everything about the administration of the Empire. Year by year England sends out fresh drafts for the first fighting-line, which is officially called the Indian Civil Service. These die, or kill themselves by overwork, or are worried to death or broken in health and hope in order that the land may be protected from death and sickness, famine and war, and may eventually become capable of standing alone. It will never stand alone, but the idea is a pretty one, and men are willing to die for it, and yearly the work of pushing and coaxing and scolding and petting the country into good living goes forward. If an advance be made all credit is given to the native, while the Englishmen stand back and wipe their foreheads. If a failure occurs the Englishmen step forward and take the blame. Overmuch tenderness of this kind has bred a strong belief among many natives that the native is capable of administering the country, and many devout Englishmen believe this also, because the theory is stated in beautiful English with all the latest political colour.

There be other men who, though uneducated, see visions and dream dreams, and they, too, hope to administer the country in their own way—that is to say, with a garnish of Red Sauce. Such men must exist among two hundred million people, and, if they are not attended to, may cause trouble and even break the great idol called "Pax Britannic," which, as the newspapers say, lives between Peshawur and Cape Comorin. Were the Day of Doom to dawn to-morrow, you would find the Supreme Government "taking measures to allay popular excitement" and putting guards upon the graveyards that the Dead might troop forth orderly. The youngest Civilian would arrest Gabriel on his own responsibility if the Archangel could not produce a Deputy Commissioner's permission to "make music or other noises" as the license says.

Whence it is easy to see that mere men of the flesh who would create a tumult must fare badly at the hands of the Supreme Government. And they do. There is no outward sign of excitement;

306

there is no confusion; there is no knowledge. When due and sufficient reasons have been given, weighed and approved, the machinery moves forward, and the dreamer of dreams and the seer of visions is gone from his friends and following. He enjoys the hospitality of Government; there is no restriction upon his movements within certain limits; but he must not confer any more with his brother dreamers. Once in every six months the Supreme Government assures itself that he is well and takes formal acknowledgment of his existence. No one protests against his detention, because the few people who know about it are in deadly fear of seeming to know him; and never a single newspaper "takes up his case" or organises demonstrations on his behalf, because the newspapers of India have got behind that lying proverb which says the Pen is mightier than the Sword, and can walk delicately.

So now you know as much as you ought about Wali Dad, the educational mixture, and the Supreme Government.

Lalun has not yet been described. She would need, so Wali Dad says, a thousand pens of gold and ink scented with musk. She has been variously compared to the Moon, the Dil Sagar Lake, a spotted quail, a gazelle, the Sun on the Desert of Kutch, the Dawn, the Stars, and the young bamboo. These comparisons imply that she is

beautiful exceedingly according to the native stan-
dards, which are practically the same as those of
the West. Her eyes are black and her hair is
black, and her eyebrows are black as leeches; her
mouth is tiny and says witty things; her hands are
tiny and have saved much money; her feet are
tiny and have trodden on the naked hearts of many
men. But, as Wali Dad sings: "Lalun *is* Lalun,
and when you have said that, you have only come
to the Beginnings of Knowledge."

The little house on the City wall was just big
enough to hold Lalun, and her maid, and a pussy-
cat with a silver collar. A big pink and blue
cut-glass chandelier hung from the ceiling of the
reception room. A petty Nawab had given Lalun the horror, and she kept it for politeness' sake.
The floor of the room was of polished chunam,
white as curds. A latticed window of carved
wood was set in one wall; there was a profusion
of squabby pluffy cushions and fat carpets everywhere, and Lalun's silver *huqa*, studded with tur-
quoises, had a special little carpet all to its shining
self. Wali Dad was nearly as permanent a fixture
as the chandelier. As I have said, he lay in the
window-seat and meditated on Life and Death
and Lalun—specially Lalun. The feet of the
young men of the City tended to her doorways
and then—retired, for Lalun was a particular
maiden, slow of speech, reserved of mind, and not

in the least inclined to orgies which were nearly
certain to end in strife. "If I am of no value, I
am unworthy of this honour," said Lalun. "If
I am of value, they are unworthy of Me." And
that was a crooked sentence.

In the long hot nights of latter April and May
all the City seemed to assemble in Lalun's little
white room to smoke and to talk. Shiahs of the
grimmest and most uncompromising persuasion;
Sufis who had lost all belief in the Prophet and
retained but little in God; wandering Hindu
priests passing southward on their way to the
Central India fairs and other affairs; Pundits in
black gowns, with spectacles on their noses and
undigested wisdom in their insides; bearded headmen of the wards; Sikhs with all the details of
the latest ecclesiastical scandal in the Golden
Temple; red-eyed priests from beyond the Border,
looking like trapped wolves and talking like ra-
vens; M. A.'s of the University, very superior and
very voluble — all these people and more also
you might find in the white room. Wali Dad
lay in the window-seat and listened to the talk.

"It is Lalun's *salon*," said Wali Dad to me,
"and it is electic — is not that the word? Outside of a Freemason's Lodge I have never seen
such gatherings. *There* I dined once with a Jew
—a Yahoudi!" He spat into the City Ditch
with apologies for allowing national feelings to

overcome him. "Though I have lost every belief in the world," said he, "and try to be proud
of my losing, I cannot help hating a Jew. Lalun
admits no Jews here."

"But what in the world do all these men do?"
I asked.

"The curse of our country," said Wali Dad.
"They talk. It is like the Athenians — always
hearing and telling some new thing. Ask the
Pearl and she will show you how much she
knows of the news of the City and the Province.
Lalun knows everything."

"Lalun," I said at random — she was talking
to a gentleman of the Kurd persuasion who had
come in from God-knows-where — "when does
the 175th Regiment go to Agra?"

"It does not go at all," said Lalun, without
turning her head. "They have ordered the 118th
to go in its stead. That Regiment goes to Lucknow in three months, unless they give a fresh
order."

"That is so," said Wali Dad without a shade
of doubt. "Can you, with your telegrams and
your newspapers, do better? Always hearing and
telling some new thing," he went on. "My friend,
has your God ever smitten a European nation
for gossiping in the bazars? India has gossiped
for centuries — always standing in the bazars until
the soldiers go by. Therefore — you are here to-

day instead of starving in your own country, and
I am not a Muhammadan — I am a Product — a
Demnition Product. That also I owe to you and
yours: that I cannot make an end to my sentence
without quoting from your authors." He pulled
at the *huqa* and mourned, half feelingly, half in
earnest, for the shattered hopes of his youth. Wali
Dad was always mourning over something or other
— the country of which he despaired, or the creed
in which he had lost faith, or the life of the English which he could by no means understand.

Lalun never mourned. She played little songs
on the *sitar*, and to hear her sing, "O Peacock, cry
again," was always a fresh pleasure. She knew all
the songs that have ever been sung, from the war-
songs of the South that make the old men angry
with the young men and the young men angry
with the State, to the love-songs of the North where
the swords whinny-whicker like angry kites in the
pauses between the kisses, and the Passes fill with
armed men, and the Lover is torn from his Beloved
and cries, *Ai, Ai, Ai!* evermore. She knew how
to make up tobacco for the *huqa* so that it smelt
like the Gates of Paradise and wafted you gently
through them. She could embroider strange things
in gold and silver, and dance softly with the moonlight when it came in at the window. Also she
knew the hearts of men, and the heart of the City,
and whose wives were faithful and whose untrue,

and more of the secrets of the Government Offices than are good to be set down in this place. Nasiban, her maid, said that her jewelry was worth ten thousand pounds, and that, some night, a thief would enter and murder her for its possession; but Lalun said that all the City would tear that thief limb from limb, and that he, whoever he was, knew it.

So she took her *sitar* and sat in the window-seat and sang a song of old days that had been sung by a girl of her profession in an armed camp on the eve of a great battle — the day before the Fords of the Jumna ran red and Sivaji fled fifty miles to Delhi with a Toorkh stallion at his horse's tail and another Lalun on his saddle-bow. It was what men call a Mahratta *laonee*, and it said:—

> Their warrior forces Chimnajee
> Before the Peishwa led,
> The Children of the Sun and Fire
> Behind him turned and fled.

And the chorus said:—

> With them there fought who rides so free
> With sword and turban red,
> The warrior-youth who earns his fee
> At peril of his head.

"At peril of his head," said Wali Dad in English to me. "Thanks to your Government, all our heads are protected, and with the educational facilities at my command"—his eyes twinkled wickedly—"I might be a distinguished member of the local administration. Perhaps, in time, I might even be a member of a Legislative Council."

"Don't speak English," said Lalun, bending over her *sitar* afresh. The chorus went out from the City wall to the blackened wall of Fort Amara which dominates the City. No man knows the precise extent of Fort Amara. Three kings built it hundreds of years ago, and they say that there are miles of underground rooms beneath its walls. It is peopled with many ghosts, a detachment of Garrison Artillery and a Company of Infantry. In its prime it held ten thousand men and filled its ditches with corpses.

"At peril of his head," sang Lalun again and again.

A head moved on one of the Ramparts — the gray head of an old man — and a voice, rough as shark-skin on a sword-hilt, sent back the last line of the chorus and broke into a song that I could not understand, though Lalun and Wali Dad listened intently.

"What is it?" I asked. "Who is it?"

"A consistent man," said Wali Dad. "He fought you in '46, when he was a warrior-youth; refought you in '57, and he tried to fight you in '71, but you had learned the trick of blowing men

313

from guns too well. Now he is old; but he would still fight if he could."

" Is he a Wahabi, then? Why should he answer to a Mahratta *laonee* if he be Wahabi — or Sikh?" said I.

"I do not know," said Wali Dad. "He has lost, perhaps, his religion. Perhaps he wishes to be a King. Perhaps he is a King. I do not know his name."

"That is a lie, Wali Dad. If you know his career you must know his name."

"That is quite true. I belong to a nation of liars. I would rather not tell you his name. Think for yourself."

Lalun finished her song, pointed to the Fort, and said simply: "Khem Singh."

"Hm," said Wali Dad. "If the Pearl chooses to tell you the Pearl is a fool."

I translated to Lalun, who laughed. "I choose to tell what I choose to tell. They kept Khem Singh in Burma," said she. "They kept him there for many years until his mind was changed in him. So great was the kindness of the Government. Finding this, they sent him back to his own country that he might look upon it before he died. He is an old man, but when he looks upon this his country his memory will come. Moreover, there be many who remember him."

"He is an Interesting Survival," said Wali Dad,

pulling at the *huqa*. "He returns to a country now full of educational and political reform, but, as the Pearl says, there are many who remember him. He was once a great man. There will never be any more great men in India. They will all, when they are boys, go whoring after strange gods, and they will become citizens — 'fellow-citizens' — 'illustrious fellow-citizens.' What is it that the native papers call them ?"

Wali Dad seemed to be in a very bad temper. Lalun looked out of the window and smiled into the dust-haze. I went away thinking about Khem Singh, who had once made history with a thousand followers, and would have been a princeling but for the power of the Supreme Government aforesaid.

The Senior Captain Commanding Fort Amara was away on leave, but the Subaltern, his Deputy, had drifted down to the Club, where I found him and enquired of him whether it was really true that a political prisoner had been added to the attractions of the Fort. The Subaltern explained at great length, for this was the first time that he had held Command of the Fort, and his glory lay heavy upon him.

"Yes," said he, "a man was sent in to me about a week ago from down the line — a thorough gentleman, whoever he is. Of course I did all I could for him. He had his two servants and some silver cooking-pots, and he looked for all the world like a native officer. I called him Subadar Sahib; just as well to be on the safe side, y'know. ' Look here, Subadar Sahib,' I said, ' you're handed over to my authority, and I'm supposed to guard you. Now I don't want to make your life hard, but you must make things easy for me. All the Fort is at your disposal, from the flag-staff to the dry ditch, and I shall be happy to entertain you in any way I can, but you mustn't take advantage of it. Give me your word that you won't try to escape, Subadar Sahib, and I'll give you my word that you shall have no heavy guard put over you.' I thought the best way of getting at him was by going at him straight, y'know, and it was, by Jove! The old man gave me his word, and moved about the Fort as contented as a sick crow. He's a rummy chap — always asking to be told where he is and what the buildings about him are. I had to sign a slip of blue paper when he turned up, acknowledging receipt of his body and all that, and I'm responsible, y'know, that he doesn't get away. Queer thing, though, looking after a Johnnie old enough to be your grandfather, isn't it ? Come to the Fort one of these days and see him ? "

For reasons which will appear, I never went to the Fort while Khem Singh was then within its walls. I knew him only as a gray head seen from

Lalun's window — a gray head and a harsh voice. But natives told me that, day by day, as he looked upon the fair lands round Amara, his memory came back to him and, with it, the old hatred against the Government that had been nearly effaced in far-off Burma. So he raged up and down the West face of the Fort from morning till noon and from evening till the night, devising vain things in his heart, and croaking war-songs when Lalun sang on the City wall. As he grew more acquainted with the Subaltern he unburdened his old heart of some of the passions that had withered it. "Sahib," he used to say, tapping his stick against the parapet, "when I was a young man I was one of twenty thousand horsemen who came out of the City and rode round the plain here. Sahib, I was the leader of a hundred, then of a thousand, then of five thousand, and now!" — he pointed to his two servants. "But from the beginning to to-day I would cut the throats of all the Sahibs in the land if I could. Hold me fast, Sahib, lest I get away and return to those who would follow me. I forgot them when I was in Burma, but now that I am in my own country again, I remember everything."

"Do you remember that you have given me your Honour not to make your tendance a hard matter?" said the Subaltern.

"Yes. to you, only to you, Sahib," said Khem

317

Singh. "To you because you are of a pleasant countenance. If my turn comes again, Sahib, I will not hang you nor cut your throat."

"Thank you," said the Subaltern gravely, as he looked along the line of guns that could pound the City to powder in half an hour. "Let us go into our own quarters, Khem Singh. Come and talk with me after dinner."

Khem Singh would sit on his own cushion at the Subaltern's feet, drinking heavy, scented aniseseed brandy in great gulps, and telling strange stories of Fort Amara, which had been a palace in the old days, of Begums and Ranees tortured to death — aye, in the very vaulted chamber that now served as a Mess-room; would tell stories of Sobraon that made the Subaltern's cheeks flush and tingle with pride of race, and of the Kuka rising from which so much was expected and the foreknowledge of which was shared by a hundred thousand souls. But he never told tales of '57 because, as he said, he was the Subaltern's guest, and '57 is a year that no man, Black or White, cares to speak of. Once only, when the aniseseed brandy had slightly affected his head, he said: "Sahib, speaking now of a matter which lay between Sobraon and the affair of the Kukas, it was ever a wonder to us that you stayed your hand at all, and that, having stayed it, you did not make the land one prison. Now I hear from without

that you do great honour to all men of our country and by your own hands are destroying the
Terror of your Name which is your strong rock
and defence. This is a foolish thing. Will oil
and water mix? Now in '57 —— "

"I was not born then, Subadar Sahib," said the
Subaltern, and Khem Singh reeled to his quarters.

The Subaltern would tell me of these conversa-
tions at the Club, and my desire to see Khem
Singh increased. But Wali Dad, sitting in the
window-seat of the house on the City wall, said
that it would be a cruel thing to do, and Lalun
pretended that I preferred the society of a grizzled
old Sikh to hers.

"Here is tobacco, here is talk, here are many
friends and all the news of the City, and, above all,
here is myself. I will tell you stories and sing
you songs, and Wali Dad will talk his English
nonsense in your ears. Is that worse than watching the caged animal yonder? Go to-morrow,
then, if you must, but to-day such and such an
one will be here, and he will speak of wonderful
things."

It happened that To-morrow never came, and
the warm heat of the latter Rains gave place to
the chill of early October almost before I was
aware of the flight of the year. The Captain commanding the Fort returned from leave and took
over charge of Khem Singh according to the laws

of seniority. The Captain was not a nice man. He called all natives "niggers," which, besides being extreme bad form, shows gross ignorance.

"What's the use of telling off two Tommies to watch that old nigger?" said he.

"I fancy it soothes his vanity," said the Subaltern. "The men are ordered to keep well out of his way, but he takes them as a tribute to his importance, poor old wretch."

"I won't have Line men taken off regular guards in this way. Put on a couple of Native Infantry."

"Sikhs?" said the Subaltern, lifting his eyebrows.

"Sikhs, Pathans, Dogras — they're all alike, these black vermin," and the Captain talked to Khem Singh in a manner which hurt that old gentleman's feelings. Fifteen years before, when he had been caught for the second time, every one looked upon him as a sort of tiger. He liked being regarded in this light. But he forgot that the world goes forward in fifteen years, and many Subalterns are promoted to Captaincies.

"The Captain-pig is in charge of the Fort?" said Khem Singh to his native guard every morning. And the native guard said: "Yes, Subadar Sahib," in deference to his age and his air of distinction; but they did not know who he was.

In those days the gathering in Lalun's little white room was always large and talked more than before.

" The Greeks," said Wali Dad, who had been borrowing my books, "the inhabitants of the city of Athens, where they were always hearing and telling some new thing, rigorously secluded their women — who were fools. Hence the glorious institution of the heterodox women — is it not? — who were amusing and *not* fools. All the Greek philosophers delighted in their company. Tell me, my friend, how it goes now in Greece and the other places upon the Continent of Europe. Are your women-folk also fools?"

" Wali Dad," I said, " you never speak to us about your women-folk, and we never speak about ours to you. That is the bar between us."

"Yes," said Wali Dad, "it is curious to think that our common meeting-place should be here, in the house of a common — how do you call *her?*" He pointed with the pipe-mouth to Lalun.

"Lalun is nothing but Lalun," I said, and that was perfectly true. " But if you took your place in the world, Wali Dad, and gave up dreaming dreams —— "

" I might wear an English coat and trouser. I might be a leading Muhammadan pleader. I might be received even at the Commissioner's tennis-parties, where the English stand on one side and the natives on the other, in order to promote social intercourse throughout the Empire. Heart's

Heart," said he to Lalun quickly, "the Sahib says that I ought to quit you."

"The Sahib is always talking stupid talk," returned Lalun with a laugh. "In this house I am a Queen and thou art a King. The Sahib" —she put her arms above her head and thought for a moment—"the Sahib shall be our Vizier — thine and mine, Wali Dad — because he has said that thou shouldst leave me."

Wali Dad laughed immoderately, and I laughed too. "Be it so," said he. "My friend, are you willing to take this lucrative Government appointment? Lalun, what shall his pay be?"

But Lalun began to sing, and for the rest of the time there was no hope of getting a sensible answer from her or Wali Dad. When the one stopped, the other began to quote Persian poetry with a triple pun in every other line. Some of it was not strictly proper, but it was all very funny, and it only came to an end when a fat person in black, with gold *pince-nez*, sent up his name to Lalun, and Wali Dad dragged me into the twinkling night to walk in a big rose-garden and talk heresies about Religion and Governments and a man's career in life.

The Mohurrum, the great mourning-festival of the Muhammadans, was close at hand, and the things that Wali Dad said about religious fanaticism would have secured his expulsion from the

322

loosest-thinking Muslim sect. There were the
rose-bushes round us, the stars above us, and
from every quarter of the City came the boom of
the big Mohurrum drums. You must know that
the City is divided in fairly equal proportions between the Hindus and the Musalmans, and where
both creeds belong to the fighting races, a big religious festival gives ample chance for trouble.
When they can—that is to say when the authorities are weak enough to allow it—the Hindus do
their best to arrange some minor feast-day of their
own in time to clash with the period of general
mourning for the martyrs Hasan and Hussain, the
heroes of the Mohurrum. Gilt and painted paper
presentations of their tombs are borne with shouting and wailing, music, torches, and yells, through
the principal thoroughfares of the City, which
fakements are called *tazias*. Their passage is rigorously laid down beforehand by the Police, and
detachments of Police accompany each *tazia*, lest
the Hindus should throw bricks at it and the
peace of the Queen and the heads of her loyal
subjects should thereby be broken. Mohurrum
time in a "fighting" town means anxiety to all
the officials, because, if a riot breaks out, the officials and not the rioters are held responsible. The
former must foresee everything, and while not
making their precautions ridiculously elaborate,
must see that they are at least adequate.

"Listen to the drums!" said Wali Dad. "That is the heart of the people — empty and making much noise. How, think you, will the Mohurrum go this year. *I* think that there will be trouble."

He turned down a side-street and left me alone with the stars and a sleepy Police patrol. Then I went to bed and dreamed that Wali Dad had sacked the City and I was made Vizier, with Lalun's silver *huqa* for mark of office.

All day the Mohurrum drums beat in the City, and all day deputations of tearful Hindu gentlemen besieged the Deputy Commissioner with assurances that they would be murdered ere next dawning by the Muhammadans. "Which," said the Deputy Commissioner in confidence to the Head of Police, "is a pretty fair indication that the Hindus are going to make 'emselves unpleasant. I think we can arrange a little surprise for them. I have given the heads of both Creeds fair warning. If they choose to disregard it, so much the worse for them."

There was a large gathering in Lalun's house that night, but of men that I had never seen before, if I except the fat gentleman in black with the gold *pince-nez*. Wali Dad lay in the window-seat, more bitterly scornful of his Faith and its manifestations than I had ever known him. Lalun's maid was very busy cutting up and mix-

324

ing tobacco for the guests. We could hear the thunder of the drums as the processions accompanying each *tazia* marched to the central gathering-place in the plain outside the City, preparatory to their triumphant re-entry and circuit within the walls. All the streets seemed ablaze with torches, and only Fort Amara was black and silent.

When the noise of the drums ceased, no one in the white room spoke for a time. " The first *tazia* has moved off," said Wali Dad, looking to the plain.

" That is very early," said the man with the *pince-nez.*

" It is only half-past eight." The company rose and departed.

" Some of them were men from Ladakh," said Lalun, when the last had gone. " They brought me brick-tea such as the Russians sell, and a tea-urn from Peshawur. Show me, now, how the English *Memsahibs* make tea."

The brick-tea was abominable. When it was finished Wali Dad suggested going into the streets. " I am nearly sure that there will be trouble to-night," he said. " All the City thinks so, and *Vox Populi* is *Vox Dei*, as the Babus say. Now I tell you that at the corner of the Padshahi Gate you will find my horse all this night if you want to go about and to see things. It is a most disgraceful exhibition. Where is the pleasure of saying '*Ya Hasan, Ya Hussain*,' twenty thousand times in a night?"

All the processions — there were two and twenty of them — were now well within the City walls. The drums were beating afresh, the crowd were howling "*Ya Hasan! Ya Hussain!*" and beating their breasts, the brass bands were playing their loudest, and at every corner where space allowed Muhammadan preachers were telling the lamentable story of the death of the Martyrs. It was impossible to move except with the crowd, for the streets were not more than twenty feet wide. In the Hindu quarters the shutters of all the shops were up and cross-barred. As the first *tazia*, a gorgeous erection ten feet high, was borne aloft on the shoulders of a score of stout men into the semi-darkness of the Gully of the Horsemen, a brickbat crashed through its talc and tinsel sides.

" Into thy hands, O Lord ! " murmured Wali Dad profanely, as a yell went up from behind, and a native officer of Police jammed his horse through the crowd. Another brickbat followed, and the *tazia* staggered and swayed where it had stopped.

"Go on ! In the name of the Sirkar, go forward ! " shouted the Policeman ; but there was an ugly cracking and splintering of shutters, and the crowd halted, with oaths and growlings, before the house whence the brickbat had been thrown.

Then, without any warning, broke the storm —

not only in the Gully of the Horsemen, but in half a dozen other places. The *tazias* rocked like ships at sea, the long pole-torches dipped and rose round them, while the men shouted: "The Hindus are dishonouring the *tazias!* Strike! Strike! Into their temples for the Faith!" The six or eight Policemen with each *tazia* drew their batons and struck as long as they could, in the hope of forcing the mob forward, but they were overpowered, and as contingents of Hindus poured into the streets the fight became general. Half a mile away, where the *tazias* were yet untouched, the drums and the shrieks of "*Ya Hasan! Ya Hussain!*" continued, but not for long. The priests at the corners of the streets knocked the legs from the bedsteads that supported their pulpits and smote for the Faith, while stones fell from the silent houses upon friend and foe, and the packed streets bellowed: "*Din! Din! Din!*" A *tazia* caught fire, and was dropped for a flaming barrier between Hindu and Musalman at the corner of the Gully. Then the crowd surged forward, and Wali Dad drew me close to the stone pillar of a well.

"It was intended from the beginning!" he shouted in my ear, with more heat than blank unbelief should be guilty of. "The bricks were carried up to the houses beforehand. These swine of Hindus! We shall be gutting kine in their temples to-night!"

327

Tazia after *tazia*, some burning, others torn to pieces, hurried past us, and the mob with them, howling, shrieking, and striking at the house doors in their flight. At last we saw the reason of the rush. Hugonin, the Assistant District Superintendent of Police, a boy of twenty, had got together thirty constables and was forcing the crowd through the streets. His old gray Police-horse showed no sign of uneasiness as it was spurred breast-on into the crowd, and the long dog-whip with which he had armed himself was never still.

" They know we haven't enough Police to hold 'em," he cried as he passed me, mopping a cut on his face. " They *know* we haven't! Aren't any of the men from the Club coming down to help ? Get on, you sons of burnt fathers!" The dog-whip cracked across the writhing backs, and the constables smote afresh with baton and gun-butt. With these passed the lights and the shouting, and Wali Dad began to swear under his breath. From Fort Amara shot up a single rocket; then two side by side. It was the signal for troops.

Petitt, the Deputy Commissioner, covered with dust and sweat, but calm and gently smiling, cantered up the clean-swept street in rear of the main body of the rioters. "No one killed yet," he shouted. " I'll keep 'em on the run till dawn! Don't let 'em halt, Hugonin! Trot 'em about till the troops come."

328

The science of the defence lay solely in keeping the mob on the move. If they had breathing-space they would halt and fire a house, and then the work of restoring order would be more diffi-cult, to say the least of it. Flames have the same effect on a crowd as blood has on a wild beast.

Word had reached the Club, and men in even-ing-dress were beginning to show themselves and lend a hand in heading off and breaking up the shouting masses with stirrup-leathers, whips, or chance-found staves. They were not very often attacked, for the rioters had sense enough to know that the death of a European would not mean one hanging, but many, and possibly the appearance of the thrice-dreaded Artillery. The clamour in the City redoubled. The Hindus had descended into the streets in real earnest, and ere long the mob returned. It was a strange sight. There were no *tazias* — only their riven platforms — and there were no Police. Here and there a City dignitary, Hindu or Muhammadan, was vainly imploring his co-religionists to keep quiet and behave them-selves — advice for which his white beard was pulled. Then a native officer of Police, unhorsed but still using his spurs with effect, would be borne along, warning all the crowd of the danger of in-sulting the Government. Everywhere men struck aimlessly with sticks, grasping each other by the throat, howling and foaming with rage, or beat

329

with their bare hands on the doors of the houses.

"It is a lucky thing that they are fighting with natural weapons," I said to Wali Dad, "else we should have half the City killed."

I turned as I spoke and looked at his face. His nostrils were distended, his eyes were fixed, and he was smiting himself softly on the breast. The crowd poured by with renewed riot — a gang of Musalmans hard-pressed by some hundred Hindu fanatics. Wali Dad left my side with an oath, and shouting: "*Ya Hasan! Ya Hussain!*" plunged into the thick of the fight, where I lost sight of him.

I fled by a side alley to the Padshahi Gate, where I found Wali Dad's horse, and thence rode to the Fort. Once outside the City wall, the tumult sank to a dull roar, very impressive under the stars and reflecting great credit on the fifty thousand angry able-bodied men who were making it. The troops who, at the Deputy Commissioner's instance, had been ordered to rendezvous quietly near the Fort showed no signs of being impressed. Two companies of Native Infantry, a squadron of Native Cavalry, and a company of British Infantry were kicking their heels in the shadow of the East face, waiting for orders to march in. I am sorry to say that they were all pleased, unholily pleased, at the chance of what they called "a little fun."

The senior officers, to be sure, grumbled at having been kept out of bed, and the English troops pretended to be sulky, but there was joy in the hearts of all the subalterns, and whispers ran up and down the line: "No ball-cartridge — what a beastly shame!" "D'you think the beggars will really stand up to us?" "'Hope I shall meet my money-lender there. I owe him more than I can afford." "Oh, they won't let us even unsheathe swords." "Hurrah! Up goes the fourth rocket. Fall in, there!"

The Garrison Artillery, who to the last cherished a wild hope that they might be allowed to bombard the City at a hundred yards' range, lined the parapet above the East gateway and cheered themselves hoarse as the British Infantry doubled along the road to the Main Gate of the City. The Cavalry cantered on to the Padshahi Gate, and the Native Infantry marched slowly to the Gate of the Butchers. The surprise was intended to be of a distinctly unpleasant nature, and to come on top of the defeat of the Police who had been just able to keep the Muhammadans from firing the houses of a few leading Hindus. The bulk of the riot lay in the north and north-west wards. The east and south-east were by this time dark and silent, and I rode hastily to Lalun's house, for I wished to tell her to send some one in search of Wali Dad. The house was unlighted, but the door was open, and I climbed upstairs in the darkness. One small lamp in the white room showed Lalun and her maid leaning half out of the window, breathing heavily and evidently pulling at something that refused to come.

"Thou art late — very late," gasped Lalun without turning her head. "Help us now, O Fool, if thou hast not spent thy strength howling among the *tazias*. Pull! Nasiban and I can do no more. O Sahib, is it you? The Hindus have been hunting an old Muhammadan round the Ditch with clubs. If they find him again they will kill him. Help us to pull him up."

I put my hands to the long red silk waist-cloth that was hanging out of the window, and we three pulled and pulled with all the strength at our command. There was something very heavy at the end, and it swore in an unknown tongue as it kicked against the City wall.

"Pull, oh, pull!" said Lalun at the last. A pair of brown hands grasped the window-sill and a venerable Muhammadan tumbled upon the floor, very much out of breath. His jaws were tied up, his turban had fallen over one eye, and he was dusty and angry.

Lalun hid her face in her hands for an instant and said something about Wali Dad that I could not catch.

Then, to my extreme gratification, she threw her

332

arms round my neck and murmured pretty things. I was in no haste to stop her; and Nasiban, being a handmaiden of tact, turned to the big jewel-chest that stands in the corner of the white room and rummaged among the contents. The Muhammadan sat on the floor and glared.

"One service more, Sahib, since thou hast come so opportunely," said Lalun. "Wilt thou"— it is very nice to be thou-ed by Lalun — "take this old man across the City — the troops are everywhere, and they might hurt him, for he is old — to the Kumharsen Gate? There I think he may find a carriage to take him to his house. He is a friend of mine, and thou art — more than a friend — therefore I ask this."

Nasiban bent over the old man, tucked something into his belt, and I raised him up and led him into the streets. In crossing from the east to the west of the City there was no chance of avoiding the troops and the crowd. Long before I reached the Gully of the Horsemen I heard the shouts of the British Infantry crying cheeringly: "Hutt, ye beggars! Hutt, ye devils! Get along! Go forward, there!" Then followed the ringing of rifle-butts and shrieks of pain. The troops were banging the bare toes of the mob with their gun-butts — for not a bayonet had been fixed. My companion mumbled and jabbered as we walked on until we were carried back by the crowd and had to force our way to the troops. I caught him by the wrist and felt a bangle there — the iron bangle of the Sikhs — but I had no suspicions, for Lalun had only ten minutes before put her arms round me. Thrice we were carried back by the crowd, and when we made our way past the British Infantry it was to meet the Sikh Cavalry driving another mob before them with the butts of their lances.

"What are these dogs?" said the old man.

"Sikhs of the Cavalry, Father," I said, and we edged our way up the line of horses two abreast and found the Deputy Commissioner, his helmet smashed on his head, surrounded by a knot of men who had come down from the Club as amateur constables and had helped the Police mightily.

"We'll keep 'em on the run till dawn," said Petitt. "Who's your villainous friend?"

I had only time to say: "The Protection of the Sirkar!" when a fresh crowd flying before the Native Infantry carried us a hundred yards nearer to the Kumharsen Gate, and Petitt was swept away like a shadow.

"I do not know — I cannot see — this is all new to me!" moaned my companion. "How many troops are there in the City?"

"Perhaps five hundred," I said.

"A lakh of men beaten by five hundred — and Sikhs among them! Surely, surely, I am an old man, but — the Kumharsen Gate is new. Who pulled down the stone lions? Where is the conduit? Sahib, I am a very old man, and, alas, I — I cannot stand." He dropped in the shadow of the Kumharsen Gate where there was no disturbance. A fat gentleman wearing gold *pince-nez* came out of the darkness.

"You are most kind to bring my old friend," he said suavely. "He is a landholder of Akala. He should not be in a big City when there is religious excitement. But I have a carriage here. You are quite truly kind. Will you help me to put him into the carriage? It is very late."

We bundled the old man into a hired victoria that stood close to the gate, and I turned back to the house on the City wall. The troops were driving the people to and fro, while the Police shouted, " To your houses! Get to your houses!" and the dog-whip of the Assistant District Superintendent cracked remorselessly. Terror-stricken *bunnias* clung to the stirrups of the cavalry, crying that their houses had been robbed (which was a lie), and the burly Sikh horsemen patted them on the shoulder, and bade them return to those houses lest a worse thing should happen. Parties of five or six British soldiers, joining arms, swept down the side-gullies, their rifles on their backs, stamping, with shouting and song, upon the toes of Hindu and Musalman. Never was religious en-

335

thusiasm more systematically squashed; and never were poor breakers of the peace more utterly weary and footsore. They were routed out of holes and corners, from behind well-pillars and byres, and bidden to go to their houses. If they had no houses to go to, so much the worse for their toes.

On returning to Lalun's door, I stumbled over a man at the threshold. He was sobbing hysterically and his arms flapped like the wings of a goose. It was Wali Dad, Agnostic and Unbeliever, shoeless, turbanless, and frothing at the mouth, the flesh on his chest bruised and bleeding from the vehemence with which he had smitten himself. A broken torch-handle lay by his side, and his quivering lips murmured, "*Ya Hasan! Ya Hussain!*" as I stooped over him. I pushed him a few steps up the staircase, threw a pebble at Lalun's City window, and hurried home.

Most of the streets were very still, and the cold wind that comes before the dawn whistled down them. In the center of the Square of the Mosque a man was bending over a corpse. The skull had been smashed in by gun-butt or bamboo-stave.

"It is expedient that one man should die for the people," said Petitt grimly, raising the shapeless head. "These brutes were beginning to show their teeth too much."

And from afar we could hear the soldiers sing-

ing " Two Lovely Black Eyes," as they drove the
remnant of the rioters within doors.

.   .   .   .   .   .

Of course you can guess what happened? I
was not so clever. When the news went abroad
that Khem Singh had escaped from the Fort, I
did not, since I was then living this story, not
writing it, connect myself, or Lalun, or the fat
gentleman of the gold *pince-nez*, with his disap-
pearance. Nor did it strike me that Wali Dad
was the man who should have convoyed him
across the City, or that Lalun's arms round my
neck were put there to hide the money that Nasiban gave to Khem Singh, and that Lalun had used
me and my white face as even a better safeguard
than Wali Dad, who proved himself so untrust-
worthy. All that I knew at the time was that
when Fort Amara was taken up with the riots
Khem Singh profited by the confusion to get
away, and that his two Sikh guards also escaped.

But later on I received full enlightenment; and
so did Khem Singh. He fled to those who knew
him in the old days, but many of them were dead
and more were changed, and all knew something
of the Wrath of the Government. He went to
the young men, but the glamour of his name had
passed away, and they were entering native regiments or Government offices, and Khem Singh
could give them neither pension, decorations, nor

influence — nothing but a glorious death with their backs to the mouth of a gun. He wrote letters and made promises, and the letters fell into bad hands, and a wholly insignificant subordinate officer of Police tracked them down and gained promotion thereby. Moreover, Khem Singh was old, and anise-seed brandy was scarce, and he had left his silver cooking-pots in Fort Amara with his nice warm bedding, and the gentleman with the gold *pince-nez* was told by those who had employed him that Khem Singh as a popular leader was not worth the money paid.

"Great is the mercy of these fools of English!" said Khem Singh when the situation was put before him. "I will go back to Fort Amara of my own free will and gain honour. Give me good clothes to return in."

So, at his own time, Khem Singh knocked at the wicket-gate of the Fort and walked to the Captain and the Subaltern, who were nearly gray-headed on account of correspondence that daily arrived from Simla marked "Private."

"I have come back, Captain Sahib," said Khem Singh. "Put no more guards over me. It is no good out yonder."

A week later I saw him for the first time to my knowledge, and he made as though there were an understanding between us.

"It was well done, Sahib," said he, "and greatly

338

I admired your astuteness in thus boldly facing the troops when I, whom they would have doubtless torn to pieces, was with you. Now there is a man in Fort Ooltagarh whom a bold man could with ease help to escape. This is the position of the Fort as I draw it on the sand —— "

But I was thinking how I had become Lalun's Vizier after all.

THE ENLIGHTENMENTS OF
PAGETT, M. P.

"Because half a dozen grasshoppers under a fern make the field ring with their importunate chink while thousands of great cattle, reposed beneath the shadow of the British oak, chew the cud and are silent, pray do not imagine that those who make the noise are the only inhabitants of the field — that, of course, they are many in number — or that, after all, they are other than the little, shrivelled, meagre, hopping, though loud and troublesome insects of the hour."—*Burke:* "Reflections on the Revolution in France."

THEY were sitting in the verandah of "the splendid palace of an Indian Pro-Consul," surrounded by all the glory and mystery of the immemorial East. In plain English it was a one-storied, ten-roomed, whitewashed mud-roofed bungalow, set in a dry garden of dusty tamarisk trees and divided from the road by a low mud wall. The green parrots screamed overhead as they flew in battalions to the river for their morning drink. Beyond the wall, clouds of fine dust showed where the cattle and goats of the city were passing afield to graze. The remorseless white light of the winter sunshine of Northern India lay upon every-

thing and improved nothing, from the whining
Persian-wheel by the lawn-tennis court to the long
perspective of level road and the blue, domed
tombs of Mahommedan saints just visible above
the trees.

"A Happy New Year," said Orde to his guest.
"It's the first you've ever spent out of England,
isn't it?"

"Yes. 'Happy New Year," said Pagett, smiling at the sunshine. "What a divine climate
you have here! Just think of the brown cold fog
hanging over London now!" And he rubbed his
hands.

It was more than twenty years since he had
last seen Orde, his schoolmate, and their paths in
the world had divided early. The one had quitted
college to become a cog-wheel in the machinery
of the great Indian Government; the other, more
blessed with goods, had been whirled into a simi-
lar position in the English scheme. Three suc-
cessive elections had not affected Pagett's position
with a loyal constituency, and he had grown in-
sensibly to regard himself in some sort as a pillar
of the Empire whose real worth would be known
later on. After a few years of conscientious attendance at many divisions, after newspaper battles innumerable, and the publication of intermin-
able correspondence, and more hasty oratory than
in his calmer moments he cared to think upon, it

occurred to him, as it had occurred to many of
his fellows in Parliament, that a tour to India
would enable him to sweep a larger lyre and address himself to the problems of Imperial administration with a firmer hand. Accepting, therefore, a general invitation extended to him by
Orde some years before, Pagett had taken ship
to Karachi, and only over-night had been received
with joy by the Deputy-Commissioner of Amara.
They had sat late, discussing the changes and
chances of twenty years, recalling the names of
the dead, and weighing the futures of the living,
as is the custom of men meeting after intervals of
action.

Next morning they smoked the after-breakfast
pipe in the verandah, still regarding each other
curiously, Pagett in a light gray frock-coat and
garments much too thin for the time of the year,
and a puggried sun-hat carefully and wonderfully
made; Orde in a shooting-coat, riding-breeches,
brown cowhide boots with spurs, and a battered
flax helmet. He had ridden some miles in the
early morning to inspect a doubtful river-dam.
The men's faces differed as much as their attire.
Orde's, worn and wrinkled about the eyes and
grizzled at the temples, was the harder and more
square of the two, and it was with something like
envy that the owner looked at the comfortable
outlines of Pagett's blandly receptive counte-

nance, the clear skin, the untroubled eye, and the mobile, clean-shaved lips.

"And this is India!" said Pagett for the twentieth time, staring long and intently at the gray feathering of the tamarisks.

"One portion of India only. It's very much like this for 300 miles in every direction. By the way, now that you have rested a little — I wouldn't ask the old question before — what d'you think of the country?"

"'Tis the most pervasive country that ever yet was seen. I acquired several pounds of your country coming up from Karachi. The air is heavy with it, and for miles and miles along that distressful eternity of rail there's no horizon to show where air and earth separate."

"Yes. It isn't easy to see truly or far in India. But you had a decent passage out, hadn't you?"

"Very good on the whole. Your Anglo-Indian may be unsympathetic about one's political views; but he has reduced ship life to a science."

"The Anglo-Indian is a political orphan, and if he's wise he won't be in a hurry to be adopted by your party grandmothers. But how were your companions unsympathetic?"

"Well, there was a man called Dawlishe, a judge somewhere in this country, it seems, and a capital partner at whist, by the way, and when I wanted to talk to him about the progress of

India in a political sense [Orde hid a grin which might or might not have been sympathetic], the National Congress movement, and other things in which, as a Member of Parliament, I'm of course interested, he shifted the subject, and when I once cornered him, he looked me calmly in the eye, and said: ' That's all Tommy Rot. Come and have a game at Bull.' You may laugh, but that isn't the way to treat a great and important question; and, knowing who I was, well, I thought it rather rude, don't you know; and yet Dawlishe is a thoroughly good fellow."

" Yes; he's a friend of mine, and one of the straightest men I know. I suppose, like many Anglo-Indians, he felt it was hopeless to give you any just idea of any Indian question without the documents before you, and in this case the documents you want are the country and the people."

" Precisely. That was why I came straight to you, bringing an open mind to bear on things. I'm anxious to know what popular feeling in India is really like, y'know, now that it has wakened into political life. The National Congress, in spite of Dawlishe, must have caused great excitement among the masses ? "

" On the contrary, nothing could be more tranquil than the state of popular feeling; and as to excitement, the people would as soon be excited over the ' Rule of Three ' as over the Congress."

344

"Excuse me, Orde, but do you think you are a fair judge? Isn't the official Anglo-Indian naturally jealous of any external influences that might move the masses, and so much opposed to liberal ideas, truly liberal ideas, that he can scarcely be expected to regard a popular movement with fairness?"

"What did Dawlishe say about Tommy Rot? Think a moment, old man. You and I were brought up together; taught by the same tutors, read the same books, lived the same life, and thought, as you may remember, in parallel lines. *I* come out here, learn new languages, and work among new races; while you, more fortunate, remain at home. Why should I change my mind — our mind — because I change my sky? Why should I and the few hundred Englishmen in my service become unreasonable, prejudiced fossils, while you and your newer friends alone remain bright and open-minded? You surely don't fancy civilians are members of a Primrose League?"

"Of course not, but the mere position of an English official gives him a point of view which cannot but bias his mind on this question." Pagett moved his knee up and down a little uneasily as he spoke.

"That sounds plausible enough, but, like more plausible notions on Indian matters, I believe it's a mistake. You'll find when you come to consult the

345

unofficial Briton that our fault, as a class—I speak
of the civilian now — is rather to magnify the progress that has been made towards liberal institutions. It is of English origin, such as it is, and the
stress of our work since the Mutiny — only thirty
years ago—has been in that direction. No, I think
you will get no fairer or more dispassionate view
of the Congress business than such men as I can
give you. But I may as well say at once that
those who know most of India, from the inside,
are inclined to wonder at the noise our scarcely
begun experiment makes in England."

"But surely the gathering together of Congress
delegates is of itself a new thing."

"There's nothing new under the sun. When
Europe was a jungle half Asia flocked to the
canonical conferences of Buddhism; and for centuries the people have gathered at Puri, Hurdwar,
Trimbak, and Benares in immense numbers. A
great meeting, what you call a mass meeting, is
really one of the oldest and most popular of Indian institutions. In the case of the Congress
meetings, the only notable fact is that the priests
of the altar are British, not Buddhist, Jain or Brah-
manical, and that the whole thing is a British con-
trivance kept alive by the efforts of Messrs. Hume,
Eardley Norton, and Digby."

"You mean to say, then, it's not a spontaneous
movement?"

"What movement was ever spontaneous in any true sense of the word? This seems to be more factitious than usual. You seem to know a great deal about it; try it by the touchstone of subscriptions, a coarse but fairly trustworthy criterion, and there is scarcely the colour of money in it. The delegates write from England that they are out of pocket for working expenses, railway fares, and stationery — the mere pasteboard and scaffolding of their show. It is, in fact, collapsing from mere financial inanition."

"But you cannot deny that the people of India, who are, perhaps, too poor to subscribe, are mentally and morally moved by the agitation," Pagett insisted.

"That is precisely what I *do* deny. The native side of the movement is the work of a limited class, a microscopic minority, as Lord Dufferin described it, when compared with the people proper, but still a very interesting class, seeing that it is of our own creation. It is composed almost entirely of those of the literary or clerkly castes who have received an English education."

"Surely that's a very important class. Its members must be the ordained leaders of popular thought."

"Anywhere else they might be leaders, but they have no social weight in this topsy-turvy land, and though they have been employed in clerical

work for generations, they have no practical knowledge of affairs.　A ship's clerk is a useful person,
but he is scarcely the captain; and an orderly-
room writer, however smart he may be, is not the
colonel.　You see, the writer class in India has
never till now aspired to anything like command.
It wasn't allowed to.　The Indian gentleman, for
thousands of years past, has resembled Victor
Hugo's noble:

> "Un vrai sire
> Chatelain
> Laisse ecrire
> Le vilain.
> Sa main digne
> Quand il signe
> Egratigne
> Le velin."

And the little *egratignures* he most likes to make
have been scored pretty deeply by the sword."

"But this is childish and mediæval nonsense!"

"Precisely; and from your, or rather our, point
of view the pen *is* mightier than the sword.　In
this country it's otherwise.　The fault lies in our
Indian balances, not yet adjusted to civilised
weights and measures."

"Well, at all events, this literary class represent the natural aspirations and wishes of the people at large, though it may not exactly lead them,
and, in spite of all you say, Orde, I defy you to

find a really sound English Radical who would not sympathise with those aspirations."

Pagett spoke with some warmth, and he had scarcely ceased when a well-appointed dog-cart turned into the compound gates, and Orde rose, saying:

"Here is Edwards, the Master of the Lodge I neglect so diligently, come to talk about accounts, I suppose."

As the vehicle drove up under the porch Pagett also rose, saying with the trained effusion born of much practice:

"But this is also *my* friend, my old and valued friend, Edwards. I'm delighted to see you. I knew you were in India, but not exactly where."

"Then it isn't accounts, Mr. Edwards," said Orde cheerily.

"Why, no, sir; I heard Mr. Pagett was coming, and as our works were closed for the New Year I thought I would drive over and see him."

"A very happy thought. Mr. Edwards, you may not know, Orde, was a leading member of our Radical Club at Switchton when I was beginning political life, and I owe much to his exertions. There's no pleasure like meeting an old friend, except, perhaps, making a new one. I suppose, Mr. Edwards, you stick to the good old cause?"

"Well, you see, sir, things are different out here. There's precious little one can find to say against the Government, which was the main of our talk at home, and them that do say things are not the sort o' people a man who respects himself would like to be mixed up with. There are no politics, in a manner of speaking, in India. It's all work."

"Surely you are mistaken, my good friend. Why, I have come all the way from England just to see the working of this great National movement."

"I don't know where you're going to find the nation as moves, to begin with, and then you'll be hard put to it to find what they are moving about. It's like this, sir," said Edwards, who had not quite relished being called "my good friend." "They haven't got any grievance — nothing to hit with, don't you see, sir; and then there's not much to hit against, because the Government is more like a kind of general Providence, directing an old-established state of things, than that at home, where there's something new thrown down for us to fight about every three months."

"You are probably, in your workshops, full of English mechanics, out of the way of learning what the masses think."

"I don't know so much about that. There are four of us English foremen, and between seven and eight hundred native fitters, smiths, carpenters, painters, and such like."

" And they are full of the Congress, of course ? "

"Never hear a word of it from year's end to year's end, and I speak the talk, too. But I wanted to ask how things are going on at home — old Tyler and Brown and the rest ? "

"We will speak of them presently, but your account of the indifference of your men surprises me almost as much as your own. I fear you are a backslider from the good old doctrine, Edwards." Pagett spoke as one who mourned the death of a near relative.

"Not a bit, sir, but I should be if I took up with a parcel of babus, pleaders, and schoolboys, as never did a day's work in their lives, and couldn't if they tried. And if you was to poll us English railway-men, mechanics, tradespeople, and the like of that all up and down the country from Peshawur to Calcutta, you would find us mostly in a tale together. And yet you know we're the same English you pay some respect to at home at 'lection time, and we have the pull o' knowing something about it."

"This is very curious, but you will let me come and see you, and perhaps you will kindly show me the railway works, and we will talk things over at leisure. And about all old friends and old times," added Pagett, detecting with quick insight a look of disappointment in the mechanic's face.

351

Nodding briefly to Orde, Edwards mounted his dog-cart and drove off.

"It's very disappointing," said the Member to Orde, who, while his friend discoursed with Edwards, had been looking over a bundle of sketches drawn on gray paper in purple ink, brought to him by a *Chuprassee*.

"Don't let it trouble you, old chap," said Orde sympathetically. "Look here a moment, here are some sketches by the man who made the carved-wood screen you admired so much in the dining-room, and wanted a copy of, and the artist himself is here too."

"A native?" said Pagett.

"Of course," was the reply, "Bishen Singh is his name, and he has two brothers to help him. When there is an important job to do, the three go into partnership, but they spend most of their time and all their money in litigation over an inheritance, and I'm afraid they are getting involved. Thoroughbred Sikhs of the old rock, obstinate, touchy, bigoted, and cunning, but good men for all that. Here is Bishen Singh — shall we ask *him* about the Congress?"

But Bishen Singh, who approached with a respectful salaam, had never heard of it, and he listened with a puzzled face and obviously feigned interest to Orde's account of its aims and objects, finally shaking his vast white turban with great significance when he learned that it was promoted by certain pleaders named by Orde, and by educated natives. He began with laboured respect to explain how he was a poor man with no concern in such matters, which were all under the control of God, but presently broke out of Urdu into familiar Punjabi, the mere sound of which had a rustic smack of village smoke-reek and plough-tail, as he denounced the wearers of white coats, the jugglers with words who filched his field from him, the men whose backs were never bowed in honest work; and poured ironical scorn on the Bengali. He and one of his brothers had seen Calcutta, and being at work there, had Bengali carpenters given to them as assistants.

"Those carpenters!" said Bishen Singh. "Black apes were more efficient workmates, and as for the Bengali babu — tchick!" The guttural click needed no interpretation, but Orde translated the rest, while Pagett gazed with interest at the wood-carver.

"He seems to have a most illiberal prejudice against the Bengali," said the M. P.

"Yes, it's very sad that for ages outside Bengal there should be so bitter a prejudice. Pride of race, which also means race-hatred, is the plague and curse of India and it spreads far." Orde pointed with his riding-whip to the large map of India on the verandah wall.

"See! I begin with the North," said he. "There's the Afghan, and, as a highlander, he despises all the dwellers in Hindustan — with the exception of the Sikh, whom he hates as cordially as the Sikh hates him. The Hindu loathes Sikh and Afghan, and the Rajput — that's a little lower down across this yellow blot of desert — has a strong objection, to put it mildly, to the Maratha, who, by the way, poisonously hates the Afghan. Let's go North a minute. The Sindhi hates everybody I've mentioned. Very good, we'll take less warlike races. The cultivator of Northern India domineers over the man in the next province, and the Behari of the North-West ridicules the Bengali. They are all at one on that point. I'm giving you merely the roughest possible outlines of the facts, of course."

Bishen Singh, his clean-cut nostrils still quivering, watched the large sweep of the whip as it travelled from the frontier, through Sindh, the Punjab and Rajputana, till it rested by the valley of the Jumna.

"Hate — eternal and inextinguishable hate," concluded Orde, flicking the lash of the whip across the large map from East to West as he sat down. "Remember Canning's advice to Lord Granville, 'Never write or speak of Indian things without looking at a map.'"

Pagett opened his eyes; Orde resumed. "And

354

the race-hatred is only a part of it. What's really the matter with Bishen Singh is class-hatred, which, unfortunately, is even more intense and more widely spread. That's one of the little drawbacks of caste, which some of your recent English writers find an impeccable system."

The wood-carver was glad to be recalled to the business of his craft, and his eyes shone as he received instructions for a carved wooden doorway for Pagett, which he promised should be splendidly executed and despatched to England in six months. It is an irrelevant detail, but in spite of Orde's reminders, fourteen months elapsed before the work was finished. Business over, Bishen Singh hung about, reluctant to take his leave, and at last joining his hands and approaching Orde with bated breath and whispering humbleness, said he had a petition to make. Orde's face suddenly lost all trace of expression. "Speak on, Bishen Singh," said he, and the carver in a whining tone explained that his case against his brothers was fixed for hearing before a native judge, and — here he dropped his voice still lower till he was summarily stopped by Orde, who sternly pointed to the gate with an emphatic Begone!

Bishen Singh, showing but little sign of discomposure, salaamed respectfully to the friends and departed.

Pagett looked inquiry; Orde, with complete re-

covery of his usual urbanity, replied: "It's nothing, only the old story: he wants his case to be
tried by an English judge — they all do that — but
when he began to hint that the other side were in
improper relations with the native judge I had to
shut him up. Gunga Ram, the man he wanted to
make insinuations about, may not be very bright;
but he's as honest as daylight on the bench. But
that's just what one can't get a native to believe."

"Do you really mean to say these people prefer
to have their cases tried by English judges?"

"Why, certainly."

Pagett drew a long breath. "I didn't know
that before." At this point a phaeton entered
the compound, and Orde rose with "Confound
it, there's old Rasul Ali Khan come to pay one
of his tiresome duty-calls. I'm afraid we shall
never get through our little Congress discussion."

Pagett was an almost silent spectator of the
grave formalities of a visit paid by a punctilious
old Mahommedan gentleman to an Indian official;
and was much impressed by the distinction of
manner and fine appearance of the Mahommedan
landholder. When the exchange of polite ba-
nalities came to a pause, he expressed a wish to
learn the courtly visitor's opinion of the National
Congress.

Orde reluctantly interpreted, and with a smile
which even Mahommedan politeness could not

save from bitter scorn, Rasul Ali Khan intimated that he knew nothing about it and cared still less. It was a kind of talk encouraged by the Government for some mysterious purpose of its own, and for his own part he wondered and held his peace.

Pagett was far from satisfied with this, and wished to have the old gentleman's opinion on the propriety of managing all Indian affairs on the basis of an elective system.

Orde did his best to explain, but it was plain the visitor was bored and bewildered. Frankly, he didn't think much of committees; they had a Municipal Committee at Lahore and had elected a menial servant, an orderly, as a member. He had been informed of this on good authority, and after that committees had ceased to interest him. But all was according to the rule of Government, and, please God, it was all for the best.

"What an old fossil it is!" cried Pagett, as Orde returned from seeing his guest to the door; "just like some old blue-blooded hidalgo of Spain. What does he really think of the Congress after all, and of the elective system?"

"Hates it all like poison. When you are sure of a majority, election is a fine system; but you can scarcely expect the Mahommedans, the most masterful and powerful minority in the country, to contemplate their own extinction with joy. The worst of it is that he and his co-religionists,

who are many, and the landed proprietors, also of
Hindu race, are frightened and put out by this
election business and by the importance we have
bestowed on lawyers, pleaders, writers, and the
like, who have, up to now, been in abject sub-
mission to them. They say little, but after all
they are the most important faggots in the great
bundle of communities, and all the glib bunkum
in the world would not pay for their estrangement.
They have controlled the land."

"But I am assured that experience of local self-
government in your municipalities has been most
satisfactory, and when once the principle is accepted in your centres, don't you know, it is
bound to spread, and these important—ah'm—
people of yours would learn it like the rest. I see
no difficulty at all," and the smooth lips closed
with the complacent snap habitual to Pagett,
M. P., the "man of cheerful yesterdays and con-
fident to-morrows."

Orde looked at him with a dreary smile.

"The privilege of election has been most reluctantly withdrawn from scores of municipalities,
others have had to be summarily suppressed, and,
outside the Presidency towns, the actual work
done has been badly performed. This is of less
moment, perhaps—it only sends up the local
death-rates—than the fact that the public interest
in municipal elections, never very strong, has

waned, and is waning, in spite of careful nursing on the part of Government servants."

"Can you explain this lack of interest?" said Pagett, putting aside the rest of Orde's remarks.

"You may find a ward of the key in the fact that only one in every thousand of our population can spell. Then they are infinitely more interested in religion and caste questions than in any sort of politics. When the business of mere existence is over, their minds are occupied by a series of interests, pleasures, rituals, superstitions, and the like, based on centuries of tradition and usage. You, perhaps, find it hard to conceive of people absolutely devoid of curiosity, to whom the book, the daily paper, and the printed speech are unknown, and you would describe their life as blank. That's a profound mistake. You are in another land, another century, down on the bed-rock of society, where the family merely, and not the community, is all-important. The average Oriental cannot be brought to look beyond his clan. His life, too, is more complete and self-sufficing and less sordid and low-thoughted than you might imagine. It is bovine and slow in some respects, but it is never empty. You and I are inclined to put the cart before the horse, and to forget that it is the man that is elemental, not the book.

"The corn and the cattle are all my care,
And the rest is the will of God."

Why should such folk look up from their immemorially appointed round of duty and interests to meddle with the unknown and fuss with voting-papers? How would you, atop of all your interests, care to conduct even one-tenth of your life according to the manners and customs of the Papuans, let's say? That's what it comes to."

"But if they won't take the trouble to vote, why do you anticipate that Mahommedans, proprietors, and the rest would be crushed by majorities of them?"

Again Pagett disregarded the closing sentence.

"Because, though the landholders would not move a finger on any purely political question, they could be raised in dangerous excitement by religious hatreds. Already the first note of this has been sounded by the people who are trying to get up an agitation on the cow-killing question, and every year there is trouble over the Mahommedan Muharrum processions."

"But who looks after the popular rights, being thus unrepresented?"

"The Government of Her Majesty the Queen, Empress of India, in which, if the Congress promoters are to be believed, the people have an implicit trust; for the Congress circular, specially prepared for rustic comprehension, says the movement is '*for the remission of tax, the advancement of Hindustan, and the strengthening of the British Govern-*

ment.' This paper is headed in large letters —
'MAY THE PROSPERITY OF THE EMPRESS OF INDIA
ENDURE.' "

"Really!" said Pagett, "that shows some cleverness. But there are things better worth imitation in our English methods of — er — political statement than this sort of amiable fraud."

"Anyhow," resumed Orde, "you perceive that not a word is said about elections and the elective principle, and the reticence of the Congress promoters here shows they are wise in their generation."

"But the elective principle must triumph in the end, and the little difficulties you seem to anticipate would give way on the introduction of a well-balanced scheme capable of indefinite extension."

"But is it possible to devise a scheme which, always assuming that the people took any interest in it, without enormous expense, ruinous dislocation of the administration and danger to the public peace, can satisfy the aspirations of Mr. Hume and his following, and yet safeguard the interests of the Mahommedans, the landed and wealthy classes, the conservative Hindus, the Eurasians, Parsees, Sikhs, Rajputs, native Christians, domiciled Europeans and others, who are each important and powerful in their way?"

Pagett's attention, however, was diverted to the gate, where a group of cultivators stood in apparent hesitation.

"Here are the twelve Apostles, by Jove!—come straight out of Raffaele's cartoons," said the M. P., with the fresh appreciation of a new-comer.

Orde, loath to be interrupted, turned impatiently towards the villagers, and their leader, handing his long staff to one of his companions, advanced to the house.

"It is old Jelloo, the Lumberdar or head-man of Pind Sharkot, and a very intelligent man for a villager."

The Jat farmer had removed his shoes and stood smiling on the edge of the verandah. His strongly marked features glowed with russet bronze, and his bright eyes gleamed under deeply set brows, contracted by life-long exposure to sunshine. His beard and moustache, streaked with gray, swept from bold cliffs of brow and cheek in the large sweeps one sees drawn by Michael Angelo, and strands of long black hair mingled with the irregularly piled wreaths and folds of his turban. The drapery of stout blue cotton cloth thrown over his broad shoulders and girt round his narrow loins, hung from his tall form in broadly sculptured folds and he would have made a superb model for an artist in search of a patriarch.

Orde greeted him cordially, and after a polite pause the countryman started off with a long story told with impressive earnestness. Orde listened and smiled, interrupting the speaker at times to

362

argue and reason with him in a tone which Pagett could hear was kindly, and, finally checking the flux of words, was about to dismiss him when Pagett suggested that he should be asked about the National Congress.

But Jelloo had never heard of it. He was a poor man, and such things, by the favour of his Honour, did not concern him.

"What's the matter with your big friend that he was so terribly in earnest?" asked Pagett, when he had left.

"Nothing much. He wants the blood of the people in the next village, who have had small-pox and cattle plague pretty badly, and by the help of a wizard, a currier, and several pigs have passed it on to his own village. 'Wants to know if they can't be run in for this awful crime. It seems they made a dreadful charivari at the village boundary, threw a quantity of spell-bearing objects over the border, a buffalo's skull and other things; then branded a *chamar* — what you would call a currier — on his hinder parts and drove him and a number of pigs over into Jelloo's village. Jelloo says he can bring evidence to prove that the wizard directing these proceedings, who is a Sansi, has been guilty of theft, arson, cattle-killing, perjury and murder, but would prefer to have him punished for bewitching them and inflicting small-pox."

363

"And how on earth did you answer such a lunatic ? "

"Lunatic ! the old fellow is as sane as you or I ; and he has some ground of complaint against those Sansis. I asked if he would like a native superintendent of police with some men to make inquiries, but he objected on the grounds the police were rather worse than small-pox and criminal tribes put together."

" Criminal tribes — er — I don't quite understand," said Pagett.

" We have in India many tribes of people who in the slack ante-British days became robbers, in various kind, and preyed on the people. They are being restrained and reclaimed little by little, and in time will become useful citizens, but they still cherish hereditary traditions of crime, and are a difficult lot to deal with. By the way, what about the political rights of these folk under your schemes ? The country people call them vermin, but I suppose they would be electors with the rest."

" Nonsense — special provision would be made for them in a well-considered electoral scheme, and they would doubtless be treated with fitting severity," said Pagett with a magisterial air.

" Severity, yes — but whether it would be fitting is doubtful. Even those poor devils have rights, and, after all, they only practise what they have been taught."

"But criminals, Orde!"

"Yes, criminals with codes and rituals of crime, gods and godlings of crime, and a hundred songs and sayings in praise of it. Puzzling, isn't it?"

"It's simply dreadful. They ought to be put down at once. Are there many of them?"

"Not more than about sixty thousand in this province, for many of the tribes broadly described as criminal are really vagabond and criminal only on occasion, while others are being settled and reclaimed. They are of great antiquity, a legacy from the past, the golden, glorious Aryan past of Max Müller, Birdwood and the rest of your spindrift philosophers."

An orderly brought a card to Orde, who took it with a movement of irritation at the interruption, and handed it to Pagett: a large card with a ruled border in red ink, and in the centre in school-boy copper-plate, *Mr. Dina Nath.* "Give salaam," said the civilian, and there entered in haste a slender youth, clad in a closely fitting coat of gray homespun, tight trousers, patent-leather shoes, and a small black velvet cap. His thin cheek twitched, and his eyes wandered restlessly, for the young man was evidently nervous and uncomfortable, though striving to assume a free-and-easy air.

365

" Your honour may perhaps remember me," he said in English, and Orde scanned him keenly.

" I know your face, somehow. You belonged to the Shershah district, I think, when I was in charge there ? "

" Yes, sir, my father is writer at Shershah, and your honour gave me a prize when I was first in the Middle School examination five years ago. Since then I have prosecuted my studies, and I am now second year's student in the Mission College."

" Of course : you are Kedar Nath's son — the boy who said he liked geography better than play or sugar-cakes, and I didn't believe you. How is your father getting on ? "

" He is well, and he sends his salaam, but his circumstances are depressed, and he also is down on his luck."

" You learn English idioms at the Mission College, it seems."

" Yes, sir, they are the best idioms, and my father ordered me to ask your honour to say a word for him to the present incumbent of your honour's shoes, the latchet of which he is not worthy to open, and who knows not Joseph; for things are different at Shershah now, and my father wants promotion."

" Your father is a good man, and I will do what I can for him."

At this point a telegram was handed to Orde,

who, after glancing at it, said he must leave his young friend, whom he introduced to Pagett, "a member of the English House of Commons who wishes to learn about India."

Orde had scarcely retired with his telegram when Pagett began:

"Perhaps you can tell me something of the National Congress movement?"

"Sir, it is the greatest movement of modern times, and one in which all educated men like us *must* join. All our students are for the Congress."

"Excepting, I suppose, Mahommedans, and the Christians?" said Pagett, quick to use his recent instruction.

"These are some *mere* exceptions to the universal rule."

"But the people outside the College, the working classes, the agriculturists; your father and mother, for instance."

"My mother," said the young man, with a visible effort to bring himself to pronounce the word, "has no ideas, and my father is not agriculturist, nor working class; he is of the Kayeth caste; but he had not the advantage of a collegiate education, and he does not know much of the Congress. It is a movement for the educated young-man"—connecting adjective and noun in a sort of vocal hyphen.

"Ah, yes," said Pagett, feeling he was a little

367

off the rails, "and what are the benefits you expect to gain by it ?"

"Oh, sir, everything. England owes its greatness to Parliamentary institutions and we should *at once* gain the same high position in scale of nations. Sir, we wish to have the sciences, the arts, the manufactures, the industrial factories, with steam-engines and other motive powers and public meetings and debates. Already we have a debating club in connection with the college and elect a Mr. Speaker. Sir, the progress *must* come. You also are a Member of Parliament and worship the great Lord Ripon," said the youth, breathlessly, and his black eyes flashed as he finished his commaless sentences.

"Well," said Pagett, drily, "it has not yet occurred to me to worship his Lordship, although I believe he is a very worthy man, and I am not sure that England owes quite all the things you name to the House of Commons. You see, my young friend, the growth of a nation like ours is slow, subject to many influences, and if you have read your history aright —— "

"Sir, I know it all — all! Norman Conquest, Magna Charta, Runnymede, Reformation, Tudors, Stuarts, Mr. Milton and Mr. Burke, and I have read something of Mr. Herbert Spencer and Gibbon's 'Decline and Fall,' Reynolds' 'Mysteries of the Court,' and —— "

Pagett felt like one who had pulled the string of a shower-bath unawares, and hastened to stop the torrent with a question as to what particular grievances of the people of India the attention of an elected assembly should be first directed. But young Mr. Dina Nath was slow to particularise. There were many, very many demanding consideration. Mr. Pagett would like to hear of one or two typical examples. The Repeal of the Arms Act was at last named, and the student learned for the first time that a license was necessary before an Englishman could carry a gun in England. Then natives of India ought to be allowed to become Volunteer Riflemen if they chose, and the absolute equality of the Oriental with his European fellow-subject in civil status should be proclaimed on principle, and the Indian Army should be considerably reduced. The student was not, however, prepared with answers to Mr. Pagett's mildest questions on these points, and he returned to vague generalities, leaving the M. P. so much impressed with the crudity of his views that he was glad on Orde's return to say good-bye to his " very interesting " young friend.

" What do you think of young India ? " asked Orde.

" Curious, very curious — and callow."

" And yet," the civilian replied, " one can scarcely help sympathising with him for his mere youth's sake. The young orators of the Oxford Union arrived at the same conclusions and showed doubtless just the same enthusiasm. If there were any political analogy between India and England, if the thousand races of this Empire were one, if there were any chance even of their learning to speak one language, if, in short, India were a Utopia of the debating-room, and not a real land, this kind of talk might be worth listening to, but it is all based on false analogy and ignorance of the facts."

" But he is a native and knows the facts."

" He is a sort of English schoolboy, but married three years, and the father of two weaklings, and knows less than most English schoolboys. You saw all he is and knows, and such ideas as he has acquired are directly hostile to the most cherished convictions of the vast majority of the people."

" But what does he mean by saying he is a student of a mission college? Is he a Christian?"

" He meant just what he said, and he is not a Christian, nor ever will he be. Good people in America, Scotland, and England, most of whom would never dream of collegiate education for their own sons, are pinching themselves to bestow it in pure waste on Indian youths. Their scheme is an oblique, subterranean attack on heathenism ; the theory being that with the jam of secular education, leading to a University degree, the pill of moral or religious instruction may be coaxed down the heathen gullet."

"But does it succeed; do they make converts?"

"They make no converts, for the subtle Oriental swallows the jam and rejects the pill; but the mere example of the sober, righteous, and godly lives of the principals and professors, who are most excellent and devoted men, must have a certain moral value. Yet, as Lord Lansdowne pointed out the other day, the market is dangerously overstocked with graduates of our Universities who look for employment in the administration. An immense number are employed, but year by year the college mills grind out increasing lists of youths foredoomed to failure and disappointment, and meanwhile trade, manufactures, and the industrial arts are neglected and in fact regarded with contempt by our new literary mandarins *in posse*."

"But our young friend said he wanted steam-engines and factories," said Pagett.

"Yes, he would like to direct such concerns. He wants to begin at the top, for manual labour is held to be discreditable, and he would never defile his hands by the apprenticeship which the architects, engineers, and manufacturers of England cheerfully undergo; and he would be aghast to learn that the leading names of industrial enterprise in England belonged a generation or two since, or now belong, to men who wrought with their own hands. And, though he talks glibly of manufacturers, he refuses to see that the Indian manufacturer of the future will be the despised workman of the present. It was proposed, for example, a few weeks ago, that a certain municipality in this province should establish an elementary technical school for the sons of workmen. The stress of the opposition to the plan came from a pleader who owed all he had to a college education bestowed on him gratis by Government and missions. You would have fancied some fine old crusted Tory squire of the last generation was speaking. 'These people,' he said, 'want no education, for they learn their trades from their fathers, and to teach a workman's son the elements of mathematics and physical science would give him ideas above his business. They must be kept in their place, and it was idle to imagine that there was any science in wood or iron work.' And he carried his point. But the Indian workman will rise in the social scale in spite of the new literary caste."

" In England we have scarcely begun to realise that there is an industrial class in this country, yet, I suppose, the example of men like Edwards, for instance, must tell," said Pagett thoughtfully.

"That you shouldn't know much about it is

natural enough, for there are but few sources of information. India in this, as in other respects, is like a badly kept ledger—not written up to date. And men like Edwards are, in reality, missionaries who by precept and example are teaching more lessons than they know. Only a few, however, of their crowds of subordinates seem to care to try to emulate them, and aim at individual advancement; the rest drop into the ancient Indian caste groove."

"How do you mean?" asked Pagett.

"Well, it is found that the new railway and factory workmen, the fitter, the smith, the engine-driver, and the rest are already forming separate hereditary castes. You may notice this down at Jamalpur in Bengal, one of the oldest railway centres; and at other places, and in other industries, they are following the same inexorable Indian law."

"Which means ——?" queried Pagett.

"It means that the rooted habit of the people is to gather in small self-contained, self-sufficing family groups with no thought or care for any interests but their own—a habit which is scarcely compatible with the right acceptation of the elective principle."

"Yet you must admit, Orde, that though our young friend was not able to expound the faith that is in him, your Indian army is too big."

"Not nearly big enough for its main purpose. And, as a side issue, there are certain powerful minorities of fighting folk whose interests an Asiatic Government is bound to consider. Arms is as much a means of livelihood as civil employ under Government and law. And it would be a heavy strain on British bayonets to hold down Sikhs, Jats, Bilochis, Rohillas, Rajputs, Bhils, Dogras, Pathans, and Gurkhas to abide by the decisions of a numerical majority opposed to their interests. Leave the 'numerical majority' to itself without the British bayonets — a flock of sheep might as reasonably hope to manage a troop of collies."

"This complaint about excessive growth of the army is akin to another contention of the Congress party. They protest against the malversation of the whole of the moneys raised by additional taxes as a Famine Insurance Fund to other purposes. You must be aware that this special Famine Fund has all been spent on frontier roads and defences and strategic railway schemes as a protection against Russia."

"But there was never a special famine fund raised by special taxation and put by as in a box. No sane administrator would dream of such a thing. In a time of prosperity a finance minister, rejoicing in a margin, proposed to annually apply a million and a half to the construction of railways and canals for the protection of districts liable to scarcity, and to the reduction of the annual loans for public works. But times were not always prosperous, and the finance minister had to choose whether he would hang up the insurance scheme for a year or impose fresh taxation. When a farmer hasn't got the little surplus he hoped to have for buying a new waggon and draining a low-lying field corner, you don't accuse him of malversation if he spends what he has on the necessary work of the rest of his farm."

A clatter of hoofs was heard, and Orde looked up with vexation, but his brow cleared as a horseman halted under the porch.

"Hello, Orde! just looked in to ask if you are coming to polo on Tuesday: we want you badly to help to crumple up the Krab Bokhar team."

Orde explained that he had to go out into the District, and while the visitor complained that though good men wouldn't play, duffers were always keen, and that his side would probably be beaten, Pagett rose to look at his mount, a red, lathered Biloch mare, with a curious lyre-like incurving of the ears. "Quite a little thoroughbred in all other respects," said the M. P., and Orde presented Mr. Reginald Burke, Manager of the Sind and Sialkote Bank, to his friend.

"Yes, she's as good as they make 'em, and she's all the female I possess, and spoiled in consequence, aren't you, old girl?" said Burke, patting the mare's glossy neck as she backed and plunged.

"Mr. Pagett," said Orde, "has been asking me about the Congress. What is your opinion?" Burke turned to the M. P. with a frank smile.

"Well, if it's all the same to you, sir, I should say, Damn the Congress, but then I'm no politician, but only a business man."

"You find it a tiresome subject?"

"Yes, it's all that, and worse than that, for this kind of agitation is anything but wholesome for the country."

"How do you mean?"

"It would be a long job to explain, and Sara here won't stand, but you know how sensitive capital is, and how timid investors are. All this sort of rot is likely to frighten them, and we can't afford to frighten them. The passengers aboard an Ocean steamer don't feel reassured when the ship's way is stopped and they hear the workmen's hammers tinkering at the engines down below. The old Ark's going on all right as she is, and only wants quiet and room to move. Them's my sentiments, and those of some other people who have to do with money and business."

"Then you are a thick-and-thin supporter of the Government as it is."

"Why, no! The Indian Government is much

too timid with its money—like an old maiden aunt of mine —always in a funk about her invest-ments. They don't spend half enough on railways, for instance, and they are slow in a general way, and ought to be made to sit up in all that con-cerns the encouragement of private enterprise, and coaxing out into use the millions of capital that lie dormant in the country."

The mare was dancing with impatience, and Burke was evidently anxious to be off, so the men wished him good-bye.

" Who is your genial friend who condemns both Congress and Government in a breath?" asked Pagett, with an amused smile.

"Just now he is Reggie Burke, keener on polo than on anything else, but if you went to the Sind and Sialkote Bank to-morrow you would find Mr. Reginald Burke a very capable man of business, known and liked by an immense constituency North and South of this."

"Do you think he is right about the Govern-ment's want of enterprise?"

"I should hesitate to say. Better consult the merchants and chambers of commerce in Cawn-pore, Madras, Bombay, and Calcutta. But though these bodies would like, as Reggie puts it, to make Government sit up, it is an elementary considera-tion in governing a country like India, which must be administered for the benefit of the people at

377

large, that the counsels of those who resort to it for the sake of making money should be judiciously weighed and not allowed to overpower the rest. They are welcome guests here, as a matter of course, but it has been found best to restrain their influence. Thus the rights of plantation labourers, factory operatives, and the like, have been protected, and the capitalist, eager to get on, has not always regarded Government action with favour. It is quite conceivable that under an elective system the commercial communities of the great towns might find means to secure majorities on labour questions and on financial matters."

" They would act at least with intelligence and consideration."

" Intelligence, yes; but as to consideration, who at the present moment most bitterly resents the tender solicitude of Lancashire for the welfare and protection of the Indian factory operative ? English and native capitalists running cotton mills and factories."

" But is the solicitude of Lancashire in this matter entirely disinterested ? "

" It is no business of mine to say. I merely indicate an example of how a powerful commercial interest might hamper a Government intent in the first place on the larger interests of humanity."

Orde broke off to listen a moment. " There's

Dr. Lathrop talking to my wife in the drawing-room," said he.

" Surely not; that's a lady's voice, and if my ears don't deceive me, an American."

" Exactly; Dr. Eva McCreery Lathrop, chief of the new Women's Hospital here, and a very good fellow forbye. Good morning, Doctor," he said, as a graceful figure came out on the verandah; " you seem to be in trouble. I hope Mrs. Orde was able to help you."

" Your wife is real kind and good; I always come to her when I'm in a fix, but I fear it's more than comforting I want."

" You work too hard and wear yourself out," said Orde, kindly. " Let me introduce my friend, Mr. Pagett, just fresh from home, and anxious to learn his India. You could tell him something of that more important half of which a mere man knows so little."

" Perhaps I could if I'd any heart to do it, but I'm in trouble, I've lost a case, a case that was doing well, through nothing in the world but inattention on the part of a nurse I had begun to trust. And when I spoke only a small piece of my mind she collapsed in a whining heap on the floor. It is hopeless !"

The men were silent, for the blue eyes of the lady doctor were dim. Recovering herself, she looked up with a smile half sad, half humorous.

" And I am in a whining heap too; but what phase of Indian life are you particularly interested in, sir?"

" Mr. Pagett intends to study the political aspect of things and the possibility of bestowing electoral institutions on the people."

" Wouldn't it be as much to the purpose to bestow point-lace collars on them? They need many things more urgently than votes. Why, it's like giving a bread-pill for a broken leg."

" Er — I don't quite follow," said Pagett uneasily.

" Well, what's the matter with this country is not in the least political, but an all-round entanglement of physical, social, and moral evils and corruptions, all more or less due to the unnatural treatment of women. You can't gather figs from thistles, and so long as the system of infant marriage, the prohibition of the remarriage of widows, the lifelong imprisonment of wives and mothers in a worse than penal confinement, and the withholding from them of any kind of education or treatment as rational beings continues, the country can't advance a step. Half of it is morally dead, and worse than dead, and that's just the half from which we have a right to look for the best impulses. It's right here where the trouble is, and not in any political considerations whatsoever."

" But do they marry so early?" said Pagett, vaguely.

"The average age is seven, but thousands are married still earlier. One result is that girls of twelve and thirteen have to bear the burden of wifehood and motherhood, and, as might be expected, the rate of mortality both for mothers and children is terrible. Pauperism, domestic unhappiness, and a low state of health are only a few of the consequences of this. Then, when, as frequently happens, the boy-husband dies prematurely, his widow is condemned to worse than death. She may not re-marry, must live a secluded and despised life, a life so unnatural that she sometimes prefers suicide; more often she goes astray. You don't know in England what such words as 'infant-marriage, baby-wife, girl-mother, and virgin-widow' mean; but they mean unspeakable horrors here."

"Well, but the advanced political party here will surely make it their business to advocate social reforms as well as political ones," said Pagett.

"Very surely they will do no such thing," said the lady doctor, emphatically. "I *wish* I could make you understand. Why, even of the funds devoted to the Marchioness of Dufferin's organisation for medical aid to the women of India, it was said in print and in speech that they would be better spent on more college scholarships for men. And in all the advanced parties' talk—God for-

give them — and in all their programmes, they
carefully avoid all such subjects. They will talk
about the protection of the cow, for that's an
ancient superstition — they can all understand
that; but the protection of the women is a new
and dangerous idea." She turned to Pagett im-
pulsively:

" You are a member of the English Parliament.
Can you do nothing? The foundations of their
life are rotten — utterly and bestially rotten. I
could tell your wife things that I couldn't tell you.
I know the life — the inner life that belongs to the
native, and I know nothing else; and, believe me,
you might as well try to grow golden-rod in a
mushroom-pit as to make anything of a people
that are born and reared as these — these things
are. The men talk of their rights and privileges.
I have seen the women that bear these very men,
and again — may God forgive the men!"

Pagett's eyes opened with a large wonder. Dr.
Lathrop rose tempestuously.

" I must be off to lecture," said she, " and I'm
sorry that I can't show you my hospitals; but you
had better believe, sir, that it's more necessary for
India than all the elections in creation."

" That's a woman with a mission, and no mistake," said Pagett, after a pause.

" Yes; she believes in her work, and so do I,"
said Orde. " I've a notion that in the end it will

be found that the most helpful work done for India in this generation was wrought by Lady Dufferin in drawing attention — what work that was, by the way, even with her husband's great name to back it! — to the needs of women here. In effect, native habits and beliefs are an organised conspiracy against the laws of health and happy life — but there is some dawning of hope now."

"How d'you account for the general indifference, then?"

"I suppose it's due in part to their fatalism and their utter indifference to all human suffering. How much do you imagine the great province of the Punjab, with over twenty million people and half a score rich towns, has contributed to the maintenance of civil dispensaries last year? About seven thousand rupees."

"That's seven hundred pounds," said Pagett quickly.

"I wish it was," replied Orde; "but anyway, it's an absurdly inadequate sum, and shows one of the blank sides of Oriental character."

Pagett was silent for a long time. The question of direct and personal pain did not lie within his researches. He preferred to discuss the weightier matters of the law, and contented himself with murmuring: "They'll do better later on." Then, with a rush, returning to his first thought:

"But, my dear Orde, if it's merely a class

movement of a local and temporary character, how d'you account for Bradlaugh, who is at least a man of sense, taking it up?"

" I know nothing of the champion of the New Brahmans but what I see in the papers. I sup-pose there is something tempting in being hailed by a large assemblage as the representative of the aspirations of two hundred and fifty millions of people. Such a man looks 'through all the roaring and the wreaths,' and does not reflect that it is a false perspective, which, as a matter of fact, hides the real complex and manifold India from his gaze. He can scarcely be expected to distinguish between the ambitions of a new oligarchy and the real wants of the people of whom he knows noth-ing. But it's strange that a professed Radical should come to be the chosen advocate of a movement which has for its aim the revival of an ancient tyranny. Shows how even Radicalism can fall into academic grooves and miss the essen-tial truths of its own creed. Believe me, Pagett, to deal with India you want first-hand knowledge and experience. I wish he would come and live here for a couple of years or so."

" Is not this rather an *ad hominem* style of argu-ment?"

" Can't help it in a case like this. Indeed, I am not sure you ought not to go further and weigh the whole character and quality and up-

384

bringing of the man. You must admit that the monumental complacency with which he trotted out his ingenious little Constitution for India showed a strange want of imagination and the sense of humour."

"No, I don't quite admit it," said Pagett.

"Well, you know him and I don't, but that's how it strikes a stranger." He turned on his heel and paced the verandah thoughtfully. "And, after all, the burden of the actual, daily unromantic toil falls on the shoulders of the men out here, and not on his own. He enjoys all the privileges of recommendation without responsibility, and we —well, perhaps, when you've seen a little more of India you'll understand. To begin with, our death-rate's five times higher than yours — I speak now for the brutal bureaucrat — and we work on the refuse of worked-out cities and exhausted civilisations, among the bones of the dead."

Pagett laughed. "That's an epigrammatic way of putting it, Orde."

"Is it? Let's see," said the Deputy Commissioner of Amara, striding into the sunshine towards a half-naked gardener potting roses. He took the man's hoe, and went to a rain-scarped bank at the bottom of the garden.

"Come here, Pagett," he said, and cut at the sun-baked soil. After three strokes there rolled

385

from under the blade of the hoe the half of a clanking skeleton that settled at Pagett's feet in an unseemly jumble of bones. The M. P. drew back.

"Our houses are built on cemeteries," said Orde. "There are scores of thousands of graves within ten miles."

Pagett was contemplating the skull with the awed fascination of a man who has but little to do with the dead. "India's a very curious place," said he, after a pause.

"Ah? You'll know all about it in three months. Come in to lunch," said Orde.